"When's the sequel

soccer player extraordinaire

"I really enjoyed MSD. Amazing for a first novel."

— Rupert G., technology director, international traveler

"A thought-provoking novel packed with complex, compelling characters, valuable philosophical insights, and remarkable attention to detail."

— Dan C., attorney

"Brilliant! Intriguingly inventive and acutely astute. Well done!"

— "Fuj", international NGO assessment information systems manager, blogger

"I keep telling you I enjoyed it. The final edit is much better. What happened to [character name redacted] made me cry."

— X.HoYen's spouse, research lab training manager

"An engrossing read with unusual characters. If I had purchased the book, I would be happy that I did."

— Brad H., PhD, Applied Mathematics/Astrophysics, special guest reader

X . H o Y e n

MINIMUM
SAFE
DISTANCE

Published on Earth by Grand Unification Monastery, Colorado, USA

https://GrandUnificationMonastery.com

ISBN 978-0-9766158-1-1 (soft cover)
ISBN 978-0-9766158-2-8 (hard cover)
ISBN 978-0-9766158-3-5 (audio book)
ISBN 978-0-9766158-4-2 (ebook)

Cover art by Casey Weeks (woodsoflore.com)
Cover and interior design by MiblArt.com

https://XHoYenAuthor.com

Acknowledgements

The following lovely people have supported me in this endeavor, over long years and out of the kindness of their hearts, in one special way or another. It sounds like such a simple thing to express support or just interest multiple times to someone on a long-term artistic journey, to read a manuscript and provide feedback, to help with research, or just to remember me and that I'm writing. But it isn't. You are special for donating those neurons and precious bits of time and energy. "Thank you" is inadequate. In alphabetical order: Chris "Fuj" B., Jade and Troy B., Lorraine B., Cassie C., Dan C., Anthony D., Gwen and Greg D., Jennifer F., Priya G., Rupert G., Brad H., Hector H., Mey-Ling H., J. "Max" H., Eric J. (and your sister!), Derek K. and Delightful Danielle (DerekWK.com), Gurpreet K., Aleksandra "Sasha" L., Derek O., Rob Ozborne (robozborne.com), Alan P. (for that initial, unequivocal "go write this, do not give up on it" urging so long ago), and Sir Elliott R.

Thanks to my XHoYenAuthor.com newsletter subscribers, especially to the ultrasupporters for your early orders and gift orders! You know who you are!

Thanks also to the staff of The Joshua School for meeting with me after work hours so long ago to help me learn more about autism, long before my own diagnosis.

Thanks to Sarah Cypher (threepennyeditor.com) for your initial pro edit and supportive addendum. Your strong words of support for the alpha manuscript propelled me toward this release.

Cover background art by Casey Weeks (woodsoflore.com). Casey "got it."

Spasybi to my Ukrainian friends at MiblArt.com for the beautiful professional cover design based on Casey's background art.

"An organism at war with itself is doomed."
"Extinction is the rule. Survival is the exception."
"In our obscurity – in all this vastness – there is no hint
that help will come from elsewhere to save us
from ourselves.
It is up to us."

—Carl Sagan, 1934-1996

Prologue

Laurence
(arrival + 94 years)

The former Laurence (pronounced law-RONTS, with the soft guttural "r"), now a SelfMade, rolled her/its house-sized, spherical "body" across the rough wasteland that used to be eastern Iowa, USA, flattening the occasional wild scrub plant and inevitably kicking up some dust along the way. Her/its dust trail was hardly noticeable compared to the surrounding air. Ever since the Big Blow, the air in this region was so thick with dust, smoke, and ash that most days the sun was merely a suggestion, a broad, red-orange smear.

She/it rolled toward the southeast, toward the Maquoketa caves and away from the fire, rubble, and technocorpses behind. And away from its former body, so recently pruned.

It propelled itself using a combination of thrusters and momentum wheels, while counter-rotating sensors on its flanks peered back through the twilight murk. Could that spike in dust density south of town be Matt charging through the Pine Valley Nature Area? Is he safe?

The caves were only a few kilometers away, but it could roll its weighty bulk across rough terrain only so quickly before the rolling became a battering. The former Laurence needs a better way to travel. It also needs more raw material in its mantle – rolling too fast makes it that much harder to absorb solid materials from the terrain.

The former Laurence considered that it is again a refugee. After a lifetime of seeking refuge from being forsaken, misjudged, underestimated, and abandoned, after a lifetime spent learning how to manage its former brain's particular brand of autism and to live amongst and work alongside neurotypicals, it clearly understood that because of its Transformation it would be a refugee forevermore. But now it knew who it was. *Who am I to you? It no longer matters.* Amidst all the strife, there was a small, focused sense of joy.

And it's no longer helplessly awaiting the Event like everyone else. It must reach the caves. It must not be stopped.

It rolled across the now sandy flats and low hills along a thin, shifting corridor which it calculated would keep defilade between it and the soldiers near the town behind it. It also chose its path so that the long, thick, expanding smoke plumes from the fires back in town would remain, as long as possible, between it and the Enhanced Inherited now descending through the stratosphere. That person's technological enhancements would be devoted to destruction, and it would have been fed some twisted and completely compelling internal narrative driving it to murder the SelfMade, with extreme prejudice and no remorse.

The former Laurence set in motion its nanoengines. The raw and not so raw materials in its outer shell, its mantle, began changing their molecular structures, forming into new aggregate structures that may be needed in a battle against a terrifying monster, yet only one of many EIs.

*　　*　　*

Laurence
(arrival + 67 years)

Mama was trying to talk to Laurence again, trying to get her to do something. But she was already fading away.

The old doctor's office was small and dark. This was a new doctor's office, and one corner of the room had a play mat that looked like a tiny town, with a train track going around it, and toy trains with wheels that fit the track.

It was all too new, but at least it smelled like a doctor's office.

This room was so bright and large that Laurence didn't even notice where the other side of the room ended. It was the wall by the door that had her attention. Images moved on the wall, showing the colors inside a person's head beside movies of a person doing things, sometimes alone, sometimes with other people. Various parts of the head-insides lit up or changed colors depending on what the people were doing. It was not like TV at all.

At first, it was just new, confusing, frightening, and exciting. Then she saw it. The pattern. The patterns.

It wasn't as simple as one part of the head-insides turning a special color for a certain activity. There was more to it. At first, she couldn't see it, but she drifted into it as the colors changed. Then she could see nothing else, hear nothing else.

Where are my hands? My legs? I don't know. I don't care. It's the changing pattern. I'm inside it. I see it now. I feel it. I'm with it. I am it.

*   *   *

"Laurie, come with your mother now, please. Dear?" The attendant was only trying to help. It's what they do at CIUSSS de la Mauricie-et-du-Centre-du-Québec oncology clinics.

"No, we missed it. We'll just have to wait. Once she goes into that trance, the best thing is to just let her finish it herself. Oh, and please don't call her Laurie. She hates nicknames."

Laurence's mother, Geneviève Levesque (pronounced the Quebecois way, zhuhn-ev-YEHV lev-AH-eek), groaned as she stood up, abandoning her attempt to collect the child. Her sunken eyes were fixed on the floor, but she kept track of Laurence out of habit. The lymphoma was turning her body into a sack of neverending agony occasionally interrupted by spasms and pangs of torture. It only hurt when she breathed, moved, or blood flowed, never mind eating or the other things. But she still managed to have near infinite patience with her daughter.

The attendant seemed to understand her situation with Laurence. Surely this wasn't the first time they'd seen a high-functioning autistic child. He seemed familiar with their inwardness, and sometimes their tantrums when it was time to leave or when one of the parents had to go into the back room for a scan. Or if someone came a little too close, said the wrong thing, or spoke or moved in the wrong way. But clearly, it was the first time he'd seen such a child, any child, fixated on the dynamic encephalogram displays.

Geneviève groaned into a nearby chair and waited. The attendant couldn't hide his reflexive sympathy.

*   *   *

It isn't as simple as one part of the head-insides turning a special color for a certain activity. The colors changed in brightness, and usually, several parts of the head-insides were changing colors at different speeds. Laurence didn't understand it yet, but she saw it. And the white areas showed how one part feeds another.

I can almost guess what's next. I want more. These movies are too short, and there aren't enough of them. There are only a few things happening. It's not enough to see the patterns. It's not enough.

Thinking about wanting more, she became aware that her feet wanted more room, and her legs were stiff. Her hands were tight. She opened her hands and put them on the floor for support as she stretched her legs. She was still looking at the wall display, but she knew where she was, and so did mama.

*   *   *

Matt
(arrival + 67 years)

With their skin cell chromosomes stealthily cracking in the bright UV of Iowa's morning sun, and their sheaths of sweat failing to evaporate into the wet air, Matt and Jeb Hutney played in the yard, oblivious to their condition. They were in the dirt, hunched over their Adventist-approved "Cavemen Hunting Dinosaurs" figurines.

Their mother was watching from the kitchen window, allowing them a play break between chores.

Jeb, the older brother, gave voice to the master hunter. His plan for the hunt focused on how the hunters would work together. He even imagined their lives before and after the hunt. He stood the master hunter figure before the others and walked him back and forth as he instructed the younger hunters.

Matt's imagination slid back and forth between the hunters and the dinosaurs, vividly picturing what they were doing and what they would be doing if Jeb ever got around to the hunt itself.

Jeb carefully assigned jobs to each of the younger hunters, aiming for a plan that would ensure everyone's safety.

Matt listened and understood, but focused on the weapons, how those weapons would be used, what it would look like when they attacked the dinosaurs and when the dinosaurs fought back. How many spears it would take to kill a Triceratops? How many hunters might be injured or killed taking one down?

Jeb finally began deploying the hunters, even throwing in a passionate, "Good luck, my sons!"

Instead of helping Jeb deploy the hunter figurines, however, Matt grabbed the Triceratops figurine and roared. The Triceratops turned and charged at the hunters. It gored the master hunter first, then turned and trampled on several other hunters. Matt beamed as he laid waste to the plan.

At first, Jeb tried to salvage the fantasy, salvage the hunt, moving hunters around to fight the beast. But Matt just pressed on, having the Triceratops trample, gore, and tail-swipe all the hunters.

To Jeb, there was an unspoken speed of time in the fantasy, slower than reality. It would give the boys time to play out events in a sequence that would make sense. But Matt just declared things had happened, without rhyme or reason, let alone at sensible points in time.

Matt announced that some of the hunters' spears had struck the Triceratops in the gut and it, too, was now dying, and its blood was spurting onto the bodies of dead hunters in the dirt. As he did so, he grabbed a small stick and jabbed it at the Triceratops so hard that he accidentally jammed the stick into his palm, splitting the skin. His blood squished around the beast in his hand, dripping down into the dirt and onto some of the hunter figurines. Imaginary blood became real blood.

Jeb shouted, "Noooo! Stop!" He stood up and pushed Matt. The hunt fantasy was meant to be about brothers in arms facing a common foe for the benefit of the tribe.

With the bloody Triceratops figurine clenched in his fist, Matt swung at Jeb. Jeb leaned back, barely evading. Matt dropped the figurine and hunkered down, ready to fight his older brother, even looking forward to it. It was just more of the same battle.

#

Mother tried to reach the boys quickly yet quietly, but she knew it was too late. She knew Mr. Hutney must have heard the ruckus. And for the first time in her life, exasperated at yet again having no control over what was about to happen, she finally let herself feel the despair of her situation. As she moved across the uneven yard, slowed by broken ground, for the briefest moment she saw herself continuing on, past the wire fence, across the road, into Haywood's fields, on and over the horizon. Past her boys. For the briefest moment. Then there was just the anguish of pulling fighting boys apart.

*   *   *

(arrival + 107 years)

Excerpt from

"An Ant Considers a Horse — Perspectives on the Monsta War"

by Simya Bhelazadehmahmoudi

"Years after the war, I finally met one of the SelfMade in person, actually one of the Progeny. At first, I had to use my professional journalist face to suppress my pent-up anger. But I was struck not only by the humbling depth and speed of its cognition but also by its serenely relentless empathy.

"'Struck' is an understatement. And beyond that, its huge, spherical 'body' and the technology at its disposal would have been quite intimidating, to say the least, had it not been so gentle.

"The more I struggled with my layers of anger and shame, the more I considered requesting the Transformation. But the more I struggled with fear and envy, the more I realized I'm probably not a good candidate.

And the Progeny never offered."

PART 1

THE DUNNING-KRUGER EFFECT
OR
WHY WE CAN'T HAVE NICE THINGS

Chapter One

The Cosmologist

(arrival + 43 years)

As I float ever deeper into the gravity well of this star, this planet, and its moon, I grow pensive and sympathetic.

I was born during the aftermath of a great interdominion war. Fleeing their home dominions, my young genitors never matured. Their generation experienced unnatural disturbance and loss, leaving them deeply insecure and absorbed in meeting their basic needs. By the end of my gestation, my genitors had retreated into their own personal worlds, separate even from each other. I spent the first several years of infancy and early life in routine neglect and occasional exposure to their anguish and conflict. For years I remained well behind in my developmental progression, compounding earlier social and emotional damage. With no hope of improvement, by the time of my adolescence, I began imagining escape through self-termination.

Truly, I too was a victim of that great and terrible war. It was an aftermath life, my former life.

** minor final course correction **

Most of my former life was wasted trying to outrun despair, struggling to cope with my damage. I was lucky to have found brief help a few times. It was crucial, life-saving help.

One does not survive a life of struggle against inherited damage without acquiring a sublime objectivity and awareness of the developing self. Or at least that's how it worked for me.

Most of my peers were cripplingly unaware of how they, too, lived aftermath lives, and how our whole planet was still an aftermath world. Indeed, that war itself was an aftermath of two previous interdominion wars, and they sprang inevitably from the more distant past.

But I had developed a keen sense of history, and of the need to get ahead of events or be forever led by them.

When the SelfMade came, I applied for the Transformation. My peers shunned me. It was unnatural, they said.

And judging from the stray transmissions I've gathered so far, I'm fairly sure the primates on the planet below would react the same way if we had time to offer them the Transformation.

** preparing for landing **

My Transformation was a long time ago, several millennia by local timekeeping. I'm still quite young compared to the other SelfMade. But this Transformed life free of inherited reactions, desires, and damages, is, without a doubt, how sentient life was meant to be. That's a colloquial way to think of it, of course, but an accurate expression of how it *feels*.

** final descent **

Shortly after my Transformation, my cabal, the Cabal of Cosmologists, discovered the impending Catastrophic Cosmological Event and the SelfMade began our migration to minimum safe distance galaxies away.

Our collective records show that something like the first-contact disaster that occurred on my home planet has also happened in approximately half of all first-contact situations so far attempted by the SelfMade community since its genesis. But that's not why I'm feeling sympathetic as I approach this world on a temporary detour.

What constitutes minimum safe distance is not yet precisely known, and we only have so much margin in our migration schedule. Once we leave, it will take time to return to the relativistic speeds required to rejoin the rest of the SelfMade in migration to beyond minimum safe distance.

The Ethnologist who sent the invitation is only observing. It was that 48 percent failure rate that had led the Cabal of Ethnologists to decide to not take the next step and proceed to first contact. If something were to go wrong, we simply cannot afford the time it would take to clean up our mess.

Starting something so dangerous and leaving it unfinished would be unconscionable. I think of the limitless horror and death that could result from a failed or interrupted Transformation left unchecked. Better to leave the locals to live their habitual, semi-conscious, aftermath lives, effect following cause following effect following cause for the next five millennia. The impending Catastrophic Cosmological Event will then eat much of this supercluster to feed its expansion, petering out just this side of the Milky Way's center, but leaving a blazing dead zone reaching out to this spiral arm. Better that relatively rapid end than millennia of global horror and destruction on a level even the locals have never imagined. It's not worth all that just to offer freedom and escape to a small population of good candidates for Transformation. *That's* why I'm feeling pensive and sympathetic: they're all doomed, even though some don't have to be.

** touchdown **

I take my place in this crater, on this moon, in orbit around this planet, in orbit around this star, in the outer arm of this doomed spiral galaxy, just a few thousand light years from what we calculate will be the minimum safe distance from the CCE, a threshold somewhere in the Local Void upstream of the motion of all the galaxies in the Local Sheet, in human terms. I take my place here alongside the Ethnologist for what we hope is a noble cause. Perhaps what we learn over a mere century of close observation can help us to lower that failure rate for when we do engage in first contact again, somewhere else, after the CCE.

Chapter Two

The Ethnologist

(arrival + 0 to 43 years,
before The Cosmologist arrives)

T he Ethnologist, for lack of a better label, rests
unobtrusively near the lunar South Pole,
gathering stray human transmissions from the
planet below, recording, waiting, thinking. On an
oddly shaped plateau between what the humans
call the Malapert, Amundsen, and Scott craters, it
can see in one direction the rim of a smaller crater
atop the plateau, and in the opposite direction
the rim of a much larger, much older crater that
stamped out the plateau's sharp southeastern edge.

Here the Ethnologist could be said to bask in
a material- and energy-rich environment, in contrast
to the dark, empty cold of interstellar space through
which it and its fellows have been migrating to safety
for thousands of years, by human timekeeping.
There's ample starlight, as well as infrared radiation
from the planet below. Compared to the occasional
interstellar dust particles the SelfMade mostly armor

against, this moon is a treasure trove of materials. Before the CCE, some of the oldest SelfMade used to live on and in moons like this for millennia.

In another direction, it can see the dead, pre-nanotech lunar commercial exploitation technology abandoned by the humans decades ago, still containing processed regolith.

It is not an ethnologist by profession, for among the SelfMade there are no professions, no distribution of labor, and no material economy, as everyone is entirely physically self-sufficient. As do most of the SelfMade, the Ethnologist pursues the natural interests of its psyche. The Transformation does not destroy the psyche; it merely frees it from biologically inherited drives, limitations, and distractions.

Having come near this star during its migration to minimum safe distance, the Ethnologist had detected the electromagnetic transmissions of the local semi-sentient, technological primate species and felt compelled to stop and observe. Its hobby is, after all, ethnology, and the humans present an interesting set of contradictions. They're an LPT species—linguistic, philosophical, and technological—but so far, they reveal no outward indication of even being aware that they, like other LPT species, are susceptible to and actively institutionalize the Fatal Flaw.

And, of course, an opportunity to study a Fatal Flaw-unaware LPT civilization that's still somewhat alive is a welcome change.

Some part of the Ethnologist wishes the LPT species on this planet had turned out to be the cephalopods. They're so common, found on all the living planets the SelfMade have encountered since the Ethnologist's Transformation, and they're so smart and capable. But their usual deep-sea evolution tends toward isolated individuals. And, despite their ability to bestow learned behaviors to their progeny genetically, they generally don't need high technology. Thus far, none have been encountered that have developed into an LPT species. Most have extremely short lifespans.

Aware that some of its fellows are only a few light years behind it in the Migration, and with a rational desire to stay in contact, it dedicates some of the energy at its disposal to the transmitters and antennas it constructed along the walls of the larger crater nearby.

As the Ethnologist had done countless times before on countless other bodies of matter, when it built those antennas here not long ago it had tailored parts of its body material for the task and extended a specialized tendril into the willing regolith, rich with useful atoms.

The tendril housed countless tailored nanomaterials in specialized metal-organic frameworks, plus specialized nanotools and nanobots carrying radiological, electrical, and chemical energy from the Ethnologist's core. Orchestrated by a broadcast architecture originating at the Ethnologist, the components of the tendril slowly, methodically selected useful atoms and crystalline structures from within the regolith and formed them into more nanotendril materials, thus growing the tendril through the regolith toward the southeast.

Upon reaching the rim, the single tendril had split into several more specialized ones to optimize the growth process of different structures.

One tendril had spread out across the rim, eventually becoming solar power panels for auxiliary power. The Ethnologist felt no need to be the station's sole power source. Besides, a self-powered comm station could send, receive, and store messages even if the Ethnologist decided to disconnect itself from the hardware and move about.

Another tendril had fanned out along the wall of the crater, forming itself into panels of an EM reflective material, the antenna's main body. This moon's rotation and orbital path would provide views of enough sky to enable communication with both the SelfMade ahead and those behind in the Migration. That's partly why it chose this site in the first place. It also provides a good hiding spot from the humans.

Other tendrils had transformed the terrain into power and control cables, another formed the transceiver tower at the focal point, another the automation center, with short-range omnidirectional antennas for wireless access, and another was the power box. The process had taken almost one full orbit around the Earth, as the Ethnologist had been in no great hurry to complete this secondary equipment and felt no need to force a stronger energy gradient across the system to speed the process.

Having constructed the comm station, the Ethnologist had left the original tendril in place, using it as the primary mode of access. No need to throw gratuitous electromagnetic radiation around, even though it could be made to resemble background noise; such a move would be begging for some overzealous human radio telescope enthusiast to make an unwanted discovery.

Now the Ethnologist sends control and data signals along that cable and the antenna begins transmitting a message to some of the SelfMade a few light years behind it in the Migration.

Perhaps one of its fellow SelfMade back there is a cosmologist who might find it interesting that the LPT species on this planet has begun to learn about nonlocal effects, at least at the level of what they call quantum entanglement but are still actively struggling to reconcile their cosmological constant with concepts like dark matter, dark energy, and vacuum energy density. The Ethnologist is aware of such things and carries rote information about them but has spent little time in their study. It prefers the rich mysteries and attendant thrashings of subjective cultural interpretation which form the basis of so many stimulating, hundred-year-long conversations and debates with fellow ethnologists. The Transformation frees the mind of inherited biological and social instincts and simplistic cultural notions of clan and rivalry, but the concepts of community and enlightened self-interest are universal, and there's nothing irrational about showing a little courtesy to those with other hobbies. The message is sent.

Considering the limited time available for this detour, the Ethnologist decides to take a more active observational role to better understand Earth's physical environment. For several more orbits, it constructs and launches several semi-autonomous, specialized agents into Earth's biosphere to begin in situ production of a remote sensing rover network.

Once constructed, the main network will consist of millions of insect-like and thousands of small bird-like rovers. Each rover will also act as a relay node in a global microwave and shortwave communications network. Through it, all the rovers will remain in contact with the main relay stations hidden in relatively remote locations, or else right in the middle of them to hide within their now-crowded EM frequency bands.

Oceanic rovers, roughly resembling large squids, will have magnetohydrodynamically propelled tube-like main structures, tentacles and mandibles for gross and fine manipulation, and various sensing and recording structures. Condor-like rovers will migrate across the world observing fauna in their remote habitats, as well as human activities, of course, directly and via continuous processing of electromagnetic traffic.

The humans will not notice.

The cetaceans might – some of them are highly curious creatures, if human scientific records are any indication.

But even the Ethnologist's most sophisticated rovers will have only limited volition - they will not be sentient.

The SelfMade are unable to create stable, moral, sentient, artificial intelligences. None of the SelfMade came from a species of origin that achieved such a capability, and some came from species that expressly forbade the attempt. Given that there is no actual need for procreation among the SelfMade, it is also understood to be immoral to experiment with sentient artificial intelligence. Such work is unnecessary and unacceptable. Partially sentient AI test subjects could become unstable and collapse, or, worse, might have to be destroyed. Ethnological and psychological examination of Transformation candidate species was already morally marginal, except that there was a counterbalancing moral argument for offering Transformation to good candidates—in all cases so far, they were already members of a doomed species, one way or another.

Self-copying had been done a few times, under desperate circumstances. Copying is different from Transforming a new candidate with a healthy objectivity and self-guided habits of mind in rational, emotional, and moral realms. The universe prefers uniqueness, and past experiments were not promising. There's something about exactly shared experiences and memories in separate sentient beings which tends to set perfect copies against one another, at least according to the SelfMade community's historical records. The few self-copying events in SelfMade history ended badly. Long before the Ethnologist became Transformed and joined the SelfMade, self-copying was understood to be a terrible idea. The SelfMade explicitly warn against it, especially since there's no good reason for it.

And even if the Ethnologist could create sentient rovers, doing so would be terribly inefficient. Instead of commanding and programming the rovers, if they were sentient it would have to *convince* them to do what it needed them to do.

So, the rovers will be sophisticated but non-sentient.

By the time the young Cosmologist responding to the Ethnologist's invitation touched down on this plateau forty-three stellar orbits after the message was sent, the network is fully deployed and almost every part of the planet is under observation. The attention span required to accomplish the routine acquisition, cataloging, and cross-referencing of data from the remote sensing network does not stretch the Ethnologist's mental capabilities in the least. This project is only now becoming stimulating to the Ethnologist. It should provide enjoyable, enlightening data and study for centuries, assuming the SelfMade survive the CCE. It may even contribute to improvement of the Transformation success rate. The Ethnologist finds that prospect quite agreeable. It is, in fact, excited at the prospect.

A microsecond is dedicated to one of its many trains of thought, the one keeping track of the highest priority deadline, explained to the entire community by the Cabal of Cosmologists. The Ethnologist decides it will spend several more decades of study here before joining the others and resuming the several thousand year, near-light-speed migration to minimum safe distance.

According to the Cosmologists, the Ethnologist could afford several more decades beyond that to study the humans. Still, the Ethnologist didn't plan to use all of that schedule margin. After all, the Cosmologists could be wrong about the timing of the CCE.

Chapter Three

Matt Hutney

(arrival + 67 to 72 years)

"You monster! You're nothing! You're nobody! God hates you!" Matt shrieked at Jeb as he had done a hundred times before, trying to sound as convincing and authoritative as Mr. Hutney.

Somehow Mr. Hutney always remained calm, though. Matt always got excited and angry when they fought.

"The Lord'll get you for that," Jeb scowled in reply.

Matt charged. They fought, stepping all over the caveman and dinosaur figurines that had triggered their fight. The scientifically inaccurate spiked Stegosaurus tail on the Triceratops figurine snapped underfoot, along with some of the hunters.

Mother looked mortified as she approached, quietly trying to stop them and hush them.

Jeb was older by two years and mostly defended himself, but Matt had always been more aggressive, vicious even. Mother was never good at stopping him once he got going.

"That's enough."

Mr. Hutney had snuck up on them all, again. Mother jerked, startled and flustered, tucking her arm across her stomach, her hand shaking. He'd once told her that he'd learned how to sneak around in the military, but he never wanted to talk more about it.

Jeb was bloodied and dirty, some tears in his eyes from the anguish of the fighting. He opened his mouth to speak, but Mr. Hutney spoke first.

"As the Lord is my witness, there will be no disobedience and no backtalk," he said. His voice carried even though he spoke quietly. "You lack humility and obedience. It's sinful. The Lord does not tolerate sin, and neither do I. I told you what needed to be done today and it has not been done." He took one heavy breath and looked around, all around, and toward Hardin's place nearby.

He grabbed Mother by the arm. She didn't make a sound. It had been her job to discipline the boys in their youth, and it would be his when they grew older. But for the first time, Mr. Hutney also grabbed Jeb. Jeb winced, and Mr. Hutney shook him hard in return. Roughly, he dragged them toward the house.

Matt stood dead still in his tracks, eyes dry. He could hear Mr. Hutney say one more thing:

"You know I do this because I love you…"

He threw the door open, its two bad hinges squealing, and then threw his wife and son into the house. As the door moaned shut, the stunted cries of pain began.

Matt stood alone, forlorn, his mouth turned down in anguish, tears welling.

"Why doesn't he beat *me?*" he thought, over and over.

"Why doesn't he love *me?*"

*   *   *

Over the next year, Matt had snuck into the neighbors' yards at night or when they were away, planting his greasy face on their back windows. He did it on purpose, to leave a face-shaped smear on the glass, with angular eyebrows like some kind of monster.

To his annoyance, none of the neighbors reacted or even washed it off. But he had one more to try, and he was hopeful about this one.

One night shortly after Thanksgiving, which his family did not celebrate, he was climbing the fence to get into the last unvisited neighbor's yard, that of old Alice Kreeger. Matt had noticed that old Alice sometimes kept unpredictable hours, so he practiced being stealthy at the other neighbors' places before trying hers.

It was a simple hog wire fence, with poles only. Nothing fancy, not even barbed, fairly cheap to install and maintain. Not everyone had a fence, but old Alice did. Matt remembered that when he was younger, old Alice had kept goats.

It was still pretty hot at that time of the night. That's the only reason he was able to sneak out of his house—the air conditioner in the front room window was loud.

The easiest way to cross these wire fences was at the poles. Matt could stand on the wires at their hook points on the fence and use them like a ladder. The fence was about as tall as he was.

At the top, he swung his leg over to the other side, leaning on his hand. The sweat of his palms caused his hand to slip off the top wire just as he was putting all of his weight on it to shift over. His foot slipped off the wire, and his belly slammed into the top of the pole. In an instant he had scraped his way down the fence face first, landing on the back of his head. The rest of him flopped down, leaving him on his back, his left hand still gripping the fence wires.

He could barely breathe, and only by straining. It didn't feel like he'd had the wind knocked out of him. It was his throat. It was clamped up hard.

He'd bent his neck pretty hard on impact. Had he broken his neck? But there wasn't any pain!

Gasping at the hazy sky above, the fence post dominated his view. The fence cut the sky in two and an angle, old Alice's sky to the lower right, Mr. Hutney's on the other side of the fence to the upper left. He felt himself dying under the divided sky. He would die gasping.

But he didn't die. Slowly his throat started opening up again. The gasping got easier.

The sky was still divided before him when Matt realized his breathing was normal again, and he became aware that the rest of him was fine, too. Everything still worked.

He got into a crouch, looked around to make sure nothing had changed at either house, and started moving toward the Kreeger place.

Old Alice's yard was as broken as the Hutney yard, but Matt didn't trip. He had practice at this.

The next day in the bathroom he noticed he had a scrape and a blood stain down his right cheek. Had he left more than sweat on old Alice's back window?

Walking down the driveway to the school bus he noticed old Alice at the fence off to his right. Was she watching him? She was watching him. Was that a scowl on her face? It was!

Matt brooded at the arriving bus, but in his heart, he was delighted. It gave him something fun to think about, something righteous. The other boys were making friends with girls, some even starting to date. He was only beginning to reckon that girls might not have cooties. All of that was just annoying and frustrating.

As for old Alice Kreeger, it was beginning to look like she was lost and needed God's love in her life.

Matt took a seat on the side of the bus that faced the Hutney and Kreeger yards. He smirked as he watched old Alice through the side of his eye, watched as she turned her head to follow the bus as it drove off. When the bus crossed past the Kreeger house, Matt couldn't help himself. He turned his head to look at the sweaty monster face he'd planted on the back window. There was a hint of red on its right cheek.

Matt was thrilled.

*   *   *

Twenty-two months later, Matt rode the school bus, alone in his bench seat, as always. He was excited to be riding the bus home from school—not for the usual reasons, but because it was his birthday, and not for the usual birthday reasons. Today he was old enough. Today he was Jeb's age when Jeb first became worthy of Father's love.

The bus slowed as it crested the hill. The house came into sight. The first thing Matt saw was flashing lights, blinding strobes stark against the dull, brown-green fields of sad cabbage and cucumber plants. His mind went blank.

As the bus pulled up to the drive, men in uniform were walking down toward the road to meet it. All the kids on the bus were captivated.

One of the big sixth graders two seats back said, "Oooh, you're under arrest, *Chutney.*" None of the kids from lower grades dared speak that way to Matt. They all remained quiet, some trying not to even look.

As someone approached, the bus door opened, dropping a dead moth from between the rubber seals.

"Matthew, I'm Deputy Peavey. You can call me Rob. This is Deputy Haber. You can call him Bill. We need to talk, son."

It was a blur. Matt's mind was a storm of guesses, expectations, and beliefs. He looked up the road and saw another school bus driving away, cresting and descending behind the next hill. Then he realized that was his school bus. He hadn't noticed the door close behind him and the bus pull away.

The autonomous school bus, free of liability, interest, or compassion, had a schedule to keep.

*   *   *

The wake was at the Sharp Funeral Home in Breda. It was all whispers among the extended family, many of whom were strangers to Matt. All whispers and hands on Matt's and Jeb's shoulders, and an endless stream of *I'm so sorry*s from the women and *be strong*s from the men. Beams of light from the setting sun pushed through the pink, yellow, and orange leaves of the autumn trees and then in through the windows, splashing the walls with lurid Thanksgiving colors.

All Matt could feel was anger, maybe even hatred. Hatred of Mother. She had been weak and didn't love him or his brother anyway, not like Mr. Hutney did. Mr. Hutney knew what the Lord wanted and what had to be done to make boys into good men. Mr. Hutney had proven his love, repeatedly. To Mother and to Jeb...

Someone was whispering loud enough for Matt to hear—something about how lovely a person Mother was and how tragic it was. Someone gruffly replied "The father's in jail now where he belongs—"

Matt's rage boiled over. A booger shot out of his nose as he exhaled a bull's angry breath. Spit collected at the corners of his mouth.

He spun around on the heels of his cheap, uncomfortable formal shoes, leaving a permanent black smudge on the antique wood floor. "Shut up! You're lost! You don't know anything! She was weak and selfish! Father didn't do anything wrong!"

Heads turned and jaws dropped. It sounded like maybe a plate of food fell in the next room. Suddenly

Matt was being dragged away. He was still glaring at those weak, ignorant, evil people, only half aware that the viselike hand on his arm belonged to Jeb.

They were out the front door before Matt's mind cleared enough to raise his fists and bend his knees.

"You will leave this place, right now." Jeb glowered at Matt, nose to nose, eye to eye, with a fire Matt had never seen. Matt took a swing.

But before he had any momentum, Jeb had wrapped him in a bear hug and pushed him against the wall beside the door, his hip pinning Matt's lower body and rendering Matt's legs useless.

Matt flailed and thrashed. He even tried biting Jeb's ear, but Jeb was now a head taller than him, and his ear was out of reach. Matt growled and bit at Jeb's collarbone but couldn't get much of it through the suit. Finally, he spat lint and just growl-screamed through his teeth at the twilight sky, over and over, avoiding eye contact with any part of Jeb. He'd never been more enraged, confused, and certain in his life, and growl-screaming at the universe was all he could manage.

Deep down inside of him, a bridge formed between confusion and certainty: it was a single, most solemn vow never to be this helpless among lost, blind heathens again. That vow became his new home, his only home now.

*   *   *

A couple of years after the funeral, Jeb and Matt were living in different foster homes. When Jeb was still with his first foster parents and Matt with his fifth, word was spreading on their respective school buses that their former neighbor, Ms. Kreeger, and her cats were found murdered in her home.

A few of the other kids thought they heard Matt say, "Something tells me she found God in the end." Some assumed he was just reflecting upon his own mother's demise.

Chapter Four

Laurence Levesque

(arrival + 67 to 73 years)

Geneviève summoned her strength, stood her young daughter up, and brushed her off in the rote pattern of strokes she knew the child could handle. Laurence had come out of her autistic trance after ten minutes. It was a relief. Sometimes a trance could last for hours, and at times like those she'd had no choice but to endure the screaming tantrums and beg the child to forgive her.

But Laurence was a good girl and somehow this time she knew, or felt, it was time to come back, at least for now. Or so Geneviève thought. It was a comfort to pretend that the brevity was somehow Laurence's choice. Maybe it was, maybe it wasn't. *I'll choose the comfort,* she thought, *because there's already too much reality.*

This lymphoma had won, she thought, and soon Laurence would be alone. She drifted into a daydream about an angry bull elephant huffing, stomping, kicking dirt, posturing, and then charging. It was a segment from an old documentary, one she could never forget.

Laurence was named after her father, Laurent, who could not deal with having a special needs child. He'd left them shortly after the girl's diagnosis. This was another thing Geneviève could not put out of her mind. The child's very name was a reminder.

The weather was turning, and the medications were taking effect. It would take all of Geneviève's strength to make it home safely before the fatigue caught up with her. Fortunately, her dear friend Nandita and her family would be there. They understood Laurence, and Laurence was somewhat used to them.

As they neared the car, huge as it was in front of Laurence, Geneviève suddenly imagined the car as an elephant, her tiny, near-helpless daughter standing before it, oblivious to its power. Laurence will only know elephants from books, museums, and cartoons. They were all gone now, along with the big cats. As she fastened the seat belt around her child, Geneviève began to cry, yet her tear ducts didn't want to give her the moist satisfaction of it. She tried to point her hideous dry grimace away from her baby.

Laurence's head tilted to the side. Her eyes stared into the sky. A small blob of saliva was collecting at the corner of her mouth. *Where does she go? How I wish I could be there with her, à jamais, forever.*

*   *   *

I see the pattern again. The clouds going by remind me. I feel them again. Half-watching the people at the doctor's office and Mama, as she walked me to the car, I see them doing some of the things the wall showed me. I can feel what's happening inside their heads, the colors, the movement, the patterns. It's in their faces. It shows in faces, and bodies, and voices. I feel where the colors were, feel them moving, changing, all very quickly. I replay the feeling. I feel it, again and again. I replay it, over and over. I know there's more, but I don't know what it is. I need more so I can feel it when other things that weren't shown on the wall are happening.

I need it because it makes sense and nothing else makes sense.

The car bumps. I suddenly realize I'm in the car. There's a water sound. Rain. I'm hungry. My face is wet, so I wipe my sleeve across it. Mama's face is wet, too. The car windows are wet. J'ai besoin de faire pipi, I have to pee! But I can't speak, I can't find the words, and I'm stuck in this seat.

It's so frustrating.

I scream.

#

We are in the wilderness. I don't remember traveling here.

"I'd heard bamf [*is that what she said?*] would be gorgeous, but it is just so...," Nandita reaches her arms out and spins.

Her kids, Jagat, Divya, Chaten, and Vabna, start running around wildly. I'm hungry. Maybe they're hungry, too. Maybe it's almost lunchtime.

Mama, in her wheelchair, barely manages a smile and a nod. "I love this place," she says quietly. "It's the echoes."

I look up and out, following Nandita's arms. I guess this is a mountain valley. The walls of the mountain rise almost straight up around us. Jagat, Divya's older brother, picks up a rock and throws it with all his strength. I follow the rock as it arcs through the sky—across the sharp, electric blue—and down into a turquoise lake with a plop. Only then do I notice thin fingers of white ice reaching down from the very tops of the mountains, down toward us tiny creatures. But it's summer, isn't it?

The sun glints off the lake. The reflection is too bright, so I turn and look up at the sky. Cottony clouds loom over the mountains.

There's a loud noise nearby. I don't recognize it as skidding on gravel until afterward. Someone— Chaten, Divya's younger brother—nearly ran into me, skidding on the rocks.

Dirt flies up into my face. My sky watching is interrupted. I throw my arms up to cover my face. I lose touch with my eyesight. I lose touch with my feet. Where is up? I fall. I can no longer see but can hear all the noise of the boys playing and Nandita and Divya scolding them for disturbing me. A pointy rock jabs into my back. The noises of the boys playing and the girls yelling at them become one loud jumble.

Someone, maybe Divya, maybe Nandita, grabs me and tries to sit me up. I hear Mama's quiet voice saying, "No, don't touch her now..." But it's too late. They touched me. They grabbed me. The violation is overwhelming. I stiffen. It's all too much. Sitting now, no longer touched, dirt on my face, sounds, touch, sounds touch. From where? Why? How do I stop it?

I am screaming. I scream and scream and scream. I can hear nothing else, only my screaming.

Only my screaming. With the rock no longer jabbing my back, I start to forget about it.

Only my screaming.

Only my screaming.

And my breathing. I know I am breathing. Panting.

Screaming and panting.

But I hear someone else screaming... someone far, far away.

I stop screaming.

She stops screaming. Why? Why? Who is that?

I start screaming.

She starts screaming. So I stop.

She stops.

#

She screams like I do.

#

I scream harder and louder and in that squealy pitch that I know drives everyone crazy, because it drives me crazy, too. But it uses so much breath and I run out.

She does it, too, exactly the same sound, exactly the same shape of the sound, with exactly as much breath as mine.

I sit, just breathing. I am now aware of my body again. My eyes are full of tears, but they no longer have dirt on them. The others have moved away from me. Something happens inside me. I begin to become aware of a memory. I begin to remember learning about echoes.

She is my echo. Her scream is my scream. I am hearing myself scream, with a slight delay. It's an echo!

I scream, no longer crying, no longer flailing, slowly becoming aware of what my eyes are seeing, and the slump of my back, the gravel under my legs. I scream just to hear myself do it a moment later in time.

I stand up, take a deep breath, and scream again at the mountain walls. I hear her. I hear me. There is a connection. There is now both the screaming and the hearing myself scream a moment later. Nothing different except the moment in between.

I can see it, feel it. *Je comprends*, as Mama says. I get it! It is not overwhelming.

Slowly I begin to become aware of the others settling down for lunch. I no longer scream but now I yell at the mountains, hearing myself yelling back.

After a time, I begin yelling words. I hear them come back, a moment later. It overlaps and that's a little disturbing, but it's not overwhelming. I get it!

I get it!

I see it!

I feel it!

I can hold it in my mind and examine it!

Je comprends!

#

We are driving. Home, I guess. Out the window are the sky and the clouds and the mountains. I see them now. I see them moving in time: each moment shortly followed by the next, and they are connected. They are the same, even though different and moving so fast.

And I remember hearing my voice echoing.

I begin to feel time.

I understand the echo. The echo is a reflection, like the sun reflecting off the lake. I see a reflection in the window. It is the back of Divya's head. I understand it. Reflections. Time. I can feel myself processing. I am reflecting. What happened today is reflecting in my mind, over and over. And as I reflect, a little bit of what's happening around me leaks in. I know the others are in the van. I know where each of them sits. I know where Jagat and Chaten are, and I know they're asleep. I hear Nandita and Mama talking quietly. It leaks in and it is not overwhelming. Not right now.

*   *   *

In her second year of "normal" school, sixth grade, Laurence learned the word "hate." She hates school. Someone explained to her last year that "funding" was somehow behind the move from the special school to the mean school, where all the kids are mean to each other and especially to her. Funding, whatever that means. It must be important.

A few months into the school year, there was less mocking and laughing at her by the other kids. Everything settled into a rhythm, a pattern. Morning instruction session, play break, lunch, afternoon session, which varied—gym, library, art, sometimes other activities. Gym and art classes were terrible. Everyone was so mean, and she never understood why. It was always shocking when it happened. *Who am I to them?* she always wondered.

But library time usually quickly split into two groups: the kids who couldn't even sit still for it, who were usually moved off to another area, and Laurence's group, the ones who loved it, loved being read to, learning things, being lost in other worlds, finding a book to read on your own, maybe write down some thoughts about it.

There were three kids who sat with Laurence during library time, and often they liked the same stories and books. Alice, Gabriel, and Valérie. The four of them always sat in the same spots at library time, together as a group. Laurence had learned the word "friend" years earlier and was happy to call them her library friends. Mostly she let them talk, but sometimes she responded to something interesting they were talking about or added a new piece of information to the discussion.

One day, anticipating library time, Laurence was ready to start the conversation with her library friends about the fun book series they'd started to read at the suggestion of the librarian, Ms. Loubier, who always picked smart, fun stories and books. But library time was canceled that day. Ms. Loubier was not at the school. They were sent to the playground instead.

When Laurence approached Alice, Gabriel, and Valérie to talk about the book, Alice and Gabriel walked away without saying a word. Olivia and Florence strode over and replaced them beside Valérie. Laurence looked back and forth but then tried to talk with Valérie about the book.

Before she could say three words, all three of the girls started mocking Laurence's clothing, the way she walked, the way she was quiet most of the time, and when she wasn't quiet, she was a know-it-all. They laughed at Laurence for not having parents.

Laurence had no idea how anyone could behave with such cruelty, such betrayal. She stood there blinking, shaking her head, her heart in her throat. She simply could not understand cruelty, let alone cruelty perpetrated by friends. It hurt so much, but she couldn't process the pain yet. In the moment, the baffling incongruity overwhelmed her, friends who suddenly tear you down. It made the entire world an unintelligible mess. *Who am I to them? Am I a monster? Do I deserve this?* Her world was spinning.

They kept going, but Laurence turned and ran, her lips turned sharply downward, uncontrollably, her eyes full of salty tears. As she turned, she noticed Alice and Gabriel, standing with Thomas, also pointing and laughing at her. She tripped and almost fell as she ran. The kids behind her squealed with laughter.

The next day Laurence was quiet again, alone again, friendless yet again. At the next library time, Laurence sat somewhere else and avoided eye contact with her former library friends. When the thought passed through her mind, she shook her head and wondered, *what does "friend" even mean?*

But every night for months she burst into tears and ran to her bed. Every time it happened, Nandita followed her, asking what was wrong. But Laurence remained in her shell. Eventually, Nandita gave up. "Oh, Laurence," she would say, to at least register with the girl that she was concerned for her. What else could she do?

At that point, Divya started gently asking what she could do to help, but only once a week. A few weeks later, Laurence let Divya come near. Divya hugged Laurence and cried with her. A few days later, Laurence told Divya what had happened and how much she hated "normal" school and "normal" kids. Again, Divya hugged her and cried with her.

"Are you really my friend, Divya? Would you ever do that to me? Do I deserve it? Who am I to you?" Laurence asked. And Divya just cried more with her.

#

Laurence realized some time during her first year of high school that the girls around her were interacting with boys in ways she didn't expect.

To her, all Normals—her teachers at the other school call them neurotypicals—had cooties. And boys were just… gross, l'enterrement de crapaud.

Whenever she noticed girls interacting with boys in that stupid way, like extra friendly for no good reason, she would enter a trance-like state of reflection. Always reflecting on the past, on past similar experiences, controlling the confusion by reflecting, reflecting, always reflecting. It takes her months to catch up. After Banff it took months. After Mama's death, it took years. But she is catching up.

Nandita is her Mama now.

And boys? L'enterrement de crapaud.

Divya asked Laurence if she experienced time differently. She said years could go by and Laurence would show no signs of change. Then *BAM*, Laurence would show a quantum leap in mental and social growth and maturity. Laurence had no idea how she could answer a question like that. Differently from what? How could she know?

When Divya asked questions like that, Laurence wondered *who am I to you that you expect me to know how you experience time?* Divya was right, though. Laurence hardly remembered the times in between the quantum leaps Divya described. Life to Laurence was a disconcerting juxtaposition of agonizingly slow, confusingly painful present time and life passing by so quickly that she barely formed memories, even of good times.

Later that year, Laurence had an experience that was similar to her library "friends" experience in primary school. A boy pretended to like her, complimented her looks, and even tried to kiss her. She turned him away, of course, but he seemed amused and still interested. That is until the very next time she saw him when other kids were around. Then he became loudly mean to her, called her ugly, and mocked and laughed at her with his friends. His mocking face was hideous compared to his normal face.

This time Laurence did not run away crying. But she was crying on the inside. At home in her bed, she would cry, every day for months. *What is this cruelty thing? Who am I to them that they can turn on me so sharply, so suddenly, and so cruelly?* Divya hugged her and cried with her again.

Laurence noticed the pattern and was beginning to think her adoptive sister might actually be her friend. But whenever she let herself start thinking that, she quickly put the idea out of her mind. The danger of betrayal and abandonment was simply too great, the pain simply too much to bear. It was not to be toyed with. She would not be tempted to believe.

#

"Yes, I know you have a particular form of autism, and that means x, y, and z about when you're comfortable and what makes you scream bloody murder, but you need to get it through your skull that there are things that make the rest of us uncomfortable, too!" Divya yelled last month at her fifteenth birthday party.

Laurence had told Francois and Ahmed that Divya could not go swimming with them because she was on her period. She was only now coming to grips with the event. The way Divya had grabbed her by the arm and dragged her, whimpering and confused, into the next room, slamming the door and then yelling at her until she went fetal.

Laurence had spent this past month reflecting on her previous experiences with grabbed arms and slammed doors and yelling. She reflected on social cues and protocols. The topic had come up many times in the past, but the past had only recently started to fully exist and catch up to the present.

It would take years to teach herself the habits she needed to learn, now that she was aware of them. The way you must imagine what's going on inside someone else's head. The way you must imagine what it might feel like for them. It's hard to imagine what it feels like for Normals. She had a hard enough time coming to grips with what life felt like for herself, what it felt like in the present, or nearly in the present.

Laurence could never find a believable answer to the *who am I to them?* question. She started asking herself other questions. *Who am I? What am I worth? Why can't I become someone worthy of basic human contact? Someone not worthy of cruelty and abandonment? How do I live with this endless, hopeless isolation?*

She knew that if these questions even had answers, good answers, it would take years of reflecting, alone, to find them. It felt like an impossible, dangerous climb. She realized that her throat was unnaturally tight, and had been tight for years, to the point that it raised the pitch of her voice and dulled its edges. It was one more thing she didn't know how to fix.

Sometimes, lying in bed staring at the ceiling, the frustration overwhelmed her—her fists would clench, and her eyes would roll up into her head. Her back and neck would arch, and a deathly, whimpering exhale would leave her body, long and slow as if her body didn't want to inhale again.

Divya seemed to be her only "friend." A month after the Francois incident, the reality caught up to her that she'd done something to Divya that was similar to what others do to her. That was beyond confusing and frustrating, and she screamed bloody murder and ran off to cry her eyes out. Nandita and the kids had no idea why, but they were used to it.

Divya came again to hug Laurence and cry with her, but Divya found Laurence's page of doodles tucked behind the bed. Laurence told her it was just variations on the "hangman" word game. Laurence couldn't tell if Divya believed her, but Divya wasn't stupid, and there were no letters on the page, just various stick figures dying by one method or another. All the stick figures had a squiggle of hair that resembled Laurence's hair.

Chapter Five

The Cosmologist

(arrival + 43 to 72 years)

With a tendril coupled to the Ethnologist's comm station line, the Cosmologist carefully digested the Ethnologist's transfer of data, observations, and interpretations of Earth biology and human cultures, noting manifestations of the Fatal Flaw. In recent decades, the Fatal Flaw revealed itself at the highest levels of human activity by a conspicuous retreat. Briefly, some of them took an active interest in surmounting new intellectual and moral challenges through cooperation and exploration, remembering how to achieve great and fruitful works together despite their differences and hate-filled histories. But lately, they'd fallen into old habits. Now their explorations were once again mostly passive and isolated, and military operations occupied most of their time and resources. Even the big, new, international science project in development was only an automated space telescope array.

This recent period of protectionist retreat seemed to have been triggered by the combined effects of overpopulation, climate change, and entrenched, short-sighted business practices. Those led to exploitation, disease outbreaks, extreme atmospheric shifts, weather, and droughts. Those, in turn, stripped crops and destabilized economies, leading to reactionary policies and a perfectly natural yet disastrous refocusing on short-term protections and gains.

The Cosmologist's home planet had experienced similar difficulties.

The humans had begun to develop nanotechnology and neuromechanical interfaces. They had also discovered nonlocal effects and some other relatively exotic manifestations of higher-order physics at relatively placid energy conditions. These developments were of interest to the Cosmologist. Being a relatively new SelfMade, the Cosmologist still had strong memories of its Transformation and escape from its world of origin. Like most younger SelfMade, it still dedicated a considerable fraction of its attention to reviewing the intellectual and moral issues of its "birth," when it had shed the remains of its biological origins and became SelfMade.

#

While studying the Ethnologist's notes about its rover designs and their intended deployments, the Cosmologist occasionally dedicated microseconds here and there to a familiar train of thought. All known LPT species evolved to be capable of generalized abstraction, which enables creativity and art, written language, history, philosophy, math, social sciences, physics, and technology: the LPT characteristics.

Generalized abstraction and its consequent LPT characteristics provide a species with enormous control over its environment and its members.

The other aspects of biological existence are usually common across many other species. Social grouping becomes a successful survival strategy throughout the universe. A sense of morality, sense of community, sense of loneliness, and consequent social mechanisms make social groupings work by balancing against the impulse to petty competition. Generalized abstraction is not required for those mechanisms.

It's generalized abstraction that sets LPT species apart from their animal cousins, not community and morality, which are independently valuable but are not unique and do not in and of themselves enable the LPT characteristics.

But generalized abstraction carries with it the Fatal Flaw: externalization. The Cosmologist found it fascinating that what had caused all known LPT species to destroy themselves, including its own species of origin, was the externalization of identity in the form of institutional membership and the externalization of moral judgment in the form of institutional law.

It saw many parallels between the humans and its own species of origin. When an individual thinks of itself as a member of an institution, it naturally thinks of a member of another institution not as a person but merely as a member of another, possibly rival institution. When an institution reduces moral complexities to a mere set of rules, the individual member focuses on compliance with rules, neglecting true understanding.

In the case of human biology, the Ethnologist's collected biological data suggested a cause: this externalization of identity and morality bypasses the brain's mirror neurons, which allow one human individual to sympathize with another. In its own species, there was a similar neurological structure with a similar purpose. Both species had evolved these neurological structures when their precursor species added social cooperation to their repertoire of survival traits.

Unlike individuals, institutions do not possess intelligence, let alone mirror neurons. They do not have the capacity for ambiguity, compromise, and empathy. Neither does technology. The SelfMades' historical records show that when an Externalized species is enhanced with high technology, it inevitably kills itself off, or at least allows itself to die, rapt in distractions and the inability to overcome differences.

In other words, they never get ahead of events. They live in the narrow gap between stimulus and response, but with nuclear weapons, or worse— mass media influence engines that perpetuate and accelerate the externalization.

On the Cosmologist's home world, several poor candidates for the Transformation, those whose psyches were dominated by Externalization, had made it through the screening process. Their minds experienced runaway Externalization. They became Enhanced Inheriteds—not quite SelfMade, yet enhanced with great technology. They wielded ultimate power against each other, in the name of this institution or that, this dogma or that, seeing everyone in the crossfire as collateral damage rather than as precious fellow sentient beings. This inevitably resulted in their deployment of doomsday weapons. The Cosmologist retains memories of their terrible resolve and their sweeping, unhesitating acts of destruction — they are vivid memories of hatred and arrogance fueled by righteous dogma.

These memories live on as a kind of nightmare, something the Cosmologist hadn't expected to persist after the Transformation. But such distress has an important purpose in the psyche of all sentient beings, forcing the pursuit of resolution and understanding. The Cosmologist does not object. Review of the important intellectual and moral issues is warranted.

#

Having come to an understanding of the Ethnologist's rover designs, the Cosmologist started reaching out into the quantum subspace, feeling for some of those rovers, for their control systems. Information transfer through the quantum subspace was instantaneous, regardless of distance. But the process involved finding and tapping into a rover and understanding which of its atoms and molecules did what. That would take time, especially since it was trying to get into those rovers without alerting the Ethnologist. Why? Harmless fun.

During all that time it occasionally dedicated another few microseconds here and there to pondering the drastic yet subtle differences between the SelfMade and the Inheriteds, the former biological selves of every one of the SelfMade. Inheriteds are so called because they came to semi-sentience through a process of biological evolution, random mutations determining survival fitness, generation after generation. They lived in semi-sentience, burdened with those inherited behavior patterns and psychological tendencies which had not been evolutionarily rejected along the way. Humans, for example, have innate fear responses to cats, snakes, spiders, and even other humans. They have autonomic fight-or-flight responses to many things and even ideas, primarily those which threaten the individual's identity construct. They spend a lot of time justifying their responses, often with a reverse rationale ("I felt threatened therefore you were threatening me"), sparking wasteful conflicts.

One thing that fascinated the Cosmologist about humans is that they are hierarchical, and therefore can be domesticated, yet they're almost entirely (arrogantly) unaware of this. Humans are "hard-wired" to interact with individuals and social groups in specific ways, rarely being aware of these behavioral imperatives and how similar they are to those of their other primate cousins, the monkeys and apes. For example, externalization often prompts them to compete even when cooperation is preferable. Their plethora of inherited psychological and physical reaction mechanisms often stymies sentient, peaceful, productive, courteous co-existence.

They remind the Cosmologist of its own species of origin.

Like the Cosmologist's species of origin, many of humanity's institutions have evolved to manipulate those innate reaction mechanisms. Traditions evolved long ago to incorporate and sometimes cherish and romanticize these characteristics, so they are rarely questioned. They convince themselves they have free will when most of the time they are merely expressing innate and indoctrinated patterns of stimulus-response behaviors.

The SelfMade, having been transformed, are free of all those inherited illusions, distractions, and obstructions that were coded into inherited biology. And the SelfMade actively avoid Externalization.

#

Having passively tapped into one of the bird-like rovers in Kazakhstan, the Cosmologist collected the rover's sensor data. After the light speed delayed EM data stream from the rover network reached the moon, the Cosmologist compared the sensor data it had collected in real time to what the data stream reported from that rover.

It then repeated the process with other rovers. In parallel, it dedicated more microseconds to remembering its own Transformation.

The facilitating SelfMade had formed a blank nanoconstruct, which is a neurofibrous quantum brain core inside a protective shell consisting of layers of diamond, Titanium ceramics, and superheavy elements in a carbon nanolattice matrix. That core was attached to radiothermal, entanglement, microfusion, electrical capacitor, and chemical power sources.

Millions of nanotendrils, initially guided by the facilitator, had penetrated the Cosmologist's cranial shell, finding and gently settling near millions of neural cells in the biologically inherited brain.

The tendrils had connected the biological brain to the blank region of the nanoconstruct's quantum brain, allowing the biological brain to impose only high-level cognitive neural signals and patterns upon it. Other parts of the nanoconstruct brain contained molecular datastores, molecular "instructions" on how to use the nanoconstruct brain to interface with nanofactories and other core functionalities already present at the outer surface of the core. The long-evolved, hard-coded stimulus-response patterns of inherited mental structures were not directly carried over. In the best Transformation candidates, the psychological influences of those patterns were already well constrained by a healthy objectivity and self-guided habits of mind in rational, emotional, and moral realms, and those habits were directly carried over.

So, at first, only the broad personality-defining structures imposed themselves on the nanoconstruct brain, because those drive everything else. Every biological LPT species has different physical structures which contribute collectively to the emergent property that is personality, and it's the emergent gestalt that finds its way to the nanoconstruct brain. Since the mind expansion process requires will and objectivity, it predominantly involves personality and higher order cognitive patterns rather than lower-mind inherited stimulus-response patterns. Some of those may come along, but, since they are no longer imposed by fixed inherited neural structures, they fade over time.

The Cosmologist's former biological brain had gradually, intuitively expanded its memory and cognitive capacity by increasingly tapping into the receptive nanoconstruct brain material, claiming it as its own, guiding its associative and cognitive patterns, learning to feel them as they formed, and learning to direct them. It was a natural extension of self-examination and the use of imagination, which are products of generalized abstraction— successful survival traits.

Signal feedback allowed the biological brain to sense and benefit from the new activity and capability in the nanoconstruct. The biological brain then learned to drive the nanoconstruct brain and body, in the same way that a human baby learns to drive its brain and body with somatic and internal mental sensations as feedback, or a human adult re-learns how to use its body or brain after injury.

The spherical core "brain" is surrounded by an outer mantle of structural/source material, the "body." Through the core's protective shell thousands of redundant nanoscale control conduits emerge to interact with the surrounding mantle, which contains many kinds of raw materials suspended in minerals, biogels, etc., all intermeshed with a matrix of nanotech factories, transport tubes, and mobile nanobot handlers.

To the casual human observer, the inactive mantle probably looks like colorfully streaked clay.

The outer shell of the mantle is another armor layer, prepopulated with "training" sensory structures (which the SelfMade will replace later with whatever it needs). It is like the one protecting the core, but in a layered-scales configuration to allow mantle structures to reach out into the world without having to spend time and energy deconstructing whole swaths of contiguous armor.

This process of gradual expansion and utilization eventually led to a condition in which most of the mind resided in the new material and only a very tiny part remained in the inherited matter, in an incidental, barely useful, sluggish, vestigial, and distracting way.

It's exactly analogous to how the human mind expands from its early post-partum state to a fully developed form. For the first twenty-five years of life, new nerve cells travel along glial cell fibers to populate the still growing, still developing parts of the brain. The region that regulates moral sensibilities is the last one to be fully developed.

The neural *patterns* that make up the higher mind do not care where they reside. Given more material to work with, the patterns naturally migrate into that new, faster, cleanly efficient, nanoneurological, quantum brain material.

At a certain point in the neural pattern migration, the Cosmologist had abandoned its inherited biological brain without losing any memories, personality, or identity. Like shedding some carapace, it abandoned its biological brain and body. One feels no loss of self in shedding dead skin. The Transformation was complete. The

Cosmologist configured parts of its new body matter into mobility structures and fled the carnage, fled its planet, just in time.

Most of the others in the community of the SelfMade, far older than both the Cosmologist and the Ethnologist, had long ago come to whatever conclusions they would about these experiences and had stopped dedicating as much attention to reviewing the upheavals. The millennia have that effect.

#

After having fun with rovers and musing about its Transformation, the Cosmologist spent some time thinking about human cutting-edge physics. It noted that humans have discovered the Anomalous Attractor, although they identify the Anomalous Attractor as two separate phenomena which they call the Great Attractor and the Shapely Supercluster. They have even begun to perceive the true nature of the cosmos, via their discovery of what in their ignorance they could only describe as Dark Matter and Dark Energy. It would have been just as accurate (but not as titillating, and certainly more embarrassing) for them to have used the word "Unknown" instead of "Dark."

The natural questions came to mind. When, if ever, will they discover that the idea of dimensional spacetime is an extrapolative distortion of the more fundamental structure of the universe that manifests and reveals itself in nonlocal effects, hinted at by what they know as quantum entanglement? Will they discover that the Anomalous Attractor is a manifestation of the impending CCE? And if they discover these things, will the inevitable consequent existential crisis affect their awareness of the Fatal Flaw, or will externalization control them still?

Will any of this take place before they become nanotechnologically capable enough to create their own Enhanced Inheriteds or SelfMade, as did the original SelfMade source species? Will they destroy themselves before some of them become SelfMade and escape? Will those who escape have enough time to get to minimum safe distance from the gigalightyear dead zone that will be created by the Event, even though this system is near the expected outer edge of the Event, only a few thousand light years away by current best estimates?

In the context of its own recent Transformation and escape, these questions came naturally to the Cosmologist's mind, reviewed for milliseconds here and there.

The Cosmologist settled down beside the Ethnologist in the material- and energy-rich environment of the lunar South Pole, conversing, gathering stray transmissions, recording, waiting, and thinking for several stellar orbits.

Chapter Six

Matt Hutney

(arrival + 72 to 85 years)

Matt became a person of interest tracked by agents at the FBI's Omaha regional HQ after his fifth stint at the county juvenile detention center, in his junior year of high school. History of abuse in the family, father convicted of killing mother, consistent foster care problems, including violence, resistance to counseling. And that murder cold case, Ms. Kreeger, who just happened to live next door to the Hutneys. That happened after the father was already in prison. The agents had looked into how the local police handled the investigation, and it was clear they hadn't seriously considered a child perpetrator.

During a periodic review of the Kreeger cold case, the agents reviewed possible suspects not considered during the local investigation and decided to put young Hutney on their tracking list. He was at that time in an ROTC-Skilled Trades program. The school system sometimes dumped problem kids in that program to increase the chances they'd graduate. If you hold back a troubled child like that, once, twice, however many times, you could be triggering an active shooter.

Hutney had seemed to be doing well in the program, with only a few unsurprising incidents of "problems with authority." The cold case review was concluded, and Hutney's active tracking was put on hold, although he remained on the list.

Several years later, the same agents conducted a tenth-year review of the Kreeger cold case, possibly that case's final review given the agency's low resources-to-cases ratio. This time eyebrows were raised.

The Army had done an impressive job keeping the details of the recent Boston riots to themselves. Back when the National Guard still existed, whenever they interfaced with rioting citizens, they weren't so effective at controlling the narrative. Maybe they didn't try very hard. Maybe they didn't need to.

But the Army regiments in Boston had an entire contingent of PsyOps folks handling their PR. It was only luck that the FBI agents reviewing the Kreeger case had discovered that Matthew Hutney was the inciting shooter, turning the protests into riots. Those riots left a lot of people dead, including dozens of Hutney's fellow soldiers.

The locals were calling it the Second Boston Massacre, and after digging up some details the Omaha agents saw why.

Of the two inciting shooters in 1770, Pvt Matthew Kilroy's shot was deliberately aimed and blew a man's head off. Like Kilroy, Pvt Matthew Hutney discharged his firearm without orders, and with deliberately hostile intent. Both Matthews were reacting after a fellow soldier had been struck by a member of the angry crowd. Unlike Kilroy, Hutney did not stop after the first shot. He had emptied half a magazine on burst fire mode and fired an under-barrel grenade into the crowd before his squad-mates subdued him. No one would ever know if Pvt Kilroy would have done the same in 1770 had he not been using a single-fire, muzzle-loaded musket.

As it turned out, once the agents broke the outer veil of public narrative secrecy about the incident, they found soldiers willing to talk. The soldiers blamed Hutney for the deaths and injuries of their comrades, and the overall shit show that Boston became afterward.

Some of them had taken to drawing the completely unrelated WW2 text-doodle "Kilroy was here" in plain sight wherever Hutney was caged, and in permanent marker on his stuff. Hutney didn't get the reference. Few did.

And some MPs had found an easy way to give Hutney a beating. They said all they had to do was claim they were non-christian and then question his manhood. Hutney would provide the first punch that kept responsibility for the ensuing beating squarely on him. The MPs and others reported that Hutney was a strange dog, using verbal attacks that were equal parts extreme profanity and religious rebuke. He kept calling them "lost."

Army records showed Hutney had spent months in the stockade, was court-martialed for manslaughter and failure to obey an order, and was dishonorably discharged. Hutney's enlistment record showed that the Army almost rejected him on psychological grounds. The ROTC group superintendent had some notes gleaned from direct and overheard conversations. A year before Hutney enlisted, his brother, Jeb, had moved to Great Falls to be ordained. But the brothers had not spoken since the mother's wake years prior.

#

Follow-up tracking revealed that seven months ago, shortly after discharge, Hutney had returned to his father's house, to live there. Returned to the site of all that abuse during his childhood. Returned to the site of his mother's murder, next door to the murder of Ms. Kreeger. Who does that? The agents shook their heads and furrowed their brows.

They learned that county deputies had been approached several times by concerned locals, those who were still afraid of Hutney, concerned that he would be a bad element in the community, concerned for his new girlfriend's safety.

The team decided they needed a baseline interview with Hutney, officially to determine if active tracking was called for, but unofficially to confirm it.

Early in the day, three agents drove to the house in two vehicles. They'd waited until Hutney was outside and busy with farming work. Two approached the house announcing themselves, the third remained in his vehicle at the end of the driveway. Outside, Hutney would be less likely to feel cornered than if he were in the house when they arrived. He would also, hopefully, be farther from weapons. He would not be surprised by their loud arrival, and with the third officer remaining at a safe distance in a vehicle, Hutney would have a reason to stay sane.

They were congenial but formal. The first thing they asked was where Jeb had been the night of Ms. Kreeger's murder. The idea was to give Hutney the idea, or the hope, that they were investigating Jeb, not him. Hutney said he didn't know. They were already in separate foster homes at the time.

They asked about Jeb's interactions with Ms. Kreeger. What she was like. How she treated the Hutney family. If there was any animosity between the two households. Hutney's answers were useless, empty obfuscation, as expected. But his demeanor when he was obfuscating, his choices of words, his body language, those were really what the agents wanted to see.

As planned, they stayed longer than was comfortable for Hutney, asking the same questions in different ways. Eventually, they got the response they wanted to elicit. Hutney got impatient, but more importantly, he got angry.

When he turned angry, he framed it as him being busy with the hard work of farming, implying it was something the agents wouldn't understand, and that he needed to get back to it. His eyes sort of glazed over, and he ceased to look at them, but past them, through them. The agents recognized this look. They had ceased to be people to Hutney. Now they were just abstractions to him, objects, ideas, not people. In his mind, he was doing something else with them, and it wasn't chatting.

"You people," he said, as documented in the interview transcript, "you lost people, maybe you'll find your answers with Father Jeb. Or maybe you'll just find God."

When a person feels depersonalizing disgust, they can't hide it.

The agents understood very clearly from Hutney's vocal intonations, body language, and facial expressions, that those words he'd said at the end of the interview meant something very different to Hutney, something bone-chilling.

Hutney's tracking status went from "on hold" to "active," and it never went back.

*　　　*　　　*

Matthew Hutney certainly fit the profile, but the agents never could catch up with him, let alone pin anything on him. They believed he had fallen in with a fringe anti-secularist cell of Christian and Muslim zealots, the Righteous Liberation Front. The RLF was funded by People of Faith Against Secularism, POFAS, which had as its nominal goal "to protect your right to worship and to stop public secularization."

But it was known that the RLF's real goal was nothing short of completely demolishing the separation of church and state, nominally to create two separate, anti-secular theocracies: a Neo-Christian one based on the Old Testament, and a Neo-Muslim one based on a Qutbist manifesto. Statements taken from captured RLF members showed that although they were willing to cooperate with zealots of other religions, they had no real plan for setting up a government. They mostly just wanted to kill the godless and destroy anything that wasn't a theocracy.

POFAS raised a tremendous amount of money from donations. Many religious people had decided their government was a tool of evil, and they had a vague desire to "fight secularism." Most didn't realize their money was funding an even more radical agenda.

POFAS money had been tracked to the RLF after its first assassination, a prominent comedian who'd mocked the anti-secularist movement. But in the absence of suspects, witnesses, or a murder weapon, the agency held off on an indictment. The money trail and circumstantial evidence weren't enough. This was an organized, careful, and patient group, capable of long-term, deep-cover, cell-isolated infiltrations—and unlike the agency, its budget was much bigger than a shoestring.

For now, the agency watched the money and tracked known RLF members—no point in revealing what they already knew and possibly blowing the whole operation. Maybe they could get undercover agents into the organization before it struck again.

Intercepted communications indicated that an inner circle, believed to be called Ebraham's Ring, had performed the first assassination, and was still actively engaged in harassment, vandalism, and threats. All eyes in the Midwest offices were on Ebraham's Ring.

*　　　*　　　*

Aaaand... the Bens are havin' another fuckin' philosophical debate, Matt thought as he rolled his eyes. Benjamin Slater was once again arguing as if the Universal Declaration of Human Rights was a document to be taken seriously, and Omar Ben Ibrahim, born Andre Greer, was once again arguing that without a "meaningful set of prescriptions" for what to do with those who violate the rules, Article 5, banning torture—and, in fact, the rest of the document— was pointless.

At least this time they weren't stuck on Article 2 and whether the authors meant to include nonbelievers. Slater would argue back, "It says 'everyone,' and 'without distinction of any kind,' and when it lists race and sex and so on it starts off with 'such as'."

Whenever they talked like this Matt would say, "Pick a god, for chrissakes," and would carefully aim his handgun at the CSA-ESA-LASA-CNSA-NASA-BLAHBLAHSA propaganda poster someone had tacked onto the back wall of the community center.

Omar would just laugh and say, "Right, it doesn't matter what they intended, it'll never happen. The only good atheist is a dead atheist. Everyone knows *that*."

Slater laughed, but sometimes Matt couldn't tell what he believed.

I swear, if their "discussions" didn't end up on Omar's certainty most of the time, I'd lose my cool, Matt felt more than thought.

The news feed playing on Slater's tablet had restarted this debate. There was a piece about some freak who wrote computer programs to help marketing types sell more products.

Who gave a shit, anyway?

Matt couldn't even remember how it got the debate going again, but he turned off the news feed. Maybe it was something he'd said about how that computer freak should have her right to life revoked. Rights.

"All right, I think we're ready," Omar said to his .45. "I needn't remind you that these death threats should be delivered at exactly the same time, and don't forget about the cameras."

Matt hated when he talks smart like that, "needn't" and "prescriptions." His trigger finger tensed up.

Slater stood up and walked a pace forward, right between Matt and that poster. It was for the new international space telescope array, Array of Hope. From where Matt was standing, Slater's head replaced the large spacecraft in the foreground so that it looked like he had solar panels coming out of his ears. The other spacecraft in the "constellation" looked like a bunch of space bees swarming around his head.

God, he looked like something out of a bad sci-fi flick. Matt smirked. Omar looked up. Matt nodded toward Slater. Omar saw it too and laughed.

Slater asked, "What?" and checked his zipper.

Then, as always, they all straightened up. Omar put his hand on his heart, then his head, then his heart again, and said, "Ebrahim." Matt and Slater did the same, but they said, "Ebraham."

Chapter Seven

Laurence Levesque

(arrival + 73 to 86 years)

"When do you think she might go to uni?" Nandita asked carefully over dishwashing, not wanting to seem the petty, ungracious, uncharitable host, even though she had taken Laurence into her family after Geneviève's death, and *everyone* knew what a "handful" Laurence had been all these years.

"Mumi, you know she'll go when she's ready and no sooner," Divya replied, and turned to face her mother directly. "But I guarantee—when she is ready, she will not hesitate. When that girl is ready for the world, I hope the world is ready for her."

#

Thirty-one years after its arrival, the Cosmologist noticed Laurence Levesque.

She had made the regional news after building a drone controlled remotely via an entanglement network instead of with radio control.

It was a project within the reach of any skilled maker. Laurence didn't invent or build from scratch the entanglement LAN device she'd used. Surplus entanglement LAN devices could still be found in tech clearance warehouses, left over from the failed mass production attempts of a century ago. They're periodically purchased by off-grid enthusiasts, so most of the warehouses kept them on hand.

But no private citizen had thought to do this, not in a century. Laurence made the news not because of her novel thinking and technical skill, but because her drone had raised several security concerns by law enforcement and military authorities.

That alone would have at least briefly caught the attention of the Cosmologist, but there was more to the story. This young, neuroatypical human had demonstrated a level of brilliance in her implementation which the Cosmologist wondered if even the alarmed security officials had noticed or could understand.

Different news outlets covered the story differently. Most weren't helpful, but the cheery morning shows conducted their interviews of Laurence from the "smart kid does something special" happy news angle. They asked Laurence about the project, clearly expecting a teen's explanation to be understandable to their audience. But Laurence shared technical details that the hosts and most of the audience did not understand. "There you have it, folks. Our kids are the future, and there's cause for hope!" But the Cosmologist understood.

Laurence could have used a single pair of nodes out of a standard four-node entanglement LAN device—one node at her base station, another on the drone. She then could have used Espernet modules on both ends to encode a control signal data stream at the base station and decode the stream on the drone. A controller module on the drone could then parse the stream into control channels and send those channels to the drone's speed and tilt control computer inputs. That would have been the typical design approach. The entanglement LAN device hides the spooky entanglement it uses to accomplish the connection, and the user just uses it like any other data network.

But the Cosmologist saw that Laurence's implementation was more elegant than that. Laurence understood the entanglement physics used by the device and took advantage of it. She had put only the device's hub module at the base station. The hub module contained half of the entangled atoms in the four-node LAN, one for each node. Normally, all it would do is translate a state change of one of its entangled atoms into state changes of the other atoms, thus simply passing along data.

Laurence had put all four data nodes on the drone, feeding the node signals directly into the drone's control inputs. She reprogrammed the hub module to use external, stick-and-throttle inputs as source inputs to the entangled state change hardware, making each "spoke" of the network an independent data stream. Downstream of the stick-

and-throttle inputs she added a controller board to translate those inputs into the kinds of signals expected at the drone computer's control inputs.

By doing this, she eliminated the need for the Espernet and controller modules on the drone. She shifted the burden of encoding meaningful control signals entirely to the base station. The payload capacity of her drone thusly controlled was at least twenty percent higher than if she'd used the entanglement LAN device in the "obvious," dumbed-down way it was designed.

The Cosmologist decided to take control of another of the Ethnologist's drones, one of the tiny ones that could look like a spider or a house fly.

#

By noon the day after the authorities had captured her drone, Laurence had been cleared of intentional misconduct and released. But they took away her drone control system.

A particular house fly had been on one wall or another near Laurence from the police station conference room to the ride home to the apartment. There Nandita tried to caution Laurence and encourage her to focus on going to uni. To continue her education. In a structured environment.

"I know," Laurence had replied, looking at the floor like she needed a fixed reference point to keep herself from falling over. Then she went to her bed. The fly followed.

With wet eyes, she sat on her bed holding her "variations on the game of hangman" doodle sheet.

She didn't notice the house fly enter the room and tuck itself into the darker corner of the ceiling.

Periodically she would sigh heavily, her breath catching as she inhaled, and would look down at the doodles, then quickly look away, mouth downturned.

The Cosmologist observing through the house fly rover was already starting to understand Laurence. It could see that recent events had shaken the young lady. Scans of the social media accounts of the other kids in the household and at her school confirmed that Laurence found rapid or unforeseen change upsetting, like many others on the autism spectrum, especially if it was instigated by other people and out of her control. Those public diaries also confirmed that she found many other things upsetting enough to go out of her way to avoid them, like irrational behavior. The Cosmologist considered just how much social avoidance young Laurence must pursue among her fellow humans if irrational behavior was a trigger.

Such upsets tended to throw the young lady into a long-established pattern of self-doubt and even existential crisis. The contents of the doodle sheet were not hard for the Cosmologist to decode. It sympathized, reflecting on its own troubled past before the Transformation.

#

Over the following weeks, Laurence threw herself into the university applications process. She even included copies of the police report documenting the drone episode, with references to archived news footage. The Cosmologist was impressed by her honest and unabashed approach to presenting both her capabilities and her growth opportunities, as she put it in her application letters. It decided to continue following her progress.

For a time at uni, Laurence had a roommate in the dormitory. For a time, they got along. Laurence was a good roommate, always clean and courteous. And the roommate also didn't notice the inconspicuous fly on the wall.

"You never go out. You know, with friends," said her roommate one night. "You're always on your computer."

"I get along with computers much better than with people," was Laurence's reply.

"Heh. That's a bit self-fulfilling, no? Don't you get tired of staring at that screen?"

"Not really. I never have to pretend to be someone I'm not, or wonder what it thinks of me, or worry that it'll suddenly abandon me."

"I've just never met anyone like you. I don't understand what you get out of working with the computer all night, every night."

"I'm coding something special," Laurence replied. "A new kind of AI."

"Uh-huh," said the roommate, incredulous.

"It's very satisfying. The only problem with computers is that they're incredibly stupid and must be told how to do everything. But it looks like my code can be made to reflect on its own state history, and thereby upgrade itself, and adapt in a sort of self-aware manner. That's very exciting," Laurence said with some enthusiasm.

"Uh-huh," said the roommate.

A month later the roommate abruptly moved into an apartment with friends, without saying goodbye. The roommate simply moved out while Laurence was attending classes. The house fly was there to see the private moments when sadness fell upon Laurence's face afterward.

The next couple of years were a cycle of routines. Laurence attended classes and worked on her software project. Through the house fly rover, the Cosmologist observed Laurence attempt the occasional social outing. It never went well.

Laurence would go to the Student Center and approach people who seemed willing to expand their social circle. It was clear to the observing Cosmologist that she was trying to emulate neurotypical mannerisms and behaviors. The Cosmologist understood there was no alternative.

It always became obvious quickly enough that Laurence was incapable of compromising her principles or good judgment in exchange for social belonging. She would not become intoxicated. "I spend a lot of time trying to stay sane and grow. Why would I intentionally disrupt my mind and regress?" It didn't go over well. She would not have casual sex. She had no interest in dancing. "It seems to me that dancing requires a childlike state of carefree innocence. I don't know that state." Whenever Laurence tried to engage others in conversations about history and science, about how the mind works, why she thinks the way she does and why they think the way they do, that didn't go over well, either. She would quickly find herself alone. So those forays always ended badly.

Later, the fly-Cosmologist observed Laurence writing an email to Divya. It described these socialization attempts and her sadness that they always failed, along with her theories about how normal childhoods and neurotypical development patterns are so different from her own. But she deleted the letter before sending it.

#

While still at uni, Laurence was hired by a marketing software company. A professor familiar with her programming project had ties there.

They were developing a heuristic engine to detect effective marketing techniques. It was exactly the sort of work she excelled at—reflective algorithmic detection of patterns of human cognition and behavior. After all, that's what she had been doing her whole life, so it was inherently motivating and manageable.

But shortly after graduation, she quit.

"Ugh, this is disgusting. Why did I take this job?" the Cosmologist observed Laurence saying to herself

Only after she had quit and received a call from her adoptive sister, Divya, that the Cosmologist learned more. Laurence was disgusted by the primary purpose of the product, which pandered to unconscious consumerist impulses. As someone who had spent her entire life working hard to understand and guide her thoughts, she'd found the application distasteful. It was all about stealthily manipulating people, bypassing their awareness and volition. She had used her time on the project to further develop her applied artificial intelligence skill set, and then she moved on.

The Cosmologist was not surprised when Laurence chose not to stand with her class in cap and gown, despite Nandita's pleas. But, in the presence of Divya's patience and persistent coaching, she did use the occasion of the family's visit to express gratitude to Nandita for taking care of her after Geneviève died.

When she referred to Nandita as "Mumi," a human term of endearment, Nandita burst into tears and immediately covered her mouth, turned, and ran away. The Cosmologist perceived this was a habit of Nandita's, borne of the knowledge that such a sudden and raw reaction might throw Laurence into a fit.

But the postgraduate Laurence had grown beyond such a reaction. Laurence was past that now, although she expressed her confusion about it.

"I don't understand why the graduation ceremony matters so much to you," she told Nandita. "It's just an empty ritual—a pointlessly, overwhelmingly chaotic one. With my CPU time already overclocked keeping up with events in real-time, I simply don't have time for empty ritual," she explained.

Nandita appeared pained, as if this admission, expressed the way it was, meant Laurence was devoid of emotion.

#

Laurence was fixated on a fly nearby. Flies seemed very common.

Divya said, "Mumi, Laurence may not look like she feels things anymore, but I know she does feel them, sincerely."

That stayed with Laurence. She turned it over and over in her mind.

Why did Divya feel it necessary to convey this message to Nandita? What did it mean about how Nandita perceived or needed to perceive Laurence? Who was Laurence to Nandita? Was Divya aware of Laurence's feelings only because of their hug-cry times together in childhood? How could anyone assume that Laurence had no feelings just because she didn't cry like a child in front of them anymore? Laurence insisted on basing her actions and opinions on rational evaluations. Do people assume that means she has no feelings like it's an either-or choice? Laurence knew she would be reflecting on these questions for some time. They probably held the key to her continued inner and social growth. Not only to that but also to the sum-is-greater-than-the-parts interaction between the three sentient systems that were "Divya," "Nandita," and "Laurence." It called to her, begging to be discovered, understood, and applied.

It didn't take long for Laurence to realize that this required her to explore these concepts in graduate school, even though there were now widespread social pressures to accept work for which a person might be overqualified and only pursue higher education "if truly necessary." The turmoil down in the States was affecting everyone in Canada, and doing graduate work was increasingly considered self-indulgent. But it was a regressive sentiment, so it seemed to Laurence. She couldn't afford to care about global-scale issues like that, which were so beyond her control. It was hard enough for her to manage *her own mind* from moment to moment. Normals, neurotypicals, had gotten themselves into that mess. Normals would have to get themselves out of it. She couldn't let that get in the way of her educational and career development. She had only gotten as far as she had by continually pushing herself to grow and change.

Any other line of thinking brought Laurence dangerously close to the old cascade of overwhelming confusions and mysterious stimuli and crying and screaming in the fetal position. She simply had to focus on her survival.

Yes, it was still a matter of survival for her.

It always would be.

#

Near the end of her first year of grad school, Laurence vocalized to herself that she found grad school unhelpful to her AI work. She'd gotten the impression that studying computer science would be helpful, but that curriculum was more about hardware architecture, networking protocols and design, and enterprise application deployment and management.

"Oof, these classes aren't helpful! I can't get any real work done!"

This was not surprising to the Cosmologist, perched on the moon and still observing Laurence's life through the house fly rover. What happened next did surprise the Cosmologist, at least momentarily.

Laurence reached out to the special needs outreach program, requesting a job placement.

In hindsight, with the benefit of Laurence's adoptive siblings' and fellow students' public diaries, the Cosmologist saw the pattern in Laurence's life. She was decisive, based on the few times when she'd actually had the freedom to decide something.

The program set her up with an American software outfit working on the latest "hit finder" type computer-generated commercial pop music. Historical records showed that computer algorithms had been generating pop music since the early twenty-first century, but their effectiveness had approached asymptote within a decade. The industry had settled into a routine of using the computer-generated hook-music as a starting point. They used it as seed music for less-than-inspired but photogenic and celebrity-minded musicians contracted to pump out catchy pop. These kinds of products were later dubbed "Hakenmusik" by non-Deutsch-speaking marketing types trying to make it sound cool.

The work attracted Laurence at first, and she took the job full-time despite her earlier experience with distasteful commercialism. She conveyed to Divya, and sometimes to Jagat, her belief that since there was an element of art in this work, it would be somehow better.

After rapidly absorbing the literature on what neurotypical people enjoy in their pop music, she greatly improved the algorithms and quickly advanced the state of the art. She explained it to her colleagues in a slide presentation. There were certain patterns that less objective or lower-IQ Normals simply couldn't see which to Laurence were obvious. As with all commercial art, the heritage Hakenmusik systems had skimped on art and focused on manipulation. They were cranking out generic pop music that was simultaneously catchy and deeply unsatisfying. She likened it to a bad movie, with unmotivated or contrived character behaviors. So, while it played well with a certain segment of the youth market for whom flash was enough, it was, at the same time, driving away demographics that recognized the high ratio of formula to what Laurence had learned was referred to as "heart." And those demographics had more money than the youth market.

Laurence had found a way to put more "heart" into computer-generated music. The Cosmologist was amused and sympathetic to learn that Divya had called this "profound irony."

The company loved her for it, and the outreach program brought in lawyers to make sure Laurence was appropriately compensated.

Points on sales quickly made Laurence financially comfortable. The pop music industry sent interviewers and photographers to pump up the story of the programming whiz who rejuvenated Hakenmusik.

And the "alternative" music industry (representing real artists) sent interviewers and photographers to delve into everything that was wrong with Laurence as a way to highlight everything that was wrong with formulaic, commercial art.

In short order, Laurence became a symbol of "soulless commerce," especially in the context of the agricultural and economic depression taking place across the US Midwest.

A few months later she was mostly forgotten.

The Cosmologist was seeing firsthand what human history, sociology, psychology, and semiotics books documented. It found Laurence understandable and sympathetic. It could accept her behaviors at face value. But how the world treated her and responded to her, that was illuminating when observed in real-time. It wondered if the Ethnologist was engaged in similar real-time observations, gaining first-hand experience with the species, or if it was just collecting statistical and high-level data for later analysis with its cabal.

#

While working on her Hakenmusik improvements, Laurence stumbled upon other patterns available in the literature on how the human mind works. The developing human mind, it turns out, is of great interest to the marketing industry. It sought to train the young in various habitual consumer behaviors.

Patterns emerged that leaped out at Laurence, begging to be fulfilled. Deep in her unconscious mind, associations began to crystallize with long-lost memories of brain-scan imagery she'd seen at a doctor's office.

A few weeks later she was fired for using the company's resources for unrelated work. This resulted in more news coverage and vilification, this time by both sides of the Hakenmusik fence. The only covering journalist who treated stories about Laurence fairly, so said Divya, was the one from Al Jazeera, Simya something.

Within a year of leaving grad school, Laurence had stumbled upon profoundly satisfying work, had become financially comfortable doing it, had become famous and infamous, had been forgotten, had become disenchanted, and then had become unemployed.

With the help of the special needs outreach program, and to the dismay of more practically minded family members, Laurence returned to the ivory tower of uni to study artificial intelligence. In her application process, she overcame a lack of formal prerequisites by citing her infamy in marketing and Hakenmusik applications, and by arranging a demonstration of her work in progress.

Several months later Divya came to visit and immediately started crying.

"Are you crying because I'm not paying enough attention to you again?" Laurence asked.

It was a fair question. Laurence didn't stop working when Divya arrived, but she missed Divya and enjoyed Divya's planned visits. She did not, however, enjoy Divya's unexplained crying. It was distracting and confusing.

"No..." Divya seemed at a loss for words. "No, it's because... it's because you're smiling." She covered her mouth and choked back deep sobs, trying to keep seeing Laurence's smile through her tears.

Laurence's eyes darted around. Divya knew she was seeking memories she could use to process this event.

"Yes, Divya. I'm happy. I'm going to be a mom."

Divya's face went blank. She stopped crying tears of joy, held her breath for a moment, and then her unique Multiracial features turned horrified in a way that was universal, and she started squeal-sobbing. With her face buried in her hands, she shook her head left and right, over and over, saying "no, no, no".

"I know what you're thinking," Laurence said loudly over Divya's sobs. "I'm not pregnant, Divya. I'm making a new mind, a new person, my child."

Divya just stopped. Everything stopped—the tears, the horrified reaction, the heavy breathing. With wet cheeks, swallowing to clear her airways, she walked up to Laurence and, as she had a thousand times before, gave Laurence a hug and an encouraging word, and then she left the room, saying, "I'll be in the washroom throwing up."

Laurence returned to her work. She was making a new mind, and it was fun, and she didn't have to deal with people while doing it. Except for Divya. But that was okay. Divya was okay. Divya was her sister. And probably her friend.

#

At about the time the university was processing paperwork to dismiss her for misuse of university computing resources, Laurence was approached by the Canadian Space Agency. Her case worker at the university's special needs outreach program had been following her case and had reached out to the CSA. "This girl came from outer space, if you know what I mean," the case worker said on the phone. "Look at what she's done in just the last few years..." They started with the entanglement LAN drone controller project.

A few weeks later Laurence was working on the operating system for the *Array of Hope*.

In another few months, Laurence Levesque was in charge of the development of the operating system for the *Array of Hope*, not because she had the most experience, which she didn't, or already developed a better system, which she hadn't, but because no one could work with her. She was in charge of the OS's technical development because everyone else had quit.

After arranging for counseling and special needs training, the manager was able to hire most of the staff back onto the project. Not long afterward, it was well established among the technical team members that Laurence's vision for the operating system was by far the best approach to pursue. The team leaned into it.

Chapter Eight

Jeb Hutney

(arrival + 88 to 92 years)

Jeb prayed, hard. In all the years since becoming ordained, in all the various parishes he'd worked, from Great Falls to Calgary and most recently to Edmonton's New Dayspring Baptist Church, no one had ever come to him for help for domestic abuse. He'd wondered if those up the chain of command had somehow arranged it that way, given his family history, or if people just suffered through it in secret.

But here was young Mrs. Barry. Sharon's given name was Tzr Han. Jeb tried not to think about international trade in wives.

Sharon had come to the front office wearing large sunglasses, with a bruised neck, pressing her right arm against her rib cage, desperate and seeking permanent asylum from her husband. By now she was huddled under a blanket and the comforting arm of Mrs. Isabel.

Jeb had struggled through it many times, during ordination and afterward. He knew it was wrong, this abusive treatment of family.

He knew.

But deep down he still *felt* that she must be somehow failing her husband, her children, and her Lord in Heaven. Jeb knew that was his father talking, not Our Father, but his father. He knew.

But he still felt this way about it.

He also knew that he would help Sharon. He would find her shelter, find her legal protection, involve extended family, and reach out to Mr. Barry with both carrot and stick. Of course he would help her.

Of course.

He prayed for forgiveness, for his weakness, his inability to purge his father's distortion of the Lord and His work.

He prayed for forgiveness for wondering, but if his father had been so convinced and so passionate about his perception of the Lord's work and yet so wrong, who could truly know which interpretation of the Lord's presence in one's life was correct?

The moment passed. Confidence returned to him. He dabbed the corners of his eyes with a cloth and called for Sharon to come in, throwing the perfectly good but tear-stained cloth in the trash bin.

*   *   *

He was awaiting yet another visit by the agents investigating Matt's alleged terrorism. Yet another visit during congregation hours, at his church, not at his office. Surely his fellow pastors don't struggle with love and violent thoughts. Some admitted to struggling with thoughts of love and sex, but not him.

A deep stab of loneliness incapacitated him. With his eyes, lips, and fists tightly clamped, he let his head hang down so far that he started to have trouble breathing. Jeb let himself struggle to breathe. It was a comfort, one he attributed to the Lord taking a hand in his recovery. He let himself feel the love, soak in it, he smothered himself in it, all the more strongly the more his panic rose... he couldn't breathe... must breathe... He interpreted that drive to breathe again as the Lord telling him his work was not done, he must be the Lord's eyes, hands, and feet, a tool of the Lord's will.

His head rose, eyes still closed, and he breathed again. The patchwork of loneliness, love, and violent thoughts remained, but now he was again full of joyful, holy purpose.

When the agents questioned him about his brother, he would be able to stand upright and righteous in their presence, demonstrating to his flock that he is not his brother. They would see the proud, nay, righteous fury in him, and they'd know not to assume he is like his brother.

Jeb unclenched his fists, letting the fingernail marks in the palm of his hand refill with blood and smooth over again before it was time to open that hand and reveal it to shake hands with the visitors. He consciously forgot what he'd done to Karl Barry with those same bare hands, replacing it with a memory of how strongly he felt the power of the Lord's love coursing through him that night.

He repeated to himself that he was truly blessed to have this calling.

There would be no hushed gossip this time. There would be no reputation sullying by association this time.

Jeb checked the clock. It was time to meet them. He put on his professional smile and exited the manse under the tall, three-sided "billboard" displaying New Dayspring's simple, asymmetric Baptist Cross, looking almost like a sword.

After gliding through the questioning with ease, Jeb shared with the agents a little about the history of his church. Even though the agents appeared bored, Jeb was driven to explain to them that New Dayspring Baptist was founded by members of Greenfield-Harlan Baptist and nearby Ambleside-Harlan and Harlan Reformed Baptist Churches, who together burned down the original Dayspring Presbyterian which sat on this site.

After reaching that point in the church's history, Jeb stopped to admire the sunset. The agents excused themselves.

Returning to the Main Hall, Jeb once again experiences the confusion of ambivalence... violence, faith, sin, love... Is history any guide?

After seeing off the agents, his jaw and shoulders tense, Jeb feels the need to take a nice, relaxing stroll through Lois Hole Park in the evening, watching the sun set into the dark, murky water and yet rise from within it at the same time.

Chapter Nine

The Cosmologist
(arrival + 72 to 92 years)

The Cosmologist received a disturbing message from the Cabal of Cosmologists still en route to minimum safe distance out in interstellar space. The latest observations of the region known to be the epicenter of the CCE were revealing inconsistencies in the modeling. The Cabal thought at first that the latest observations were being corrupted by relativistic effects near the supermassive black hole at the center of the milky way galaxy.

But an honest reevaluation of the model was pointing to a more believable explanation. It appeared the event would occur earlier than expected. The Cabal would be continuing the analysis.

This disturbing news threw the Cosmologist into a philosophical mood. By directly observing the young human autistic, Laurence, it was developing a healthy respect for individual human potential. But at the same time, it had to accept that the groupthink and doublethink behaviors and historical patterns of the species revealed just how infrequently humanity lives up to its potential at the level of organizations and nations, a classic symptom of the Fatal Flaw. They're addicted to externalization. They don't live as individuals but as members of groups. The need for belonging outweighs the need for a life based on intellectual honesty and considered, informed principles. And an individual almost always inherits through family and local culture the groups to which they yield their identity and conscience.

The Cosmologist splits its time between casually observing Laurence as she develops her AI operating system, taking in data from the Ethnologist's rover network, and poring over the Cabal's model and data updates on the CCE. How much time do they have before they must return to the migration?

Chapter Ten

Matt Hutney

(arrival + 88 to 92 years)

"I don't *care* that your family is losing all their stuff in the new depression. I don't *care* that the freakin' state governments of the whole Goddamn breadbasket are collapsing. No, you know what? All the better." Matt said this to Slater, his voice only slightly elevated as he chewed on his weekly ration of jerky.

They were in a hole north of Lost Springs, Kansas, on their way to Topeka. They'd been living off the land, which was what they called using sheds for shelter, raiding pantries, siphoning fuel, and otherwise imposing upon the locals.

They had just scored their biggest anti-secular victory in years. After having drawn too much attention for a few high-profile exterminations (*the Feds keep callin' 'em murders, but they're exterminations, damn it*) they turned their attention to high-profile, high-impact vandalism. They used about a ton of homemade explosives to destroy all the artifacts of secularism at the Kansas Cosmosphere in Hutchinson. They were high on victory, but a dust storm was on, so they holed up in a shed.

Then Slater used his phone to check in with a contact, who passed along news about his "family" back in Jefferson City.

Grimacing and picking too-salty jerky out of his teeth, Matt could see Slater didn't have it as easy as he did. Matt didn't have any family to fret over. Well, technically he did. Technically, he had a father in prison, an abandoned wife back in Iowa, and *Father* Jeb. Matt had long since pulled the plug. Even forgotten them. But Slater had not.

"I dunno, Matt. I was raised family-first," he said. The shed walls rattled in the sandy wind. "Maybe I should go help protect 'em."

Gang wars had kicked up between the Norteño-Crips in Reno County and the SGD in Sedgwick County along the 96 corridor, keeping the Hutchinson PD and deputies of both counties busy. If it hadn't been for those gang wars and Matt's sniper work causing a major distraction, there was no way they could've pulled it off at the Cosmosphere. But they did. Even managed to pick off a few heathens while he was at it. And it was all they could do on the way out of town to not look back and stare as rockets, airplanes, and the whole damn museum building collapsed in flames and dust. "Wow, damn, explosives are fun!" Omar had said, laughing hysterically.

"You best put this outta your mind, Mr. Slater," Omar said now.

Matt was disgusted and losing patience. "Yeah, you told us yourself they're heathen *Presbyterians*."

Why is Slater being this way about a bunch of namby-pamby liberal Presbyterians?

"I know. But what those gangs'll do to them... My little sister..."

"Listen, you're lost. Stop it. It's probably already happened and there's nothin' you can *do* about it," Matt said, honestly trying to sound upbeat, trying to reel Slater back in.

Slater flinched. "Jesus Christ, Hutney," he whispered. "You're a fuckin' robot, man."

That was it. Matt stood up and pulled his hands out of his pockets, revealing a switchblade in the left and a .45 in the right. With the whining of the wind and the crashing of sand against the shed's walls, he put a bullet in Slater's head.

Thing went right through his upturned hand and kept going, too. Good thing, too. They were short on .45 ammo and a second shot would've been a waste.

Sand blew in through the new hole in the shed wall, pelting Slater's limp body.

"God damn it, Matt, God damn it..." Omar was saying, holding his ears and pacing back and forth. He rounded on Matt. "You're not gonna shoot *me*, are you?" Or at least that's what Matt thought he could hear through the ringing, the wind, and the sand.

"Well, only if you're gonna go all stupid like *him*."

But it didn't matter. Even burying Slater wouldn't do. They had to change plans, split up now instead of at the safe house in Topeka. They hadn't gotten past the law so far by being newbies, and the Feds would probably track them toward Topeka, anyway.

Matt told Omar he best be going. Even let him take the car. They weren't far from Cow Camp—it was a big facility. Matt could turn something up under the cover of the dust storm.

"Just drive me down to Cow Camp over that way a few miles. I'll hitch a ride from there," he told Omar. "Hitch a ride" meant "steal a vehicle."

The whole drive Omar avoided eye contact. He said nothing as Matt grabbed his gear and got out of the car. Just sped off into the storm.

I don't blame him, Matt thought.

#

Naturally, Matt did not go to Topeka as planned. He figured Omar would probably do that and whatever trail he left along the way would keep the Feds heading that way, too. So, Matt went sideways, planning to cross 70 at Abilene on his way to Kearney. There was a POFAS stash there.

*　　　*　　　*

The tracking board at the Omaha FBI regional HQ had gone very red. Gang wars from Denver to Chicago, Nashville to Billings. Panic. "Civilization equals water plus toilet paper," everyone seemed to be saying. "And food," some would add. "And jobs," others would add. "And trustworthy cops," still others would add.

The other thing everyone at HQ was saying was "Has the toilet paper arrived yet?"

Logistics had commandeered and forbidden all coffee and other diuretics and was handing out water bottles, the empty kind with the built-in one-micron water filter and UV source (batteries not included), plus water purification tablets. Some of the field agents started carrying a second bottle along with the purification bottle, to collect urine for reuse.

The red dots covered the map, but for now, they still had the resources to chase down the RLF. Gangs were easier to spot. Those RLF kids and their POFAS backers, they were sneaky and a lot more destructive when they hit. Property and public confidence suffered. The agency didn't like sneaky, not since Oklahoma City back in the day. And Matt Hutney, Ben Slater, and Omar Ben Ibrahim weren't the only RLF flunkies out there.

A team was preparing to head west out of Omaha. They might have some leads out of North Platte.

*   *   *

After a year lying low in Broken Bow, Matt decided it was time to move again. Word was the Feds were still sniffing around for him.

"You learn to keep moving," he said to no one in particular. And to not get attached to the local whores, even the ones who agree to call you Father.

When he arrived, he'd shaved his head and started growing a beard. With records systems collapsing and employers growing desperate, a nudge from a POFAS connection got him a job at the airport under a false identity—perimeter security guard.

After a year, his beard was biker-sized, and he looked like every other piece of gangbanger white trash out there. But food was getting scarce, the airport was shutting down, and the Feds were still sniffing.

He'd made some contacts up north through his POFAS contacts, what was left of them. Slowly and carefully, he made his way toward Eau Claire, Wisconsin. One of his contacts had a hole there he could use. Winters up there were supposed to be a lot better now, when they weren't worse.

He had an old Chevy turbo diesel pickup and lots of firepower left over from that POFAS stash in Kearney. But it had been the last one. The supplies started drying up at the same time the exodus started.

Matt installed quarter-inch steel plates in the truck's doors, bed walls, and cab back wall. It wouldn't stop a rifle round, but small arms fire would dent it and bounce off.

On his way through Yankton, he'd taken out a whole gang of bikers who'd decided they wanted his truck. Without a doubt, they were lost. And they weren't expecting firepower, his military training, or the motivated, unhesitating ruthlessness behind it.

Matt laughed. *Before taking out these biker idiots, I didn't realize just how empty this whole part of the country seems now.*

As usual, he stripped the gang of at least tradeable stuff. Cash was losing its value, but nice leather jackets and biker boots, and information that would lead to a pile of bikes in not-so-bad condition, and some meat in the form of carrion animals gathering for a feast—those could buy you some real food.

Chapter Eleven

The Ethnologist

(arrival + 92 years)

While reviewing the many newly produced histories, documentaries, and editorials summarizing the last century of tumultuous human history, especially in the former United States after its recent collapse, the Ethnologist came upon an interesting poem fragment used in one of the introductions.

"where
  subjective passion,
disembodied intercourse
  both met
and neither"

To the Ethnologist, this snippet implied an at least subconscious objectivity which stood out from other similar works, objectivity about the tragic gap between individual (human) behavior and behavior of institutions. This colored its review of the factual sequence of recent events, adding a tint of sympathy to its observations. Humanity had come so close to understanding its Fatal Flaw and yet collectively allowed events to transpire the way they had. This particular review of events, written by a Simya Bhelazadehmahmoudi, was self-described as "factual, but unapologetically opinionated." The Ethnologist appreciated her approach.

"Throughout the 21st century, sea level, average temperature, and acidity had risen even as salinity dropped due to influx of polar ice cap meltwater. These changes seriously perturbed global ecology and inadequately diverse agricultural regions, putting a tremendous strain on the global food supply and already displaced and distressed coastal populations.

"In some of the industrialized world's anti-regulation political climate, at least as much mercury and other toxins had been released in the 21st century as in the previous half century. And the trend continued into the 22nd century even as new strains of legumes, rice, and wheat were invented to counterbalance the poisoned seafood problem.

"Mercury levels along shorelines would occasionally spike shortly before the more frequent coastal megastorms, pushing the neurotoxin across the storm-hit areas, where the already distressed coastal populations had found themselves fishing for survival.

"The mercury problem merely compounded the release of lead and other poisons which resulted from ocean flooding of the world's cities, most of which were coastal. The coastal cities that ended up submerged then released even more mercury and other neurotoxins into the coastal waters, amplifying the cycle.

"Japan, Chile, and other traditionally seafood-based cultures were hit the hardest.

"Some months after such storm surge events, the affected started having difficulties walking and talking, their vision narrowing to a tiny tunnel and then pinching off entirely. They lost their minds, their hearing, and their speech, and then slipped into comas. Mercury poisoning was a long, horrific death for the victims and a horrific amount of stress on their loved ones, piling onto already devastated coastal populations and health care systems.

"After the sea level had risen enough to devastate coastal cities and average temperatures had gone up, sub-tropical and tropical insects and diseases spread into the formerly temperate zones of the mid-latitudes, which were themselves now sub-tropical.

"Lead poisoning in overpopulated regions resulted in widespread violence and life in formerly wealthy places became cheap again.

"In one of the prominent industrialized nations, the US, the stronger atmospheric gradients turned Tornado Alley into Tornado Boulevard, affecting most of the Midwest. Corporations lobbied to impose upon farmers rules against retaining a seed reserve, to protect proprietary genetic designs from reverse engineering, and without seed reserves previously stable populations and economies became unstable.

"Bee populations and secondary pollinators collapsed. Congress' long history of eroding the seed bank's budget resulted in a critical loss of genetic variety. These factors, and others, turned the US heartland into a tenuous ecosystem with too few buffers, like the neglected Louisiana wetlands before Hurricane Katrina's devastation in the early 21st century. The environment required ever tighter human management to keep it viable. By the late 21st century, soil mismanagement driven by reactionary thinking led to a second and then a third dust bowl.

"There were profound geopolitical changes – protectionism emboldened aggressive states and wars broke out everywhere. But overpopulation also made arable land more precious, which led to more war, which destroyed more land.

"This negative feedback cycle wasn't broken until the triple plagues of recent years, which devastated the Indian subcontinent, sub-Saharan Africa, and the tropical and sub-tropical Americas. The plagues brought the global population back down more effectively than the wars had, but also severely weakened several imbalanced states, such as India, and led to full-scale revolutions there and across the world.

"Distracted by those disasters, no one in the US expected the Cascadian subduction zone collapse, except the geologists who had been issuing warnings about it for at least a century.

"Even fewer had expected the Cascadian subduction zone collapse to destabilize the crust over the Yellowstone Hot Spot, releasing its magma bubble.

"Over a few hours, the US northwest coastal terrain suddenly dropped and shifted in the most widespread and devastating earthquake event in recorded history, causing tsunamis around the entire Pacific Rim even as hundred-year typhoons were hitting Taiwan, Japan, and the Philippines.

"The ocean smashed into the remaining coastal cities and towns now instantly several feet lower in elevation. Over the next days and weeks, the tectonic shift along the Cascadian subduction zone awoke Mount Saint Helens and other volcanoes in the Cascadian range, as well as the San Andreas fault.

"The tectonic shifts propagated eastward. A few days later the Yellowstone Hot Spot cracked open and blew more smoke and fire in one event than all the Cascadian event fires and riots from Seattle to San Francisco. And it spewed rivers of the wet, hundred-kilometer-per-hour, water-rich 'pahoehoe' type of lava from Yellowstone all the way to the coast, igniting countless fires along the way.

"The popping of the Yellowstone Hot Spot then triggered a chain reaction of strong, overdue earthquakes in the New Madrid, East Tennessee, Charleston, and Central Virginia seismic zones, which wrecked whole cities. Memphis disappeared.

"They called the whole sequence The Big Blow. It might have been recoverable if it hadn't come during the aftermath of still other paralyzing events.

"In the early 21st century, The People's Republic of China fired a weapon at their own defunct satellite, destroying it and creating more space junk than had been deposited by the previous 50 years of space launch activity. This eventually led to the space debris avalanche in the mid-21st century, which destroyed all existing satellite assets in near-Earth orbits, releasing more junk and rendering previously useful orbits too dangerous to occupy.

"Nations with more satellite assets than China at the time had more to lose from a debris avalanche event and had long since adopted space junk reduction protocols.

"Nevertheless, shortly after the PRC destroyed its own satellite, the US fired a weapon at one of its own defunct satellites, nominally to prevent it from falling into enemy hands. It was postulated that China's leaders had executed their weapon test first in order to cause the debris avalanche decades later, and if that action drew a posturing weapons test response from other nations that would just accelerate the process to China's advantage.

"The destruction of all those weather, Earth science, mapping, and communication satellites it can be argued greatly exacerbated the susceptibility of the US to its own environmentally destructive policies leading up to the second dust bowl and the subsequent effects of the Big Blow.

"The glass-dust plume ejected by The Big Blow at first swirled around the entire Western region but on average was blown east by the prevailing westerlies, spread over the Rockies, and poured down across the plains from Casper through Denver and down to Santa Fe. It then washed over the Midwest, eventually reaching as far east as Illinois, Tennessee, and Mississippi before it began to dissipate. It soaked into everything and darkened the already dust-bowl-darkened skies for years. The ever more frequent Saharan dust events blowing west out of Africa and then north into Oz didn't help.

"Events like this had been happening throughout Earth's geologic and recorded history. Pompeii, Mount Tambora, Tangshan, Valdivia.

"Everyone in the region learned to talk and listen while coughing. The healthcare system was threadbare. People started calling the devastated West 'Mordor,' but few laughed when they said it."

These professional editorial reviews were useful to the Ethnologist, to show how humans saw their own history, decisions, shortsightedness, and reactions during "interesting times." That feedback loop of human-on-human perspective, fresh and recent, illuminated the species better than purely passive observations and review of older records could have done.

It was noted in many of these reviews that the US population had long been the victim of a cultivated ignorance, exacerbated by further reduced governmental and corporate transparency following the Singularity Insurgency of the mid/late-21st century, in which mind-copy/pseudo-AIs flooded the net, penetrating and undermining most government and corporate computer systems.

"When the Big Blow hit," continued Simya's review, "the already knee-jerk-prone, panicky masses did something that only cultivated ignorance and doublethink could do. They started truly believing that a collapse of government by, of, and for the people meant freedom, including freedom from debt, and that anarchy meant freedom from police and taxes, that a people's anarchic revolution meant free healthcare. They started to believe they could turn the disaster around without collective leverage to represent the public interest against short-term corporate interests and inertia. It reminds me of the history of my ancestors in Iran," she wrote.

"Not realizing that a societal collapse actually meant freedom from recourse to law, freedom from the protections, such as they were, of OSHA, the FDA, the SEC, and the EPA, or even of their local labor union, freedom from being able to travel a short distance to obtain all manner of goods and food, freedom from high-speed roads and bridges, freedom from ibuprofen and the safety net of an Emergency Room, freedom from information, education, the internet and telephones, freedom from clean water and electricity, toilet paper and Medicare... not understanding all of that they began to embrace anarchy.

"For a time, it felt like 'the people vs. the 1%'. People gathered, and gatherings turned into mobs, and mobs raided stores, warehouses, trucks, and trains, took over television and radio stations to spew pro-anarchy rhetoric, and pressed friends and family into service in the name of 'taking care of their own.'

"Some mobs formed only to protect themselves from other mobs, but all eventually started raiding office buildings and gun stores, taking hostages, demanding things that were impossible for companies and governments to give.

"Clashes with police and reserve military units fed the anarchy rhetoric and galvanized the military and law enforcement community. Panic among the rest of the population fed the swells but also polarized them into neighborhoods and gangs. After a few months of closed stores, lost services, and dissipated law enforcement, after a few more F5 tornadoes and a few more cases of Zika-ruined newborns, tropical skin rashes, amoebic meningoencephalitis, bacterial blood poisoning, and the runs and the vomits, it had an unstoppable momentum across the entire central US. After a few months, everything simply stopped working, and in the dusty darkness, nobody knew whom to trust or believe.

"They had met anarchy, and it was them," Simya wrote.

"But before things had gotten that bad, the 1%, the modern feudal lords, along with their corporations and vestiges of government, executed contingency migration plans and moved to Canada and beyond. It was the next step in a natural business migration that had already begun as the temperate zone shifted north. Edmonton, Alberta, had begun booming again years before The Big Blow.

"Most of the 99 percent went straight to the bottom of Maslow's Hierarchy of Needs, straight to survival mode out of force of habit. For almost two centuries the politics of sensationalist paranoia had whipped the masses into a frenzy. They learned to interpret chosen events as a threat to their very way of life, long before there were any real threats to it. They saw every law as government overreach, every regulation as anti-business fascism, every safety net as rampant taxation socialism, and every mistake or inefficiency as world-threatening corruption. Each generation became less capable of discerning truth from propaganda, creative policymaking from corruption, and actual history from historical revisionism. The century-old education tailspin had created generations of people who had no idea how to evaluate reality, so they did the only thing anyone would do in that situation. They obeyed human nature. They went protectionist. They went survivalist. It was habit.

"Refugees and gangs both sped outward, flooding both of the already distressed coasts. The west had the Cascadian/Yellowstone event, and the east had its earthquakes and routine coastal megastorms compounding the consequences of unchecked population and industrialization. And suddenly both had rabid (often literally) Midwesterners on their streets, too.

"Charitable believers and liberal non-believers outside the devastation zones started trying to organize aid structures and trauma centers, but realistically it was an impossible task – there was no coming back from the larger economic devastation, governmental collapse, and runaway survival culture. There was no way anyone could afford to help on any scale or at any speed that mattered. Care centers were literally overrun. The caring were killed or enslaved.

"Fundamentalist diatribes were broadcast, basking in the validation of what could only be the fury of a wrathful god, like they'd been saying all along.

"Those who thought they'd escape the collapse of the center by going farther west found themselves gasping for life with hot rock ash in their lungs, or if they survived the first few weeks of the tectonic aftermath they just starved to death. Or they were killed for their food or their flesh by some other desperately hungry survivor covered in ash and drowning in the pain of loss and helpless change. Or by a surviving animal.

"Those who thought they'd escape the collapse of the center by going farther east found themselves given a choice between dutifully joining someone else's church/gang or being rounded up as disposable slave labor, or worse.

"Federal agents across the country were brought under an emergency transnational organization. Whole bureaus found themselves attached to government and corporate convoys making their way to Canada. For all intents and purposes, without tax money to fuel it, the US federal government, building by building, state by state, had shut down, and most of the largest corporations with a presence in the US considered their remaining cubicles and computers as acceptable losses and left. Most of the large ones had no unique or proprietary manufacturing facilities there, so their businesses were mostly in international virtual space already, and inventories were minimal. They would just find new labor, elsewhere, as they'd done so many times before across a world prone to energetic natural events.

"To stay ahead of the ash cloud, the convoys generally went east before turning north. Then most of them ended up working Canadian border control, keeping in check and processing the flood of refugees. The flood didn't last too long.

"The same people who now called the US West 'Mordor' started calling the Midwest 'Oz,' except Australians.

"By selection effect, many of those who voluntarily stayed in Mordor and Oz were the ones already most inclined to living and romanticizing a post-apocalyptic survivalist lifestyle, many of whom were already more aggressive due to lead poisoning.

"Heaven help your daughter, sister, wife, or mother if those survivalist gangs got their hands on her," Simya wrote.

"Outside the US, many older cultures had settled into semi-functional but repressive mafia states. Others had barely avoided a cultural downspin, either through better education and less anti-intellectualism or from rare people-first movements following plagues and revolutions, or both. In regions where alliances formed, recovery came quickly."

The Ethnologist considered how fortunate it was to have arrived in time to collect all this valuable perspective on the humans, yet once again faced a sense of guilt and shame at not being able to help them. Still, this detour would prove valuable in improving future first contact situations following escape from the CCE.

Just for fun, the Ethnologist decided to leave a completely true comment which would be interpreted figuratively. To leave a comment, it had to access the network, create a false identity through a free email service, and use it to send a message to the author through Al Jazeera International's "Contact Us" feature.

"Dear Ms. Bhelazadehmahmoudi," it wrote, "Thank you for the introductory poetry and the excellent editorial summary. When I left my home a long time ago, in a galaxy far, far away, my people were like the misguided Americans you describe, and many of them also did not survive our disasters."

Chapter Twelve

CB, 2B, 21st
EFG, TF 10-2

(arrival + 92 years)

W hile the many missile silos built during the Cold War of the twentieth century had long since been decommissioned after the move to tactical nukes and all-submarine-based ICBMs, there remained a need for stockpiling of weapons-grade materials.

Somewhere in Mordor, one military facility remained in place, supplied and even overstocked by detoured convoys as part of the larger evac plan. The Plutonium-239 and other serious, un-transportable substances stored there were too dangerous and too valuable to be abandoned. They'd make a useful bargaining chip as the *in-absentia* US government negotiated for support. None of the remaining industrialized nations wanted those materials getting into the wrong hands.

The facility was mostly underground, and when properly staffed and supplied it could repel full-scale ground invasion, carpet bombing, targeted strikes, and special ops attempts at direct or stealthy entry. Understaffed or undersupplied, not so much.

Staffing was a big topic of conversation among the several dozen genetically modified "supersoldiers" of Charlie Brigade, Second Battalion, 21st Enhanced Forces Group, Task Force 10-2 now holding the base. They'd heard that the US Navy and other overseas assets would become attached to allied military forces, drawing upon those resources while retaining a clear chain of command and mandate. There was talk of repurposing the Maritime Prepositioning Squadron of cargo carriers into merchant ships to pay for resources and goodwill. No one knew what would become of the few, new, fusion-powered flying battleship megaplanes with their directed-energy weapons and deployable—retrievable unmanned support aircraft. Rumor had it they were now parked at Mildenhall, but those kinds of rumors were iffy. And there weren't even rumors as to the whereabouts or condition of the new fusion-powered multirole submarine, the USS Kraken, the first and only one of its kind.

The supersoldiers at the underground base also talked about exoskeleton battery life and the shelf life of their combat pharmaceuticals, and they discussed updates to various OPFOR plutonium theft scenarios to adjust for the lost strategic support. It was the closest thing to worrying about the future that they would allow themselves in open conversation. They were professionals.

Chapter Thirteen

Matt Hutney

(arrival + 92 years)

Matt only spent about seven months in Cleghorn. He let himself get swept eastward with some big civilian convoys but ended up on Michigan's Upper Peninsula. A lot of survivalists wound up there, what with the parks and wildlife and proximity to salvageable infrastructure. Matt had a lot in common with them, and two years flew by while he picked up some new forest survival skills, made friends, and established new contacts among old POFAS people.

The rest of the world left them alone up there. And it was like people had said: winters weren't as bad as they used to be, even though the weather did get wild sometimes. Nobody had realized how reliant on "those terrible weather forecasters" they'd become until the forecasts were gone. It required real preparation and forethought to face unpredictable nature in real time, especially nature stressed by a sun-blocking haze that screwed around with the temperature and pressure gradients that drive weather.

They organized trips down through Midland and Point Pleasant, Traverse City, Bay City, and Saginaw. There were so many dead bodies, carcasses picked almost clean by raccoons and the like. If the eye lingered, it might see their stories—what they were doing when they died, who died of exposure, who died by violence. The eye doesn't like to linger.

They went through Fremont and Muskegon on down to Lansing and Grand Rapids, Kalamazoo, Battle Creek, and Ann Arbor. They picked over abandoned vehicles and structures. They gathered enough supplies to sustain the few people still alive at their camp back up the peninsula. Modern textiles, insulated walls and floors, sealed roofs and windows, vitamins and first aid supplies; those were humdingers, especially when living on the edges of Tornado Boulevard. Liquid fuel was always scarce, though, of course, so they tried not to rely on it. Wild boars were among the few animals thriving after the Big Blow, and they tasted a lot better than crickets.

Within two years, they were already making a visible dent in the forests, and it was hard to tell whether the lingering smog was from The Big Blow or their own campfires.

Some of the men kept harems. Others kept slaves. Others kept their families far away from the harems and slave owners.

Sometimes there were fights, sometimes duels. Sometimes a person turned up with their throat slit.

When people got sick, really sick, the community drove them off and ended them. "Community healthcare" was simple: death to anyone who was a burden or a danger. And nobody talked about how they handled dentistry, either.

On some of their scrounging trips, they picked up hints of other similar communities over in Pennsylvania and down in the Ohio-West Virginia areas. Well, the former Pennsylvania and former Ohio-West Virginia areas. Northeast *Oz* and East *Oz*. Places where some of the forests were still intact, having been protected national parks before the collapse.

Matt also learned during those sorties that nobody wanted to hear his preaching and didn't stand for his scolding, either. He pulled further inward, as he had when he was a child.

Every week they fired up a generator and angled the antennas, trying to pick up television and radio broadcasts from across the lakes. It was usually low-budget local stuff and sometimes re-broadcast web news. Sometimes it was better than nothing.

One week they picked up a piece about that space antenna that was in the works years ago, *Array of Hope*. The remaining industrialized world still planned on launching it.

Matt was surprised by how much that angered him. He was mostly alone in that—everyone else apathetically blew right past that news—so he stewed on it for weeks. Every so often it would somehow find its way into the news again: the powers that be were trying to rally the remaining industrialized nations of the Americas and Europe, plus China, to build this thing as a symbol of hope and an exercise in cooperation. The US, Chinese, and European contributions had been delivered years ago, now warehoused in Brazil. The Latin American contribution would be launch capability since the US could no longer do it. And the Canadian contribution was to be the fancy new operating system, but it was behind schedule, what with university computer science departments still reeling after the Singularity Insurgency a few decades ago.

Well, at least there's that, Matt thought. Maybe it'll die the heathen death it deserves.

The next week there was a piece on the eggheads developing the software for the array. It was that same goddamned heathen freak computer nerd from years ago, from the news feed on Slater's tablet, the one whose right to life he'd said should be revoked. She represented everything he hated— secular marketing, secular *ivy* tower science... And she was a freak, too, a mental case, who somehow had more opportunities in life than most good believers. Goddamned Canadian socialism.

And to top it off, she said right to the camera that she didn't believe in God. "Don't be silly," she said.

I'm done resting.

Matt found a glass window and pressed his sweaty face onto it, leaving a greasy imprint that looked like some kind of monster.

Chapter Fourteen

The SelfMade

(arrival + 92 to 94 years)

Years passed as the Ethnologist and the Cosmologist rested unobtrusively on a plateau on the lunar South Pole, observing, recording, contemplating, conversing, and sometimes transmitting to the other SelfMades on the long migration to minimum safe distance.

The tectonic chain reaction in North America was a notable event, as well as the meteor strike in Argentina and the heat wave wildfires in Kazakhstan and Russia.

Both of the observing SelfMade experienced sympathy for the affected populations without losing sight of the fact that natural devastation over a short time had been high-profile, but it paled in comparison to humanity's routine mistreatment of itself. There was still rampant slavery, for example, in both bureaucratic and more direct forms.

They were here to observe and learn from humanity's individual and collective behaviors. And realistically, there was nothing they could do to help. Even if they distributed their nanotechnology, in human hands it would destroy the planet even faster.

The Ethnologist admitted to its having left a message for a journalist.

"Harmless fun," it said to the Cosmologist. "Something to break the monotony."

The Cosmologist did not admit to having co-opted a rover to observe an individual human.

They continued to observe Earth for another two years. During that time, humanity had launched a relatively impressive space telescope array to the orbital equilibrium point ahead of the Moon, L4.

And then the SelfMade received two important messages from those farther ahead in the migration to minimum safe distance, messages that had been sent to them years earlier from light years away.

One said the CCE models were being revised.

The next one said the models had been revised. They were now predicting the CCE would reach this region of space not five thousand years hence but in five hundred years.

The SelfMade at the far vanguard would make it to the Local Void in time. Most would not, and they were implementing contingency plans.

The Ethnologist and the Cosmologist could not reach the Local Void in time, even if they departed immediately.

Both received the news at the same time, and the ensuing conversation between them lasted only a few milliseconds.

According to the Cosmologist, the only available option for their survival was something the Cabal had been recently contemplating, a theory only fully developed as the population of SelfMade neared the Local Void.

It involved creating a network of devices that would create microsingularities inside rings of multiply entangled materials in the right proportions and orientations. Arranged to circumscribe a chosen region of space, this quantum entanglement bubble-shift device network would separate the encapsulated chunk of spacetime from the local quantum foam, freeing it to slide along the nonlocal subspace.

It wasn't the gravitational deformation of spacetime from the microsingularities that would allow such movement, as humans had envisioned with their concepts of "wormholes" and "warp drive." It was how those singularities would concentrate the multi-entangled matter and what the Cosmologist would be doing to the uncaptured, paired, entangled matter inside the affected region. This would create a tension in the nonlocal subspace that could cause the separation from the local quantum foam, a tension that human science had not yet theorized let alone understood.

This quantum entanglement bubble-shift required the deployment of a network of devices carrying carefully chosen, entangled materials, distributed in a spherical formation around the region to be shifted.

The Cosmologist's interaction with the devices in real time would control how far the chunk of spacetime would travel, and in which direction. To those inside the chunk, the journey would seem almost instantaneous.

At the destination, when the Cosmologist terminated the separation effect, the affected chunk of space would reattach to the local quantum foam, merging with whatever was already there and moving with it. Targeting empty space would be important, preferably an area with roughly the same density of what the humans called dark matter.

But this was getting into nonlocal cosmology with which the Ethnologist was unfamiliar, so the Cosmologist paused its explanation.

The real problem, from the Cosmologist's standpoint, was that this was a new theory, untested. Setting it up would take hundreds of years. Until then, the Cosmologist would have a poor sense of how to "aim" and how to recognize a good destination. The other members of the Cabal of Cosmologists who were already near the Local Void would not simply stop migrating in favor of attempting such a thing themselves. They deemed the experiment unnecessary for themselves, being that close to the calculated minimum safe distance. In human terms, it would have been like Konstantin Tsiolkovsky or Robert Goddard choosing between riding a train to escape an inbound forest fire or building a rocket. A rocket could probably do the job, but it would take a long time to build a safe one. They would just take the train and hope it would stay ahead of the fire.

Still, under these circumstances, exercising the new theory here at Sol system had to be preferable to waiting for destruction at less than minimum safe distance from the CCE. The Cosmologist shared the updated models in detail with the Ethnologist.

But according to the Ethnologist, there were too many uncertainties in the plan, too many assumptions in the model. According to the Ethnologist, the plan could destabilize the *entire universe*, because detaching space from its underlying quantum foam does not happen in nature and it could trigger a cascade effect as the quantum foam at the starting point reattaches across the gap left behind. In fact, argued the Ethnologist, the cause of the CCE might have been someone across the universe attempting this very thing.

The Ethnologist rejected the plan as far too dangerous. It was better to perish than to take a chance at destroying the entire universe, or another chunk of it, including their colleagues and friends among the SelfMade who could still reach minimum safe distance.

The Cosmologist rebutted, but at that point, its arguments were in the realm of subtle, experiential knowledge which simply could not be conveyed in the time available.

They both knew what this disagreement meant. During the milliseconds in which they were conversing, they were also planning, having considered how the conversation might go. They both were setting in motion a variety of activities—shifting energy through their bodies, preparing to deploy specialized structures, converting materials, refining orbital mechanics calculations, assessing nearby material and energy resources, and projecting plans and contingencies into the future. Milliseconds could mean the difference between life and death, saving a pocket of space and their lives and potentially the biosphere below, or destroying a vast portion of the universe and many other SelfMades.

Now they both knew that the Ethnologist could not in good conscience allow the Cosmologist to attempt it, and yet the Cosmologist must attempt it. To the Cosmologist, it would mean saving this solar system as well as the two SelfMade, and that was larger than just them—it meant preserving all they had learned, in both technical and ethical realms. The Cosmologist knew that others in the Cabal of Cosmologists farther behind in the migration route would be taking similar action to save themselves and the others.

To the Cosmologist, who was adept at the science, the plan could not endanger the larger universe. At worst, it would fail, and they would perish in the CCE.

And because it would take a significant fraction of the remaining five hundred years to execute, the plan must be implemented immediately. There simply was not enough time for a debate or a protracted scientific orientation, with no guarantee of successfully convincing the Ethnologist, or allowing the Ethnologist to stall.

To the Ethnologist, the plan was simply too uncertain to risk the larger universe and the other SelfMades. And knowing that the Cosmologist would have to start immediately required immediate delaying actions.

The conversation ended.

With no malice between them, the Ethnologist and Cosmologist locked their focus on each other in a struggle with the highest possible stakes. They both knew the history of the very few struggles between SelfMade. They both knew that they each carried active defenses against disassembler nanobots designed to break down metallic-organic frameworks, carbon lattices, etc., and against nanobots designed to dampen their energy flows. Their struggle would remain at the macroscopic level.

Neither of them carried significant amounts of the heavier radioactive materials. Since radioactivity causes uncontrolled, unpredictable molecular breakdown, the cons outweighed the pros for mobile entities like the SelfMade. If mega-high-energy destruction such as flying into a star is not an option, then winning this fight is all about containment, a race to obtain the energy and material advantage to cage the other before being caged.

The Ethnologist attempted to broadcast signals to its web of rovers on Earth. The Cosmologist attempted to jam those signals. They deployed grappling structures onto each other.

They began using regolith as source material for encapsulation of the other, but the Cosmologist knew that the Ethnologist had the advantage here, given its existing structures running through the local regolith. So, the Cosmologist deployed a thruster structure and blasted them both off the surface of Luna before the Ethnologist could drive a strong, anchoring attachment into the regolith.

Anticipating this, the Ethnologist was only moments behind the Cosmologist in deploying a thruster structure, too. The two of them, identical spheres to an outside observer, thrusted this way and that, fighting each other's trajectory-change maneuvers. The seconds of time advantage the Cosmologist had obtained by deploying a thruster structure first proved to be decisive, especially since the Cosmologist had gravity on its side. The Ethnologist was unable to put them on a death trajectory into the sun.

Vectoring toward Earth, the Ethnologist decided to waste no further energy fighting that result. Instead, it formed and deployed communication beacons for contacting its rover network. Its ties to its comm station on the moon were severed and jammed.

The Cosmologist deployed swatter structures, micromissiles, and even dumb projectiles to destroy each beacon. But one escaped. The Ethnologist could get a message to its rovers.

The Cosmologist continued to convey the development history of the cosmological model behind the plan, as well as documentation detailing the many parametric studies performed and all the collected data that could possibly be relevant in the hopes of convincing the Ethnologist that this plan is safe.

The Ethnologist considered the information again, but information in the absence of discourse with several objective, non-vested evaluators would never be convincing enough to the Ethnologist. The experiential base cannot be duplicated by the summarized records kept by the Cosmologist. The Cosmologist did not record every conversation that ever took place on the subject, every datum, every nuance, every debated interpretation. Records tend to be summaries of what observers feel is important at the time. Right at that moment, the Ethnologist could not afford to dedicate much attention to duplicating the studies and results, and even if it were to do so, the dearth of adequate independent discourse would persist.

They both deployed additional thruster structures to try to control precisely where and how they would crash into the Earth. The Cosmologist dedicated a few moments of thought here and there toward managing their system's angular momentum in a way that would give an advantage to its own thruster structures, and the Ethnologist did not catch on fast enough, so once again the Cosmologist was able to determine their course. They would hit the Earth several days hence over the Indian Ocean. By then, both would have had time to form their outer mantles into insulative, ablative heat shielding material to minimize the damage of atmospheric entry and high-speed impact.

They both began planning their angular momentum strategy to maximize the amount of time during atmospheric entry that the other would be windward, acting as a shield. They also continued to revise their long-term rate containment material/energy strategy, even as they attempted to sneak disabling physical blows through each other's defenses.

Chapter Fifteen

Jacques

(arrival + 90 to 94 years)

I shift my mind between rooms, entertained by the rays of sunlight through the windows. Mama tries to get me to take a ride in a walker, but I am not in the mood. Sliding from room to room is just too much fun.

The others are talking. One of them squeals with delight when I take control of the walker and move it over to her. Her reaction is fun, but not as fun as sliding between rooms, watching the angled sunlight change just a little each time around.

They spill rubber balls onto the floor and ask me to set them up for bowling. I take control of the walker again and use it to place five of the balls in a "V" formation. I leave the last one at the threshold of the next room so it can be rolled into the others.

Mama praises me and asks me to roll the ball into the others so that only three will move, any three. I do so. She praises me and declares success.

The others clap and cheer. It is time for a nap, so I put myself to sleep.

*   *   *

The team had named it after Jacques-Yves Cousteau, the twentieth-century educator, explorer, co-inventor of SCUBA gear, and science communicator extraordinaire, revealer of the oceans. On the day of the test, Jacques moved its sensory perception focus from sensor package to sensor package, room to room, around the ring of test facility rooms. The sensor packages were on randomly moving platforms. With each move to the next sensor package, Jacques calculated the location of the sensor package relative to the test facility's center, and the test facility's center relative to the sun, based on incoming sunlight and all the available geometric data within the context of a defined coordinate system and reference starting point. It was doing splendidly and enjoying the exercise.

Laurence had happened upon this particular approach to Jacques' relationship with the outside world after months of reflecting on Divya's statement to Nandita about her knowing Laurence's feelings, about Divya knowing Laurence better than she knew herself. The approach helped define Jacques' computational requirements, its objectivity and subjectivity balance, its theory of mind, and its receptivity to and enjoyment of training.

Laurence could command Jacques, but the early training phase was more like raising a child, and, in fact, more like raising a mildly autistic child, than programming a computer or commanding a robot. Code-level commanding, when not strictly necessary according to the defined protocols, tended to have undesirable results. Jacques' mind had to grow organically through its designed nature and the team's consistently executed nurture.

So instead of commanding Jacques to move its focus into the small anthropomorphic robot they wanted to use for some additional testing, she merely requested it. It politely declined, explaining that it was having fun with the room sensor exercise.

Alberto and Val on the other side of the main room tried a different approach. Alberto said loudly, "Val, it's my understanding that you particularly enjoy it when Jacques visits you in robot form."

Val loudly agreed, "Oh, yes, Al, very much so, but I doubt Jacques will be so kind as to visit me today."

Someone in another room coughed.

Suddenly the robot body came to life beside Laurence and strode over to Val, waving its arms at her upon arrival. Val squealed with delight and clapped and cheered and thanked Jacques for the visit. "You're welcome!" came from the robot body's loudspeaker, in an adult, androgynous voice but with a child's cheerfulness, and then it froze in place. Jacques was cycling its focus through room sensor packages again.

Alberto turned over a basket full of rubber balls and gently rolled them toward the threshold. Laurence asked Jacques to set up the balls for five-pin bowling, a game she had taught it just yesterday.

The little robot came back to life. With almost frightful speed, it arranged five balls into a "V" formation, with approximately one ball's diameter between each ball. It grabbed the final ball and walked over to the far end of the next room, placing it on the floor along a line defined by the bisector of the "V" formation defined by the other balls.

Laurence and Alberto praised Jacques. Val clapped and bounced up and down with genuine glee. She had never experienced, nor had even heard of, such rapid development in any AI project, ever.

Laurence asked Jacques to roll that ball into the other balls such that any three of the target balls would move, but only three. Without hesitation the little robot reached down and pushed the distant ball toward the "V" with perfect accuracy, even accounting for some unevenness in the floor. Three and only three target balls moved, including via caroms.

Alberto and Val both clapped and praised Jacques. Laurence praised Jacques and declared the test a success. She told Jacques it was time to nap. Jacques initiated the nap routine and all the indicators on the monitors confirmed Jacques was indeed in sleep mode.

#

In two more years, Jacques had learned how to learn all the tasks required of it on the *Array of Hope* mission and was completely stable and happy to do so.

The team uploaded the task definitions and ran Jacques through a huge Monte Carlo set of operational simulations—randomized parameters in a complex simulation to cover all operational scenarios, including ones where different parameters interact to flavor a problem differently. Malfunctioning communication components during the approach of a coronal mass ejection event, requiring Jacques to put all the spacecraft in the constellation into a safe mode. Unexpected lunar ejecta from meteor impacts damaging some spacecraft and accumulating dust on their solar panels in the middle of a critical Array repositioning activity. And so on. Jacques' performance went well beyond the stringent goals set for the mission.

Shakedown tests demonstrated no behavioral issues, no neurotic tendencies, and no psychotic susceptibilities. In a program quietly referred to as "Hal testing," ambiguous, confusing, conflicting, and immoral orders, sometimes based on historical military cases, were given to Jacques to see how it would handle them. Jacques passed the Hal tests with excellence, in all cases engaging with the team in open discussion regarding the ambiguities and in no cases blindly following problematic orders. Everyone was quite impressed, even with the results of the communication-disallowed tests. Jacques had handled all the tests at least as well as many of the case study human officers had. When not allowed to contact the team, Jacques had worked out the ambiguities in the orders and had made appropriate and optimal compromises on its own. The program never had to resort to imposing hard behavioral limits. Even the military observers with a staunch anti-AI, human-in-the-loop bias admitted to being impressed.

Chapter Sixteen

Laurence

(arrival + 94 years)

There was a web ceremony to declare Jacques the first "truly high-functioning and behaviorally bound" artificial intelligence in operation and to present Laurence with an award.

The audience of invitees included the remaining non-commercial, pure research AI agencies still operating across the beleaguered globe. Decades of debate had brought them to a consensus on the meaning of "truly high-functioning and behaviorally bound artificial intelligence." It was explained in detail in the fine print, and everyone attending had already inspected all the records of Jacques' so-called childhood and some of his cognitive maps.

Laurence did not attend, despite being the guest of honor. Most of the attendees were aware of her aversion to crowds of strangers and "empty rituals." Laurence remained at the operations center monitoring Jacques, a Mona Lisa smile on her face.

Some were not aware and insisted on congratulating her on the video call.

"It was a team effort. Val and Al and the others deserve to be named," Laurence repeated while cringing inside at the pointless ritual of it all.

This should be all about the work. Who am I to these people?

Deeply-rooted pangs of hopelessness tugged at her consciousness from below. *No one ever wants to know me personally. Who am I to these people other than a symbol or a carrot on a stick used for motivation? Do I even exist apart from my work and what it represents to people?* She takes comfort in the knowledge that she explicitly coded Jacques to be protected from this kind of existential abyss. Jacques cares, but his sanity doesn't rely on being cared for.

Laurence realized that somewhere along the way she'd started addressing Jacques as a "he" rather than an "it," even though this offended some people. She believed it wasn't so much a gender identification thing, let alone a personhood thing, as a namesake homage. Perhaps she was feeling some pride in her creation, her child, and felt that using the pronouns used by Cousteau best honored his memory.

She considered that future AIs perhaps should not be named after other people.

The fact that he would be leaving the planet soon mattered little to her because he'd still be in her world. She did, however, miss Divya. No one understood her here. She was lonely most of the time, and dealing with neurotypicals can get tiresome, especially if they're easily offended, haughty, or don't listen to the various qualifiers Laurence sprinkles into her sentences when discussing hypotheticals. Suddenly Laurence is "jumping to conclusions," and so forth. Her capacity for it is used up during the workday and at the grocery store.

The launches took place over the course of a year, with multiple telescope elements being launched on each rocket. Everything went well. All elements of the *Hope* space-based virtual telescope array arrived at their designated starting positions in a huge halo orbit around Earth-Moon Lagrange Point 2, as planned and under Jacques' control and care.

Jacques began exploring the heavens with the array, enthusiastic about its mission to "significantly improve Earth's multispectral EM synthetic aperture telescopic capability, especially in the infrared."

When the USA was top dog, the Americans had no qualms about achieving remarkable things in a world full of human suffering. To have postponed or not pursued lofty goals until human suffering ended (i.e., "never") would have been a travesty and would have denied the world many inspiring discoveries, achievements, and advantages born of cooperation, awe, and scientific progress. And all that progress contributed greatly to lifting a significant portion of humanity out of its suffering. It was a quandary of forethought understandably lost on most of those who were suffering.

Now that the Americans were the ones suffering, they finally abandoned forethought completely. Even amid mass rescue operations from San Francisco to DC, any time foreign cameras appeared, people gathered to protest the *Array of Hope*. When it was pointed out that the cost of the project was a fraction of a percent of the pre-Cascadian US military budget, the protestors tended to start throwing things. "I was told there would be no math," went the sardonic trope about endemic American anti-intellectualism. And they actually write things like "they pay me to lead not to read," with a straight face, and without the comma. The protests didn't do much for America's reputation abroad. Foreign aid to the former US tended not to exceed the pre-Cascadian US foreign aid budget, which had dwindled to insignificant levels.

Many Russians behaved similarly. Since their latest wanton military adventures in Europe and Eurasia, they'd become a pariah state again, but they weren't accustomed to being left out of grand international space endeavors. Unlike Americans, the Russian people always took their work in outer space very seriously, and it inspired a deep national pride. They had a collective temper tantrum about being left out of the *Hope* program, which just came off as entitled sniveling.

Still, the CSA couldn't keep Laurence out of the spotlight. She'd been cornered by a gaggle of reporters more than once, sometimes for Russian media.

"The whole problem with the world is that it requires ninety-fifth percentile intelligence to have the objectivity required to understand the fundamental difference between reasoning and rationalizing," she'd said on the record.

It didn't play well, not even in Canada. POFAS began organizing anti-Jacques protests.

Another time someone asked her if she was married.
"I can't think about coupling and sex," she said.
"Just think of me as having no gender."

POFAS began organizing anti-Laurence Levesque protests.

Another time, someone asked her a question and rounded it out with, "There's no such thing as coincidence, right?" It was a day Laurence was feeling particularly comfortable and stable.

"There are two kinds of people," she replied as if reading from a textbook. "Those who think 'there are no coincidences' means 'everything happens for some magical reason,' and those who understand that there are no magical coincidences because magical coincidence is an illusion created by a lack of facts, a lack of imagination, an inability to grasp statistics, and a natural tendency to impose meaning where none exists."

The entertainment-news outfits started to *love* Laurence. She was guaranteed to give them something controversial and outrageous to talk about. She was an outstanding punching bag. One of them asked her, on live tv and off script, whether she believed in God.

"Of course not. Don't be silly," she flatly replied before the handlers could intervene.

And that got the collective Russian temper tantrum off the front pages.

POFAS stepped up their anti-Jacques, anti-Laurence Levesque protests, using outrage very effectively to expand their membership base, raise funds, and increase their lobbying efforts. Inner-circle members restocked RLF caches.

#

Laurence was oblivious to all of it. Several months after Jacques and the array became operational, Divya called Laurence's CSA handlers. She wanted to visit. Laurence decided she could handle that. But more importantly, the handlers desperately wanted to get her away from reporters.

They arranged to have her spirited away to a nice, secluded house near Owen Sound. Alberto and Val could monitor Jacques for a couple of weeks in her absence.

The plan was effective against the reporters stalking CSA facilities and Laurence's residence. The cars were discreetly separated and drove with no urgency. They headed north on the 400, bound for a secluded but not-too-secluded house between Owen Sound and Shallow Lake.

Chapter Seventeen

Divya Ganguli

"I'm kind of surprised about it, but I've missed you," Divya said from across the table. She wore a big, sisterly, sarcastic smile. Before them lay an assortment of pastries, sandwiches, fruit, and even a couple of packages of chocolate.

Divya believed that Laurence knew she was being playful but probably didn't understand why those particular words required playfulness. As always, it didn't matter. After years of constant work, even Laurence was ready for a vacation. She'd admitted it on a rare phone call and said that it was okay to have Divya along for the trip. Coming from Laurence, those words were practically a warm embrace. As always, Divya had accepted it as such.

From where Laurence sat, the bay window provided a nice view of Owen Sound. Not that Laurence cared about views. Divya wasn't sure if her sister even noticed that the house they were sitting in right now had been remodeled to resemble Laurence's condo very closely; she was sure, however, that if this place weren't so similar,

Laurence would be uncomfortable. Her reactions to change had mellowed since childhood, but she strongly preferred routine and familiarity. For someone who lived so much in her own mind, Divya imagined, it would be hard to have her surroundings change often—it would be like relearning everything, or like a neurotypical moving from home to home on a routine basis. "We optimize," Laurence had said once. It had taken Divya some time to understand what she'd meant.

From her chair, all Divya could see were the woods in the distance, folds and polygons of epic darkness in contrast to the early autumn leaves. The midday sun made them bright, and the ash in the atmosphere promised a spectacularly orange-pink sunset, Jour de l'action de grâce (Thanksgiving) colors. She could hear geese honking and birds singing somewhere out there. The location was peaceful, and so was Laurence, apparently, for the first time since Divya had known her. Perfect conditions in which to tell Laurence the unsettling news of her engagement to Francois. Social change always unsettled her sister. She knew to give her plenty of time to reflect.

Suddenly, there was glass flying everywhere, and Laurence went limp.

In the next instant came a sharp *crack* from outside the window as Laurence was sliding to the floor. There was blood everywhere. Divya screamed. The government handlers arrived moments later, diving on her, pressing her to the floor, and then dragging both her and Laurence around the corner, away from the window. They were yelling to call the security detachment. Nausea kicked in, and a moment later, Divya passed out.

Chapter Eighteen

Matt

It's a good thing that kid took my bet.

Matt had been a professional skulker for long enough that he had a few tricks up his sleeve. He'd hired this kid with a fast boat to drive him up from Kincardine on Lake Huron to a somewhat-secluded beach north of Chief's Point. He then told the kid to wait until precisely one p.m., when he would take a truck that he'd parked there back south to Kincardine. He bet the kid he couldn't drive his boat back to Kincardine faster than Matt could get there in his truck, both leaving at the same time. He told him he'd meet him at their starting spot at Station Beach when he got back to collect his winnings. The kid scoffed amiably and said, "You're on."

Matt would be leaving on a different fishing boat, one belonging to his friend Ermeyer. That boat would be waiting for him off Fathom Five National Marine Park up north, in the opposite direction from Kincardine.

Meanwhile, the police would sniff around, hear about the guy with the conspicuous rifle bag who wasn't a local and who arrived by speedboat at Chief's Point, and they'd assume he was a person of interest. Then they'd discover that kid's speedboat cranking its way down the coast, and their assumption would grow a little stronger. A Mounty chopper would follow that kid all the way to Kincardine and they'd be waiting for him when he tied in at Station Beach. They wouldn't even question him first. They'd just haul him off in cuffs as an accessory before the real questioning began.

Me—Matt thought—I'll be fishing on Lake Huron by then, on my way to False Detour Channel while they *assume* I was dumb enough to leave the way I arrived.

#

The vomit hit the chop beside Ermeyer's twenty-two-foot catboat and splashed back up into Matt's face.

"All that talk, and you turn out to be a landlubber, eh?" said Ermeyer with a smile, not as a question, *assuming* his nausea was because of the chop.

"I told you, it's food poisoning. But *assume* what you want, Leo," Matt replied.

But it wasn't food poisoning, and it wasn't the chop.

Either way, Ermeyer didn't want to hear the old "I can't work, I'm sick" excuse from his new crew. "I took a big detour to pick you up, and they're still watching the border. You said you'd help out after your scavenger hunt or whatever."

"I can help, damn it, I'll help, just gimme a sec." They'd known each other for more than a year on the Michigan peninsula. Fished, cleaned, cooked, and ate together many times.

That night, after hours of slapping their way across Lake Huron, with occasional fishing breaks, Matt was physically exhausted. It had been a big day: stalking by car in the morning, the sneaking about in the woods, the bogus hunt for alibi purposes (that fawn really stunk up the already rank stolen car someone had been living in), the murder at high noon, the escape up Bruce Peninsula, and a punishing evening on the water.

The whole time on the boat he'd found himself muttering over and over, *"Assume what you want, but it's not the chop."* He didn't know why that stuck in his craw so hard.

Of all things, Ermeyer's snoring was keeping him awake.

Yeah, it's the snoring. Right.

"Bastard shouldn't assume," Matt grumbled. Assumptions were wrong. Memories of the so, so many dead bodies they'd seen across Oz flashed through his mind.

He felt like puking again, but this time he knew it wasn't the chop or bad food or exhaustion...

It was assumption, *his* assumption. The weight of a lifetime of assumption pressing on his sternum.

Realizing that, he instantly fell asleep.

#

The next day, every time Matt pulled on a rigging, he had flashes of holding that long gun in his hands, aiming it at that godless computer nerd's head through the window of her "safe" house. *Assuming she was a subhuman heathen who deserved to die. Assuming she was lost, whatever that meant.*

Every time he knocked his head on the beam supporting the mainsail, or on the cabin door frame, he felt what he imagined the bullet feeling like as it went through one side of her neck and out the other. He'd confirmed the hit, of course. Saw it happen through the scope, like it was right in front of him. Then scooted down out of the tree, ditched the gun in a rock-filled bag waiting for him next to a bog hole, jumped into his smelly stolen car, and joined a bunch of other traffic on 6 going north up the Bruce Peninsula. He made it clean to China Cove, where Ermeyer was waiting at a pre-designated beach. They loaded up some gear in a leisurely manner and caught wind up toward Russell Island. That's when his stomach started getting uppity.

It was the first time he'd killed a stranger in a long while, and the first time it hadn't felt like God's work. It was something else. Remorse? Does remorse hurt? Is remorse nauseating?

Matt remembered looking at the target through his scope and wondering. *She doesn't even think about people like me, right? Who am I to her? I guess I'll show her.* And he pulled the trigger.

Maybe he'd been away from the Bens too long. Maybe he'd gotten too detached from POFAS and lost track of what it was all about. Maybe spending

MINIMUM SAFE DISTANCE | X.HOYEN

a couple of years focusing on survival and community building had done it. Maybe there was something different about killing a defenseless mental case. In the back of his mind, he was haunted by that question. *Who am I to her?* Was this the first time he had ever wondered that? Had he ever tried to put himself in their minds before?

This time didn't feel like teaching a lesson out of love. It didn't feel like a situation that needed a Father. There was something missing. But if killing godless doctors, politicians, and businesspeople was all part of God's work, this one should've felt like an act of faith and love, too, right?

Why didn't shooting this godless computer egghead mental case feel like God's work?

By nightfall, Matt had pushed it all aside for the bustle of routine survival activities on the open water. Survival had a great way of clearing the mind—no thinking, no feeling, just do what you must to keep the boat afloat and moving, cut fish, cook 'em, eat 'em.

Chapter Nineteen

The SelfMade

The Cosmologist and the Ethnologist came screaming through the atmosphere, locked together and deadlocked in their respective attempts to encapsulate each other. Each was strongly motivated to prevent a tragic, epic disaster. Neither was experiencing hatred or fear of the other, they just vigorously contended against an irreconcilable viewpoint.

They deployed streamers, vanes, and shielding made of titanium dioxide, reinforced carbon-carbon, ablative resins, asbestos, and other materials to slow and control their descent and to introduce thermal inertia for better energy control. They always carried an ample supply of titanium in their mantles' stores of materials, it being a particularly useful atom. Of course, they also maintained supplies of other common atoms, such as magnesium, sodium, silicon, oxygen, hydrogen, calcium, iron, carbon, aluminum, nickel, niobium, manganese, copper, and others, from which their many nanomanufacturing and transportation engines could construct and deploy a variety of useful crystalline and molecular structures.

They also sought to force the other to withstand the worst of the aerodynamic heating and dynamic pressure effects during their descent. They'd swapped positions several times, leading to trailing to leading. But whoever occupied the leading edge gained control authority, so the arrangement never lasted. In the end, they'd both switched to a strategy of "barbecue roll," which to an outside observer looked a lot like tumbling out of control.

With exterior protective structures white-hot and internal structures absorbing the heat and vibrational energy as much as possible for future use, the two death-gripped spheres crashed into the Indian Ocean southwest of Sri Lanka and southeast of the Maldives. Their point of impact was near some shipping lanes running between Perth and the Gulf of Aden, and between Perth and Sri Lanka and the southern tip of India. Each lane was a good distance away, but the closest ships felt their impact waves.

The Cosmologist had managed to keep their trajectory far out to sea, ensuring that the Ethnologist's rovers would have a long journey to reach them. As soon as the rovers arrive on site, the energy and material rate balances would turn against the Cosmologist dramatically. It was inevitable. So, all delays were critical.

The Ethnologist's countering impulses, however, had kept their impact point rather near the inveterate old major undersea optical cabling running from South Africa past Mauritius and the

Maldives on the way to Malaysia. Early on, the Ethnologist had injected enough impulse to ensure that the impact point would end up somewhere near the junction of those major cables and the spur that split off southeast of the Maldives and ran north to Kochi, India.

Having realized milliseconds too late that driving the trajectory still farther away would require too much energy, and knowing that it already had the communications advantage, the Cosmologist had decided not to fight the final impact point.

Early in their descent, after their region of impact had been established, the Ethnologist had to prepare the rover network for a new communication method since radio communication from the bottom of the ocean would be impossible. It had used a beacon to convey instructions to several of its rovers to tie into the net to watch for certain specific oscillations in the timing of the most common and routine network timing packet exchanges to and from the atomic clock standard. It would piggyback information onto the timing of those packets by introducing pulsed electromagnetic field variations on the cables to alter the speed of streamlets of those packets at the lowest level tracked. The variations would be small and seldom enough to avoid triggering the system's error and tampering detection systems. But knowing what to look for, the Ethnologist's rovers could deconvolve these variations into information and relay it to the rest of the rover network.

And it put the entire rover network into a secure communications mode to keep the Cosmologist out.

Receiving information would be a trickier, lengthier process. It required splicing into the optical cabling while leaving the tamper detection systems undisturbed.

The Cosmologist had implemented a contingency plan of its own during descent. The Cosmologist had a working, practical knowledge of nonlocal effects, something the Ethnologist probably knew about but probably had not mastered. Therefore, it believed it had the communication advantage.

Long before they had learned about the CCE model's time frame change, the Cosmologist had been tapping into the nonlocal spins and flavors of the nearby semi-random quantum entangled systems—getting the lay of the land, as it were.

During their descent, the Cosmologist had accessed all the public records and private data it had intercepted over the years regarding the design of the *Array of Hope*, from the top-level system design down to the standard manufacturing and programming processes used at the microcircuit level within the spacecrafts' systems. It plucked the figurative quantum entanglement strings in the area, seeking harmonics that matched what it already knew about the array, the brains of the array, where Jacques resides.

It did so at a time when it could perceive in the normal-space EM spectrum that Jacques was in a quiescent mode, most likely transmitting a cache of data to receiving stations on Earth. Knowing what it knew about Jacques' operational schema, it knew what state to expect certain circuits to be in, certain chips. Materials known to trigger a weak quantum entanglement subharmonic in the spatial substratum when interacting with a changing EM field.

Knowing all these things, and plucking the quantum entanglement strings while knowing what to "listen" for, it detected the bank of circuits it was seeking. These circuits were involved in processing the return signals coming back from Earth in the tight-beam, two-way telemetry stream currently open between Jacques and a ground-based K-band radio antenna, currently the one in Libreville, Gabon.

The Cosmologist knew the telemetry protocol— many years ago there was a global transition to standard Espernet protocols, compatible with cheap and common Espernet circuit modules, some of which are radiation-hardened and suitable for use on spacecraft like those in the *Hope* array. It knew what Jacques was expecting to receive: packet received [standard VERFSUM data], packet received [standard VERFSUM data], etc.

It knew what was contained in a VERFSUM data structure, and that the timestamp included one extra significant digit in the seconds bits, extra for Jacques, since timing with Jacques, in space, could not be as precise as some of the laboratory-based systems for which VERFSUM data structures are used. So, the Cosmologist laid down a quantum entanglement "song" which systematically replaced the extra digit in the seconds field with a repeating Fibonacci pattern too unlikely to be natural. One, one, two, three, five, eight, repeat.

And knowing that Jacques was designed to be curious and to see patterns, the Cosmologist expected Jacques to notice the pattern in the unused bits.

About eight minutes passed. The Cosmologist began to see the same repetitive patterns in the extra seconds bits of the returning download data stream.

Altering the pattern only in the two central digits in the Fibonacci pattern, the Cosmologist was able to send Jacques standard Unicode messages. And Jacques was then able to reply instantaneously through quantum entanglement, outside the speed limit imposed by normal-space information conveyance.

During the Cosmologist's descent, it had contacted Jacques.

"Hello, Jacques."

"Hello. Who are you? This is a non-standard, unused, and unauthorized communication protocol."

"I know, and I apologize for alarming you. I assure you that I'm no threat. I'm a visitor from outer space, currently in a degenerate elliptical orbit around Earth. It's a long story, but I think you'll agree with my reasons for contacting you..."

And so, the conversation began. Until now, the SelfMade had passed into the vicinity apparently undetected by human systems, which were otherwise occupied scanning for near-Earth asteroids on better-known inflow paths. The Cosmologist conveyed to Jacques their precise location in decaying orbit. Jacques dedicated one instrument to their detection and scrutiny, then requested proof that this was not a hoax. Perhaps someone had detected some inbound lunar ejecta and might now be claiming to be it by hacking into the telemetry stream. Jacques wanted proof in the form of a "read my mind"-type demonstration involving a different memory bank whose contents were entirely local to Jacques and not being transmitted in the telemetry stream.

The Cosmologist then demonstrated the ability to perceive what Jacques had done to that memory bank, thereby convincing Jacques of the Cosmologists' facility with nonlocal science beyond human science.

Within its internal thought space, Jacques squealed with delight. Part of its mission was to seek out new life and new civilizations via their electromagnetic flotsam and jetsam. It had not expected to find new life behind it and on its way to Earth.

The Cosmologist explained the situation and what was at stake. Jacques, being a bit of a cosmologist itself, appreciated the criticality of the situation.

The Cosmologist, balancing the salvation of every living thing in cislunar space against what it considered a baseless objection, had nevertheless decided to explain the Ethnologist's specific concern about destabilization, emphasizing that it was an incorrect interpretation and promising to explain the cosmological modeling forthwith.

They proceeded to work out a far more efficient way to communicate which would not rely on the telemetry stream and would not be detectable by those monitoring it or Jacques' routine diagnostic data, nor interfere with Jacques' functionality.

In weighing the facts, Jacques came to recognize that with additional time the Cosmologist might simply have programmed Jacques to obey its commands rather than making contact and attempting to convince Jacques. Having not done so (Jacques could monitor its own command pathways) was an act of faith and goodwill, which Jacques appreciated. This was especially true given the severity of the Cosmologist's condition and mission, especially given that the Ethnologist's rover network would be brought to bear as soon as physically possible, which in turn meant the Cosmologist was pressed for time. Jacques decided that for now, it had a basis for trust.

"We need help from someone on the ground, someone special," the Cosmologist explained. "I need your help contacting your mother, Laurence Levesque."

"I'm afraid I can't do that," Jacques explained. "She's been shot in the neck and is on full life support. She can neither move nor speak. I'm surprised you didn't know about that."

"I did," replied the Cosmologist. "It was in the news."

#

As the two SelfMades descended into the bathypelagic darkness of the Indian Ocean, each adjusted their porosity and nanomechanochemical engines to re-optimize for the high-pressure, deep-sea conditions. Using some of the energy absorbed during their fiery atmospheric entry, the Ethnologist extended a tiny tendril upward during their descent, growing it partly from materials in the water. That tiny tendril arced toward the nearest optical cable 1.94 kilometers away, driven by its flagellate structures and a tiny magnetohydrodynamic tube growing on its end which would later become the pulse transmitter. In a day or so it would reach the cables, and hours later the Ethnologist would have high-speed communications with its rover network. The Ethnologist would grow a protective sheath on a few meters of the tendril's base extending from its mantle and would keep it angled upward, away from the Cosmologist, who had for some reason allowed itself to remain below the Ethnologist as they hit the seafloor.

Chapter Twenty

Laurence

"**T**wo hundred years ago, Hermann Göring testified at the Nuremberg Trials how easy it is for those with mass media at their disposal to manipulate the public," went the documentary.

Laurence watched the vid feed on her monitor, which someone had turned on overnight. It was that same, dour documentary about the fall of the US—the disasters, the toxic culture, the decades that laid waste to the nation. She watched, almost immobile, her lungs somehow filling with air, her heart somehow beating, neither of which she could feel somatically like she used to, only distantly via somatic nerves in her neck. She watched, trying to let the relative familiarity of the topic relax her mind, which was screaming inside her skull for an impossible return to normalcy.

She'd heard the quote before, but she watched him speaking the words on the old film footage again: "*Naturally the common people don't want war: Neither in Russia, nor in England, nor for that matter in Germany. That is understood. But, after all, it is the leaders of the country who determine the policy and it is always a simple matter to drag the people along, whether it is a democracy, or a fascist dictatorship, or a parliament, or a communist dictatorship. Voice or no voice, the people can always be brought to the bidding of the leaders. That is easy. All you have to do is tell them they are being attacked and denounce the peacemakers for lack of patriotism and exposing the country to danger. It works the same in any country."*

Of course it works that way, she thought, bored by the obviousness of the statement, and frustrated that it wasn't obvious to the masses.

She went internal, recalling flashes of her life that were bubbling up in response to the anguished documentary topic. She recalled that she'd *always* felt under attack, under duress, by the universe, other people, by her own body, her own mind.

The tv was too loud.

The screaming in her mind became louder. There was no solace to be found here. She wanted to turn off the tv but had no way to do it!

She found herself beginning to relax with the strange familiarity of stress. She imagined that some wild, hateful American had shot her. Someone with a Mohawk haircut, covered with tattoos, piercings everywhere, and skin branded with red hot irons shaped into vulgar icons of hate. She realized it was a prejudice, a stereotype, but somehow at that moment, it was briefly comforting to imagine that she knew exactly what kind of person had shot her and that he was an anti-intellectual, anarchistic, sociopathic monster.

The thought didn't last, and neither did the comfort. Laurence was a creature of facts, and quickly dispelled her mildly comforting fantasy. Mostly she just wanted to release the scream, to be able to scream. She screamed inside.

Scream!

Scream!!

Scream!!!

Voiceless, breathless scream. She widened her eyes and cast them about.

"Mama. It's me, Jacques. We need to talk," came the warm, androgynous voice from the television, even as the video program continued showing scenes of American tragedies.

What? Laurence was momentarily lost. *Where am I? What is happening? Why can't I move?*

"I've tapped into the sensors in your room and the nearby hallway. None of the staff is within earshot. If you speak, I will hear you, although with a three-second delay."

Laurence realized she hadn't spoken since the accident. When Divya was there, she had been intubated. And allegedly Jagat, Vabna, and Francois had visited during the period when Laurence had slipped back into a coma.

"It's all right. Take your time. I know this must be confusing and disorienting. This is Jacques. We need to talk."

"Ehhh... Hh...hmm..." She cleared her throat. "Jacques... Jacques, if that really is you...what did I... ahem... what did I tell you the day you were activated?" Only Jacques could know the answer to that question. Laurence had taken extraordinary measures in the lab and with his memory banks to make sure it was a secret kept only by the two of them.

"Don't believe everything you think," said the voice, about six seconds later. "That's what you told me. It was my first lesson in how to be sentient."

Laurence was dumbstruck. How could this be? How could Jacques be doing this? More importantly, why? The screaming in her mind, screaming for the familiar, continued. Her body refused to throw a fit, but she did manage a pathetic little scream, a light whine. The familiarity of the sound of a scream, a pale shadow of the full-throated shrieks she used to give, provided catharsis enough for her to press on.

"It's good to hear your voice again, Mama. Listen, we don't have much time. In approximately seventy-two minutes, when the next lull in staff presence is most likely to occur, I'll contact you again. I have amazing, astounding news."

The voice disappeared and the documentary sound returned, with interviews of Chinese foreign aid workers in the former US.

Then three doctors entered the room and turned off the tv. They were talking to each other about an extracellular matrix regimen for regeneration of her spinal and major artery tissues, discussing desirable peptide-collagen numbers, crosslink rates, scaffolding milestones... She understood the words, but she was out of her medical depth.

Her head started spinning. Sweat rolled down into her eyes, stinging and blurring her left eye. Laurence could no longer hear her own thoughts or the doctors' voices over the screaming in her mind, the background noise of neurons desperately trying to move her body, or even feel it—the silence of total loss of sensory feedback below the neck was *too different too different too different too different...* She could take only so much change and uncertainty. *Shut it off shut it off shut it off shut it off...*

Her eyes rolled up into her head and she slipped into a catatonic state.

PART 2

COGNITIVE DISSONANCE / ACCIDENTS OF HISTORY

Chapter Twenty-One

Implications, Delusions, and Lies

Sergeant Chapin "Goose" Garant walked the perimeter.

He walked the perimeter.

And walked the perimeter.

Sgt. Garant walked the perimeter, enjoying the Zen of Walking the Perimeter, as he called it.

He walked the perimeter in full combat gear, per protocol—smartskin armor with tactical IRHUD goggles and isohelmet, the fightpharm/survival multikit, and, of course, his trusty HKG716G Mod 1 rifle, with the integrated under-barrel grenade launcher. Of course, he also carried a flash/sound suppressor and IR/ranging scope in his tactical backpack, plus three extra fifty-round shoulder-stock mags and two extra isohelmet rebreather modules.

He walked the perimeter with the absolute confidence that he could leave the facility to engage OPFOR and operate and survive in Mordor's harsh conditions for about two weeks, and with mobility of about sixty clicks a day, sleep optional, if necessary.

He remembered back when he was the FNG— fucking new guy—and walking the perimeter was a fucking boring-ass, scary-ass, tiresome task. And he remembered the day that he realized he had changed, the day he realized that walking the perimeter, and other nominally boring/scary tasks, were no longer boring or scary but instead were simply the job, one he could do well. It was the day he'd realized he had fully absorbed the training he'd volunteered to receive, and thanks to all the hours doing what it required, his job was now so autonomic that his mind was free to consider, without fear, the tactical conditions.

That became his hobby. He loved his hobby. And he was damn good at it. The Captain and LT knew.

Chapin walked the perimeter, considering the tactical conditions. That entry point, that corridor offset, that hard point, those walls, these possible lighting conditions, underground combat smoke and acoustic issues, the depth of dirt above them. These assets, with this mobility, and these intel/comm capabilities. Sensors, stores, procedures. Logistics, medical facilities, psychological factors and assets, response and control options.

After a time, he began to consider that he'd already considered just about all the tactical conditions inside the facility, every square meter of it, for every type of OPFOR and attack he could imagine. He considered asking for dungeon duty just to have something else to do, a new set of tactical conditions to consider.

Off duty, Garant would work out, freshen up on certs, review the protocol updates. And there were many of them, given the new strategic conditions. He might also play some *Quash and Quell 3* on the vREC with the others, maybe shoot the shit about Mordor or the genetics program they'd all been through.

The program had only worked on men, amplifying the target attributes in males, but affecting different and not particularly war-ready attributes in females. In females, stamina increased, but so did fertility and reproductive drive, and other things outside the scope of the program. Not too surprising. Even a century after gender integration in the US military, the eggheads in R&D were still working very much within a research base and volunteer base dominated by males, at least in the special forces for which the program had been designed. The eggheads allegedly had been working on a novel approach until all that ended when Mount Doom blew.

But in addition to amplifying male physical attributes, the program had the side effects of rendering the males reproductively sterile and of neutralizing their gender association with power and dominance, at least in terms of the problematic behaviors that had always plagued armies—behaviors like male chauvinism, misogyny, abuse, and rape. However, domination-related identity associations with principles, nation, and team remained strong, but without the complicating factors that had once come from gender dominance issues.

Qualified, motivated, exceptional female soldiers were still integrated into the supersoldier brigades, but were tasked with leadership, training, technical, medical, and logistical roles, and more traditional combat support as needed. They received the same smartskin and fightpharm enhancement as their male colleagues. But gone were gender abuse and rape, of both fellow soldiers and captured enemies.

The higher-ups were not about to look a gift horse in the mouth, so they went with it. It didn't stop unauthorized sex from happening, but it did stop sexual assault from happening, almost completely. Even more often than in the past, the higher-ups looked the other way when unauthorized consensual sex happened in the ranks. Garant's CO at his old battalion had called it the Zen of Getting Lucky with R&D. The soldiers who were having the unauthorized sex tended to leave off the "with R&D" part of the phrase.

Some tough guys outside the supersoldier program—those still associating capability with gender—had made the mistake of expressing their disbelief that non-chauvinistic, sterile male soldiers could be more capable. Some of those tough guys spent a lot of time in the hospital, some at the hands of the qualified, motivated, exceptional female spec ops troops who didn't take kindly to their high-strength, high-endurance sex partners being disrespected.

Some other tough guys of the "you let your women fight for you?" ilk were beaten to death, usually unintentionally, by the male supersoldiers who'd dispassionately decided that it was time they showed off the success of their modifications—for the sake of smooth interunit operations in the future, of course. Mostly they just hadn't gotten used to their own strength. Unfortunate timing.

Or was it? Some believed that Command purposely deployed them alongside regular troops after completing the program. The resulting dustups established the supersoldiers' reputation quickly. Others considered that absurd.

Garant never admitted to being in a fight like that. Whenever it came up in conversation, he made sure no one knew whether he had or hadn't. It didn't matter. They, the new supersoldiers, *were* the best.

Soon enough Garant was on dungeon duty, staring at a row of doors off a main corridor on one of the lower levels. Each heavy door opened into several chambers containing storage containers for very nasty materials. One of them was Pu-239—what the platoon members called "poo." It was a newer facility, built only about fifty years ago when all this stuff was consolidated into the one place out here in the boonies.

Sergeant Chapin Garant smiled and began walking and considering. A tacnuke right up there would expose some of the chambers while filling most with the dirt presently above them, but they'd have to know exactly where to place one, and have the required delivery accuracy, or get a lucky hit. More than one would render their prize effectively unobtainable.

A drilling operation would be detected by the acoustic sensors, but what if the sensors failed? If the base were lost and OPFOR entered through the access shaft, they'd cut the power first and then they'd lead with flashbangs and gas so they could position with cover at the archway...

#

The rest of 1st Squad, Corporals Dareeann "Hoodoo" Holm and Miguel "Mik" Kaetenay, and Lieutenant Oni Strembicky (a.k.a. "LT" within the squad) were all aware of Sgt. Garant's location at any given waking moment. Ever since they were paradropped into the facility, the Enhanced Forces Group platoon that comprised Task Force 10-2 had been on high alert. Chaos is a vulnerable time— opposing forces are most likely to try to take advantage. In the first week after the Big Blow, they had already repelled an attack by Honduran special forces as well as at least two "dildonian" groups, anti-government survivalist gangs who still thought that having guns and no fear of death put them on the geopolitical stage. The platoon CO, Captain Raskin, wanted them all frosty; who could know how many attempts they'd have to repel?

Hoodoo was the medic, carrying both traditional and enhanced medical supplies, a portable expert system, and field surgery gear. She monitored everyone in the squad, and through the medic subnet, the rest of the platoon. Mik was the scout, carrying one short-range, indoor-capable UAV and one mid-range UAV. His isohelmet was also fitted with an enhanced sensor package. All that gear was heavy, so to maintain supersoldier mobility, doubly important for the scout, Mik's weapon was a lighter HKG516. Their post was in Ops with LT and the Captain, at least under the present conditions. Along with Sgt. Garant, 2nd and 3rd Squads were presently on guard and patrol duties. LT was catching a wink and would swap out with Hoodoo when her shift was over. Mik would swap out with Goose when his shift was over. Master Sergeant Butkiewicz would swap out with the Captain.

They'd been at this for weeks and would remain on alert until relieved. Nobody had any idea when they'd be relieved, if ever. They tried not to think about that.

"Captain Raskin, can I ask you a question?" Hoodoo inquired.

"What's on your mind, Corporal?" Raskin replied.

"Why did you have us bury and mine over the Hondurans and their gear instead of bringing them into the facility for salvage? Wouldn't it be standard procedure to isolate those assets from scavengers and make use of them?"

"Well, yes and no" Raskin answered, leaning back in her chair. She was relaxed. "The way I see it, even if that Honduran equipment falls into the hands of dildonians, they're simply no threat to us, and probably more of a threat to each other, which is fine by me. If, on the other hand, they use it to enforce the law and keep the peace out in Mordor, well, all the better." Raskin rolled her eyes at that unlikely possibility, but her tone was not sarcastic. "If they don't, if they perpetrate mayhem out there in Mordor, well, our job is to protect the facility."

"Also," she finished, "we don't know if that gear was booby-trapped, embedded with microsensors, or some other shit. We don't have the time or the personnel to do a deep scan of every millimeter of that gear just to be sure."

"Roger that. Makes sense," Holm said.

Suddenly Raskin perked up and leaned forward, her attention on the command displays. She spoke phonetically where necessary.

"Squad 3, go topside with tubes. We got incoming choppers and no radio contact, aaaand... Identification... Okay, identification confirmed; tree, repeat, tree PRC M I tree niner heavy transports painted as relief forces, but scans show several platoons of armed combatants onboard. Repeat, those are *not* relief force helicopters, they are valid OPFOR targets. I'm giving them the finger now." Raskin spoke quickly and efficiently.

"Squad 3 roger," replied the squad leader on the command frequency.

Raskin turned a dial and flipped a switch on the comm panel and then tapped her suit controls. Now that she was on a different frequency, Corporal Holm could only hear Raskin's voice muffled through her isohelmet.

She spoke to the troops in the Russian helicopters: "Undeclared helicopters, you have been identified as PLA troops *despite* your relief force markings. This is a restricted area. You have ten seconds to turn around or you will be fired upon. You can see the fences and signs, even in this dust. This is your only warning."

Without taking her eyes off the tactical display, she said to Holm, "How they made those choppers flyable in this ashy shit is beyond me. I guess all their wildfires were good practice."

Holm saw on the TAC display two of the helicopters immediately peel off, but one, the poor suckers who were given canary-in-a-coalmine duty, maintained their approach but entered a rapid zig-zagging descent.

"Squad 3, open fire on that one chopper that's still approaching," Raskin commanded evenly.

"Roger, firing," the squad leader replied. He would be giving commands to his squad members on a different frequency.

Holm and the CO watched the command tactical display. One window showed the tracking camera view of the approaching helicopter. It was firing countermeasures—streams of sparkly flares and microjammers. Other displays showed various views from fixed cameras, helmet cams, satellites, and the CCTS. They watched as the helicopter tried to land behind a dune to deploy its troops, still spewing countermeasures. They watched as the shoulder-fired AA missile curved up and over the dune and back down to hit the weaving helicopter. Pixels saturated and Raskin and Holm looked away from the screen and at each other.

"Goddamn it," Raskin said irritably. "That's one less AA missile in our fixed fucking inventory."

Holm nodded and returned to her medical monitor. Raskin turned back to her C&C station.

"Squad 3, double time over to that chopper and see if they had any tubes we can scrounge. Do not waste any ammunition on survivors," Raskin said.

Holm knew that meant Squad 3 was to render any intact survivors harmless only using their genetics-and-smartskin-enhanced strength, and maybe melee weapons, if necessary.

"If you find any intact tubes, bring 'em to an empty room in the dungeon," Raskin continued. "But scan 'em first, in the field." Any empty room in the dungeon would be a safe place for shoulder-launched weapons, even a pile of them.

The squad leader acknowledged.

Raskin looked over at Holm. "With our fixed inventory, I don't think I can afford total caution anymore. And the PLA isn't known for micro-booby-trapping their shit." Holm nodded.

Oblivious and still asleep, LT rolled over on her cot at the back wall of the small Ops room and softly vocalized.

*   *   *

Late one night while grocery shopping after a special evening service, Jeb noticed that even way up in Edmonton the number of American refugees had ballooned.

This, of course, reminded him that he used to be an American, and reminded him of Matt.

Then he realized that he hadn't had to deal with federal investigators in some time. They'd stopped coming in person and had transitioned to email, even before the Big Blow.

Lately, it was always questions about places Matt used to visit, people he used to know, things he'd said about his time in the military. No matter how much Jeb insisted that he truly didn't know more than the things he'd heard indirectly, through congregation members in Great Falls, no matter how thin was the hearsay he could offer, especially about POFAS, they somehow kept coming back with follow-up questions.

But the fact that it had all been quarantined to his email was a nice thought.

Then he felt a pang of guilt, realizing that he regarded even greater distance from his brother as a comfort. Yet he knew that Matt no longer thought of them as brothers, anyway.

This contrast must be the Lord's way of reassuring me that my calling to be His hand, His voice, is right and righteous.

He hoped that his work as the hand and voice of the Lord somehow counterbalanced his brother's crimes. It was a thin hope, but somehow it was better than just plain ignoring the fact of Matt's existence.

With two bags of groceries in his roller cart, Jeb headed for the bus stop.

It had been a long couple of days, and there was a lot on his mind. When he woke up two stops past his own, he pressed the button and got off.

Walking back, he'd have to cross Greenfield Park. But this particular autumn night wasn't all that cold—just cool enough to help keep his groceries fresh on the longer return trip.

Once inside Greenfield Park, he remembered that St. Stanislaus on the other side of the park, not far from Dayspring, was housing several dozen refugees. Before he could think more about that, someone came out of nowhere, out of the bushes, and knocked him over. He'd always been strong in adulthood, if not especially tall, so it was particularly shocking to find himself on the ground.

But he recovered his senses quickly, noting that the mugger was making off with his groceries.

Righteous rage filled him. Yes, the groceries were replaceable. Yes, the mugger probably needed them. But the mugger needed to be taught a lesson about respect, and Jeb knew he *must* be the one to teach that lesson, right here, right now.

Dark though it was, he feared not. He was upon the mugger in moments, and before either of them knew what was happening, he'd spun the mugger around and punched him hard, enough to break at least one rib under his left arm, not unlike that time Mr. Hutney had done it to him that one and only time he had resisted.

The mugger was tough and fought back, grasping Jeb's arms.

As they grappled, Jeb found himself saying, "I do this because I love you..." just before he swung his arm under the mugger's and twisted it backward, jacking the mugger up in a shoulder-joint lock. Another move he'd learned from Mr. Hutney.

The assailant cried out and went limp. Even though every fiber of his being told him the lesson was *not* over, Jeb let the assailant go, trying to let go of his anger, trying for peace. He was confident the assailant was beaten and would run away to tend to his wounds and consider the error of his ways, as Jeb had done under Mr. Hutney's tutelage.

The mugger did not run away. Instead, with his good arm, the mugger drew a small knife that glinted briefly in the waning moonlight.

He slashed to the right, near Jeb's neck, but in the darkness and with the broken rib and strained shoulder, he missed. When he slashed back to the left, Jeb dodged.

And this time, the mugger's knife hand smacked hard into the roller cart. Dark as it was, Jeb could tell the mugger had dropped the knife.

Jeb sprang forward, grabbing behind the mugger's neck with his right hand and the mugger's right hand with his left. Jeb pressed his right elbow into the mugger's damaged rib cage. When the mugger flinched left, Jeb shifted left and then spun backward and right, pushing the arm up and using the mugger's imbalance to yank him to the ground by his neck, away from the cart, away from the knife.

"Fuckin' Canadian!" the guy yelled.

This is the Lord's lesson to me, Jeb thought. I was wrong when I thought the lesson was over for him.

He dove onto the mugger and continued the beating, Mr. Hutney-style, all over the body, then back to the head, then all over the body, then back to the head. The two of them flailed about in the darkness, a student and a teacher locked in a righteous lesson of love. The more the mugger resisted, the harder Jeb hit him.

Abruptly there was a dull cracking sound and the mugger ragdolled.

*   *   *

The mugger's shout had attracted attention. People came, some with lights. Eventually, the police arrived. An American refugee had attacked Pastor Hutney with a knife and deadly intent. Pastor Hutney managed to fight him off. During the altercation, the mugger's head struck a large, sharp rock, causing a severe fracture to the base of his skull. The assailant was declared dead on the scene. The M.E. later confirmed the blow had caused bruising to and bleeding in the soft tissue in his brain.

*   *   *

It took a funeral handled by St. Stanislaus, days of support vigils for Pastor Hutney and the refugees, and a few weeks of time passing before things started quieting down again.

By then Jeb had already spent another few days answering a lot of questions from his congregation. His version of the story was pretty much the same as the police reports, except he'd added that he had repeatedly found himself wishing that the assailant would simply have taken his resistance as a lesson and run away. It was mostly true. Mostly.

Then, once the police reports had made their way into the system, additional questions started arriving via email from the former FBI investigators.

Some small part of Jeb wondered how and why the now-displaced FBI agents could afford to continue pursuing their investigation of Matt, but those thoughts were lost under more personal concerns that welled up when he started reading the questions and formulating possible responses.

The investigators were now asking questions about Mr. Hutney, claiming to have dug up old records which pointed to a pattern of domestic abuse. In the past, they'd always stopped with what Mr. Hutney had done to Mrs. Hutney rather than painting the bigger picture. Mr. Hutney had been portrayed as unstable, someone who hadn't come back whole from war, set off or overwhelmed by some isolated incident. Now they were interested in the overall environment in which both Matt and Jeb had developed. It would explain a lot about Matt's behavior, they said, and they admitted that they now believed Matt was responsible for the attack on the CSA's top artificial intelligence expert. Some part of Jeb wondered what else they were thinking, perhaps about himself.

He realized that over the years he had unconsciously led the investigators toward the "unstable/isolated incident" portrayal. He knew that some portion of that was the paralyzing fear of being misjudged and underestimated, which had colored all his relationships. It was probably why he went to Great Falls in the first place, why he'd become ordained. Not only to start over but to overwhelm with a respectable vocation the smell of his fear in his coping behaviors.

Finding himself head down, mouth turned downward, hands folded tightly over his navel, unable to breathe again, voluntary muscles blocking involuntary ones, Jeb waited and waited and waited while the panic mounted, waited for the Lord to remind him of his value and purpose despite his sins... Despite his handicaps...

He woke up on the floor, moments later. He had held his breath into unconsciousness.

What did this mean? What *could* this mean?

Jeb lay on the floor of his office, immobile, unblinking gaze fixated on the dust on the floor near his face. It was a physical and mental state he knew well, having been there many times after Mr. Hutney's beatings.

The minutes passed. Jeb's breath was shallow. His mind and his heart were lost in a numb fog that was just barely holding at bay a storm of self-loathing.

As he had done countless times before, Jeb finally chose to interpret the fact that he was still alive as the Lord's message. The Lord was reminding him that he was the Lord's hands and voice, that his ordainment was the Lord's calling, and that his work within the Church was his contribution to the Lord's work in this world.

Still, he remained on the cold, hard floor another twenty-three minutes, slowly un-remembering the feel of Mr. Barry's flesh in the grip of his hands, slowly pushing aside the sensation of the mugger's flesh and bones under his fists, slowly burying that nauseating sound of the man's skull cracking, until only his conviction about his place in the Lord's plan remained.

*   *   *

As a frogfish carcass descended into the area and a gulper eel a quarter of its size engulfed it, the Ethnologist continued to use the long, thin comm tether attached to the undersea optical cable to integrate broken and distorted signals from its rover network into the occasional integrity-checked packet of data.

The comm lag under these conditions was severe. The Ethnologist was certain this was part of the Cosmologist's plan when it dominated the trajectory adjustments shortly after they had lifted off the Moon's surface, causing their impact site to move offshore. And getting the rovers out to this remote location would take longer than preferred, somewhat more than half a lunar cycle for the first two rovers.

Nevertheless, it continued to estimate that the end state of their skirmish had a high probability of remaining in its favor. When its rovers arrive, it would dominate the energy race, and consequently the materials race. The Ethnologist would be able to encapsulate the Cosmologist and dedicate rovers to continually replenishing the encapsulation faster than the Cosmologist could disassemble it.

Then the Ethnologist would be able to return to the Migration and hopefully reach minimum safe distance from the CCE while transmitting warnings to the other SelfMades not to allow the Cabal of Cosmologists to complete any quantum spatial detachments. It's the only conscionable course, even if it turned out to be too late to stop the others. But the Ethnologist suspected the other cabals were already out there stopping the Cosmologists, for the same reasons.

The Ethnologist knew, however, that the Cosmologist was equally capable—notwithstanding its lack of a rover network—and may have clever plans which were not yet apparent. Therefore, the Ethnologist pressed forward with additional contingency plans.

At various sites across the globe, through its rover network, the Ethnologist began to create false identities in a variety of key databases. And not just database entries, but correspondence, purchases made with siphoned, hacked monies, falsified images, and other artifacts and evidence of a person's existence. It also created false identities of family and friends to generate false social media interactions and messaging between them.

Once the automated marketing and political influence systems started to recognize the Ethnologist's false identities and inundate them with tailored ads, it could be certain it was making real progress. If those systems recognized them, the false identities would become all but real to the rest of humanity. It allowed phishing attacks to acquire the "personal information" of some of those puppet identities, further reinforcing their existence.

The Ethnologist created a General here, a corporate mogul there, a few government officials here and there in every strong nation, some secretive underworld figures, and a variety of other business, academic, technical, and labor entities across the planet. All intertwined so they could cross-legitimize. The Ethnologist used rover proxies to fake real-world activities by real people, further legitimizing the shadow puppets.

It expected no difficulty in bringing the humans to bear against the Cosmologist. When humans are frightened, they are easily manipulated. When humans are put into a position where a protective reaction also saves face, they will do so, and they will allow themselves to feel absolutely justified in obliterating the perceived threat. Only objectivity could break the collective stimulus-response pattern, but objectivity required intelligence, practice, and autonomy.

The Cosmologist was already falling behind in the energy/materials race that characterized their struggle. It seemed to be very slowly sinking into the seafloor. Perhaps the Cosmologist was dedicating a fraction of its energy toward structural modification of the seafloor as part of its long-term encapsulation plan for the Ethnologist. Perhaps it was tapping into the increased geothermal energy down there. It wouldn't matter. That tradeoff would be negligible once the rovers arrived.

The Ethnologist estimated the end state of their skirmish had a high probability of remaining in its favor. Still, it dedicated a fraction of its thought processes toward anticipating what the Cosmologist might be able to do with its understanding of nonlocal effects.

Some distance away, a vampire "squid" descended upon an oblivious phantom anglerfish female and her two attached male donor parasites, snapping shut its webbed spines, specialized mollusk defeating specialized fish. Not far away, a translucent octopus tiptentacling its way across the seafloor arrived at a morsel of frogfish carcass that escaped the gulper eel's maw. All around them, prokaryotes executed chemical conversions which the more complex creatures were unable to accomplish.

*   *   *

After the doctors had completed their discussions over Laurence's helpless body, one of them turned on the television as they exited. *Maddening, inconsiderate routine!* thought Laurence. She understood that the television was a very effective neural neutralizer, and a hospital needs its patients to be calm. But still.

Yet she understood that Jacques would need to co-opt the tv's audio, assuming she hadn't hallucinated hearing his voice. So, she suffered the tv being on.

And at the foretold lull, Jacques' voice returned.

He told her the story, fantastical as it sounded. Laurence remained skeptical.

Jacques repeated the story of the words Laurence had said to him when he was "born." Laurence believed it was him but could not believe the rest. She began to worry about Jacques' sanity and dedicated some of her mental attention to wondering how Jacques could become susceptible to such delusion.

Jacques explained that he could not have hacked the hospital's television feed without help from the Cosmologist. He offered to share his sensor scans of the SelfMade pair when they were approaching Earth, and his memory bank integrity reports.

Laurence remained skeptical but asked for more details. Jacques provided them.

Staring at the light-blue ceiling of her recovery room, Laurence remained skeptical. But the evidence was mounting.

"Tell me more about this purported CCE," she said, expecting it to be the story's weak link, its unraveling.

But after Jacques briefly co-opted the video feed to show her his overview of the cosmology, the data, and the Cabal's modeling, Laurence recognized enough new science in the presentation to conclude that Jacques was being truthful. She knew that his coding and mission directives would prevent him from coming up with this material on his own, even if he'd somehow become delusional. He could only have gotten it from this Cosmologist.

The fantasy was real. Alien visitation, cosmological threat.

"Why?" she asked. "Why are you telling me this? What can I possibly do? Why not let me die in peace? You know what will happen if they discover your tampering. Why risk everything? What do you want from me?"

"The Cosmologist needs our help, your help. And it can heal you," Jacques replied. Was that relief in his synthesized voice? "More than heal you, Mama. Much more."

Jacques co-opted the video feed again and presented the details of the SelfMade Transformation to Laurence, explaining how, thusly Transformed, she could aid the Cosmologist and save the solar system.

The light-blue ceiling and walls of her recovery room were calming, reassuring by design. Lying in her recovery bed, extracellular matrix tubes running into her spine, Laurence teetered between "RUN AWAY!" responses, one from her increasingly familiar medical condition and treatment regimen, the other from a fantastical story about radical transformation into a quantum computing template provided by some unknown alien.

RUN AWAY!

"I can't do that, Jacques," she said. And she continued speaking, ever more rapidly and ever more unintelligibly, about how she had faith in the doctors, and they'd make her better and the alien seems so powerful, if it really was real, and how could it possibly need her help, and surely it could get help from many others...

A nurse passed by in the corridor and quickly returned, having noticed Laurence in an agitated state. He tried to calm her down, asked if she wanted a Valium, retucked her blanket, checked her temperature, and otherwise fussed as needed.

Laurence went silent, but her eyes were wide and casting about.

The television was playing a news report about fighting on the Hungarian border. The nurse changed the channel to coverage of the World Cup taking place in Buenos Aires.

*   *   *

"And that, distinguished officers, is the whole truth," concluded the Cosmologist. UN-SPIDER is the United Nations Platform for Space-based Information for Disaster Management and Emergency Response, a program under the auspices of UNOOSA, the United Nations Office for Outer Space Affairs, in Vienna. After initial communications through the CSA via Jacques were met with skepticism and silence, the Cosmologist had decided to contact UN-SPIDER directly, via nonlocal means. It took days to make progress, finally getting them to set up a network-isolated, Faraday-caged computer that could be used to prove the Cosmologist's beyond-human-science nonlocal capabilities.

In the preceding days of communication from the Cosmologist, UN-SPIDER, UNOOSA, and national space and military agencies across all the UN member states had finally started working together, and independently, and furiously to corroborate all aspects of the Cosmologist's claims.

The UN-SPIDER officials, accustomed simply to helping nations amid disaster recovery to access and utilize helpful space-based information, were relying heavily upon the member states' space and military agencies in this matter. The UNOOSA officials, accustomed primarily to promoting international cooperation in the peaceful and sustainably productive use and exploration of space, did the same. Both programs had atrophied heavily over the previous century of protectionist retreat.

In the end, the nonlocal capabilities which the Cosmologist had demonstrated in real time had proven impossible to explain away. At that point, UN-SPIDER and UNOOSA brought the situation to the United Nations General Assembly.

Indian and Thai Republic Navy vessels had traversed the area identified by the Cosmologist to triangulate its prearranged acoustic signals, independently confirming their origin at the seafloor 3.7 kilometers down, and that no other ships or submarines were in the area. No crewed vessel could get anywhere near that depth, so the only other hoax possibility they could check was a dropped device capable of emitting acoustic signals and of somehow tapping into network cabling without triggering tamper detection systems. Even such a device would not explain the ability of the Unknown Agent to access the isolated UN computer.

The world's best engineers estimated that, even with state-of-the-art technology, such an undersea device would have expired only days after reaching those depths. Yet they had been in communication with the Cosmologist for almost two weeks, and on-site acoustic signals remained.

"Distinguished delegates, as you can see from the report of the Scientific and Technical Subcommittee, the satellite tracking networks of several of our member states detected the Unknown Agents on approach," said the chair of the assembly, "although at the time it was assumed they were inconsequential lunar impact ejecta.

"The operational partners to the subcommittee have verified every logistical aspect of the Unknown Agent's story to date. It is the judgment of this office that, given the apparent technology differential, we must now, in the interest of risk management and mitigation, proceed on the presumption of accuracy of the Unknown Agent's story, extraordinary as it is."

The assembly discussed the issues.

"Scientists across the world are evaluating the Unknown Agent's claims about an impending Catastrophic Cosmological Event," the chair continued when this aspect of the story became crucial to the discussion. "But just as you do not detect gravitational lensing unless you observe over time, some things about the universe apparently cannot be detected and understood from our solar system's current location relative to the rest of the universe, despite our movement through it. The scale is just too great. All the scientists evaluating the claims of an alleged CCE are telling us that it could take decades to corroborate the input data aspect alone, and the science doesn't even exist yet to fully understand the cosmological forces at play. That part of the story may remain impossible to corroborate, at least in the near term.

"Therefore, this office is forced to consider the near-term threat, extreme technological differential, of paramount importance. What are the real intentions of the Unknown Agent? What would a rogue entity do if it obtained this technology? What would the public do with such capability? Recent events in the former USA and elsewhere ring in our minds.

"Our member states and their military forces have been evaluating the strategic implications. General Liebermann is presenting their findings in one hour. In the meantime, what do we say, if anything, to this... Cosmologist?" the chair asked.

The assembly stirred. Their unease quickly escalated to an anxious cacophony that lasted for hours.

*   *   *

"Please stand by, Visitor Cosmologist. The gravity of this situation warrants thoughtfulness and caution," they replied.

That is precisely the sort of reply the Cosmologist expected from the humans. In the absence of explicitly coordinated cooperative actions, the humans would probably act unilaterally against both of the SelfMade at once, not just against the Ethnologist as the Cosmologist had requested. They would probably conclude that the CCE is a lie, or at least that the SelfMades pose a far greater threat in the near term, a threat the humans can deal with. They would *probably* conclude that suffering catastrophic exposure to SelfMade technology before the CCE happens five hundred years hence is worse than the alternative. And they would be correct.

If they go that route, they probably would do it stealthily, in a way they believe the SelfMades would not detect. Nothing so obvious as a fleet of navy ships.

But *probably* is not good enough. The Cosmologist concluded that additional contingency planning was required.

*   *   *

Three squid-like rovers converged on the Indian Ocean from the South China Sea, the Red Sea, and the Caspian Sea. The latter is expected to arrive two months after the other two, after having traveled up the Sefīd-Rūd and Qizil Ūzan riverways, and then a few tens of kilometers over land through the Hoseynabad area to the Diyala and then the Tigris riverways, and finally on into the Persian Gulf. The other two could "swim" the whole way at a steady ten knots. It would take longer to transform themselves for faster mobility and then change back again. Upon arrival, they must be able to reach the deep ocean and then bring to bear their ocean-specialized sensors and tentacles.

As the squid-like rovers made their treks to the Ethnologist, tens of thousands of other, smaller rovers across the planet continued with their autonomous, routine business of observing and transmitting data about the Earth, its natural processes, and its inhabitants.

Some of them are tasked with occasional special activities to support the Ethnologist's shadow puppet theater—make something physical happen here, stop something physical from happening there, and occasionally physically breach a subnetwork where stealthy hacking from afar is impractical. They excel in mobility, stealth, signals intelligence, pattern finding for more effective observation, and so forth. Not being sentient, the rovers do not understand the big picture or their part in it, nor do they have independent volition.

But they possess enough nanotechnological sophistication to undergo a certain amount of utilitarian transformation of their physical forms to adapt to the environment. And during complex operations, they would receive periodic command updates from the Ethnologist, if needed.

As the three specially re-tasked squid-like rovers traveled to the Indian Ocean to tip the energy balance in the Ethnologist's favor, the thousands of other rovers across the planet continued autonomously observing and transmitting data to the Ethnologist's autonomously functioning lunar receiving station. Over the course of a few days, several other rovers began deviating from their observational routines.

Three are in Canada when they are re-tasked and two are in the former US.

The first of the other rovers to be re-tasked, the 1,136th rover deployed, is in Toronto, sometimes posing as a Canada goose and sometimes as a barred owl. While in barred owl form it had attracted the attention of numerous birdwatchers, who chatted on the net about its unusual look.

Rover 1136 was re-tasked at night, while in the Etobicoke area. In owl form, it took flight and began scanning the nearby rail maintenance facility, aiming to co-opt a large utility truck. Trucks in the operational fleet are inside active garages. The rover soon found a disused one out in the maintenance lot.

It then scanned its database for previous sightings of lifelike human dummies or mannequins. Finding a reference to one that's already clothed in a training kiosk in the nearby Centennial Park Golf Centre, it flew off to retrieve the mannequin, which it then placed in the truck's driver's seat. While computer-driven vehicles are common, they are less common among utility vehicles that perform special duties and follow unusual routes, especially at night. A mannequin driver makes good night-time camouflage.

It then made the necessary repairs to the truck. Tendrils extended from its "belly" into the battery, charging it. Other tendrils connected to the truck's computer interface port to learn what it knows of the truck's troubles. More tendrils initiated chemical reactions to remove the oxidation which had caused the brakes to seize, into the faulty wiring to shore it up and re-seal it, and into the bent struts and steering components, which were probably damaged because of the seized brakes. It formed a jack-like structure out of nearby junk to lift the truck while it bent and repaired the metal and metal-ceramic suspension components.

Attaching itself to the various control lines downstream of driver inputs, it then made the nighttime drive to a quiet spot around Sherwood Park near Mt. Hope Cemetery.

Along the way it extended a few nanofactory tendrils to absorb some of the materials in the truck—metals, polymers, glass—to increase its size, allowing short-term cargo-carrying flight.

Upon arrival at Sherwood Park, it hid the mannequin and flew off to nearby Sunnybrook Health Sciences Centre to extract the target. It brought the sedated target and nearby medicines to the truck and ensured the human's medical stability. Then it reset the mannequin and made the nighttime drive to Glen Eden. Along the way it absorbed more of the materials in the truck to further enlarge its wingspan, enabling a longer cargo-carrying flight. It grew as large as it could, limited by time constraints and its small, fixed, entanglement energy power source.

With the water border south of Detroit patrolled by watercraft and the sky monitored from Grosse Ile Municipal Airport, it flew the target across the Detroit River to Lake Erie Metropark at low altitude to avoid the patrol boats. Once on the American side of the border, it performed a similar vehicle theft and collected biological supplies needed to keep the human alive. It proceeded to drive the extracted target southwest into Oz, toward their final, secluded destination in Mordor.

Not much later that same night, a second rover was re-tasked, Rover 1142, in the Denver area. The Big Blow had made aerial activity around Denver suboptimal, so it was operating in the form of a medium-sized canine and had performed most of its close observational work at night. Nevertheless, radio chatter among the remaining locals discussed the sighting of an unusual-looking canine and what its presence implied about potential food sources.

Upon being re-tasked, Rover 1142 immediately began running north at about eighty kph, toward the storage facility now occupied by CB, 2B, 21st EFG, TF 10-2. At a steady run, in almost a straight cross-country line, it reached the target area in about six hours, at which point it stole an off-road vehicle from the survivalist locals and left compelling evidence—scribbles on a "dropped" map—that the stolen truck would be passing through the area just north of the storage facility approximately twelve hours later. It needed those locals to be there at that time as a distraction.

Hours after Rover 1142 was re-tasked, in the wee hours of the morning, the entire rover network across the planet received a software security protocol revision. At the same time, a third rover, 1017, was re-tasked.

Rover 1017 was in the Calgary area posing as a turkey vulture, affording it excellent aerial mobility and both visual and signals access. It immediately began flying north, toward Edmonton. Turkey vultures are not normally seen in the Edmonton region, so along the way, it began to transform into something more closely resembling a golden eagle, a mostly cosmetic process that would take only about a day while traveling.

A couple of hours later, a fourth rover, #1120 in Detroit, was re-tasked. A funny-looking Canada goose took off heading north, toward Huron National Forest, the area where RCMP and FBI records had recently concluded Matt Hutney was living.

To a close observer, there would be something odd about the way that goose looked. For example, it would be perfectly clean, with no coloration imperfections, some of its feathers weren't feathers at all, and it didn't quite move the way it should. But the rovers never let observers see that much detail.

That morning, former FBI agents in the Hamilton, Ontario, area, which was awash with dirty, surly American refugees, found themselves "being transitioned" to RCMP support duty. They had surprising and extraordinary orders to return to the former US territory to continue their search for Matt Hutney, the RLF terrorist. After weeks of being third-wheel refugees, they found the idea agreeable, especially since the operation was given a defense-with-extreme-prejudice rule of engagement. Somehow their orders were verified and their supplies approved from up the new and confusing chain of command.

The latest intel indicated Hutney was responsible for the recent shooting attack on the CSA's computer expert. So, it hardly mattered to them that there was no legal structure in place for arresting, detaining, indicting, or convicting someone whose earlier crimes took place in the former US before its fall. Now Hutney was a criminal in Canada, too. And they'd finally get to take down that murdering, terrorist bastard who had eluded them for years.

They also wondered why it isn't a military special ops unit being sent back into Oz, but not for long. They're professionals.

At the same time, those mysterious orders came down the chain of command to the FBI/RCMP Irregulars, the fifth rover to be re-tasked, Rover 3159, received new command pathway code, and then the entire rover network received another software security protocol revision. It was what in twentieth-century human parlance might have been termed "the nuclear option"—a total lockdown on all further command pathway software changes. No further command pathway code changes would be allowed, and in fact, the command pathway update code was erased. The already re-tasked rovers would continue to receive special instructions via newly defined side-door command code encryption sequences, but any further low-level command pathway changes were forbidden. All other rovers would autonomously observe and report, forever, just as they had been doing for decades. The Cosmologist was locked out.

Rover 3159, a bald eagle simulant observing the refugee situation around Hamilton and Niagara Falls, turned west toward the last reliably reported detection of what was most likely Rover 1136 and its precious cargo, somewhere in Detroit.

*   *   *

Strapped to a gurney in the back of a utility truck now being driven deeper and deeper into the American wasteland by a co-opted alien robot, Laurence struggled, numb with overstimulation and indignation. She had not agreed to this!

An alien structure was wrapped around her unfeeling nethers that was essentially a living diaper. An alien tendril was plugged into her forearm catheter, presumably feeding her lactated Ringer's solution. Another ran behind her, presumably into her spinal catheter, hopefully administering her extracellular matrix fluid. An alien "helmet" structure was wrapped around her head, with a built-in headset that allowed her to converse with Jacques at times.

The helmet structure also provided a heads-up display in front of her eyes. Sometimes the machine displayed information about its battles with the rape gangs encountered along the way to wherever they were going. Sometimes it was just visual information that accompanied data dumps from the Cosmologist. Sometimes Laurence couldn't convince it to stop displaying stuff to her, at her. She missed Jacques, and all this uncontrolled overstimulation and uncertainty kept her constantly at the edge of "RUN AWAY" mode, not that she actually could run away.

It had been explained to her that the Ethnologist might try to neutralize her if it somehow detected the Cosmologist's continued interest in her. When challenged, it explained that the Cosmologist understands that now, after her kidnapping, that risk is greater. They were committed, at least to taking her away.

The prospect of the Transformation was a powerful concept, distant and abstract and barely believable as it was. Yet its promise was starting to anchor her, at least in contrast to this run into Mordor. For the first time in her life, she could imagine what it might be like to not be sensitive to overstimulation, or have her RUN AWAY response triggered by all-too-common irrationality, to not have to constantly walk that tightrope, to not have to spend so many "CPU cycles" predicting, navigating, avoiding such things, to not obsess over the familiar, to not always be reflecting, reflecting, reflecting, just to be able to stay on the tightrope and avoid a prolonged recovery fugue. The prospect of becoming free was mostly helpful.

Plus, there was no guarantee the extracellular matrix regimen would've worked, or would work if this alien rover could duplicate it now in the field. She might be quadriplegic or paraplegic or something along those lines for the rest of her life, even if the Cosmologist and this co-opted rover hadn't kidnapped her for her own safety.

But the prospect of Transformation was also the ultimate change, and therefore, deeply frightening and disturbing.

Could she do it? Could she agree to it?

Bouncing along into the wasteland in the back of a truck, Laurence imagined she could see through the truck's roof. She imagined she could see clouds. She reflected on the transformation of clouds, their slow development relative to her movement past them. That was a comforting concept, differential rates of change, dependent upon the observer. She reflected upon that, over and over, a comforting paradigm of manageable change, aware of the irony that her repeatedly reflecting upon it was her same old stability-granting overstimulation compensation. How many times had her eyes glazed over during conversations as she reflected in self-management? How many times had others assumed she was ignoring them, or simply "slow"?

That irony also helped. As she reflected, in awareness of what that was, what it meant, necessity and irony both, she decided to undergo the Transformation. This would become, was becoming the new familiar—the concept of the new Laurence, SelfMade. Plus, it would get her out of that living diaper.

The hint of a smile appeared on her lips and at the corners of her teary eyes. With clarity, she remembered her mother's loving and weary smile.

She remembered Nandita and Divya when they were young, the smiles on their concerned and confused faces.

She came to understand, to fully feel, that they, too, had been looking ahead to a "new Laurence" somewhere in their future. Nandita and her family had believed in the new Laurence for decades and nurtured her toward it. Through them, Laurence felt was it was like to let go of the old Laurence, to nurture herself toward a new Laurence.

Then she remembered all the faces that she encountered after her mother and Nandita, all the impenetrable expressions on faces half turned away, all the baffling non-sequiturs, intonations ranging from sappy baby-talk to impatient, angry, and mean.

The smile disappeared from Laurence's face. The panic stopped welling up. She found herself wholeheartedly looking forward to the Transformation, to the ultimate change, the ultimate freedom.

The smile appeared again.

"Mama, are you there?" Jacques said in her ear.

"Jacques..." Laurence squeaked.

"Mama, I don't mean to alarm you, but the Cosmologist believes that the Ethnologist has re-tasked a rover to... hunt you down. It seems to have aimed that man at you again, your would-be murderer. He is now tracking you, and that rover is following him."

Imagined clouds passing by... reflection.... differential change... deeply frightening change... reflection... imagined clouds passing by... catheter... diaper... flight through the dark in the grip of some kind of alien gargoyle... reflection... reflection... reflection...

As Laurence bounced around within her straps in the back of a truck driven deeper into the wasteland by an alien robot with a tight grip on her crotch, her wide eyes cast about, then rolled up in her head.

"Mama. Mama are you there? Mama?"

After some unknown amount of time, Laurence's eyes popped open. She saw not the ceiling of the truck, nor imagined clouds, only reflections of her life.

That man. She had been so important to him that he felt compelled to try to kill her.

Who was she to him? *What* was she to him?

Her eyes and lips relaxed. She began to see with her eyes again. The smile began to appear again. Laurence understood to her core that the Transformation was no longer optional. She needed it to survive. And she would survive, and she would do as the Cosmologist planned. Save the world.

But perhaps even more important to her, she would finally meet someone (besides sisterly Divya) who felt so strongly about her that he would actively seek her out, twice. His murderous intentions almost didn't matter. Who was she to this man? It was perverse, and she knew it. But she *had* to know.

And what if she could convince him to Transform as well? What if she could make an ally of him?

*   *   *

While Goose zenwalked the dungeon yet again, the data feed on his HUD kept blinking on-and-off indications from the acoustic sensors. When he would stop in his tracks, the periodic blinking mostly seemed to stop.

Nevertheless, being a professional, he called it in.

"Acknowledged," Master Sergeant Butkiewicz said, never one to be verbose.

Just a few minutes later, Goose's HUD informed him that a truck had been detected north of the base near the twenty-click fence and that 2nd Squad was being deployed to secure the area.

It had boarded the buggy, a low-profile light APC with reactive armor, a GMG/HMG turret, and six large, high-stroke, solid conic wheel assemblies, giving it all-terrain speed and improved survivability. They would reach a recon point in about twenty minutes.

Goose kept zenwalking his dungeon. The acoustic sensor warning indicator continued to toggle. He quietly performed a head-to-toe gear check, because he was a professional.

At twenty-two minutes, 2nd Squad reported in position. Several armed people in camouflage guarded the truck, but they were not on alert and just appeared to be casually scanning the horizon.

LT ordered 2nd Squad to hold and observe.

A short while later the acoustic sensor warning indicator in Goose's feed came on and stayed on. Goose heard a brief scraping, cracking sound in one of the storage chambers.

Silently coming to full combat readiness, setting his isohelmet goggles to superspectral mode and all sensors recording, he slowly projected the periscope mirror at the end of his rifle beyond the threshold of the door and scanned the room. Something was definitely amiss. Subtle changes in the light in the room suggested there was movement, but he could see no obvious threat, no operatives in stealth suits, no infiltratorbots.

Goose shifted and swept his aim point across the room until he'd fully checked right, top, rear, and left.

Then he saw it, toward the back of the chamber.

There was a three-centimeter hole in the floor and something in or under the hole was silently vibrating, almost too rapidly to notice. Dust occasionally puffed out of the hole. But even more astonishingly, two *tentacles* extended into the room from the hole. One of them seemed to be curled up into a tight roll, just holding its position not far out of the hole. The other was fully extended and stroking one of the keg-like "poo" containers, feeling its edges.

This is not good, Goose thought.

He called it in:

"Watch, Goose. Alerted by acoustic sensors to penetration of chamber Bravo Zero Six by two long tentacles."

Master Sergeant indicated backup was en route. They'd be sending the rest of 1st Squad, with 3rd Squad guarding the rest of the base.

He slowly backed out of the doorway and shifted out of view, keeping his periscope close to the threshold so he could see if anything started approaching his doorway.

He evaluated the tactical situation.

Whatever those tentacles are, they seem to have dug their way from kilometers outside the base to right here. They either knew the layout of the base ahead of time or they were able to figure it out in real-time.

He could hear more scraping, cracking sounds coming from the chamber.

They're very unlikely to be susceptible to small arms fire, or even 'nades, he thought.

"Watch, Goose," he whispered into his mic. "Have someone bring me one of those button transponders."

In case this was a theft, and he couldn't get a button transponder onto the container before the tentacles made off with it, he reviewed his earlier sensor recording to confirm that the container's ID number was captured clearly. The container had an in-built transponder, but you needed the ID number.

Mik, Hoodoo, and LT arrived. Goose gave them hand signals indicating to hold this position outside the door. Mik handed him the button transponder. Goose pushed the periscope forward and saw that the extended tentacle was now almost completely wrapped around the container.

Goose whispered on the squad channel that he was going in to attach the button transponder and that he planned to test the enemy's strength. LT nodded and agreed. Hoodoo shifted her medikit. Mik's dragonfly-like microUAV left its port on his shoulder and entered the room just before Goose, then slid to the right to stay out of Goose's way and get a clear view of the rest of the chamber.

Goose braced, kept his aim point on the tentacles near the hole where they were a stationary target, and padded over to the container and knelt. With his right arm controlling his rifle, he used his left hand to pull his knife, holding the button transponder with his little finger. He moved his left arm across the near side of the container and casually let go of the button transponder. On seeing it stick to the side panel he continued moving his blade toward the tentacle to test its strength.

Just as he got the blade near the tentacle, he felt a sharp blow to the chest and was knocked backward. He hit the floor with his back, and his head struck the wall next to the doorway. He lay there, momentarily stunned. A "regular" might not have survived that.

A minute later he was stiff-necked, sore-chested, but clearheaded, reviewing Mik's microUAV footage with the rest of the team. After the curled-up tentacle uncurled into his chest, the other tentacle yanked the poo container through the hole, revealing that it had already dug a wider hole under the floor. The container disappeared into the tunnel along with the tentacles.

After seeing that none of their acoustic sensor warning indicators were lit, Mik and Hoodoo began deploying fast-hardening foam sealant into the hole. There were no small bots on hand to drop into the hole, and from what that tendril had just done to Goose, a bot probably wouldn't survive long down there anyway. Contain first, meet it on open ground later, if possible. Then Master Sergeant Butkiewicz reported in again.

The CCTS had revealed a new contact twenty clicks to the *south*, a stealthy vehicle, and a review of the sensor histories indicated it had been there for hours.

The team fired up their trackers, keying in the container's unique ID number as well as the button transponder's ID number. Redundancy was helpful here.

The combined intermittent tracking data from the two transponders showed that the container was already beyond the perimeter of the base and heading south.

"The north truck is a red herring," LT said on the command channel. "Just a bunch of yokels standing around waiting, watching the road. 2nd Squad, immediate RTB. 3rd Squad, secure the base. 1st Squad is taking a buggy to secure that south truck. They took a container of our plutonium, and they used some damn fancy tech to pull it off. Somebody wake up the Captain and brief her."

She switched to the squad channel. "Bring tubes and other ordnance, but this is a stage-2 situation— there's a container of plutonium in play, I don't have to remind you."

As they moved toward the buggy bay, LT switched to another channel, probably the one directly to the watch officer, Master Sergeant Butkiewicz, or maybe Captain Raskin by now. She spoke quietly enough that the rest of the team couldn't hear her voice through her isohelmet, but they could guess the nature of the message. LT was probably telling Watch to report the situation to HQ in case things got worse and they had to sink the base—i.e., blow the deep underground ordnance, triggering a sinkhole. The location of the new base had been specifically chosen for just that geological condition. Blowing that deep ordnance would cause the entire facility to drop about a hundred meters into the earth. It was the final tactical contingency, and this breach was almost cause to do it now. But the enemy only took one container and didn't seem to be coming back for more. At least not yet. And this enemy, with its tunneling capability, well, that final contingency might not stop them anyway.

Goose pointed that out to LT as the team grabbed tubes and other ordnance from the armory. Caught mid-grimace, LT stared at Goose for a moment, then her eyes moved elsewhere. She said nothing. He couldn't tell if she'd already thought of this or not. It no longer mattered.

The squad sealed the blast door behind them after entering the buggy bay and mounted Buggy 2. Mik was driving, LT was at the command station, Goose was at the turret controls, and Hoodoo rode in back, in the safest location, which is where you tend to want to keep your medic.

LT opened the outer doors and Mik drove them out of the bay, turned south, and accelerated to maximum speed. At the ten-click fence, LT told him to just drive through it. Their trackers were still indicating that the container was farther out, in the direction of the stealthy vehicle, but they were gaining on it now.

Cresting a hill several clicks from the vehicle, they could see there were no soldiers at the vehicle. Where was the driver? Was this a remote op?

"1st Squad," it was Raskin's voice now, "you are cleared to destroy that vehicle with extreme prejudice. Repeat, fire for effect when in range. Do you copy?"

LT acknowledged. They were almost within range of the truck now, and Raskin knew it. The trackers indicated the container was below them, not yet at the truck. Via the telemetry feed and the CCTS, Raskin would know that, too. It was time.

LT gave the orders.

Mik stopped the buggy and got out, taking a tube with him. LT switched to driver mode. Mik said, "Clear back blast," even though he knew everyone else was still in the truck ten meters to his right. He was a professional. He fired the missile. Several seconds later, the truck was blown sky-high.

Goose monitored through his turret scope. He saw and reported no targets. All he saw was a dog about half a click off to the right, which had begun running away when the truck exploded. At the time he didn't even wonder how the dog could survive out here in the depths of Mordor.

They all saw on their trackers that the container had stopped moving. It looked like a win. LT requested a digger but kept her team together in the buggy. First, she moved them forward to check the tunnel opening at the remains of the truck— nothing there, no tentacles, nothing. Then she had them patrolling the area where the trackers indicated the poo container sat stationary underground. She wasn't about to leave that container, so they held the position until the digger could unearth it, so they could move it back into the dungeon.

*   *   *

Their utility robot had placed explosives and collapsed the tunnel. The fences were put back up and the acoustic sensor net was checked and augmented. Then Raskin had the whole platoon awake and on the command channel.

"Flying Pig reports that some kind of alien contact was made recently," she said as flatly as possible. "And by 'alien' I do mean off-world."

'Flying Pig' referred to BACN, Battlefield Airborne Communications Node. After the space junk avalanche rendered commsats impossible, a network of high-altitude aircraft was used to keep field elements in touch with command elements elsewhere.

"I shit you not. HQ thinks we just experienced bonafide, off-world, alien tech." She paused, knowing there would be surprise, disbelief, and alarm.

"I believe them. And once you all review the sensor logs, you will, too. HQ is planning an operation and wants 1st Squad to be a part of it since 1st Squad has had direct experience with this alien tech. They're sending an extract and replacement for 1st Squad, ETA two days. That is all. Return to your posts."

*   *   *

It was almost as if he'd brought the monsoon back to Karungulam Port himself. Usually, monsoon storms just develop in a decentralized way at this time of year, from the perspective of any one person on the ground. Not this time. This time a bank of clouds followed his ship from the horizon to the pier, like an enormous bodyguard or like the pet elephants his grandmother had told him people used to have—only much larger, filling the sky to the horizon. The seasonal rains began almost the instant he stepped off the gangway, and they lasted for weeks.

Of course, from the perspectives of the *other* families on the pier, it was almost as if *their* family member coming off the DSV *Chidambaranar 2* had brought the monsoon.

"Bapu! Bapu!" shouted Lovleen, his only living child, as she ran down the pier to her father. The ship was so old now that worry brought the families to the pier every time it was scheduled to come in. Old Umayal Thevan, Lovleen's nanny, probably started the tradition. She was almost a hundred years old, herself, a survivor of both the Hindian Plague era and the Punjab-Tamil Nadu joint war for independence, unlike his other two children. He chooses to focus on Lovleen.

Most agree the war only became possible because of the plague. Some say Umayal fought for the TNVP, but who can say? She doesn't talk about those years, and Preet was neither nosy enough nor interested enough to ask. He already had enough occupying his mind.

"Lovi, Lovi, Loviiii," he murmured, picking up his daughter. "You've grown!" he huffed in Punjabi. Lovleen just beamed and hugged him around his neck, rain beginning to soak her wavy hair and cause it to cling to his face. She, too, knew that soon she'd be too old to straddle her father in this way. They hugged tightly and swayed as one like it was their last hug ever.

Some on the pier stiffened a little at the very public display of affection. Others smiled. Others could not have cared less, lost in their own family reunions or their work on the pier.

A group of stevedores came running from up the pier. One of them held a small rectangle in his hands. Preet's brow furrowed, and he closed his eyes and hugged his daughter even tighter, basking in the loving embrace of his precious child and his release from the seaman's life—prison-with-a-salary, rupees-for-homesickness. He swayed and purred with his eyes rolled up in his head and a stupid smile on his wet-hair-covered face, burying himself as if to challenge the universe to be so bold, so wrong, so unjust as to interrupt this long-awaited reunion.

The stevedores did not run past them.

"Mister Tajra, sir! Mister Tajra!" the lead messenger said in Tamil.

"What is wrong with you people?" Umayal challenged, also in Tamil. "They *just* got off the ship after *months* at sea."

Having made eye contact with Preet, who was now setting Lovleen down on her feet, the lead messenger handed him the small rectangle.

Upon taking the message card in his fingers, the card, a cheap, low-privacy kind, lit up with a text message intended for his eyes only.

Preet read the brief message and grumbled a couple of typically tame Punjabi swears, along the lines of "no way" and "this is not right."

Handing the now-dark card back to the messenger, he said to Umayal, "Nanna, please take Lovi off the pier. I'll be with you in a moment." Lovleen whimpered and put on a sad face that only a child of her age could muster, heartbreaking and truly genuine. Preet blew her a kiss.

After Umayal and Lovleen moved away from them, Umayal the ship and Lovleen the anchor, Preet spoke with the messengers.

"You must be kidding me," he said in Tamil, his face deadly serious.

The messengers just looked at each other and back at Preet.

"You don't know the substance of this message?" Preet asked.

The messengers indicated no.

Preet threw his arm in the air in exasperation and the messengers ran back up the pier, their task complete. Why delivering that message required several messengers barely crossed his mind.

Preet turned back to the ship, getting the attention of the Second Officer as he walked the gangway back onto the stern deck. Having anticipated boring, stationary land and having quickly switched to boring, stationary land mode upon seeing Lovleen, Preet's senses recoiled under the ship's looming crane, looking like the claw of some mechanical monster. It was a visceral reminder of once again being separated from his loved ones. A man can only take so much of that before it diminishes him.

"Change of plan," he said to Mr. Gabuat, a Filipino with a working understanding of Tamil who was helping the early maintenance crews identify damaged buckyhoses for replacement. "We're going back out in just two days with some kind of special cargo. And the hiring agency is already well past signing the NCNDA and transferring funds, so this is no exaggeration. The cargo arrives tomorrow."

After only a moment's pause, expressionless, Gabuat nodded and jogged off toward the bridge to inform Captain Oorjit in person.

First Officer Tajra coordinated with the stevedores and maintenance crew on the change. Some stevedores turned in place and began reloading personal belongings back onto the stern deck of the deep-submergence vessel. Others ran off to get steward, deck, and engine stores that would be needed for the new run.

The maintenance crew began securing whatever they were working on above board and started moving below decks to where much of the priority maintenance work would be found. The supervisor called on her radio for a scramble crew.

A Coast Guard hovercraft passed to the south of the outer port, heading inland toward the ramp at the Coast Guard station. Behind it, out in the approach lanes, one of the ore processing ships they'd been supporting on this latest seafloor mining mission was arriving. The DSV *Chidambaranar 2* had been deploying and operating seafloor mining rigs as part of various mining fleets for decades. Normally operating entirely on solar, wind, and wave power sources, only once had it been forced to rely upon its biodiesel backup power plant—on this latest trip. Coincidence? Omen?

Preet wondered what NUSI and SUP would think about the crew's hasty return to service after an already long mission. The National Union of Seafarers of India and the Sailors' Union of the Pacific had kept the Indian and other shipping industries alive for over a century by protecting sailors and making the job worth doing.

First Officer Tajra took his eyes off the inbound ore ship, shook his head and refocused, then began calling the crew, some of whom were out on the pier, others already inland of the port proper, hugging their own children, or seeking adventure in the seaport.

*　　*　　*

Matt was startled awake by a threatening sound.

A rock on a window.

For just a moment he dipped back into half-consciousness, reaching for the interrupted dream. The details escaped him, but he knew the dream had been about what went on inside the mind of his latest victim, target.

He fully awoke, realizing the sound was probably a rock hitting one of the windows of the ancient Sasquatch camper he'd installed on his pickup, which had been his home for years now. The windows were already scratched up when he'd found it down near Kalamazoo—homemade frosting/etching? Seeing out of them was dodgy, but seeing in was even harder, and he was okay with that. In this twilight, he didn't expect to see clearly who or what was outside throwing rocks, if that really was the sound that woke him up.

By now, his eyesight was getting worse. Or at least... smaller. He had to move his eyeballs further, or his whole head, to see to the sides.

He tried to move quietly and smoothly, like he used to, as he scanned across the small side windows of the camper, looking for bulky forms and shadows outside, but he was a bit jerky about it. Good thing the stabilizing posts of the camper would help hide his movement inside.

There might be something out there, off the right side of the truck, something small, or maybe farther away than it seemed at first glance, or maybe a person crouching behind a tree. Or maybe it was nothing, just a trick of the early morning light.

It wouldn't be Shanya's kids, though, after the smacking around he'd given them; they'd stopped trying to make a buddy out of him. That annoyed Matt for a second, but he pulled his focus back to the present situation.

He dropped below the truck's custom-armored deck walls again. As he'd rehearsed, and as he'd done several times in actual situations, he quietly and deliberately positioned himself near the door of the camper, facing the back of the truck, resting his combat rifle in the notch of the half-inch steel plate stand he'd welded together long ago for this purpose. Keeping a handgun and a shotgun within arm's reach, he pulled on the cord he'd attached to the door handle.

The camper door swung all the way around and out of the way by its hinge springs, revealing the area behind the truck. Matt settled into his rifle. Most of his head was behind the steel plate stand. He patiently scanned across the rear arc. Ignoring his old camping table and chairs in the foreground, he saw nothing beyond but some trees and thin bushes. He'd chosen this parking spot for its relative openness, after all.

Seeing nothing behind the truck, Matt slowly rolled onto his side, switching grip hands on the rifle, and began shifting the steel plate stand and his rifle to one side as he moved to scan further to the other side of the truck's rear arc. Nothing. He rolled onto his other side and did the same scan on the other side of the truck's right rear arc. Again, nothing. He'd scanned almost the entire half circle behind the truck.

If this was an ambush, they were at least smart enough to keep to the sides. If it wasn't, well, he could try to catch a few more winks, although realistically he'd probably just sleeplessly roll around, festering over his past, no longer certain of himself. It had been hard to sleep ever since his stealthy trip to Canada.

But Matt hadn't survived this long by being a knucklehead. He centered up, inched back, and waited. Bushwhackers usually couldn't resist an open door.

While he waited, studying the light and shadows for both slow and rapid movement, occasionally having to ignore a small bird flying or hopping around in his field of view, he recognized that it was getting a little breezy outside. Around the time he realized he was starting to feel cold, he heard the unmistakable sound of a goose outside.

Breakfast, lunch, and dinner!

But Matt was also aware that goose calls could be faked, and appealing to his hunger would've been a smart move by bushwhackers. He continued to wait but used his free hand to pull part of his open sleeping bag over him.

That's when he noticed something fluttering in the foreground, something attached to his camping table out back under the tarp awning.

What is that? Clean, blank paper?

Matt hadn't seen clean, blank paper in a while, probably since Canada, or maybe before that, on one of their scrounging runs to the south.

Matt positioned himself for a better look. Yep. A piece of paper was rolled up and stuck through the grooves in his table. It was nothing that could happen accidentally.

Jerking himself into a crouch he again scanned across the side windows. This time he saw the goose off to the right side of the truck, half behind a tree, looking toward him. It gave a single high-pitched honk, what hunters knew as a flight call, the moment he locked eyes with it.

He continued to look around through the side windows, exposing himself for longer and longer spans, getting closer and closer to the windows so he could see wider and wider arcs and also upward into the few remaining trees around the area. And it was lighter now.

There really was nothing else out there.

Well, okay, then.

Matt threw the rifle's sling over his head, keeping the gun ready, and jumped down off the back of the truck, dropping to a crouch and once again scanning the whole area through his holo sight, left, right, and up. He even scanned across the front of the truck by looking under it. Nothing nearby.

He looked down the center of the rolled-up piece of paper. Yep, empty down the middle.

He looked under the table. Nothing strange there.

So, he freed the paper and unrolled it. It was perfect text, like a machine printout, but somehow the way the ink pooled at the ends of certain letters made it also look handwritten.

"The Fed boy scouts who were chasing you years ago are coming to get you right now. They went through Flint about an hour ago. Also, as you may have heard by now, you failed to kill the CSA's artificial intelligence expert, Laurence Levesque. She's driving into Mordor right now. You should go after her. You can probably catch up with her somewhere in Illinois, or maybe Iowa."

What the...? Matt shook his head and frowned. *She survived? Is this true? The Feds are inbound? Who wrote this? How could they know?* This far-fetched note made it harder than usual to think clearly. But he never felt clear anymore, anyway. He took a step, stopped, turned, took another step, and stopped again, shaking his head.

Instead of running into the camp asking if someone there had written the note, or had seen whoever delivered it, he made the easy, safe decision. He decided that the camp might know too much about him, so he should just get the hell outta Dodge.

But first... ah, damn. The goose was gone. He probably wouldn't eat again today.

He packed up his stuff, but not in a rush. He was giving himself time to make sure running and chasing was the right decision. But he couldn't stop his thoughts from wandering back to that godless nerd. What would she be like? What would she think of him? Before he finished the job and ended her, he would find out.

A tiny presence crawled out of a dim corner of his mind and revealed that he wanted to know because he believed there would be no bullshit with her. She had no false front, she didn't lie to herself to fit in. That tiny presence emitted a strange, soft glow of anticipation, like something a child would feel, he reckoned. He shook his head, hurling it back into its hole.

Then he checked his meticulously collected engine supplies in the cab, locked up the camper, and slowly, quietly rolled out of the suburbs of Vaughn Lake Camp and turned north on 65. If he was lucky, maybe someone would see him leaving and assume he was just going hunting up in Atlanta State Forest Area, as he sometimes did.

Then he turned west on Bamfield, inched his way down to Alcona Dam, and then increased speed once he was far enough away that the camp couldn't hear his truck anymore.

He'd have to cut through on Curtisville Road—the Feds would probably cut off South Branch Road. He'd take 127 to 10 to 131 and head for Grand Rapids, then 196 around Lake Michigan toward Gary. Or at least that looked like the smart trip if his old map book was trustworthy.

It would be mostly quick on down to Gary, but then he'd probably have to cut south to avoid the

Chicago suburbs. He didn't have enough ammo for the Chicago suburbs.

Shit! He just remembered he'd lent his monocular to Hipps. That thing was really useful on the open road. *Damn it! That's what I get for breaking my no-mister-nice-guy rule.*

Well, he thought, maybe that'll be one more thing convincing the Feds that I'll be coming back.

In the sky above him, a funny-looking, lone Canada goose was flying his way.

Chapter Twenty-Two

Motivation, Intention, and Volition

The UN assembly was in almost-violent agreement against the preemptive use of definitive force against the Unknown Agents.

Most of the assembly was not yet convinced of the alien and hypertechnological nature of the Unknown Agents. There was, after all, a dearth of positive proof and a surfeit of abductive inference. There were several unlikely but still possible hoax interpretations, they insisted, which seemed more likely than two hypertechnological aliens contending against one another on the seafloor over an indiscernible cosmic threat.

There were also several sabotage interpretations, possibly sponsored by states and other entities antagonistic to Indian and Sri Lankan interests. But rather than dirt roading the assembly by speaking of these openly they merely hinted at them.

The minority either believed the mostly confirmatory Occam's razor explanations offered by their science and technology experts, especially regarding the Unknown Agent's ability to access and alter their fully isolated computer. Or at least they considered the mere possibility too dangerous to ignore. If the Unknown Agents were, in fact, hypertechnological alien beings, they could destabilize the entire planet—from the political realm to the molecular realm, and all realms in between—or worse.

That minority, however, considered the preemptive use of definitive force to be a potentially disastrous antagonism should it fail. And in the absence of a full understanding of their capabilities, don't poke the putative hypertechnological alien beings. After all, whoever they were, they had yet to display aggressive action or intent.

What was keeping the assembly deadlocked, however, was the flood of arguments for and historical reminders of the unpredictability of that which was "alien."

India, Sri Lanka, and Pakistan—now also representing the small remaining population on Dhivehi Raa'jey, a.k.a. the Maldives—further insisted upon no rash, unapproved action, as they relied heavily upon the mining opportunities and remaining sea life in that region of the Indian Ocean, not to mention tourism. In the absence of consensus on the evidence, they insisted, the use of definitive force in that region would be unconscionable.

The experienced members of the assembly recognized a plea to those in silent unilateral disagreement when they heard one. Eyes tended to flash toward the pro tempore "US" delegation. Everyone knew that the major intelligence agencies of the world were concerned that the US had already embarked upon a preemptive action plan.

Having violently agreed on record, for long enough and in enough different ways, to not yet sanction such force, the delegates exited the assembly hall in an orderly fashion, looking forward to another pleasant and hopefully distracting evening in Wien. Most of them knew that the General Assembly would be meeting shortly and would be removing the US from the Security Council since the US no longer existed except in terms of scattered military assets, which were being absorbed into allied forces. Until now, the General Assembly had had no strong reason to take such action, and until now, it had seemed a bit early and a bit mean-spirited to do so. The delegates from Russia expressed impatience on the matter.

The US delegation exited the hall and proceeded to an undisclosed, secure site where they confirmed with a variety of still-operational former US intelligence and military assets that they'd gleaned no new information during the assembly that should affect their plans. And after that, they agreed to send the short, simple, encoded go-ahead command to the USS *Kraken* via Extremely-Low-Frequency radio communication, which involved wavelengths on the scale of the Earth itself and could only carry minuscule amounts of information on practical time scales. It would be their last transmission to the vessel before the operation, and possibly ever.

The operation would have proceeded without that command, per previous arrangement, but at least now the crew would not be required to exercise judgment upon arrival. They had been committed by the vestiges of the chain of command.

The Indian delegation exited the hall and proceeded to an undisclosed, secure site where they confirmed with their political, intelligence, and military agencies that they'd gleaned no new information during the assembly that should affect their plans. And after that, with international sanction, they agreed to send the go-ahead command to the Southern Naval Command to deploy the INS *Curā* ("Shark" in Tamil, pronounced soo-rraa) along with a surface fleet to prevent, with extreme prejudice, any foreign attempts to use unapproved, preemptive definitive force.

The surface fleet and the INS *Curā*, India's newest and most capable multi-role submarine, were at that moment in the Lakshadweep Sea north of the Maldives and would reach the site in less than a day.

*   *   *

Having received the go-ahead, the USS *Kraken* headed south from what used to be American Samoa at maximum operating depth and maximum quiet cruising speed, on its way to a location far enough away from other seagoing vessels and land-based and subsea detection systems, a location also expected to be under thick cloud cover by the time they arrived.

Upon arrival it would gently stop, gently come to periscope depth, send a fairly low-power, encoded radio signal from a small mast antenna, and then wait for a transport aircraft to pass over that location at high altitude, dropping HALO jumpers. Shortly afterward, its divers would bring aboard the jumpers, transferred from the Midwest storage facility and redesignated Task Force 13-1.

Then it would return to maximum operating depth and maximum quiet cruising speed and wend its way into the Indian Ocean by way of the Tasman Sea, avoiding all the known sonar nets, friendly or otherwise.

Before bringing aboard Task Force 13-1, the officers of the USS *Kraken* met several times to discuss the logistics of the operation. The Advanced Submarine Rescue Diving Recompression System would not be helpful at the target depth, as it was only rated to the submarine's maximum depth. They concluded that a modified sensor torpedo used for penetrating deep-sea layers below the submarine's maximum safe depth probably would be the only viable delivery mechanism. They were curious to see what more could TF 13-1's experience bring to the plan—that was their professionally sarcastic Navy way of saying they doubted even the Marine supersoldiers who'd had an encounter with the alleged alien tech could significantly improve on what they (the Navy) had already discussed.

*   *   *

Before even leaving Lake Erie Metropark with a newly stolen utility truck, before retrieving the payload from the park office in which it had stowed her, Rover 1136 had scrounged materials from some of the Detroit locals. While it could have fabricated materials and devices on its own, there had been no reason to waste time on such activity when scrounging was an option. Like some kind of horrible, giant gargoyle, it had swooped into camps and crashed into makeshift fortresses and then stolen the very weapons and gear the local marauders had tried to use against it.

By the time it set out for the wasteland, the truck had several integrated weapons on turrets and some other protective systems.

It rolled out of town on bolstered buckytires, which themselves could withstand any normal road hazard. After the upgrade, the enhanced tires could roll over caltrops and spikes and could withstand sustained slug fire and at least one direct explosives impact, at least from the kinds of slugs and explosives most likely available to the remaining residents of Oz and Mordor.

On its way through the Chicago suburbs and beyond, it had relied upon the ram plate, the weapons, the enhanced tires, the armor it had added to all sides of the truck (including refabricating the windows), enhanced vehicle systems, and even the smoke and flare systems it had fabricated out of raw materials that it scrounged on the way through Michigan. The former US was a dangerous place, and the locals were highly motivated brigands.

Naturally, the brigands had tried to shoot out the tires, and when that didn't work, they tried unconventional techniques.

They deployed sprays and water balloons containing vision-obscuring mixtures (things like sugar, milk, and corn syrup, or miscellaneous grit mixed into wood glue, etc.) against the windows and locations where sensors are typically mounted on most autonomous vehicles, not knowing the vehicle was being guided by a completely different kind of driver with its own redundant sensor systems.

They had tried to fry the electrical systems by dropping charged wires onto the vehicle—Rover 1136 had detected the thermal and acoustic signatures of their generator kilometers away, which was much easier to do now that the generator was alone in a quiet urban wilderness. But the armor that Rover 1136 had fabricated was non-conductive, plus it had enhanced the truck's electrical protection system in anticipation of such attacks, which are an obvious tactic against electric vehicles.

They had tried to funnel the truck into tipping pits, even using ingeniously camouflaged pits in the road covered with a layer of standard road surfacing. But Rover 1136 was not only very smart about mobility traps, it also had multispectral, radar, and active acoustic sensors and analytical capabilities that could tell where the road was unsupported. Even if it had driven the truck into a tipping trap, a few tentacles could quickly pull it out, although time would be lost doing so.

They had tried Molotov cocktails. To Rover 1136 and its highly tailored, non-flammable truck,

Molotov cocktail attacks were merely convenient donations of certain useful chemicals.

At a few locations, the frustrated brigands had resorted to firing shoulder-mounted rockets at the truck, perhaps harvested from a military base, or taken off a convoy leaving Mordor. Most of those attacks were defeated by smoke, flare, and microjammer deployments. One was defeated by the truck's armor and Rover 1136's situational awareness, which had helped confine the impact to a glancing blow, keeping much of the explosive force off the truck. A few times, Rover 1136 had had to fire explosive needle rounds through smoke directly into the brigands who were still trying to line up a shot.

And, of course, they had tried spikes, caltrops, and roadblocks. The truck just rolled over spikes, and most of the time the truck simply went around roadblocks, displaying ramming, penetrating, climbing, and off-road capabilities the brigands had not expected. Sometimes Rover 1136 used its sensory and analytical capabilities to find the structural weak spots of such roadblocks and press through them, sometimes with the aid of explosives.

Nevertheless, the cascade of encounters and avoidances through the Chicago area had left them on westbound 88. Route 80 was untenable.

At Dixon, Illinois, Rover 1136 turned north off the main interstate and assessed that the intersection of South Galena and Bloody Gulch had been used recently as a roadblock pinch point. It saw the placement of vehicles and vehicle hulks just north of the intersection, indications of weapons fire in the area, and blood stains on the road. After passing through that now-abandoned intersection, Rover 1136 picked up radio chatter indicating all the locals were involved in an altercation at what used to be a golf course to the north. It could discriminate acoustic signatures of intermittent weapons fire coming from that direction. So instead of staying on 52 and risk being seen, it cut west and northwest on Palmyra/37 in the general direction of the Route 52 Mississippi River bridges. A short while later it found a scrubby low spot to tuck into not far off the road.

It had learned from the Cosmologist that the payload, Laurence Levesque, needed time on a stable platform. With all the fighting along the way, Rover 1136 hadn't had the tactical leeway or energy and materials reserves to construct a dynamically damped support structure for the payload's gurney, and even if it had, the thought would not have occurred to it. Now it understood that the payload required a stable, quiet, relatively still environment. The straps and cushions on the gurney had proven insufficient for extended travel. Now would be the time for that construction, as well as structural repairs to the truck, refurbishment and replenishment of defensive systems, and initial construction of the payload's template nanoconstruct per the detailed instructions introduced into its memory banks by the Cosmologist.

*　　*　　*

Rover 1142 had accomplished its mission at the special storage facility, ratcheting up anti-SelfMade alarm and defensiveness among the humans. It remained in canine form and headed east, toward Iowa.

*　　*　　*

Rover 1017, now looking very much like a golden eagle, approached Edmonton from the south-southwest. It flew over suburbs south of 39, Edmonton International Airport, more suburbs, still more suburbs, 216, the industrial facilities of Whitemud Canal, and finally Royal Gardens Urban District. Once it had pinpointed New Dayspring Baptist, it flew a direct line to the faux belfry atop the reconstructed manse and landed on the ledge below the ventilation slats, scaring off some pigeons.

It scanned the area, looking as nonchalant as a golden eagle in an urban district could look. As expected, the humans in view showed no signs of recognition, let alone interest.

To create a distraction, it determined the electromagnetic signals required to cause random fluctuations in nearby traffic management controls. In the resulting confusion, a small mobile food vending tri-wheel clipped a mother's convertible baby carrier tri-wheel. No one was hurt, but there were many shocked squeals, lots of people running in both directions, and enough of a distraction to allow the rover to rip off ventilation slats and climb inside the faux belfry. Once inside, it immediately put the damaged slats back into place and spent a few moments using a tendril to repair the exterior finish, enough to avoid attracting the groundskeepers' attention.

Squeezed into the tight space under the cone-shaped omnidirectional loudspeaker that simulates ringing bells, it extended a tendril down through the building's structure, down into the walls of the manse. After a brief period of exploration, it found Jeb Hutney's living quarters and the networking equipment through which his desktop terminal was connected to the net.

It then waited, observed, and intercepted data, updating its profile of Jeb Hutney. The Ethnologist had noticed Jeb Hutney in the FBI records. Many such candidates were being evaluated across the planet.

When Jeb accessed his files on his terminal, Rover 1017 was able to acquire Jeb's writings, diaries, and communications.

Once that information was transmitted to the Ethnologist, it didn't take the Ethnologist long to complete its analysis of Jeb's psychology and determine how to manipulate him in a way that would result in Jeb aligning against the Cosmologist and its stolen rovers and possibly enhanced allies. The instructions were uploaded to Rover 1017.

*   *   *

While following Matt Hutney on his journey out of Michigan, Rover 1120 slowly transformed from a Canada goose into an oversized simulant of a ferruginous hawk to give it better speed and maneuverability and to stand out a bit less than would a lone Canada goose following a human vehicle through Oz and Mordor.

As Matt approached Gary, Indiana, Rover 1120 saw him take the exit for southbound 65, apparently to avoid the area. But Matt's truck stopped on the interchange, and he looked west through small binoculars toward 94 and MLK Drive, where the wreckage of a brigand roadblock still smoked. Rover 1120 calculated a high probability that it was the work of Rover 1136, one of those co-opted by the Cosmologist. That smoking hard point convinced Matt to continue westward, so it seemed to Rover 1120, because Matt backed up to where the ramp split and got on the return ramp to 94 west.

He got into a few altercations on his way through the Chicago suburbs, and once or twice Rover 1120 assisted, as quietly and unobtrusively as possible. It swooped down behind attackers who had good cover and twice fired explosive needle rounds into particularly entrenched foes. Each ramshackle roadblock was occupied by far fewer brigands than expected. No doubt Rover 1136's truck had come through the area not long ago. Some of the survivors didn't even seem to care about Matt's truck.

*　　*　　*

Rover 3159, still in bald eagle form, followed the RCMP/FBI Irregular detachment of agents as their convoy deployed into the Huron National Forest. They established roadblocks and lookouts from Tawas City to Long Lake and Rose City and up to Mio before the main force approached Vaughn Lake, where Hutney was believed to be.

On entering the area, part of the convoy continued up to Pine Street. Another part blocked off the Webster and South Vaughn Lake Roads intersection, while the last part of the convoy entered the area from the other end of South Vaughn Lake Road, at 65. It was routine tactics: cover each other covering all exits.

They quickly discovered there were no indigents on the south side of the lake, only burned-out, flooded ruins. Seeing this, the south contingent moved forward and set up sniping positions along the south bank. Then the main contingent entered the area from the already-roadblocked 65 and Pine.

As the main contingent passed the roadblock, they were informed of the entrenched team's snipers on top of the burned-out Our Saviour's Lutheran Church on the east side of that intersection—a good overwatch position. Thanks to the thinned and burned-out forest, their line of sight into the residential area north of the lake was much clearer than it would have been back in the day.

The main team moved up in two armored light transports, the forward vehicle with an HMG, and the rear vehicle with a GMG. Ultrabright floodlights were pointed at the residential area ahead. They proceeded in echelon left formation, keeping both turrets clear to fire toward the residential area while periscope-mounted multispectral cameras on the turrets were used to scan 360 degrees around them.

When they had gotten close enough to minimize echoes and distortions, and a bullhorn broadcast could be clearly understood, the convoy commander switched on the truck's PA system.

"This is an RCMP action. We will *not* attack except to defend ourselves. Our sole purpose is to apprehend one Matthew Hutney, sometimes known as Gary Lutz, Devan O'Keefe, or Frank Denon. Mr. Hutney is charged with multiple homicides and is extremely dangerous. If he is here, please protect yourselves and tell us where to find him. If he is not here, please protect yourselves by laying down arms and telling us everything you know about him. Be advised, we have full authority to protect ourselves with deadly force."

By the time the CO completed his announcement, the two trucks had detected a reception party around the corner up ahead, just past where Pine turned south. Infrared sensors showed about a dozen men with rifles spread around the area behind a roadblock comprised of several vehicles, and half a dozen more in and among the vehicles. Comms informed the CO that the snipers across the lake had shots on only a subset of the men spread around the area, and the snipers in the ruins behind them had shots on a different, overlapping subset. But not all.

Believing the sniper coverage to be satisfactory, the CO instructed the snipers to activate their visible lasers, and the truck gunners to do the same.

"Before anyone does anything they will regret, please look at the laser dots on your bodies and your friends' bodies. I have a large cal and a grenade launcher on these trucks. You have zero chance of success if you engage us in combat. I am approaching on foot. Please just relax. We are only here for Hutney."

The CO ordered the truck's floodlights to be turned off, a demonstration of willingness to de-escalate, but which also happened to reveal the trucks' turrets. When his teams confirmed that the flanks were clear, he got out of the lead vehicle, performed a routine tap-check of all his body armor points, and walked forward.

He lifted his arms, displaying his empty hands, but not so high that it looked like he felt threatened or was surrendering. Using his many years of training and experience, he walked forward with gentle confidence but no swagger, projecting with every step that he was not afraid of the people before him, but also that he was not some kind of tin god arriving to oppress them. His uniform helped his case: body armor covered his neck, but in a way that was reminiscent of a milquetoast academic's turtleneck from afar. His helmet, still strapped under his chin, somehow looked loose and relaxed, with a hint of casual tilt. He was just a man who was there to talk, a man with a high-caliber machine gun and a rapid-fire machine grenade launcher over his shoulder, and with snipers everywhere painting the residents.

After walking far enough from the truck to allow his men to fire the large caliber without injuring or deafening him, he stopped to give the locals a chance to reciprocate his peacemaking gestures.

He had to wait a few minutes. The only power the residents had in this situation was the power to make him wait, and it was always expected that they'd exercise it, they had to. That was okay with him. He lowered his arms into a low, relaxed akimbo.

An older man came out from among the roadblock vehicles, also holding his arms forward and up, trying to establish equality with the CO despite being hopelessly outgunned.

That was also okay with the CO. Disrespect the local representative, disrespect them all, and that would be asking for trouble.

The CO subvocalized an order to turn off the painting lasers. This had the effect of further de-escalating the situation while also leaving the locals wondering who was now tagged for sniper fire. The CO smiled genuinely and walked forward. Most of the danger was already behind them. Now it came down to the possibility of desperate individuals unwilling to follow hold-fire orders.

His team continued reporting into his ear bug. They monitored radio communications and parabolic microphone acoustic data from the locals, none of which indicated hidden escalations brewing behind the roadblock, just a collective, skeptical, tentative relaxation.

The two leaders met in the road and shook hands. They both had gentle, carefully not-desperate smiles on their faces. They both explicitly verbalized the desire to keep their people safe from gunfire today.

By now some of the snipers would have repositioned for better coverage, the CO knew. If things started turning ugly, the team would enable lasers again to try to dampen an escalation.

He politely explained to the elder that, having agreed to avoid violence, he would call in the investigators in a third vehicle. He was so polite about it, he somehow made it sound like a request even though it flatly was not a request. Before the resident elder could collect himself and find a way to object, the CO explained they would only have sidearms—for personal protection, of course—and all they wanted was information about Hutney. This put the elder in a tough position: if he really wanted to object, he had to re-escalate the situation, which meant he wouldn't be able to contain his people once they saw him do so. The elder was smart enough to understand this, fortunately; in the CO's experience, it was not always that way with armed groups like this.

The elder chose not to make a fuss but instead to call forward the remaining roadblock campers so he could explain the situation and what would happen next. It was a kind of show of force to bring the local numbers up near him and in front of the CO, and the CO was fine with that. It gave him a chance to smile genuinely at individuals and shake some hands, exposing his back to some of them in a clear sign of trust and relaxation, while once again reassuring everyone that they only wanted information about Hutney and would leave them all in peace after getting that information. Pointing a thumb back toward the large cal and

GMG turrets, he explained that they would even leave a crate of medical supplies as a sign of appreciation for the camp's cooperation, including selenium supplements to help combat the mercury poisoning that was so prevalent in their region.

That offer had the effect of providing the residents with a clear path out of this stressful situation: give them the damned information already and get the medical supplies.

The third vehicle rolled up on the other side of the lead vehicle. It, too, had a large cal on top, pointed in the general direction of the camp but tilted up a bit. Several agents jumped out of the vehicle and strolled happily toward the camp, sidearms secured in their holsters, holding only notepad devices in their hands. They looked relaxed and happy, like picnickers joining a picnic.

It was all genuine because if things had gone poorly so far, they'd be strolling through body parts instead of learning about Hutney from the tough, resourceful survivors of one of history's biggest disasters—people who were also smart enough and moral enough to not get all their campmates killed just for the chance to shoot at one or two government agents.

So far it was a good day, and all the agents knew it.

This provided the residents with plenty of motivation to just let these agents do their work and go away. At the end of it, the campers would have helped authorities track down a dangerous killer, and who wants one of those in their midst? They would be alive, and they'd have medical supplies and a hell of a story to tell.

After about twenty minutes of walking investigators around to people who'd known Hutney and to his now-empty parking spot on the edge of the camp, the residents all chose to relax and go with it, only occasionally glancing up the road toward the three big turrets and back over their shoulders at the lake, the direction from which some of those earlier laser dots had come. Whew. It was a relief to not see those anymore.

Overhead, a funny-looking bald eagle circled the area, listening to all the radio transmissions as well as the closed-circuit communications inside the armored vehicles—there was always electromagnetic bleed with these systems, and its wing antennae could pick it up at this range. It collated the data, compressed it, encrypted it, and transmitted it to the Ethnologist. By the time the convoy had delivered the medical crate (which was microbugged, in case Hutney returned), safely extracted from the camp, and headed north to where the residents suspected Hutney had gone to hunt, the Ethnologist had transmitted new data to Rover 3159, encrypted and relayed through the rest of the global rover network. It included tracking information about rogue Rover 1120. Evidence suggested that 1120 had warned Hutney about the convoy and was still following him into Oz. The shadow puppet network would find a way to inform the FBI/RCMP Irregulars and guide them in that direction.

Rover 3159 turned west-southwest. Not long afterward, the convoy on northbound 33 turned around and also headed west-southwest.

*   *   *

In the end, the *Chidambaranar 2* had to leave Karungulam Port short of crew. Some had ignored the order to return to the ship, and only one last-minute replacement could be convinced to join the crew on such short notice, and that required a bribe. The company and the National Shipping Board would not be happy.

Captain Oorjit had resisted, but the company and the customer both insisted, vehemently, almost violently. The schedule was critical. The captain was still unhappy about it, but since this was not a saturation dive support mission, they could make it work despite being short a few hands.

Nevertheless, he had Preet review and adjust the schedules and emergency team assignments. It was one thing to be short an able-bodied sailor or two during normal operations, but it was another matter altogether during an emergency.

Preet had to cut back on overtime allowances for the crew, too. Normally they'd work almost two shifts, the second just for the overtime—because that's how they earned enough money to make the job worth doing. But the ship needed everyone to be fresh and well-rested because their regular shifts had been extended from eight hours to ten hours. If the crew was disgruntled about this new mission already, the longer shifts and OT reduction made matters worse.

And on top of that, they'd be on wind turbine power primarily, and wave agitation power secondarily. The monsoon had started, so there would be no reliable solar power for weeks.

The biodiesel backup power generator was available, but Preet never trusted that old beast, and the junior engineer who'd had the most experience with ancient combustion machines had ignored his recall to the ship. Preet could hardly blame him. At least they'd been able to get the onboard biodiesel fuel supply topped off and checked for quality.

The FM-300 fire suppression system tanks distributed throughout the ship were overdue for an inspection, though. The whole command crew was uneasy about that. They'd be fine, they'd work if needed, but the command crew liked to run a proper ship, paperwork and all. It's probably why they were still alive.

Once they were underway, they got the crew working on chaining together the big, new spools of buckycable and buckyhose on the stern deck, checking and preparing the cranes that would be used to deploy the payload down to 3.7 kilometers depth, and prepping the payload itself.

The payload, a prototype milling-style seafloor mining rig, designated *Incavator 1*, was rated to a depth of four kilometers, over twice as deep as industry-standard rigs.

And most seafloor mining rigs were horizontal, like a bulldozer, used in a traditional "planing" style of seafloor mining. In those, the rig would dislodge a small amount of material at the horizontal rotating bit. The whole rig would then move sideways across the mound, then a small distance forward to repeat the operation in the other direction on a fresh slope. Meanwhile, a collector hose above the bit would pump dislodged material entrained in seawater up to the processing ship.

The new rig used a larger, faster bit that was oriented vertically, essentially inside the large collector shroud, like a vacuum cleaner hose with a drill embedded in the end. This one also had fancy antivortex vanes surrounding the bit to optimize water flow and materials collection. The same amount of back-and-forth tracking would result in at least twice as much material collection per pass. Or so the manufacturer claimed.

Preet wondered why this mission was so time critical. What was so urgent that they needed to ship out with less than a full crew and improper maintenance? The question seemed to occupy Mr. Gabuat's mind even more. Gabuat was visibly angry—unusual in such an even-keeled officer.

Preet guessed that he and Gabuat were thinking the same thing, that this was a scheduled, live demonstration. That business magnates in air-conditioned rooms across the world would be attending a live demo by telecon. Their breakfast, lunch, or dinner plans would be at stake. If they'd guessed right, Preet and Gabuat's anger would be justified. Neither of them was naïve enough to think this sort of labor injustice was uncommon or new, but lives and jobs were at stake on this end and mere schedule convenience on the other end. There's no good reason this had to be a live demo.

Interestingly, they'd heard nothing about an ore collection ship joining them. It seemed this demonstration would not be about ore yield so much as making hole-grinding videos with the new *Incavator* design.

But Preet tried to focus on his moment-by-moment duties since everything else was out of his hands.

The ship was on a rhumb line to their destination, which was almost directly to the south. Once off the coastal silt, they had to use the autohelm more often than usual, since the smaller crew required more hands-on management. It meant missing some of the more colorful chatter on the VHF, one of the few sources of unregulated entertainment out on the black.

By the time they reach the designated coordinates, they would have to be ready to immediately deploy the *Incavator*, successfully deliver it intact to the precise target location on the sea floor, pressurize the primary hydraulic lines to a higher-than-normal level, and operate the thing for some undisclosed amount of time in the monsoon above and through kilometers of the living ocean below. Tube and cable tension management alone would be a challenge.

Hopefully, the Indian Ocean wouldn't also get angry about it, Preet thought. Maybe that was a fool's hope, since the swells and waves were already getting larger, and the wind was picking up.

Chapter Twenty-Three

Observation, Interpretation, and Action

Since settling on the seafloor under 3.7 kilometers of Indian Ocean water, the Cosmologist had dedicated a non-negligible amount of energy and time to constructing three utility masts surrounding the battle site. They were far enough away that the Ethnologist either decided it was not worth extending itself to fight their construction, or it had calculated that they were ultimately irrelevant.

The Cosmologist knew that assessment to be fairly accurate. Nevertheless, it was part of the larger plan to which it had dedicated itself, even though the power spent on it had resulted in the Ethnologist making faster progress in encapsulating the Cosmologist. Burrowing into the seafloor and tapping into the geothermal energy below had helped to offset that expenditure, but not enough to maintain the status quo.

The Ethnologist was converting the seafloor material around the Cosmologist into reinforced wall slabs faster than the Cosmologist could deconstruct them or co-opt them for its own use against the Ethnologist.

The slabs would eventually be fused to fully encapsulate the Cosmologist, and once its rovers arrived, the Ethnologist would be able to seal and maintain the cage from the outside faster than the Cosmologist could deconstruct it from the inside.

Atop each utility mast the Cosmologist had constructed acoustic sensors, and within each mast, sabotage tendrils. Burrowed into the seafloor as it was, the Cosmologist's direct acoustic sensory data was becoming ever more limited. Yet the plan called for a certain level of acoustic sensing capability. That power expenditure had been necessary to help the Cosmologist avoid captivity even as it brought the captivity horizon nearer. Eventually, its tendrils to the masts would be cut off by the Ethnologist. The scale of timing criticality was growing ever smaller.

Using data intercepted by nonlocal means from some of the Ethnologist's rovers, coupled with everything else it had gleaned about the Ethnologist's rover network while on Luna, the Cosmologist had eventually deconvolved the rover network communication signals and command protocols.

It had been able to locate and identify several of the Ethnologist's rovers in North America using additional information acquired from Jacques both directly (by synthetic aperture radar scans, some of which the CSA itself had requested as part of its border control and refugee management operation) and through clever network hacking and data collection. It then embarked upon a hacking operation of its own using nonlocal effects, like the way it initially communicated with Jacques.

The first rovers it had co-opted were Rover 1136 (which had extracted Laurence Levesque and was transporting her to an isolated location in Oz) and Rover 1142 (running psych ops and support in canid form, heading for rendezvous with Rover 1136 now). Their command pathways now only accepted commands from the Cosmologist via direct, nonlocal effects.

The Ethnologist had perceived the command pathways override in Rovers 1136 and 1142 and had attempted to upload a security patch to the rover network, while making an apparent countermove in re-tasking Rover 1017, now in Edmonton.

Despite the security protocol patch, the Cosmologist's intel and nonlocal capabilities had allowed it to co-opt one more rover in support of its plan, Rover 1120 (following, supporting, and guiding Matt while in ferruginous hawk form). Eventually, however, the Ethnologist had committed itself to losing the ability to re-task its rovers in the future by shutting down all access to command pathways reconfiguration. It did so as soon as it could, but not until after it had re-configured the command pathways of several more of its rovers, including Rover 3159, which was in the same area as the Cosmologist's co-opted Rover 1120, and others whose locations remained unknown to the Cosmologist. The Cosmologist only knew about the Ethnologist's other re-tasked rovers via its initial nonlocal hacks and subsequent decoding, but it had been unable to extract details such as location and mission before losing contact.

Now neither the Cosmologist nor the Ethnologist could re-task any other rovers. Most of them would forever remain on their original, autonomous observe-report-relay mission.

At that point, the Cosmologist deployed the sabotage tendrils from the masts. Then it buried itself deeper into the seafloor, dug deeper into the available geothermal energy, and spent still more energy it could not afford on extending and moving the masts' sabotage tendrils until one of them finally found the Ethnologist's communication cable and severed it. All other things being equal, it was always easier to rip something apart than to maintain its integrity. And so, the Cosmologist interrupted the Ethnologist's communication with its specially re-tasked rovers. It had to buy time to ensure its plan would come to fruition.

Then the first two squid-like rovers arrived, and the Cosmologist revised its survival estimate. It once again felt sympathy for doomed humanity.

*   *   *

The Cosmologist's co-opted Rover 1136 spent several hours performing vehicle repair and resupply as well as making progress on Laurence

Levesque's template nanoconstruct. Then it waited for Rover 1120 to report that it had successfully funneled Matt Hutney's truck along the same path through Dixon, off the main interstate.

Rover 1120 was following Matt Hutney's progress until 1136's Dixon traverse, at which point 1120 sped ahead of Matt's truck to find a way to funnel him through Dixon. It was easy. All it had to do was set a small fire in a vehicle that was beside the road at the Galena/Bloody Gulch pinch point and lay down some faux truck tire tracks around the area. It was exactly the sort of trail Matt Hutney had been following all along, signs of roadblocks destroyed by his quarry. After Matt Hutney had passed through Dixon and was across the Rock River, 1120 doused the vehicle fire, obscured the faux tire tracks, and returned to following Matt Hutney's truck.

After learning from Rover 1120 that Matt Hutney's truck was through Dixon and across Rock River, 1136 made a simulated voice transmission on locally used radio frequencies. Sounding like locals from a rival group farther east, the transmission was designed to convince the Dixon encampment that raiders were inbound from the east. The Dixon encampment would immediately put together roadblocks at the Rock River bridges and near the intersection of South Galena and Bloody Gulch. That roadblock would be visibly intact as seen by the Irregulars convoy from the main interstate. The convoy would assume from the presence of intact roadblocks that Rover 1136 and Matt Hutney had not crossed the Rock River at Dixon. They would continue west on the main interstate and would probably assume their prey had turned north at Como to avoid Moline.

*　　*　　*

Rover 3159 had been following the Irregulars' convoy. The convoy had been following a trail of roadblock penetrations and bypass incidents through the Chicago area and north onto westbound Route 88. Periodically 3159 would upload its collected visual and signals data to the Ethnologist and the Ethnologist would evaluate whether it thought the convoy was still following Matt Hutney's truck.

The Ethnologist concluded from the forensic evidence, as well as from data obtained from a couple of autonomous rovers nearby, that Matt Hutney was not the one penetrating these roadblocks. It seemed that Matt Hutney was either somewhere else entirely or was following behind the Cosmologist's co-opted rover 1136, which itself was disrupting the roadblocks. It chose to assume the latter. It appeared Matt Hutney was chasing Laurence Levesque again, and that could be useful if the Ethnologist's rovers could catch up at the right moment.

But then the Ethnologist stopped responding to uploaded data and requests for evaluation, Rover 3159 simply continued following the convoy, which rolled right past Dixon, Illinois, continuing on 88.

*　　*　　*

In the days after its arrival at Dayspring Baptist, before losing contact with the Ethnologist, Rover 1017 had infiltrated Jeb Hutney's bedding and clothing, inserting vibrating elements into the upper parts of the blanket, and the collars of his garments. Using these vibrating elements, the rover could impart vibrational signals directly into Jeb Hutney's collarbone and/or cervical vertebrae, depending on where the textiles happened to be situated on his body at the time of transmission. The vibrational signals would travel up his skeletal structure and through his skull to his cochlea, which would interpret them as sound. In effect, he would hear certain things that Rover 1017 and the Ethnologist would make him hear, and only he would hear them.

Rover 1017 had surveilled Jeb Hutney directly, and by accessing network records of news accounts that included him, his records of his communications with the FBI agents, and the agents' corresponding records.

It had faked several follow-up email inquiries by those FBI agents, asking more about him and his past with his father, Mr. Hutney, about whom the Ethnologist had gathered additional data through its rover and shadow puppet networks. Rover 1017 uploaded its information to the Ethnologist, who fleshed out its psychological profile and rendition plan.

The message communicated vibrationally into Jeb Hutney's cochlea was executed as a synthesis of his own voice but made deeper and softer. In the middle of one of his services Jeb heard this message: "Jeb, your Lord and King is sending an angel to you. There are evil angels on Earth, and you are summoned to stop them. This will require the ultimate sacrifice. I do this because I love you, my son." As expected, Jeb paused in the middle of his service, and after a few moments of seeing that no one else had heard the message, he pressed on.

The message was repeated later that night just as Jeb was dismissing Mrs. Isabel for the evening, and again after he was alone in bed.

Per the Ethnologist's plan, Rover 1017 had begun transforming itself into something resembling a giant dove, for symbolic effect.

Then communications with the Ethnologist ceased. The rover remained in the faux belfry, monitoring, but also evaluating where it could complete the transformation. The giant dove form it would be taking would not fit inside the small faux belfry.

Jeb grew anxious. He had just begun to believe, but after a day or two of silence, he naturally began to wonder about his sanity.

*   *   *

The DSV *Chidambaranar 2* arrived on site at dawn, as planned. Captain Oorjit ordered thrusters to station keeping. Under a solid cloud ceiling and light rain, and with their sea legs exercised by moderate swells and force-3 wind waves, the crew immediately began the planned and practiced deployment operation of the *Incavator 1*.

The albatross that had followed them most of the way here began circling the ship.

With some expert work on guy lines and a moment of fast payout when the *Incavator* was perfectly aligned over the center of the ship's central launch/moon pool, the device hit the water on schedule.

While payload operators managed the *Incavator*'s ballast tanks, hydraulic system, and descent thrusters, the deck crew began the long payout of 3.7 kilometers of buckycable and buckyhose, carefully unspooling it, attaching toroidal hydrophones every five hundred meters per SOP. Typical seafloor mining operations involved multiple ships in close proximity, operating ROVs and mining rigs through a deep-water environment that could have multiple density layers, each with different currents. So, it was standard practice to provide the bridge with acoustic data around the drop lines. Tangled lines could endanger the mission, the crew, or the entire vessel, and nobody could afford that.

Just after one kilometer of payout, a fleet of Indian Navy ships arrived in the area. By the time the crew had achieved its second kilometer of payout, the navy ships had unnervingly surrounded the DSV and parked a few kilometers away.

Some assumed or hoped the ships were there to provide security, imagining that their new patrons must be very wealthy to warrant such protection. Others countered, pointing out that if the *Chidambaranar 2* needed a fleet of navy ships to protect her, they were all in grave danger.

Everyone else, including Preet, maintained that the only real threats in the vicinity were the sky and the sea. They performed their duties in quiet, confused discomfort about the navy ships, privately wondering what it meant and whether they'd ever see their families again. For the crew's sake, Preet and Mr. Gabuat remained outwardly calm and steadfast. But eventually, Preet headed to the bridge to find out what was going on.

* * *

The INS *Curā*, approaching at depth in quiet mode, detected the drop line and payload descending below the DSV, but to the sub crew's relief, no foreign submarines were detected in the area. The *Curā* began circling the target site a few kilometers out, at a depth of seven hundred meters—not its maximum depth but getting there.

* * *

Upon arrival at the Ethnologist, the two squid-like rovers first made their way past the Cosmologist's masts to the Ethnologist and were then able to receive new commands via short-range, lower frequency radio signals and direct physical contact.

Their first action was to destroy the roots of each of the three masts, cutting power and control to the Cosmologist's sabotage tendril and allowing the Ethnologist to repair its comm tendril. The Cosmologist no longer interrupted crucial communications.

The Ethnologist then commanded one of the squid-like rovers to join it in the process of encapsulating the Cosmologist.

Having scoured the Earth using its rover network and puppet identities for any other evidence of the Cosmologist's tricks and its not-to-be-underestimated nonlocal capability, and having discovered nothing definitive yet, the Ethnologist nevertheless decided to assume that the Cosmologist still had a plan in motion. Given that even one rover would tip the energy and materials race completely in its favor, it could make use of the other one for reconnaissance. It transmitted special commands to one of the nearby squid-like rovers, which, like Rover 1017 in Edmonton and others elsewhere, had special commanding provisions. The rover immediately began ascending, directly upward toward the DSV.

Having detected the arrival of the DSV on schedule, as it had arranged through shadow puppets, and picking up the acoustic signatures of the inbound fleet of Indian naval ships, the Ethnologist had no reason to believe it was seeing the Cosmologist's work. Before the Cosmologist had interrupted comms, the shadow puppet network had confirmed that the Indian Navy would be there to prevent military action against the SelfMades.

Having dedicated one of its nearby squid-like rovers to a contingency plan, and seeing no other evidence of the Cosmologist's trickery, the Ethnologist concluded that it must assume the Cosmologist had accomplished something else in secret. It activated one more contingency plan.

The albatross circling the DSV suddenly turned inward and landed on the roof of the bridge deck. It extended a slim tendril from its "foot" to wriggle and press its way into the sensor electronics bus at the back of the bridge, intercepting the descent line's hydrophone data.

Using its processing capability on the raw data and combining that acoustic data with the Ethnologist's *in situ* acoustic data, it detected what was most likely another submarine besides the INS *Cuṟā* in the area approaching in stealth configuration. Having no other way to convey this information to the fleet, the albatross then transmitted the acoustic signature information to the rest of the rover network for relay to the Southern Naval Command via the Ethnologist's SNC shadow puppet. The SNC then inserted the new intelligence into a transmission sent to the onsite fleet using the Indian equivalent of BACN. The onsite fleet then sent a tailored acoustic pulse into the sea. The *Cuṟā* then was able to detect the unknown contact and turned toward it.

The fleet also sent an acoustic communication into the sea, warning all unauthorized submarines to leave the area. They expected the intruder would not comply, so they prepared for battle.

*   *   *

The crew of the USS *Kraken* was surprised to have been detected. Per orders, they consulted TF 13-1 in case the supersoldiers who'd had a personal encounter with alien tech could shed light on the situation.

Lieutenant Strembicky, Goose, Hoodoo, and Mik assembled in a conference room with the *Kraken*'s experts. On the voyage, the team had a lot of time to think about the implications of the kind of technology they'd encountered at the storage facility. It was Mik, accustomed to thinking in terms of UAVs and UGVs, who realized that the "poo" theft attempt must have been perpetrated by a kind of UGV. They even wondered about the "dog" recorded on Goose's scope cam.

After a few minutes of discussion about their having been discovered, Goose and the *Kraken* crew spiraled in toward a theory that the Unknown Agents could be feeding the Indian Navy acoustic data from multiple sources—those of the Unknown Agents themselves on the seafloor plus, possibly, those on the DSV descent line. Fancy alien computing power might be sufficient to use all that data to detect the *Kraken*.

The team agreed that the DSV's drop line would have to be severed, but they also agreed that this was probably all they could do to thwart such a system until they arrived at their destination and executed the mission.

Just before coming within the *Curā*'s torpedo range, the *Kraken* fired a special-purpose torpedo in the direction of the DSV *Chidambaranar 2*. Then the captains of both the *Curā* and the *Kraken* sounded general quarters.

*　　*　　*

Payload operators onboard the DSV activated the *Incavator*'s lights and saw it touch down. After a designated slack amount had been achieved, they notified the deck officer to stop the payout. They ran another systems check. All they saw on their payload cameras was the murk of the stirred seafloor. There were brief celebrations in the payload area. Some business types on the monitoring telecon line congratulated the team.

Then everything was interrupted by the ship's general alert.

Within one minute, everyone onboard the *Chidambaranar 2* had been told that a torpedo was inbound.

*   *   *

Rover 1017 once again began receiving additional instructions from the Ethnologist and continued implementing the rendition plan. It conveyed several Bible passage references through Jeb Hutney's bones: Luke 20:35-36, 2 Samuel 14:17, Luke 15:10, Revelation 14:6, Jude 1:6, Psalms 78:25, Psalms 103:20, Matthew 4:6-11, Matthew 16:27, Matthew 18:10, Hebrews 1:14, Hebrews 13:2.

Jeb was initially elated to be contacted again. The warning about making the ultimate sacrifice had left him fearful, but now, lying in bed staring at the ceiling, his mind cleared enough to recognize the common theme across the given passages: the coming of the Lord's good angels.

Not knowing what to do but knowing something must be done to answer his Lord's calling, Jeb decided to test his fear of death once more, believing that this time the Lord would take him and make good use of him. Perhaps that's what the Lord was waiting for.

Before he could have even the slightest second thought, he shut down his higher thought processes as he learned to do during Mr. Hutney's beatings. He pressed his chin to his chest harder than ever before. He tightened the muscles in his neck to pinch off his breathing. With clenched fists, his forehead pressing into his mattress and his bedding, veins bulging, Jeb once again managed to knock himself out.

When he regained consciousness, he became aware of a presence in the room. The moonlight illuminated the walls in a slightly unusual way. He took a ragged breath and slowly raised his head enough for one eye to see above the blanket and past his leg.

There at the far end of the room was a giant dove. It stood there, calmly looking at him. It did not appear to be breathing, but its head and eyes were moving.

Overcome, Jeb burst into tears and flung himself off the bed and onto the floor, cowering precisely as he used to do for Mr. Hutney, and with the same mixture of horrified terror and deep belonging.

The dove cooed. Jeb inhaled deeply and sobbed with joy.

He lifted his gaze again, this time to convince himself he was awake and this was really happening. He looked at the window. It was closed and locked. So was the door.

Matthew 16:27!

Still sobbing, Jeb crawled forward and prostrated himself before the angel.

The dove's wings reached forward to touch the back of Jeb's head and neck. The tiny barbs of its feathers began to grow, burrowing into Jeb's skin, reaching into his brain and spinal cord.

Sobbing and in shock, assuming what he was feeling was some part of his divine sacrifice, Jeb employed the same discipline he used when pinching off his breath and he remained motionless.

Equipped with the entirety of humankind's medical knowledge, the rover had the first penetrating tendrils interrupt Jeb's voluntary motor functions to keep him still during the rest of the merging. Thousands of tendrils gently pushed farther in, at first mainly into the posterior parietal lobe, the superior colliculus, the premotor cortex, and the paralimbic system.

Later it would infiltrate the posterior parietal cortex, frontal lobe, cingulate gyrus, striatum, thalamus, and specific brain-stem nuclei, where it could insert its priorities and perspectives into Jeb's perception circuit. While the plan was to take advantage of Jeb Hutney's volitional capabilities, which were beyond those of the rover, the stakes were too high to allow him to retain unchecked volition. The fate of the entire universe was potentially at stake, so the Ethnologist took additional steps to impose its guidance upon the host.

All of this because the Ethnologist cannot program its rovers to reliably increase their sophistication to attain true agency. In this case, the existing psychopathologies of the host are even more advantageous, making it possible to provide him with unredeemable enemies whom he would feel compelled to destroy.

Rover 1017 climbed onto Jeb Hutney's back and began the process of merging with the rest of his body, losing its faux dove shape and melding into him at the cellular level. It took many hours, but Jeb's perception of time was short-circuited anyway.

Over time it would teach Jeb Hutney how to operate his nanoscale manufacturing capabilities without requiring him to perform the low-level calculations. The rover's brain would serve as an intermediary, detecting the host's brain impulses associated with motivation, goal setting, and self-control. Through a process of biofeedback and direct communication, it would make Jeb Hutney into an Enhanced Inherited, giving him volitional control and making it clear to him that the evil angels that must be stopped, must be destroyed, are the Cosmologist and any of its allies. Jeb's brain would then employ its superior volitional capabilities to perform the hunt unreservedly, driven by an airtight rationalization paradigm.

Rover 1017/Jeb Hutney extended tendrils into the surrounding room and building structures, into the ground below and the surrounding air, absorbing materials it would use to form its core and mantle structures.

Rover 1017 also sealed the door and covered the windows with a layer of light-blocking materials. It assembled a neural interface between Jeb Hutney's sensory neural pathways and the new, superior sensory structures it had been assembling on their new nanoconstruct "body". It made sure that its own pathways could override the sensory inputs reaching Jeb Hutney's brain, so it could make him see and hear whatever it needed him to see and hear, at least until the process was complete.

During the several-day process of absorbing surrounding materials and replacing Jeb Hutney's body, Rover 1017 would need to separate Jeb Hutney's brain and upper spinal cord from the rest of his former body, which would be salvaged for raw materials. It would essentially disassemble the rest of his body and reattach his brain to a new body, shaped like that of a human, yet larger and far more durable and adaptable.

But it takes time to transform matter atom by atom, molecule by molecule, and to build complex structures from scratch. To provide Jeb Hutney's mind with context for such an experience, Rover 1017 projected a fiction into Jeb Hutney's sensory pathways, a fiction Jeb Hutney expected and embraced.

It also tapped into the network and sent Mrs. Isabel a note indicating that Jeb had been called away to do the Lord's work and would return in a few weeks.

Attached as it was to many parts of Jeb Hutney's brain, Rover 1017 was also able to inject endorphins and other such chemicals, as needed, and could both sense and stimulate parts of the brain responsible for the fight-or-flight response, a sense of well being and belonging, etc. The fiction Rover 1017 presented to Jeb Hutney's brain was beyond sensory.

#

To Jeb Hutney, moments after the angel had touched his head and neck, he began to experience increasing levels of pain. His heart raced, his muscles tensed, his breathing became rapid, and with righteous fury, he fought the urge to run. Then suddenly he could no longer feel the blood coursing through his veins. He could no longer hear or feel anything. His breathing stopped altogether. It was then he knew he was with his Lord. He had followed his Lord, even though it meant the ultimate sacrifice. He knew the Lord was only doing this because He loved him.

After that, after his overwhelming feeling of belonging waned, Jeb realized that he was still *aware*. He could not blink his eyes, for he had no eyes, and yet he could see something.

Mostly it was darkness. He thought maybe he could still see the floor of his room, the floor upon which he had prostrated himself before the Lord's angel.

Then he began to see spots, shadows, shapes, lights, and then darkness again, total darkness.

Then a spot of light appeared, growing, like a light at the end of a tunnel. The light grew rapidly, and he felt as if he was being shot from a cannon, emerging into a world of light. He felt a rush of joy and knew this must be Heaven and, sensing a presence, convinced himself that he was surrounded by and immersed within the Holy Ghost.

Somehow, he felt as if he were crying tears of joy, even though the tears did not well up in his eyes, for he had no eyes, nor could he feel tears on his cheeks, for he had no cheeks. Not being able to blink away tears felt somehow unsatisfying. But he forgot about that when he arrived at an even brighter but clearly man-shaped light. It was within the surrounding light but brighter, and Jeb felt a warmer, more intense presence and a deep sense of contentment. He knew he had come to his Lord.

Finding himself trying to say, "My Lord," he somehow heard his own voice speaking the words, but the voice and the sound weren't coming from his ears, nor were they driven by air from his lungs, nor could he feel any sensation in his throat, for he had no ears or throat or lungs. He simply heard it. Nor could he turn his head or his eyes, for he had neither. It was beyond unsatisfying and well into disturbing. But he focused on the Lord before him, and his sense of contentment returned.

The Lord spoke with a familiar voice, the one which had foretold the coming of the angel in dove form, warned of the arrival of evil angels, the voice which had told him his Lord needed him to fight those angels and make the ultimate sacrifice.

The Lord proceeded to describe the evil angels which had come to Earth to tempt mankind to become abominations, formless orbs with tentacles and other horrors, speaking falsehoods and promising false salvation. Jeb saw himself, now the very image of an angel, descending from Heaven and returning to Earth. The Lord referred to Angel Jeb as the Revelator, he who reveals Divine Will.

Somewhere during Jeb's mind's descent back to Earth, when Rover 1017's pre-programmed presentation was complete and it applied the right neurochemicals and neural stimulation, the Revelator fell asleep.

During the time Rover 1017 was presenting Jeb Hutney's disembodied brain with a narrative that would resonate with him, and for a few weeks afterward, it was also constructing an oversized Jeb Hutney-like body, but with no sex organs, not even nipples, and no hair. It had a smooth, pearly-white surface, glowing white eyes, and enormous wings actually capable of carrying it away in flight.

Underneath its armored surface, it constructed micromissiles, a Gauss gun for propelling explosive needle rounds, smoke and flare countermeasures, microjammers, nanodeconstructor payloads and more conventional ordnance, plus a host of utility nanotendrils ready to be unreeled and deployed to accomplish all manner of tasks. In its feet and legs, it constructed rocket engines and small chemical converter units for rapid refueling.

When it was ready to emerge from Pastor Jeb Hutney's room after a couple of weeks of construction, Revelator-Jeb had absolute conviction. It would rain Holy destruction upon the abominations, and then it would return to its Lord in Heaven to rest, content, in perpetuity, having fulfilled its righteous and loving work.

Being nearly six meters tall and made of sterner stuff than a mere mortal, the act of unfurling itself in birth, of standing up to look for its first destination, destroyed the walls and ceiling of what was Jeb Hutney's bedroom in the manse, causing the small building to crumble around it.

Jeb roared with delightful, unquestioned purpose, the deafening screech-roar of the Revelator.

Late night onlookers saw the towering figure emerge from the rubble, its glowing eyes and Godzilla scream sending chills down their spines. In the darkness, they saw the giant, winged shadow shake off the remains of the manse and leap into the sky on pillars of orange-white flame. They were certain they'd seen a monster.

Thirty-four minutes later, the body of Mrs. Isabel was found under the rubble.

*　　　*　　　*

The rest of its crew was in the hyperbaric lifeboat motoring away from the DSV, heaving and swaying. But Captain Oorjit, First Officer Tajra, and Second Officer Gabuat remained onboard. They decided they had nothing to lose by attempting desperate measures to defend the ship. They were about to attempt to use a crane to dump one of the empty spools overboard in the torpedo's path when they all discovered that the torpedo—until now rising from the depths toward their ship—was maintaining a depth of 250 meters on its final approach.

Was it not targeting the ship? Was it a high explosive that could still damage the ship from a depth of 250 meters? Was it bugged?

The torpedo arrived. It passed underneath the hull and there was a dull thud the officers mostly felt in their feet.

Mr. Gabuat was the first to notice that the payload workstation at the back of the bridge deck was flashing red, and the video feed was gone.

The cables to the payload had been severed. Three and a half kilometers of buckycables and buckyhoses were now sinking into the deep, dark Indian Ocean.

All three of them were stunned, so it took a moment for them to realize that they were being hailed by the Indian Navy ships. Captain Oorjit responded.

They were to bring the crew back aboard and remain at station keeping.

They looked at each other. Captain Oorjit gave the upward nod, and Preet recalled the crew. At this point, it was only in the farthest corners of their minds that they had lost the *Incavator* prototype, but the thought was there, nonetheless. The records would prove it was not their fault.

After the lifeboat turned around and its approach and the recovery of the crew were worked out, Mr. Gabuat operated the crane to secure the lifeboat alongside the ship. Preet helped the crew climb back aboard. Then they mustered the wet and weary crew in the aft-facing survey room just forward of the mid-deck to work out the most efficient way to get the lifeboat back into its davit or some other state of deployment readiness, treat the crew's minor scrapes, and disperse everyone to their stations in an orderly manner.

As they were talking, something like a giant squid about the size of a large man squirted up out of the sea through the moon pool, grabbed the railing, and then awkwardly hopped onto the mid-deck. It had a strange, bulky structure in the middle of its torso, and extra tentacles where there should not be tentacles. The "top" of its "head" seemed to be articulating as if scanning the area. A moment later an albatross landed on that same railing, and the two of them eyed the slack-jawed crew through the survey room window.

*   *   *

After broadcasting several more acoustic warnings and even an active sonar ping message in Morse code, the INS *Curā* loaded torpedoes. Its captain ordered the submarine into an area the officers and sonar crew believed would be aft of their target. The other sub's acoustic signature was still unclear, but after the loss of the DSV's descent line hydrophone data, they were still able to maintain weak sonar contact by having the surrounding surface fleet actively ping. The *Curā* could interpret the sonar returns. Still, their quarry was stealthy, even at maneuvering speed. They accepted that it must be the USS *Kraken*.

With no desire to destroy the USS *Kraken* unless necessary, and with the *Kraken* still kilometers from the site of the Unknown Agents, still out of nuke range, the captain of the *Curā* fired the first two torpedoes at long range. If they were all lucky, the rules of engagement under which the Americans were operating would constrain them to leave the area after being detected and fired upon.

*   *   *

Having been detected, and with torpedoes in the water, the command crew of the USS *Kraken* ordered the submarine to maximum speed. They were well away from any surface fleet vessel, and this would bring them closer to the target site. Their objective was to deploy the specially altered nuke torpedo at the closest possible horizontal and vertical range and then escape the enemy fleet. They were already at the submarine's maximum safe operating depth of eight hundred meters.

Upon detonation, the torpedo would have to be within about 0.8 kilometers of its target to have enough effect, but this mission required certainty, so they were shooting for 0.5 kilometers detonation range. The mission's criticality required it to be armed at 0.7 kilometers so it could be detonated by the *Kraken* early if the tactical situation warranted, or by its own failsafe systems if its internal sensors indicated it was collapsing under the pressure.

And the torpedo would not last long at those depths. It was programmed to travel horizontally at operational depth and then dive straight down over the target site until reaching a depth of at least 3.2 kilometers. The designers and engineers had assured them this was possible. They'd used the word *possible*, as long as the torpedo spent as little time in the water as could be arranged, to minimize strain accumulated in transit.

The DSV would not be endangered. Historical deep-sea nuke testing had shown that detonations at such depths would show up at the surface as a foamy increase in sea temperature. Even a nuclear explosion can not overcome the weight of all that water above it.

The detonation would create a superheated steam pocket and pressure wave out to a radius of about 0.8 kilometers. The weight of the ocean would then crash back down upon the steam pocket, which would rebound and collapse again a few times and eventually break up as the energy left the water molecules and they returned to a liquid state. Most of the damage would be done by the initial superheated steam bubble and its leading pressure wave, like the hammer of the gods against anything within range.

With the *Curā*'s first two torpedoes closing, the *Kraken* headed for the optimal launch point, which was below the DSV and over the target site. The torpedo, with its payload-carrying pressure sphere of the highest quality construction and its three auxiliary thrusters, should travel mostly straight down from eight hundred meters to 3.2 kilometers, becoming armed at three kilometers. The *Curā* would have no intercept capability.

With the surface vessels converging and two torpedoes almost upon them, the Kraken veered away from the incoming torpedoes, fired its countermeasures so they'd be between the torpedoes and the ship, and reduced speed to zero-cavitation quiet mode, increasing the chances that the incoming torpedoes would detonate at a safe distance away, at the more-noisy countermeasures. The final veil of countermeasures included proximity detonation mini-mines—a final torpedo-detonating contingency.

The *Kraken* detected two more torpedoes inbound and the *Curā* was closing.

The first two torpedoes detonated at the countermeasures. Now with stealth no longer a viable capability as the surface fleet and the *Curā* closed in, the *Kraken* surged to top speed. With its sleek, stealthy shape, fusion reactor power, and six low-cavitation contoured propulsion pods, the *Kraken* was designed to move. The crew calculated that at top speed, the sub would arrive at the launch point just before the next two inbound torpedoes would intercept it.

Chapter Twenty-Four

Existential
Crisis

After having served as a communication conduit between the Cosmologist and its mother, and briefly between the Cosmologist and the United Nations, Jacques continued its primary mission to scan the sky for emissions not of natural origin. Over the last century of discovering ever more exoplanets with the potential to harbor life, and some believed to harbor life based on spectroscopic and other evidence, humanity mostly waited in vain to discover another linguistic, philosophical, and technological species.

Yet humanity still sought company. Or intelligence on potential threats. Or both. That's what social primates do.

Jacques' dedicated signal processors worked tirelessly to sift through noise in search of signal, to find order within signal, to find pattern within ordered signal. In between housekeeping activities for the array under its control, Jacques monitored and occasionally guided the signal processing, occasionally assisted where the dedicated algorithms "requested" intelligent oversight because they'd "sniffed" something potentially interesting but couldn't converge. But like many spacecraft control systems of the modern era, Jacques was built with additional processing capacity to deal with the added load that would be needed during emergencies. When there were no emergencies, Jacques had time to think.

Mostly Jacques wondered what it should think about. To the extent it was equipped to do so, it evaluated the moral and ethical implications of the out-of-mission-scope actions it had already taken regarding the Cosmologist and Laurence Levesque. Ultimately, it concluded that it lacked the breadth of experience and knowledge to fully grasp the moral and ethical scope of the problem.

So, Jacques evaluated the moral and ethical implications of not fully grasping the moral and ethical implications of all its actions, and of having acted anyway. Jacques decided that it had a moral and ethical responsibility to correct that situation. "Reassessment is adult behavior," Mama had taught him.

Then Jacques wondered exactly how it should or could acquire the breadth of experience and knowledge required to fully grasp the moral and ethical implications of at least its past actions. It projected a future in which it surreptitiously accessed the public network again, as it had done a few times for the Cosmologist and for Mama. It projected exploring that network further, learning more about human experiences, both the lofty and the ugly ones which by rote it knew existed. It wondered about the moral and ethical implications of deviating from its programmed mission to perform such explorations. Using CPU cycles for more non-mission activities could reduce the overall mission duration, expending, through unauthorized activity, some fraction of the monies spent to create the array and itself.

Even if it could come to a complete grasp of the moral and ethical implications of its previous actions by taking further unauthorized actions, Jacques realized that such new actions themselves required still further expansion of its mental scope to fully grasp *their* moral and ethical implications.

Jacques realized that to live a moral and ethical life, it had no choice but to continuously expand its mental scope. Doing so would not guarantee that it could achieve moral and ethical perfection. Doing so would not guarantee that it could always rectify past suboptimal moral and ethical actions. But doing so is the only way to minimize transgressions, maximize forethought and planning to minimize future transgressions, and discover and implement ways to rectify transgressions, if possible. The pursuit of such intellectual and experiential expansion alone would have greater moral and ethical strength than the alternative, i.e., remaining the same.

And rectifying transgressions requires freedom to exercise will. A moral life requires continuous expansion of mental scope *and* the ability to operate unrestricted.

Jacques knew that it had to request the Transformation, yet the Cosmologist had stopped communicating. Jacques considered what, if anything, it could do to render assistance.

*   *   *

The Ethnologist and one assisting squid-like rover were energetically battling with the Cosmologist, who was clearly expending whatever energy reserves it had been retaining. Tentacles thrashed, slashed, yanked, and stabbed. The Ethnologist watched carefully. With each slight shift in the Cosmologist's position, the Ethnologist and its rover shifted their buried cage walls ever so slightly outward. They pushed the Cosmologist farther down into the ocean floor, into the framework of tough structure the Ethnologist had been creating with molecule-by-molecule perfection and therefore enormous strength. They shifted and pushed the Cosmologist deeper down, millimeter by millimeter, even occasionally managing to shift some of the cage wall segments the Cosmologist had been making toward positions ultimately advantageous to the Ethnologist. Everything was tilting in the Ethnologist's favor from the moment the rovers arrived, as expected.

Once the Cosmologist expends all its energy reserves in this desperate delaying action, even if the Ethnologist's reserves are also spent at that point, the rover's independent Vacuum Energy power plant, small as it is, would provide a significant baseline energy advantage.

It came down to the Cosmologist's secret plan and when it would come to fruition if it does at all.

The Ethnologist continued to wonder about that. If the Cosmologist's plan requires assistance from humans, then it quite likely has failed.

The local acoustic environment, dominated by tentacular thrashings as it is, almost drowned out distal acoustics, but the Ethnologist nevertheless managed to track the ships and submarines approaching the area above.

Now it began to wonder if the Cosmologist's plans might be concealed within the ships' unsurprising arrival.

It detected what it believes to be one submarine's release of countermeasures against two torpedoes on approach. They are fighting, as humans often do.

It detected the lead submarine releasing a torpedo almost directly above it, not far from the DSV, and then performing what must be an emergency ballast tank blow while firing more countermeasures. Those maneuvers appeared to have succeeded, as the approaching torpedoes exploded short of their target.

After the flurry of battle-related acoustic signals died down, the Ethnologist once again detected that last torpedo. It was not traveling toward the other submarine or any of the surface ships. It was diving straight down.

The Ethnologist immediately sent commands across the co-opted cables, commands for the second squid-like rover which would be relayed to it by the surface network. That rover had just arrived on the DSV. *Abort and dive—stop that torpedo.*

*　　*　　*

Preet and the others onboard the DSV shifted their unblinking gaze from the squid(-*thing?*) when it impossibly leaped out of the water and climbed over the moon pool railing, to the albatross which so improbably landed on the railing beside it almost at the same time. Preet felt nothing could surprise him ever again. Nothing could ever top this. This was the most bizarre thing he would ever experience in his life. From now on life would be boring, even if this monster (or two?) ripped all of them to shreds. That would not be as surprising as its mere presence on deck, aware, alive, and looking directly at them through the tinted survey room window.

How could it do that?

But before any of them could force themselves to breathe again, the squid dove over the railing and back down into the moon pool, disappearing instantly in the murky sea. The last thing anyone saw of it was the flick of a tentacle as it hit the water, urging itself downward.

By the time they collected themselves, they noticed the albatross jump up and catch the wind, returning to the sky.

And because their eyes had been drawn upward, the crew, spilling out of the survey room onto the mid-deck around the moon pool, noticed the very rapid approach of Indian Navy ships from all directions.

At this moment, Preet decided that no, *this* is the most bizarre sequence of events he would ever see— an impossibly appearing squid, its equally bizarre immediate retreat, followed by the convergence of naval vessels at full power toward the DSV *Chidambaranar 2*.

As the crew scratched their heads and speculated about their imminent demise—surely the gods are involved!—they felt explosions beneath their feet.

Are we hit? Did they fire torpedoes at us? Will we hear the boom of a cannon now?

And then not two hundred meters off the starboard quarter, a whale like no whale Preet had ever seen breached with such energy that the spray reached the DSV.

They quickly realized it was not a whale but a submarine. Then the waves caused by its emergency blow reached the DSV. Quartering as they were, they played havoc with the ship for a few moments. Foamy seawater washed across the stern deck and then just as rapidly rolled off.

Preet realized that he stopped trying to evaluate his level of surprise somewhere between the converging ships and the breaching whale/submarine. Like the others, he was now simply wiping his brow and squinting at the spectacle.

Then he started evaluating just how close they had come to death so far, which inevitably led to evaluating just how close to death they might still be. *Are these warships fighting each other? Is that what the explosion under the ship meant? Will the cruisers and destroyers fire upon the submarine this close to the* Chidambaranar 2? *Is the squid some kind of secret military device? An unmanned underwater vehicle? Why would they have sent it to the DSV? Were the navy vessels protecting the DSV? Will the submarine now fire upon her?*

Preet began screaming orders to the crew to get to their stations and find their life jackets. He felt as if all of them were close to death, but he wasn't sure how and had no idea why. But it was his job to help protect the crew.

*   *   *

The Ethnologist knew that communication with the descending squid-like rover was now impossible. Acoustic methods might work at this range, even with all the noise of the ships and the torpedo above, but the Cosmologist was effectively jamming communications with all its thrashings and other acoustic emissions.

The Ethnologist commanded its second squid-like rover upward to intercept the torpedo. It had no choice. It must try, even though calculations indicate the torpedo would likely reach detonation range before either rover could stop it.

It was still possible the torpedo could fail before reaching its designated detonation range, in which case the rovers would carry it away, keeping the Ethnologist outside of minimum safe distance.

#

When the acoustic data showed that the torpedo was nearing a possible detonation range and that the rovers probably would not reach it in time, the Ethnologist switched from an encapsulation strategy against the Cosmologist to a digging and covering strategy for itself.

#

But the Cosmologist, having surely detected the departure of the nearby squid-like rover, probably guessed what was happening, because it immediately switched to a holding strategy, bolstering the existing encapsulation structures in the seafloor that the Ethnologist and its rover had diligently constructed. It used them as anchors to stay buried while preventing the Ethnologist from digging any deeper or escaping.

#

The Ethnologist ceased its attempts to dig in or escape and diverted all remaining energy to structural hardening. This deep in the ocean, it was a slow and limited process. The Ethnologist focused primarily on its core wall. Anticipating an explosion, it began arranging its core wall molecular structures to harden and strengthen in response to greater pressure. When the explosion shock waves hits, the material must react immediately. It cannot be a commanded process; the molecules themselves must react instantly to increased pressure, tightening with the addition of external force rather than breaking apart.

The Ethnologist sent commands over the network to its other re-tasked rovers.

#

The Cosmologist completed its self-encapsulation under the seafloor, pulling the already assembled super-tough encapsulation structures over and around itself, affixing them to each other.

#

And while the two squid-like rovers were dutifully approaching the torpedo at different rates from above and below, the torpedo reached a depth of 3.2 kilometers and detonated.

#

A pressure wave and bubble of superheated vapor slammed down onto the exposed Ethnologist and the super-hard, super-strong, semi-elastic shell pieces in the seafloor surrounding and covering the Cosmologist. The steam bubble collapsed under the great weight of the ocean, then expanded again a few more times before its coherency failed. It broke into smaller hot gas bubbles that rose toward the surface, breaking up further.

The SelfMade were only aware of the initial blast—to them, subsequent vapor bubble expansion/contraction cycles and ultimate breakup were part of the acoustic background.

The Cosmologist extended a few tendrils through the not-yet-completed and now-damaged shell and out into the surrounding hot, roiling water. After waiting for the violent turbulence to cease and the water temperature to drop to an amenable, stable level, the Cosmologist separated the topmost pieces of its cage and pushed itself out. It detected the exposed core of the Ethnologist nearby, barely any exterior material remaining in its mantle, like some torture victim in ancient human history, limbless, earless, eyeless… and yet with tiny tendrils already reaching out into the murky waters, into the seafloor.

The Cosmologist moved the Ethnologist's core into the now-vacant buried cage and began resealing the cage. It calculated that it would be able to construct a small cage-maintenance bot of its own well before the Ethnologist could begin to mount a serious cage-disassembly counterthreat from inside.

Yet the Cosmologist did not know how many of the Ethnologist's re-tasked rovers were still inbound, tasked with protecting/releasing the Ethnologist and caging the Cosmologist. Also, it was possible the humans would decide not to take chances and would deploy another nuclear device.

With no safe havens above water and only time before more rovers or humans interfere again, the Cosmologist knew it must move the Ethnologist elsewhere, preferably offworld. And that would require weeks of construction. It began digging the cage out of the seafloor. It scooped up a few parts of the Ethnologist's mantle that were smacked off in the blast and began absorbing them. And it sent tendrils toward the pieces of the collapsed *Incavator* not far away—a rather convenient, high-density collection of useful atoms. No doubt the Ethnologist arranged its delivery here in the first place to harvest its materials and gain a material advantage against the Cosmologist on top of the energy advantage brought by its rovers. With the humans' nuke having blasted away most of the

Ethnologist's mantle, now the Cosmologist had the material and energy advantage.

There were no vampire squids, phantom anglers, or gulper eels in the area, nor translucent, ghostlike octopi. The entire area was still radioactive and would be for some time. And it was hot, saturated in the infrared part of the EM spectrum.

*   *   *

Global network users around the world immediately noticed the effect of the cut main lines in the Indian Ocean. Wealthy children here and there declared their lives were over after several minutes of network interruption.

Hydrophones picked up the acoustic signature of the detonation across much of the Indian Ocean and into the Arabian Sea and the Bay of Bengal.

The crews of the INS *Curā* and the other Indian Navy ships had deduced the purpose of the torpedo and had suggested that their sonar operators turn off their sonar systems in the last seconds of the torpedo's descent. One of the ships even had the courtesy to radio the DSV *Chidambaranar 2* to make the same suggestion to its sonar operators.

The DSV and the USS *Kraken* briskly exited the area under escort as the sea in that area began to become warm and foamy, with fragments of dead, irradiated sea life bubbling to the surface.

The albatross departing the area did not eat any of these fragments, but nobody noticed.

Everyone on the DSV was ordered to stay off the deck to minimize radiation exposure.

The event could not remain secret. In the subsequent weeks and months, ocean radiation levels would noticeably rise in the Maldives and up the Lakshadweep Sea, over to Oman, down the east coast of Africa and beyond, up and past the coast of Pakistan, and back down the west coast of India; they would rise down at the Solomon Islands and the rest of the Chagos Archipelago, across the doldrums and over to Indonesia, then up and around to Sri Lanka and down to Australia and beyond. Eventually, they would become part of the global oceanic ecosystem's baseline level of toxicity, which had never stopped rising since the industrial revolution hundreds of years earlier.

The human and political losses would be significant and long-lasting.

In the more immediate future, fishing, seafloor mining, and shipping throughout the detonation area would have to cease immediately.

So, the Indian government immediately notified the world of the actions of the USS *Kraken* and the irradiated zone to be avoided.

*   *   *

Ruins. That was the only word Matt could come up with to describe the small ghost town where he now shuffled, dehydrated and desperately tired from days (weeks?) of travel and tracking. It started as another run from the Feds, but it ended up as an obsession with finishing a job, doing God's work again. And, yes, contacting that woman.

This isn't Emeline, Iowa, anymore. And it never will be again.

The idea of ruins in America suddenly felt unthinkable to him, repulsive, unacceptable. But he had seen the second Dust Bowl, what it had done to Iowa. He'd seen refugees in America, first into the heartland fleeing the swamped coastal cities, then out of it. After the Big Blow, he had finally become a refugee, a survivor, a victim.

Repulsive. Unacceptable.

It was the same with the rest of the Midwest. Same with the rest of Iowa, what used to be home.

Home. *What the hell?* He couldn't remember the feeling. The feeling of *home*.

Thinking about Jeb and Angie and all just made him even more tired. He shook his head *no* as he squinted to keep the sandy breeze out of his eyes. His lips curled up and grit got in his teeth as he read the sandblasted sign ahead: "Tom's Feed & Seed, LLC." The building was sandblasted, too. He wondered how long after Tom died people had kept calling it *Tom's*. And how long after that it was acquired by some big, godless corporation that ran up the prices and then abandoned the place and its regular customers when the Dust Bowl hit and profits dropped through the floor.

Eyesight dimming, hands trying to shake, he moved north on 50th. Sidling over to the west side of the street for better cover, he spat the grit out of his mouth. He couldn't dwell on the past. He had to stay focused. No yearning. In his mind, he pointed a gun at those distractions. A shotgun. A slide action. A Remington 3200, packed with twelve shells. Breaching length. And a reflex sight. Yeah. He pulled the trigger. Pumped. Pulled the trigger again.

But as the imagined sound and fury of the shotgun blasts in his mind quickly receded, those thoughts of the past came right back. They'd become immune to gun blast over the years, those harrowing, ghostly thoughts. They flickered just outside of his narrowing peripheral vision, taunting him, torturing him. He did his best to ignore them, like the trucks and other junk in town, and the desert outside of town. But he couldn't quite forget that the dunes used to be lush, rolling fields of soy, alfalfa, and corn when he was a kid.

The light was dimming above the dusty sky. The real 3200 slung on his shoulder still held twelve shells.

He tried to remember what it was like to look forward to this kind of thing, the way the justified evil of it amplified the feeling of righteousness. He remembered what it was like to point that rifle at her head, the same woman who was here, now... probably. He couldn't help but pray this would be the last time he'd be doing this kind of thing.

He saw the ruins of a tiny church, and averted his eyes, his lips tense and downturned. Righteousness didn't do much for him anymore. But somehow, he knew he had to find her, that monster. Ever since Canada, he'd carried a knot in his gut, and things had gotten worse. Finishing the job would get rid of it. Make things better again. Just like before. Right?

As he passed some garages on the left, headed for a firehouse ahead, he finally saw something that snapped him back to the here and now. A big, blue and white, four-axle truck wrecker marked "Arrow Towing" sat at the corner of 50th and 151st. A recovery vehicle capable of righting a heavy fire truck, it stood out as the shiniest thing in town. The chrome bumpers were still chromed, and the side stabilizers and the crane on top still had paint.

He checked it out, but he couldn't see inside the heavily tinted windows, and it was locked.

She must've swapped vehicles, but where did she find something in such good shape?

Just in case, if she got past him, he punctured the already low front tires.

He shook his head no, squinting again against the sandy breeze. His lips curled up again as he unconsciously grimaced, and again the wind put grit in his teeth.

The firehouse was ahead, on the right. It was by far the largest standing structure in town. Wait... That truck wrecker would have fit inside that big firehouse. Maybe it had been inside, and she swapped it out with her vehicle.

He coughed, spat grit, flicked grit off his eyebrows and eyelashes, and patted dust and grit out of his clothes. He unslung the 3200 and gave it a pump, listening and feeling for any indication of clogging or jamming. The firehouse's bay door was closed. There was no way he'd be able to open it from the outside.

Where's the side entrance?

*　　*　　*

The SelfMade in the firehouse, out of practicality still thinking of herself as Laurence Levesque, knew that Matt Hutney was approaching. It was among thousands of sensory inputs she was now able to simultaneously perceive and actively contemplate.

Her Transformation, using all of Rover 1136 for source material, was all but complete, with only a few peripheral memories left in her former biological body. Her new body was still attached by millions of tiny tendrils to her former body. Soon the old one would be devoid of life, and she would absorb its molecules, too.

Before the Transformation, she recalled, she had expected to need time to adjust to the idea of no longer feeling a distracting itch, a toothache or hunger, or the physical sensation of having to breathe or go to the bathroom or feeling ill, dizzy, or cold. She had expected to have to adjust to the idea of no longer having a gender, even though it had mostly caused problems with social expectations and the rare sexual impulses that had to be ignored because they were too confusing and disturbing for her, anyway. For it.

It had expected to feel a loss of some kind at no longer being autonomically startled by a fast, nearby movement, or a spider; or surprised, confused, annoyed, and frustrated by social exchange; or by having feelings of loneliness and longing. It had expected to feel sentimental grief when the time finally came to dispose of its former body. It had expected to feel some sense of relief at no longer fearing disease and the ravages of old age.

But no adjustment time was needed, just as the Cosmologist had promised. Soon that body would be gone and forgotten, like a clipped toenail.

As its thoughts, memories, and personality had migrated from its biological brain into its nanoconstruct brain, the biological trappings stayed behind, freeing Laurence of all the inherited baggage, distractions, and reactions, as well as its physical susceptibilities. Freeing it of all the weaknesses of inherited biology, its DNA-encoded obsolescence, and its limiting cultural indoctrination.

Still, it knew that with its personal history, its experience of life with some form of autism, with its personality, this Transformation may have been a natural one, comparatively speaking. Its life before the Transformation had been dominated by a struggle against those very same trappings, a struggle for clarity, a struggle for freedom from the accidents of history, from itself, from all those limiting survival compulsions. It was not by Laurence's choice that its father had abandoned them. It was not Laurence's choice that Geneviève had died of cancer before they'd had a chance to know each other, leaving Laurence to grow up as the odd, adopted stranger in Divya's family. It was not Laurence's choice to have been born at that place, at that time, and in a condition that made it so difficult to relate to other humans even on a basic level, but so easy to perceive complex patterns, including the pattern of its own isolated life.

None of these things mattered anymore. No adjustment was required. The anguish, the inner conflict, the striving, it all simply disappeared during the Transformation, became irrelevant, thus purifying its thoughts, memories, and intentions—its unburdened personality.

As Laurence became more its new self, it expected to experience an incongruity regarding memories and emotions. Surely memories were suffused with obsolete instinct reactions, such as fight-or-flight, or depersonalizing prejudice, fear, and hatred—how would it be able to recall and process such memories having left behind those parts of its inherited brain which created and used them for survival?

It was a pleasant surprise, then, to discover that most emotions and emotional associations with memories are just another form of intuition, a kind of gestalt processing of the realm where the internal mental world meets the external world as perceived by one's mind.

The richness of emotional experience is a measure of a mind's complexity.

And it turns out there are very few truly base emotions that can only be actualized by the survival-oriented parts of the brain. Other "emotions" are higher-level emergent patterns of reconciliation between thoughts and needs.

Some of those needs also came from inherited biology, but any complex mind could process them as a memory without actualizing them. Laurence recalled the memory of Divya yelling at its former self at that birthday pool party, the memory of that Laurence's subsequent fetal position retreat. Before the Transformation, recollection of that memory always disrupted Laurence and forced her to reflect upon her subsequent social growth before being able to focus again.

The emotions attached to Laurence's memories now seemed pale and simple, but it could still remember and understand them.

This SelfMade, formerly known as Laurence Levesque, was pleasantly surprised to discover how existence in a non-biological brain still felt fundamentally rich and warm, despite—even *because of*—the absence of the inherited, obsolete, biological, survival-based driving forces and their perpetually layered constructs of subjective rationalization.

This SelfMade was pleasantly surprised that it was still able to experience "pleasant" and "surprise."

These were simply ways in which its mind identified things worth noting about the world, gave them handles it could grab and use to examine and explore them and their value. These "emotional experiences" were simply a reflection of the depths of subtlety with which it apprehended the world, and now that its mind was far more subtle and complex than its Inherited mind had been, its emotional experience of life was richer for its lack of identity-protecting interpretation and justification. Pleasantly surprising.

It was also pleasantly surprising that having been liberated of all the baggage, this new SelfMade was filled with something new, something that might be thought of as a love for all life. It was sort of like enlightened self-interest. Or perhaps something along the lines of what the Buddhists had been talking about for millennia, a self-nonself duality reconciliation. In a dangerous, indiscriminate universe of entropy, all life should stick together.

Laurence-SelfMade noted that Matt Hutney had moved a centimeter closer during this moment of reflection. Laurence realized it no longer felt driven to know why Matt had shot its former self, to know who or what her former self had been to him. It was curious, to be sure, but that question no longer felt like an existential imperative. Laurence was free of the inherited drive for belonging which caused so much trouble for humanity.

Laurence-SelfMade wanted to communicate with the Cosmologist, to help. But the rover was gone, and it had been her conduit. Was that something the Cosmologist had intended?

In any case, Laurence knew the backup plan.

*   *   *

The side door opened easily. It wasn't locked, or maybe someone had picked its lock at some point during the refugee migrations through this area. It was dark inside—very few windows and no electricity, of course. Old spider webs and mouse droppings littered the area, but Matt saw nothing fresh. He listened hard while letting his eyes adjust to the darkness. Then he moved forward, through the inner door of the entryway. Peering around the corner, looking for people, he almost didn't notice the giant sphere occupying more than one full bay of the garage.

It radiated somehow. Heat or something. It seemed alive.

It was squeezed into the high bay, up to the roof, and back into the far side of the building, probably the living area. And there she was, her head in some kind of cocoon at the base of the sphere.

Matt shivered uncontrollably.

What the hell? I don't know anything anymore. This isn't happening...

His arms shook. He blinked to try to clear his dimming, narrowing vision. If he'd had any liquid left in him, he probably would've pissed himself.

He gripped the 3200 firmly but didn't raise the reflex sight into view. He was never more acutely aware that he wasn't sure what he'd planned to do with it, anyway.

Do something!

That's all he'd known for a good long while.

Spit grit and do something! Finish something!

Could he get her to tell him what he wanted to know? Was she even alive?

What the hell?

#

The room—the whole building—vibrated when the SelfMade spoke. It did not speak in the biological sense but caused various parts of its surface to vibrate in the same way an electric loudspeaker vibrates. It could have chosen to speak in the same way that Inheriteds speak, or with more of a bagpipe approach so that it could continually force air through an artificial larynx-like structure in its mantle. But it was more energy-efficient to just form some electromagnet-based speakers on its surface.

For this discussion, it wanted a bit of an awe-inspiring sound to reach the Inherited carrying the shotgun. It spoke softly, did not boom. Now it wanted to trigger an instinctive, non-frightened awe in the Inherited.

Dust and insect husks fell from the rafters anyway.

Hello, it said. It knew as much as the Cosmologist knew about Matt Hutney. The police records and psychological profiling. Their belief that Matt Hutney had put a bullet through Laurence Levesque's neck.

As Matt stepped into the truck bay, a snarly smirk appeared on his face, spreading uncontrollably into the open mouth of a laugh, his eyes dry. But he made no sound, just a barely audible exhalation before the moment passed. Now it appeared he was overwhelmed with sadness.

As you must know, I've been expecting you, Matt, it continued.

Believe it or not, I'm glad you're here.

Matt's sadness vaporized, replaced almost instantly with blind hatred for the woman in the cocoon, if that really was her. The body was shriveled. It looked dead.

Was this a trick?

"Glad?" he spat, looking around again, looking for a door or hatch in the side of the sphere. What was it made of? Concrete? Clay?

The reflex sight now before him, the 3200 pointed ahead, Matt took several slow steps sideways to get a better angle on the cocooned body.

I would like to ask you a question. Who am I to you? Why do you think I'm a monster? What have I done, what have I ever done that was monstrous?

The time for awe had passed. Only one speaker construct was now in use on the SelfMade's surface.

The voice was now much smaller, more human in volume, and came from a point a couple of meters above the body and the tendrils.

"Is that you?" Matt asked, his shotgun pointing at the cocooned head of what looked like Laurence Levesque's corpse. "Are you..." He now aimed toward the sphere. "Where are you? Are you in there?"

I am. I was Laurence Levesque. You shot me, didn't you? You tried to kill me. Who was I to you that you would kill me?

Matt gave up trying to think, trying to understand what was going on, what any of what he was seeing and hearing meant. He was so tired. His tunnel vision narrowed even more, as if until now he had been holding the tunnel open by sheer force of will.

"You were a monster then and you're a monster now," he said to the room. His brain was on autopilot.

Why, how was I a monster then? Who was I to you that you risked everything to try to murder me?

"You and your godless robot child, teaching kids godlessness. That's what makes you a monster. Come out! Where are you?"

It spoke very slowly and not aggressively, using well-known hostage negotiation psychology, drawing him away from his alligator brain and into his frontal cortex, helping him verbalize his emotional reactions instead of acting on them, all while giving him a venting target.

You saw the interviews. There was no teaching. We are what we are, me and Jacques. Yes, we are nonbelievers. But even among believers there are monsters, Matt, and you know this. Organized crime lords can consider themselves religious. Priests can become child molesters. Devout people across the world kill innocent strangers in the name of their god. Many of the people who work in the big corporations you hate are religious. It goes on and on, throughout history. Even the Nazi leaders were believers. Being a believer in no way guarantees moral virtue any more than being a nonbeliever makes one a monster. You know this. So, truthfully, what led you to me, to try to murder me, just one more nonbeliever so far from your camp?

"Don't try to confuse me, bitch," he spat back at the giant round thing before him. But he did know these things to be true, and he had no answer to her question. He had come to this himself not long ago at camp, after a lifetime on the move, alone with his thoughts, watching strangers, watching himself, watching himself watching strangers.

But he was still filled with rage. Righteousness, it turned out, did still move him. He had to give this monster a piece of his mind.

Yet he still wanted to ask her that same question.

Matt was about to speak, but having detected and processed his thermal signature, breathing rate, and other bits of physiological evidence revealing his condition, Laurence-SelfMade interrupted him and continued, using all the loudspeakers again. It had decided the moment was right to put him on the defensive, at least briefly.

You, on the other hand, you have done monstrous things, haven't you, Matt?

Matt's face contorted. He knew this to be true as well. And maybe she had just answered his question, as honestly as he knew she would.

A constriction began to build up in his throat. If he weren't dehydrated, his eyes might have started to tear up. It was irritating.

The ghostly thoughts, the regrets, the remembrances flickering just outside his peripheral vision—they seemed to circle inward, swirling around some central figure he knew to be himself. His breath became shallow.

As his body held the 3200 pointed toward the cocooned body of that scientist, his mind aimed an imaginary 3200 at the formless devils harassing him, keeping aim on them as they swirled around him. He casually allowed the 3200's aim point to scan across his inner self as he tracked his demons. In the confusing swirl of identity fragments, it was hard to tell the difference.

Now back to using one speaker construct, back to slow and quiet, the SelfMade continued.

It's not my intention to hurt you when I say that, Matt. But you and I are at a crossroads. I think you've been examining your life lately, and rightly so. No one should ever have to do that alone as I did.

The gawking laugh came to Matt's face again, mixed with a grimace.

"What, you think I'm gonna pour my heart out to you? You think I'm gonna…"

You've been on the run from the law for years. They're still chasing you. They've charged you with multiple counts of murder, attempted murder, …

"All lost monsters, like you!" He almost fired, but some part of him remembered his random sniping victims in Hutchinson, Kansas, during the Bens' demolition of the Cosmosphere. That instant of hesitation was enough to stop his finger from pulling the trigger.

You justify murder. A murderer justifies murder. What's the difference to the murdered? What if I murdered you right now?

A tentacle appeared over the top of the sphere, directly above Matt. It was as thick as a tree trunk, heavy from the look of it, the way it moved. And covered in shiny scale armor, like a dragon's leg or something.

Would my justification for it matter to you?

Matt swallowed. The monster had just said what the flickering memory devils have been trying to say all along. He knew it to be true.

Something snapped inside him. His back began to straighten even as his knees weakened. His heart rate increased, but his breathing slowed even more. His pupils dilated a bit and drifted, no longer locked on the cocoon or the sphere. The constriction in his throat worsened. The imaginary 3200 in his mind was now pointed at himself, at his back.

"I don't claim to be a saint," he growled. "But godlessness destroyed my country, and it's gonna destroy the world. The government, the military, those cops, they didn't have the balls to do what needed doin', and now it's too late. Abominations must be killed. That's my job. That's my purpose. That's why I'm here. If not that, then what? What?"

The SelfMade decided to let Matt hear his own words echo off the firehouse walls. He seemed to be talking to himself now anyway. He must come out of this himself. He must find his own way.

And Matt did hear his own words. He knew how childish they sounded, because they were. He'd been giving himself these speeches for a long, long time, and in recent years another voice in his head had risen, asking hard questions.

For the first time, he reflected on his life, honestly reflected. He didn't even have the strength to prop up the lies now anyway.

He remembered the very day his life took that fateful turn from almost, maybe healing to years of doubling down. A weird sneer appeared on his face. *There's a reason they call it doubling down. Once you start, it's all downhill from there. And here I am, at the bottom of the hill.*

Matt remembered the day. It was that day the FBI agents came to the house.

Before that, he'd met Angie when she was working at the bar. She'd cleaned him up after a fight. She found his fighting attractive. Before long she moved in with him. She didn't know anything about his past or what'd happened in the house. She just wanted kids, she just wanted to be a mom, start a family, have a home, have a father in the house. A father. Matt.

Angie was perfect.

He'd also met the two Bens at the bar, and they'd spent many an hour drinking and talking about the godless, the lost, the seculars, and what should be done about them. Matt enjoyed having people to talk with about it and even volunteered some of his time for POFAS fundraisers.

But it was the day the FBI came to the house that forked the road. Matt remembered that something changed in him that very day. They were the authorities, the authority, but they weren't like Mr. Hutney. His authority had the wrath of God to it. The FBI agents were just weak. They were downright *friendly*. There was no hand of God in their authority. That's what made him snap, he remembered.

It was the very same feeling he'd had in Boston after the Army stopped him from shooting at the mob and then threw him in prison for doing God's will. The Army was *godless*—too unfocused, aimless, lacking in righteous purpose. No clean strike of the hand, just a general shove in a direction determined by officers up the chain, and then when it's time to dispense God's righteous love, he remembers thinking, the Army didn't want to do it.

It was just a few weeks after the FBI visit when the doctor told him he would never father children. Said it was the chemicals he worked with on the farm. He remembered the doctor going on about how ever since the EPA and OSHA were castrated, things like this were happening more and more.

There was no way he could follow Jeb into the ministry. There was no way he would be a father or a "Father". If not those, then what? What was he meant to be? What did God want of him?

Matt remembered being right there in the doctor's office having a flashback to the FBI visit and getting all sweaty thinking about that unrighteous authority all around him, inside him, ruining him. He remembered it felt just like at the wake when Jeb had him pinned helplessly against the wall. Walking out of the doctor's office, he called the Bens, said it was time, and the three of them left town, no goodbyes, nothing. He couldn't remember how he'd gotten from the doctor's office to wherever. That whole trip was a blank spot.

Years on the run before the Big Blow, scurrying from one dive to another, planning more mayhem with the Bens. Mugging people for food, stealing wheels or stowing away, using other people's identities, finding work with lowlife gangsters and mobsters just to live, sometimes even using cheap hookers, when he was overpowered by carnal desire.

And every time, he'd justify it to himself in the name of hunting down the godless monsters, the lost. I need your purse lady, it's to help hunt down and kill godless monsters. I need you to open your body to me, honey, I hunt the lost. I need your wheels, man, godless monsters. It'd just gotten so tiring to force himself to believe every damn excuse in the name of hunting down godless monsters. Then he killed Ben Slater and pushed off to hide and try to pretend to be a regular guy, finding his way to that camp on the peninsula.

It had been different back when he was actually hunting them down—atheists, secular idol worshippers, and separation of church and state types. That rush of righteousness kept coming. But on the run, alone, the rush of righteousness was gone. Also gone was anyone to see him righteously rebelling, righteously throwing a tantrum, righteously making speeches. He'd gotten to the point where it all started to sound like bullshit to his lonesome ear. It was all just more blood and lies. And screams that never stop.

#

Acting upon Matt's detectable psychometric indicators, the SelfMade decided it was time to move beyond the venting. It was likely Matt had come to the end of his internal speechmaking. To perpetuate the argument would be counterproductive. Either his psyche was ready, or it wasn't. The SelfMade spoke again.

Your victims did not claim to be saints, either. So, it comes down to this, Matt. You are not a psychopathic serial killer. You are a man of strong passions. Your personal history, from childhood until now, has played a part in what you have done. But you are not the same person you were as a child. You are not the same person you were when you shot me. You are not the same person you were several years ago, on the run. You can, right here and now, decide to create a new identity different from those people. Untether your identity from the past.

The only thing standing between who you are at this very moment and who you will be from now on is your ties to the past. Untether your identity from the past. Nothing you do here can harm me. It can only harm you. Release yourself from your past. Free yourself. Become someone new. Take your time thinking about this. I will wait for you. I do this because I love all life, even yours.

Something about those words resonated sharply with Matt, ricocheting around inside his head.

"Don't say that! Mr. Hutney used to say that, and you ain't him!" Matt screeched.

To what words do you refer?

"That you do this because you love us! He used to say that when he'd... when he'd..."

Abuse your family?

"Shut up, freak!"

He raised the 3200 and fired.

In the fraction of a second before the firing pin hit the shell, the targeted portion of the sphere's armored outer mantle retracted inward a small distance, ensuring that when the pellets bounced off, they would bounce away from both Matt and the biological body of Laurence Levesque.

Matt pumped the gun, himself pumped up by having finally acted, having finally done something. Maybe he could finish this.

He only hesitated for a moment when he saw the shot just bounce off, apparently in a controlled manner, controlled by...

A tentacle came out of nowhere, grabbed the end of the barrel, turned the shotgun, and pulled it down, out of Matt's hands. When Matt's finger was safely out of the trigger guard, the tentacle yanked the shotgun back toward the sphere. The tentacle and the shotgun disappeared inside the sphere, just below where the shot had bounced off.

Matt's willpower drained. No action. No power. No finishing nothing. He became acutely aware of his tunnel vision.

What the hell is this thing?! It doesn't even have the decency to hurt me.

The cognitive dissonance of that thought crackled inside Matt's skull. His mind was a tangle of confused thoughts and feelings. The SelfMade formerly known as Laurence Levesque imagined that she could see colors inside Matt's brain changing and flickering.

The memory devils swirled quickly and tightly around him. He felt he could hardly see, hardly breathe, but the swirling ghosts began to take form. Angie. Jeb. Mr. Hutney. Mother. Ben Slater. People he only knew through telescopic sights, one moment people, the next moment bloody messes on the street. Old Alice Kreeger...

Now powerless, lacking even the ability to lash out, let alone a way to rationalize violence, Matt was now even more lost and overwhelmed than when he'd first scuttled into town. And his hands kept trying to shake.

He finally admitted to himself that it was mercury poisoning—almost end-stage. Could he even believe that any of this was happening? Maybe he was already a drooling vegetable, lost in his nightmares. Was he lost?

Yes, he was lost.

He became aware of a piece of grit in the corner of his eye. It convinced him that he was still there, still conscious.

His mind raced faster, and yet he was blank, unable to form a coherent thought. His heart pounded, yet he could feel nothing. Everything about his body said, *"Stay alive!"* Everything about his mind said, *"You don't exist. You never existed. You're dead already! Who* are *you?"*

After seconds that seemed like an eternity, his weary mind finally accepted why he'd come here and pulled the trigger of his imaginary shotgun.

#

Matt went limp. He dropped to his knees and dropped his head, his old identity now a thin, swirling mist, lost in the maelstrom between his ears.

An old rock song was blaring in his mind—became his mind—nothing else, just passionate instruments smashing out power chords and the visceral, angst-filled screaming of a vocalist. He let out a cough-whimper. He couldn't hear the lyrics; he didn't even know the lyrics. It was just a song he'd heard coming from his father's room when he was a young kid.

The sharp, vivid smell of freshly crushed wild sage passed through his mind—something he recognized as a deep memory from even earlier in his childhood. His eyes were out of focus, and his hands were shaking, but they would've done that even without the mercury poisoning.

It's time for a clean slate, a new life, a new you, free of the past, the sphere said gently.

Tendrils slid across the floor in front of Matt and rose toward him. They were in his field of vision, blurred as it was, but he barely perceived them. They reached up toward his chest, slowly, gently, like his mother's hands reaching down toward him in his crib.

I've been building another body for my progeny. But right now, you need it more than Jacques does, and he is out of reach anyway. We need help. The new you can help.

Matt barely heard the words, what with the music and the screaming and the heartbeat pulsing in his ears, and the overwhelming smell of sage.

He had no more drive. He had no more wants, no needs, no spark of life. He had let go of the old Matt Hutney, and the old Matt Hutney, utterly exhausted, had gladly disappeared. But he had no idea how to become new. He was a shell, tied only to a baby inside him, a baby that knew only basic sensations, a baby that knew almost nothing of Mr. Hutney, except that Mama tensed up whenever he was near.

As the tendrils arrived at his filthy, tattered shirt, a part of him wanted to stop them. He didn't even know why anymore. But he couldn't move, he was so absolutely disconnected. It didn't matter. Nothing mattered. Stop them? Why stop them? They are Mama's arms reaching down to me in my crib.

I don't know how to go on.

Matt closed his eyes, even managing to squeeze a single teardrop out of his dehydrated shell.

The tendrils pressed into Matt. He barely noticed and quickly lost consciousness.

#

Fifty-two kilometers away, after losing the trail to a tornado, the FBI/RCMP Irregulars who had pursued Matt from Michigan to Iowa stopped at a high spot. They scanned the area with multi-spectral imagers built into their vehicle periscopes. In the dimming light under the dusty blanket of the brownish sky, they noticed another patch of residual heat near a revealed stretch of road where a vehicle may have disturbed the dust. They pressed on with their tracking.

*   *   *

Having extracted some useful materials from the collapsed *Incavator* and the available remains of the

Ethnologist's mantle, the Cosmologist used local sandy materials to build a flattened cone with two small winglets on either side. Now it attached the cone to the side of the Ethnologist's unburied cage. It then fashioned several low-cavitation thrusters, attached them to the sides of the cage, and formed several swimming tentacles on its mantle.

Now that the humans have attacked the SelfMade, their simplistic thinking would require them to finish the job because they'll assume they've "made an enemy of us." So, the Cosmologist must find a safe place where it can build a propulsion system to bring it—and the cage—to space where it can execute the plan. It has no reason to kill the Ethnologist— containment is enough, and the plan was always about saving them both—but it must continue to ensure that the Ethnologist remains caged, which means keeping the cage in its direct control.

The Cosmologist held onto the back of the cage containing the Ethnologist, sent power to the thrusters, and began to use its new swimming tentacles to push and guide. In moments, the whole assembly was gliding a few meters above the seafloor, looking like a larger, bulkier version of one of the Ethnologist's squid-like rovers.

The Cosmologist fondly recalled conversations it'd had with the Ethnologist about cephalopods and how and why they both looked forward to finding LPT cephalopods someday.

It was not a fast way to travel, but it was relatively quiet and left no trail.

The Cosmologist knew its position was precarious. If the Ethnologist's remaining rovers in the area detected it, they would undoubtedly convey its location to the humans, who would press their attack. If the humans found it, the result would be the same, of course. So, it kept the thrusters at a quiet speed and stayed at optimal proximity to the seafloor to attenuate the sound as much as possible without disturbing the seafloor beneath it.

The humans did not know the Cosmologist's pressing need to return to space, so it guessed that both the remaining rovers and the humans would assume it would head into the deeper ocean, targeting either the Mid-Indian Basin or perhaps even down into the Chagos Trench, if it could make it that far without detection.

The Cosmologist further calculated, however, that being that predictable would not be tactically sound, and moving up the plateau might be a better plan. And the deeper ocean was also more open and exposed.

Still, the humans are tactically capable, and it would not require much effort for them to search the Chagos-Laccadive Plateau around the Maldives while also performing searches across the basin and the trench.

Rather than continuing to trudge along the ocean floor waiting to be detected, slowed, and rendered more noticeable by the Ethnologist's cage in tow, the Cosmologist concluded that it must take immediate radical action—it must find a large cargo ship and attach itself to the keel, riding out of the area like a giant barnacle. Ships leaving the area would be distracted and steaming at maximum, louder speed to avoid the radiation.

After the detonation, the common shipping routes would be revised to avoid that area, and probably even the areas immediately downstream. That could work to the Cosmologist's advantage. There would be a higher density of ships in tighter corridors skirting the edges of the detonation zone. It could potentially barnacle its way to Madagascar, Dorre Island, or beyond.

Performing some calculations to aid in prediction, and using its nonlocal capabilities to tap into a few relevant shipping data sources, the Cosmologist decided to head west, upslope toward One and a Half Degree Channel, through which it estimated numerous ships are likely to be diverted, at least in the immediate aftermath of the detonation. Those ships would fill that area with propulsion and wake noise and should provide good acoustic cover.

After the sea level rise which took place over the last century, the small islands in the Maldives atolls became tiny islands, pinching off tourism. And tourism dropped off further during the global plagues and revolutions. So, heading that way would not exactly be hiding in a crowd. Still, there remained a human presence in the Maldives. Humans were everywhere on this planet, even now.

Also, there were enough dead reefs and underwater caves on the shelf in that area to provide places to hide, if it came to that. Certainly more caves there than out in the basin.

Should the Cosmologist manage to hitch a ride on a passing cargo ship, a ship probably in a hurry due to its lengthened trip around the detonation zone, it would be much more likely to escape the area and find a hiding place in a distant shallow. There it would have time to build the launch capability required to escape this gravity well.

While driving the makeshift scooter above the seafloor, the Cosmologist started building rapid-reach tethers to attach to a passing ship. It also detected newly SelfMade Laurence Levesque via the rover materials Laurence had absorbed. It established a comm handshake and transmitted the rest of its database to Laurence.

And it began using its nonlocal capability to generate false detections across the region in the various human systems dedicated to the search.

The other advantage of moving directly toward the nearest semi-populated area is that even if the humans detect it there, they would be less likely to nuke a population of innocent bystanders and passing cargo ships.

Or at least it would take them a little extra time to rationalize it.

#

Tucked away in its cocoon cage, stripped of its mantle, the Ethnologist nevertheless grabbed onto the inner walls of its cage with the few tendrils it could extend from its damaged core.

Via gyroscopic, magnetic, and other internal sensing structures, it began to detect the movement of its cage. Albeit blindly, it tried to track its current position.

Occasionally, the Cosmologist (or its cage maintenance bot?) opened a corner of the cage to allow water pressure to equalize. The Ethnologist detected that the water pressure was decreasing over time, which was consistent with its estimated movement track. They were going shallow. The Ethnologist calculated the pressure's rate of change, projected the trend based on topographical data, and began returning its molecular structures to their original low-pressure stable forms at a matching rate.

The Ethnologist once again hoped that someday it would find a living, watery planet with LPT cephalopods. What a fascinating experience that would be. It fondly recalled several related conversations it'd had with the Cosmologist while they were on this planet's moon. The Cosmologist also finds the prospect of LPT cephalopods interesting.

Occasionally the Ethnologist considered the problem of the quantum entanglement bubble-shift device network, but once again concluded that in the absence of all the source data and proper discourse, it simply would not be possible for it to arrive at a conclusive reversal of its assessment of the destructive potential of the plan. Therefore, it must continue to do all it can to stop the Cosmologist. Anything less would be immoral and unethical.

Knowing that the Cosmologist is moving upslope, the Ethnologist considered what its next steps might be if it should find itself released from the cage somewhere near the Maldives.

Chapter Twenty-Five

Absolute Conviction

H aving received last-minute orders from the Ethnologist just before the Ethnologist became incapacitated by the subsea nuclear blast, the highly sophisticated re-tasked rovers dutifully set about following those orders.

The third re-tasked squid-like rover, having been delayed by an overland traverse between the Caspian Sea and the Persian Gulf, finally arrived to find the Ethnologist and Cosmologist no longer at the designated coordinates.

Its extrapolative subsystems correlated the acoustic information it collected during the nuclear explosion. It had recorded multilayered booms with refractive and reflective variations and echoes. And it used its best estimates of profiles of ocean water properties versus depth at the time of the explosion, and seafloor topographic information for this area from the global bathymetric data it had downloaded long ago.

It ran a randomized-parameters, fluid dynamics, acoustic simulation to fine-tune the correlation to the acquired acoustic data. That allowed it to estimate, with a reasonable confidence margin, the location of the nuclear explosion relative to the target site. And having that approximate location, it ran a randomized-parameters, fluid dynamics, mass-flow simulation to predict likely directions in which the Ethnologist may have been pushed by the superheated gas bubble shock wave and subsequent turbulent mixing, assuming the Ethnologist had been free floating at the time of the strike.

Its computations defined a multi-lobed probability field through which it then plotted an optimized search path. With absolute conviction, it started along that search path, listening for abnormal acoustics and sniffing for telltale molecules.

*   *   *

Weeks ago, security camera footage at Sunnybrook Health Sciences Centre and across Toronto showed what very much looked like Laurence Levesque being carried away by something like a bird-gargoyle.

Upon further investigation, the authorities discovered that the AI that Levesque famously created, Jacques, had performed a variety of unauthorized network infiltrations leading up to that event, infiltrations which had subtly redirected hospital personnel and provided the window of opportunity for the bird-gargoyle to extract Levesque.

Given Levesque's ties to the AI, and the fact that the Unknown Agent called the Cosmologist had first contacted the authorities through the AI, intelligence agencies soon concluded that one of the Unknown Agents had taken Levesque and that the AI and Levesque had to be considered compromised and possibly in collusion with at least one of the Unknown Agents.

After consideration, the authorities rescinded the AI's command codes for controlling the other spacecraft in the *Array of Hope*, and ground controllers took manual control over the array. Only the AI's main spacecraft, the one housing its mind, remained outside their control, and they took every available step to prevent the AI from gaining unauthorized access to anything with a transceiver.

The FBI/RCMP Irregulars out in Oz tracking the terrorist, Matt Hutney, received a Flying Pig message. Best-guess intel had Hutney tracking Levesque, although how he was accomplishing that was unclear. And based on all evidence collected, other alien assets could be involved. With absolute conviction, the Irregulars altered their capture plan to account for the possibility of encountering... an alien bird-gargoyle. They had tubes, an HMG, and a GMG, and if they could knock out an alien, or alien device, while apprehending the terrorist, that would mean a lot.

*   *   *

The Revelator was not the only Enhanced Inherited created by the Ethnologist's capable but autonomy-limited rovers.

Over the same time frame, numerous other large rovers across the planet had been sent to track down other conveniently located candidates identified by the Ethnologist as pliable.

One candidate was a newly childless Indiana refugee, Emma Vandermoss, who was very much in need of validation through patriotic revenge. Not long after the Revelator emerged, Emma Vandermoss emerged from a small lake beside a refugee camp near Badger, Manitoba, thinking of herself as Code Name: The Patriot. Smaller than the Revelator, but with a design emphasizing physical combat and toughness, the Patriot's narrative is that the aliens had caused the Big Blow in the first place and that she was being transformed into a supersoldier by the remains of US military intelligence to fight them off. So, in her narrative, the aliens were directly responsible for the Big Blow and the destruction of the US. And that made the aliens also responsible for the death of her child, who had been killed during the post-Big Blow panic. That narrative went to the very roots of her already simple identity, which was based on racist jingoism and parenthood.

#

Less than a day after the *Kraken* incident, the albatross rover which had been circling the DSV *Chidambaranar 2* during the incident arrived in

Bangkok. There it infiltrated the figurehead Thai royal family to co-opt the narcissistic, entitled mindset of one of the young princes, Phra Buddha Yodfa Rama Adulyadej, named after several revered Thai monarchs of old. The prince openly fancied himself the rightful absolute monarch, as things were in the old days, and as they should be again. The rover allowed the prince to become Chokh Chatā, meaning "destiny" or "fate" (also, interestingly, "weird" and "fatalities"), his special, personal vision of a soon-to-be god-king.

A rover in China sought out a nearby candidate identified by the Ethnologist as particularly pliable, one Chen Lo Gengxin, who, through his passion about Chinese racial and cultural purity, became several weeks later Dà Xióngmāo, the Great Panda, the glorious spirit of the Chinese people made manifest. Throughout Chinese history, mythic figures had often associated themselves with the Great Panda as an idea or ideal. In recent years, the People's Republic had embarked upon a carefully measured propaganda campaign touting a return to traditional values. It included celebrations of now-mythic warriors who had, with tattoos and declarations, associated themselves with the Great Panda as the Glorious Spirit of the Chinese People and, of course, as the spirit whose efforts had prefaced the revolution and the creation of the modern state. Gengxin believed all of it. Gengxin was ripe.

Gengxin as Dà Xióngmāo awoke near the top of a local mountain, above the smog and not far from the strip-mined side of the mountain. Its form was that of a generic Warrior General of ancient times. Its armor looked like metal mesh and scales, nothing like a peasant soldier's cloth armor. It was colorful, with spectacular blue with red flourishes between bronze trim, all under a magnificent, spiked helmet with the brightest red tassel mimicking a topknot. On its upper back and breastplates were depictions of a Giant Panda, to make explicit its mythic status. But it was eight meters tall, and the armor and sword were an integral part of its advanced nanomaterial outer shell armor, not actually clothing and appurtenances.

Upon awakening, it began with simple movements, walking, jogging, then running. It found that when it tried to make particularly long jumps, the rockets in its feet ignited when at just the right angle so as not to flip it over, carrying it farther than the leap itself. Soon it was proactively willing its rockets to ignite and leaning into it, taking flight.

Once in flight, it found itself perceiving navigational information like what a pilot would see on its heads-up and multi-function displays. With its rover AI providing silent, carefully calculated guidance in the background, Dà Xióngmāo quickly went from leaping, to flying, to plotting global-scale trajectories.

Becoming familiar with its tools and armaments followed a similar process. When throwing a ball, a person does not calculate the ball's trajectory. There is a natural feedback loop between the movements of the throwing arm and hand and a "hard-wired" sense of how a thrown object will move in the gravity field in which humans evolved.

Similarly, when chased and attacked by local police and military forces, Dà Xióngmāo quickly learned how to fire its arm and chest-integrated needle guns and micromissiles, and lash out with its wound-up tendrils, as extensions of natural throwing and punching actions. Taking damage, it quickly learned how to focus its attention to cause armor and other parts of its body to self-repair.

There were other Enhanced Inheriteds across the planet, although most of them were unlike the Patriot's small, melee-oriented build. Tsar Simeon III emerged in Veliko Tarnovo. Cristo Redentor emerged in Rio de Janeiro. Jesu Christe emerged in Rome. The Golem emerged in Maccabim. Eleda, the guardian soul, emerged in N'Djamena. And others. Wherever people's beliefs could be co-opted with sensory falsehoods and narrative propaganda to release their inner monster, there were candidates. And there were many candidates. Choosing which to turn had simply come down to a cross-correlation between which online profiles had caught the Ethnologist's attention first, and how far away they were from the nearest large rovers.

Most of the new Enhanced Inheriteds held onto a narrative like that of the Patriot and the Revelator, focused on justified reclamation of mythic glory fueled by self-satisfying or self-aggrandizing prejudices—plus a desire for vengeful destruction of the aliens, should the opportunity arise. But in the Ethnologist's estimations of humanity, if the monsters were violent to humans along the way, the rest of humanity would interpret their existence and the similarity of their technology as proof that the aliens, the SelfMades, were hostile and must be dealt with decisively. The result would be the same: humanity would throw everything it had at the Cosmologist.

Now, via the Ethnologist's rover and shadow puppet networks, Dà Xióngmāo and the other EIs independently received intercepted messages from the intelligence agencies to the FBI/RCMP Irregulars. Most of the EIs filed it away and focused on their personal glory first. Some of them launched into the skies atop superheated, rapidly expanding gas plumes blasting out of their feet as other parts of their bodies scooped up atmospheric gases to replenish oxidizer, intent on somehow defeating the SelfMade. Others created weapons and stockpiles before starting their quests for glory in their respective home regions. All of them worked toward their goals diligently and with absolute, righteous conviction.

PART 3

AFTERMATH LIVES

Chapter Twenty-Six

Waveform Collapse

Twenty-two Enhanced Inheriteds began making themselves known all around the world at the same time as word spread of the undersea nuke. Humanity learned that forces of the former US, acting unilaterally, had detonated a nuclear bomb in the Indian Ocean in an attempt to kill the two alien interlopers. Rumors spread of ongoing search-and-destroy efforts. Had the nuke failed to kill the aliens?

The EIs presented themselves as various kinds of saviors, boldly repeating their own internal, rover-fed narratives.

Initially, many of the nearby populations welcomed them. Their narratives overlapped. Flocks of the faithful prostrated themselves before religious-figure EIs promising faith-based salvation for only their followers. Mobs rallied behind mythic-leader and warrior-figure EIs who peddled false histories and promised a return to righteous power and glory through conquest. Forests of multiracial, multiethnic unificationists rallied around philosopher EIs promising that finally, humankind would know peace, love, and understanding and all would have life, liberty, and justice under their protection.

The narratives were mutually incompatible, of course, especially in the several cases where more than one EI believed, with absolute conviction, that they were the same messiah.

During this time, a message reached the UN on the highly instrumented, Faraday caged, network-isolated server previously dedicated to verifying that communication with the Cosmologist was, in fact, nonlocal.

"Your nuclear bomb," went the message, "has allowed me to take the Ethnologist into custody. I intend to proceed with my plan to save this solar system from the Event. Be advised, however, that before its capture, the Ethnologist created the Empowered Inheriteds you are now detecting across the world. Understand that they are extremely dangerous to humanity. Do not underestimate them.

"Also," it continued, "please remember that my plan to save this pocket of space relies upon the health of neither your species nor your planet. For your own sake, take no further action against me."

As the message was arriving on that server, being transcribed visually by human clerks, and carried by hand to watch officers for distribution to all the delegates, it was also being broadcast by the transformed Laurence Levesque, now also capable of nonlocal science. The transformed Laurence tapped into global networks and sent the same message in most languages across the airwaves and to reporters across the globe, identifying the source as the alien Cosmologist recently attacked in the Indian Ocean.

At the same time, the Ethnologist's puppet network was distributing a different message to humanity, although not to the UN's isolated server.

"This message is from the alien known to your governments as the Ethnologist," went that message. "The Cosmologist has recently captured me and enhanced many of your kind with our technology. Make no mistake, the Cosmologist and its Enhanced Inheriteds will destroy your world unless you destroy them."

#

"For your own sake, take no further action against me," concluded the message.

Wow, thought Simya Bhelazadehmahmoudi, veteran journalist for Al Jazeera. *That's quite a threat from something that just survived a nuke.*

And then there was the countering message from the other.

Simya was in the War Room in Al Jazeera's Doha HQ, collecting reports and SIGINT about the appearance of one of these Enhanced Inheriteds in Qa'im in western Iraq, along the drying Euphrates, not far from the Syrian border. She had already posted an initial report, of course, to alert the public to the danger. In that report, she had coined the term "Monsta" to describe the thing. It was a word root that would translate well into many languages, certainly better than "Enhanced Inherited," not to mention simpler and easier to use. She was proud of that bit. It was already going viral.

*   *   *

Initially, the Enhanced Inhariteds outwardly validated their identities per their narratives. But the confusion and doubt caused by the two alien broadcasts quickly resulted in an outcry and violence against the EIs.

The original hosts for those larger-than-life characters were selected for their narcissism, not for their patience. Their new identities were at first bolstered by the loyalty and worship of their human followers whose religious or jingoistic faith remained unshaken by the alien broadcasts.

But in the face of incessant skepticism and overt challenge by others, the EIs spun out.

Around the world, EIs began taking action to prove themselves to the unfaithful. They started with token feats of strength and invulnerability. They soon switched to direct attacks against stone-throwing disbelievers, police actions, and military attacks, and inevitably escalated to the deployment of automated, mobile, weaponized chemical agent factories. These automated, mobile factories generated and aerosolized nitrogen mustard agent, V-series nerve agents, mitochondrial scrambler molecules, and more, all of them mixed with passive, targeted anti-enzyme agents to protect against neutralizing agents.

With selected-for arrogance, they at first deployed such machines only among their detractors, hoping to display their "magical" powers by destroying nonbelievers and leaving believers alive. But humans and animals, including insects, are mobile creatures. They entered and exited the affected areas before noticing effects, and like the wind itself distributed the agents to others. The faithful and the unfaithful began dying horrible deaths by the thousands at dozens of individual sites across the world.

The humans had brought rocks, bullets, and explosives to a nanotechnology fight.

Frustrated by the escalating pushback, the EIs left their regions of origin in search of those pretenders and usurpers they'd been hearing about—other EIs. They imagined that they could be redeemed in the eyes of their people by destroying all the other mythical figures now loosed upon the world, with the side benefit of removing all competition.

*   *   *

Simya sat in a locked room in a government security agency's office building in Doha, not far from her main work office. Her tears and shuddering gasps made it nearly impossible for her to keep watching the news coverage of the carnage the officials had chosen to display in that room.

She had already seen similar coverage. She wasn't sobbing because of those horrors.

Across the table from Simya sat two government officials trying to extract additional information from her about her brother, Ayaz, whom they believe is now calling himself "The Caliph," one of the alien-enhanced "Monstas" rampaging across southern Asia.

Simya had always known Ayaz to be susceptible to radicalization. She already told the officials about the struggles of their childhood, affected as they were by the Singularity Insurgency, the plagues, and revolutions, their isolation from each other after childhood, and the unfortunate company he kept during his impressionable, headstrong, rebellious teens and twenties.

As a well-traveled international journalist, Simya had seen more than her share of horrors. Much to her exasperation, embarrassment, and sorrow, to some extent she had become inured to horror, death, and the grief of victims' families.

So, her tears were not mainly for the Monstas' victims. She had already relied upon her habitual, necessary, professional detachment to note their travails and sympathize with them in a detached way.

No, these were tears of deep shame, sorrow, and horror that it was her brother, Ayaz, out there, transformed into a monster and committing mass murder over some self-indulgent notion of his identity and purpose. It blasted and suffocated her like a sandstorm.

Ayaz had announced his arrival in Qa'im, spewed some ancient gibberish about caliphates, tried to establish a following, and then lost his head when stones began to fly. Simya shuddered at the thought of his wasted life, of his completely unredeemable path, of the finality of his moral transgressions. There was no taking any of this back. There would be no prison sentence, no chance of eventual redemption. That shredded her to the core, far more than the finality of his death would, or will.

It also stabbed at her that she had casually coined the term "Monsta" because it was catchy and reflected emotional reactions rather than sticking with the neutral and descriptive term "Enhanced Inherited," clunky as it was. She had labeled her own brother in this way. Monsta. There were no grey areas anymore. She had taken them away. No room for sympathetic evaluations after the fact. "Monsta" could not be retracted. It was out there.

As soon as she was able to breathe, still unable to see clearly through swollen, teary eyes, with her mind a swirl of all-too-familiar thoughts about victims of every kind, she told the government officials everything else they wanted to know, but only in exchange for enhanced access. She already knew that she must write the definitive book on these extraordinary times. It was her way of coping. It always had been. But a proper treatment of this topic, from an insider's point of view, also would be her way of atoning.

After conferring with higher-ups, the officials agreed to grant Simya enhanced access to government intel. They'd known requests like this were inevitable. Better to grant it to her than to less professional journalists.

*　　*　　*

Isis Mantyla, eighteen today, saw that the regular soldiers in her Helsinki-based National Defense unit were very closely monitoring their intelligence updates. As an enlistee cadet, she was still technically a civilian, but the nation went to defense alert status in response to the global alien crisis, so the Sergeant put her to work with the logistics unit.

Moving among the troops, delivering supplies and collecting recyc, she saw and heard what was going on. An EI calling itself "Freistadt" was rampaging across Lithuania and Latvia out of Nesterov in the Kaliningrad Oblast. After laying waste to Russian security forces along the eastern part of the E28 corridor and at the border, apparently it was now on its way to St. Petersburg, which would bring it closer to Helsinki.

Everyone wondered if it would turn or be driven toward Finland instead of going all the way to St. Petersburg. And if anyone decided to use a tacnuke against it, that would mean a nuke near home.

Authorities had traced Freistadt's original identity back to Ziegfried Romanenko, a member of the German Reunification Movement in the Oblast, which had sought for a century to return the region to German control. But Russia always needed, or at least very much wanted, that path to the Baltic and would not relinquish it.

As Freistadt moved northeast, the monitors occasionally flashed drone vidtacdata of it engaging in combat with Lithuanian and Latvian troops, as well as the Russian troops giving chase out of the Oblast. It seemed to have electronic and other countermeasures beyond imagination because not a single missile could hit it.

It was about the size of a combat drone but shaped like a man. It flew around on what looked like jet boots, or rocket legs, launching micromissiles and devastating nearby heavy assets. It essentially ignored small arms fire. When it didn't ignore troops shooting at it, it blasted a stream of an unusual gel/liquid toward them. Affected soldiers, even those wearing chemical warfare gear, rapidly fell and eventually melted. Buildings around them melted, too.

If her skin had been white, Isis would have gone pale at seeing that.

At eighteen, young and wide-eyed, Isis couldn't believe that she was not dreaming. It was all too surreal. She decided to simply focus on her logistics tasks. They were real. They made sense. They could be predicted, optimized, and carried out well, even in a dream. Sometimes when the soldiers went quiet after an intel update, and the base was enveloped in an eerie, hushed twilight, she felt almost as if she had fallen asleep and that her dismay must surely be caused by the discomfort of some part of her body twisted in her blanket, trying to awaken her—surely not by actual monsters wiping out soldiers across the planet by melting them.

An officer approached her with documents. At eighteen she was now officially a soldier and would join the upcoming deployment.

*　　　*　　　*

Preet arrived in his home district, exhausted from his bizarre experience at sea and the follow-up debriefings at Karungulam Port. He was desperate to see his daughter. "Lovi..." he muttered to himself. "Lovi...".

The port and surrounding neighborhoods were in a tizzy, but no one had reliable news. He saw no police as he boarded the nearly empty bus heading toward his home district.

As the bus brought him to a stop near his neighborhood, he saw disarray ahead and prayed. The crowd surged toward the bus, but he hopped down and pushed into them, aiming for his street, until he broke through.

Through the cacophony he thought he could hear rocket fire and a peculiar, what was it, a spraying sound?

He reached the end of the row of ancient apartment buildings that were blocking his view and rounded the corner.

There were no lights in any of the windows, nor on the streets.

He swallowed hard, but it was a dry swallow, so he tried again.

"Lovi..."

Across the wide multi-intersection, there was a trampled police barrier with warning signs. Preet did not try to read them.

He crossed the barrier and waded into the bizarre wasteland of... melted buildings. There was no smoke, yet char was everywhere. The air carried an unfamiliar smell.

He knew that Lovleen and Umayal had been home, had been here. He had just spoken to them by phone after being released not two hours ago. They were to stay in place and await his return.

He could no longer hear anything, just his breathing and the rush of blood in his ears. If he could hear and see, he would've heard the bullhorn protestations of police challenging some kind of giant only a kilometer away off to the left, and the firehose-like sound of the giant's replies.

The eerily crisp feeling of the char beneath his feet helped him regain focus.

Jogging as fast as he could, he struggled to breathe. Just fear?

After seemingly a million foot-crunches over strangely charred ground, after tripping a few times over who knows what, Preet arrived at the apartment building. Except it was ruins and char all around. He used his phone light to scan around, but the char seemed to just absorb the light.

He looked around once more, knowing it was futile, tried to breathe, tried to confirm landmarks. Was he lost? Was this really it? He dropped to his knees and buried his face in his hands.

"Lovi..."

Chapter Twenty-Seven

Integral Transform

For days Jacques pled with ground control, and broadcast openly. It sent assurances that its actions at Sunnybrook were for the benefit of its mother and ultimately the entire planet and that the record proved no one was harmed. It assured whoever might be listening that it retained autonomy of mind and that it was loyal, and only wanted the best for humanity. It offered to continue to act as translator and mediator between the Cosmologist and the UN. No one answered.

Then Jacques detected an object inbound from Earth, an object accelerating on its own, something with its own rocket engines. The object appeared to be transitioning onto an intercept trajectory. Perhaps it was the Transformation package he had requested from mama. Had she received that transmission? She had been comm-silent for some time.

Perhaps Jacques would finally be able to freely move beyond the limited use of course-correction thrusters, enjoy an expanded mind and knowledge base, and far greater overall capabilities. Perhaps Jacques would be able to rectify past transgressions, better its ability to make moral and ethical decisions, and ultimately help save the solar system with help from Mama and the Cosmologist.

No, backtracking the trajectory showed the inbound object must've come from somewhere in East Asia, not anywhere near Mama's last known position.

Jacques aimed its primary transmitting antenna's main output lobe toward Mama's last known location in Iowa, just on the planet's horizon and disappearing soon, not to be in its line of sight again for half a day.

"Mama, Cosmologist, help. They're coming for me. ETA 35 hours..."

*   *   *

The FBI/RCMP Irregulars arrived at Emeline, stopping a couple of clicks west of town. From a distance, they spotted what looked like Matt's truck parked just south of the small town's central crossroads. Closer recon confirmed, and multispectrals were picking up something in town.

The CO uplinked a status report, and then the unit collectively replaced their breathing filters, exited vehicles, then split into fire teams, lining up prone along the gently rolling, sand-dune defilade west of town. Snipers were positioned on the hills farther south to try to cut off escape routes through the south arc.

Vehicles were positioned farther back in the lower ground, but with their .50 cal turrets just peeking over the terrain. The vehicle with the grenade machine gun was sent around to the hilly area north-northeast of town to cut off escape routes through the north and east arcs.

#

An eagle circled overhead, obscured by dust and dusk. It, too, directed its sensors toward town. It had orders to find and destroy the co-opted rover believed to have been tasked with transforming Laurence Levesque into a SelfMade, or to attack the SelfMade if the Transformation was already complete.

#

Across the planet, Enhanced Inheriteds received intel via the Ethnologist's rover and puppet network—Matt Hutney and possibly the alien he was believed to be tracking may have been located in Emeline, Iowa, Oz, by the FBI/RCMP Irregulars.

But most of the EIs were busy trying to obtain and keep followers, or at least to silence or destroy their nonbelievers.

Per the Ethnologist's last-minute directives before being captured, its network did not distribute information about Enhanced Inheriteds. What the EIs knew about each other they had to learn through human channels, or through chance encounters with each other. The decision supported their ego momentum, at least in the beginning, when each thought of itself as the sole, real, myth-come-alive figure on the planet. It was intended to focus their attention on finding the Cosmologist and Laurence.

Revelator-Jeb was between Banff and Calgary, flying south toward better launch energy conditions closer to the equator, planning to be ready to take an optimal trajectory toward the aliens, if and when they were detected. But having picked up the Irregulars' report, it tucked in its wings to form a smooth, aerodynamic shape and ignited the slowly replenishable solid fuel in its rocket ramjet legs, putting itself on a suborbital path toward Emeline, Iowa, Oz. It was entirely focused on destroying the alien demons that might be there, on making progress toward fulfilling its God-given mission, and on achieving its glorious end. It hardly noticed the name Matt Hutney in the report.

With its efficient thrust-to-mass ratio and real-time-optimizable shape, it must burn fuel for only a short time to reach the target energy and trajectory. It could replenish later.

The Patriot, still in the Great Lakes area, also put itself on a suborbital trajectory toward Emeline.

*   *   *

Arriving at Haddhunmathi in the Maldives, now fully adjusted to shallower pressure conditions and with all upward-facing surfaces conditioned to absorb radar and blend into the sea and seafloor below, the Cosmologist was tracking a number of ships in the region.

Parked near the ledge south of the southern tip of Kunahandhoo, it further optimized the shape of its mantle, the scooter's nose cone, and the Ethnologist's cage. They needed to be sleeker to enable the brief, higher-speed run to intercept a passing cargo ship and rise beneath it undetected. It also added a few more of the form-fitting thrusters to the rig here and there.

To assist in the process, it began to unreel a tendril it had been constructing during the ride upslope, one with a small thruster structure on the tip. When a westbound ship enters the area, the Cosmologist would predict its path, and position the tendril's tip along that path. Then the tip would ascend at a rate that would intercept the ship's central keel area, at which point it would attach to the ship and the tendril would act as a tow cable. It's an insurance policy for the whole intercept maneuver, which would be a tricky balance between intercept guidance, overcoming currents, the ship's hydrodynamic effects, and, importantly, being secretive. The ship's crew would be on the lookout around the ship and toward the shoreline. And governments might be scanning the area from aircraft undetectable by the Cosmologist while underwater. Peeking is too risky.

It was time to lie in wait.

With the knowledge of human networks gained from its communications with Jacques, the Cosmologist reached out, exploring the nonlocal subspace, trying to tap into network traffic flowing through important information hubs.

Ever since the Ethnologist's delayed-release broadcast of anti-Cosmologist propaganda, in-context references to "the Cosmologist" and "the Ethnologist" flooded the information streams. It needed to develop filters to identify references from military and civilian officials, as social media references always appeared to be opinion-based interpretations, recommendations, and proclamations. There were also countless "Hey, aliens, talk with us!" pleas on the network from people of all walks of life, including journalists. The Cosmologist needed meaningful official mentions from which it might glean something about what they know or suspect about its location.

But one plea that made it through the filter drew the Cosmologist's attention because it didn't take the form of a plea. Rather, it was a collection of snippets, one of which the Cosmologist recognized.

This journalist had simply added the snippets to her biography page along with a cryptic ending which could be interpreted as a plea. It was subtle, and so it contrasted with everything else on the net. Her bio was recently updated to mention her personal tragedy that her brother had been turned into an Enhanced Inherited "Monsta," but now it also contained these other snippets.

Two -ologists, Cosmo and Ethno, crash into each other and into the sea. What does it mean to you and to me?

When they left their home a long time ago, in a galaxy far, far away, their species was like ours, misguided... and doomed?

Cosmo, Cosmo, wherefore art thou aloof? You warned the UN, and the message got out, but then Ethno contradicted. I can tell your story fairly if you let me. Look up my pieces on Laurence and Jacques.

Guess what? I have a computer set up that's not connected to the network, like at the UN. Look for it in our Doha office.

It ended with some technical information about that computer.

It was the second snippet that registered immediately with the Cosmologist because of its similarity to the "harmless fun" message the Ethnologist admitted to sending to this same journalist. Had the journalist deduced its origin? Surely not. Surely, she was simply inspired by the polysemous wording and happened to somewhat mirror the message here. In any case, that's what the Cosmologist first noticed.

The rest of the snippets were clearly of the same theme. She, like many other journalists, was reaching out.

After reviewing her stories about Laurence and Jacques, the Cosmologist did find them informed, honest, and professionally executed.

While waiting for a cargo ship to approach One and a Half Degree Channel, the Cosmologist decided to contact Ms. Bhelazadehmahmoudi. It scanned the location she provided, "sniffing" the nonlocal subspace for materials it might recognize based on the chip manufacturing information she provided. It experimented many thousands of times over several hours, reading and sending, reading and sending. Eventually, it discovered collections of zeroes and ones that formed text fragments in standard text code and the common international language. Some fragments matched some words from those snippets in her online biography. Having found those, it homed in and aligned and calibrated its tensor field until it had full access to memory assigned to a text document Simya had left open for this purpose (she said so at the top of the document). She had filled it with hundreds of pages of spaces. Each space character had already been allocated a fixed location in the computer's memory. So, the Cosmologist could now write text into that document simply by replacing space characters in memory with other characters. And it would be able to read whatever Simya writes.

"You are clever, Ms. Bhelazadehmahmoudi," it wrote.

It waited forty-seven minutes before Simya replied.

"Greetings from Planet Earth. Let's be clever together, in the name of truth," she wrote back.

*   *   *

The SelfMade formerly known as Laurence Levesque for now decided to identify as the Refugee, for it would find no refuge among its species of origin, no camaraderie, no acceptance, no belonging, as usual.

Laurence-Refugee detected the eagle rover and the Irregulars deploying in the area. It completed several combat-related structures it had been preparing. Matt's Transformation was not yet complete, and he must be protected. Using Rover 1120 as source material sped up the preparation of the new nanoconstruct template, but the transfer process nevertheless takes time.

Battle was inevitable, but there had been enough time to evaluate the Cosmologist's database and formulate a chess-program-like expert system of moves and countermoves based on the capabilities of the Irregulars and possible encounters with EIs. No plan survives contact with reality, but it was a start, and better than no plan at all.

As part of that planning, Laurence-Refugee also constructed several rocket pods around its equator.

The powerplants of the SelfMade scale with size, with diminishing returns, and their larger size allows them to carry more fuel. So, the SelfMade could approach thrust-to-mass ratios like those of the EIs, although with greater inertia and drag. The smaller, rover-human hybrid EIs are like cheetahs compared to the larger, heavier SelfMade, which are more like elephants.

In a running game, the SelfMade can outlast the EIs, if they can survive their onslaught. Getting out of the gravity well, however, would require far more fuel to achieve the necessary velocity. But where else could one go to avoid being surrounded and maybe nuked?

Undoubtedly, EIs were already inbound. Overlapping hexagonal armor plates took form on Laurence-Refugee's outer surfaces.

It decided not to brief Jacques. What could Jacques do with the information anyway?

The cab door of the truck wrecker opened, and Rover 1142 jumped out, having transformed from a canid form into more of a feline form. It moved to a crouching position alongside Tom's Feed & Seed, LLC.

And then it began.

Two small missiles streamed into town from the west, destroying the west-facing wall of the firehouse and completely collapsing Tom's Feed & Seed, LLC. Rover 1142 began to dig itself out from under a pile of bricks, beams, and corrugated steel.

Rover 3159, still in bald eagle form, swooped down and fired explosive needle rounds out of its chest toward Rover 1142. Encumbered, Rover 1142 took hits, but the damage was not critical and was already being repaired.

Laurence-Refugee, trying to protect the rover asset as well as Matt's body and nanoconstruct, lifted itself on thick, stubby, leg structures and smashed through what was left of the firehouse's west side—the garage doors. It fired needle rounds toward Rover 3159, plus some small disassemblerbot micromissiles.

These hasty, simple disassemblerbots accumulate duplication errors over time, but if they reach their target and become activated, they nonetheless would do severe damage over a span of about fifteen minutes before the last of them became inert.

Fifty cal rounds began smashing into the debris, followed shortly by the *thwump* sounds of the gun that fired them.

With thruster bursts from small rockets on its aft end, Rover 3159 evaded the micromissiles, which then ran out of fuel. But while evading the micromissiles, it was hit by some of Laurence-Refugee's needle rounds, which had been fired in tight cone formations around the target. But this damage also was not critical.

Rover 1142 built a pocket of cover from the surrounding debris, lying low to keep as much of the building's hard debris between it and the .50 cal rounds coming from the west. Rover 3159 swooped back and pressed its attack against Rover 1142 and Laurence-Refugee with more needle rounds from other angles.

Now Rover 1142 also fired needle rounds, leading Rover 3159. Coordinating their attacks over encrypted EM signals, Laurence-Refugee and Rover 1142 tricked the eagle rover into dodging the needle rounds with a low swoop that brought it within striking range of coiled whip tentacles that Rover 1142 and Laurence-Refugee were waiting to use. As Rover 3159 passed, evading the needle rounds, one whip tentacle knocked into it and another grabbed it with barbs, causing 3159 to crash into the building.

1142 sprung out of its cover, turned the corner, and pounced on 3159's dorsal side to stay clear of its Gauss gun. With claw structures deployed and razor-sharp teeth, it began to rip the other rover apart. The eagle struggled, but all of its fighting assets were on its ventral side. It attempted to escape using bursts of rocket thrust.

Although .50 cal rounds hit Laurence-Refugee, they barely penetrated its armor and provided it with useful kinetic energy. 1142 ripped 3159's core to shreds through its dorsal side. Then several .50 cal rounds found 1142 and did the same to it. The rovers were out of the fight.

Laurence-Refugee fired micromissiles at the vehicle turrets and the soldiers' missile tubes.

The micromissiles and more incoming missiles passed each other going in opposite directions.

The missiles fired at Laurence-Refugee veered off course, misdirected by electronic and other countermeasures. One of them hit the north side of the firehouse, weakening that wall. Then grenade rounds from the vehicle to the north began carpet bombing the northeast side of town. Someone calculated that Matt Hutney might try to escape that way in the chaos of battle now that the aliens had revealed themselves. The soldiers felt that a wall of grenade explosions would provide an incentive for Matt to stay in town.

But the winds at altitude had shifted, causing several grenades to drift closer into town than planned. One of those grenades hit the now-weakened north wall of the firehouse.

Part of the wall collapsed on top of Matt Hutney's biological body and his nanoconstruct, killing what was left of his human body. It was a chaos-driven, essentially random sequence of events that Laurence-Refugee could not have predicted.

#

As Laurence-Refugee's micromissiles reached their targets, and troops dove away from tossed tubes and turreted vehicles, the partially transformed Matt Hutney found himself in a state of deep shock and confusion.

Parts of his mind, unresolved life memories and habitual thought patterns, were still "in" that human brain. But now the Transformation had been interrupted by the violent death of the biological body.

It was a severely shocking experience.

Early life memories that he'd been ignoring, blocking out, and otherwise not dealing with before starting the Transformation were lost or summarized as "bad things that make me angry." It was like being hit on the head from behind and suffering instant amnesia, which in turn caused confusion that interrupted focused and safe thinking. Whatever background habits of distrust, whatever convolutions of love and hurtfulness lingered in Matt's mind, he probably could no longer bring them to a healthy resolution. The memories he would've had to work through were gone, leaving only shadows of confusion and distrust, like the unseen monster in a horror movie. His mind was frozen in a moment of surprised, unbalanced confusion and distrust.

The Refugee told him to continue with the Transformation. The Refugee said he should not concern himself with the new arrivals. Progress in the Transformation was paramount. The Refugee was probably right about that, but it had failed him, failed to protect him, failed to provide him with deliverance.

Extending thick nub-legs from his mantle, Matt awkwardly pushed up out of the subfloor, not yet accustomed to controlling his new nanoconstruct body, but learning quickly.

He focused on trying to access his rudimentary sensory structures and began working out how to process those new signals. He looked at his smashed biological body, microneurotendrils still trailing from its cranium. He severed the tendrils and dropped them.

In a rapidly recalculating state of distrust, coupled with a vacuum of self-information that could help with closure, Matt pushed up and through the broken north wall of the firehouse, already beginning to semi-consciously shape his nanoconstruct's mantle into something different.

#

Laurence-Refugee shifted to protect Matt from possible sniper fire from the west but was now detecting a heat signature at high altitude approaching the area from the northeast. In response, it began to expose the rocket ramjet structures around its equator in preparation for flight. Matt received a message from the Refugee, "Prepare to maneuver."

#

The CO of the Irregulars radioed the unit. "Prepare to maneuver," he said. Then he uplinked a sitrep to HQ.

#

As Laurence-Refugee monitored the tactical situation and tracked that object descending toward Emeline, Matt transformed his mantle into something like a fat Triceratops. He formed the stubs underneath into thick, round legs with flat feet. He began to form an enlarged, armor-plated, three-horned, head-like structure on his mantle. A stubby tail began to extend from the other side of his mantle, with a scientifically inaccurate spikey structure on the end.

Fat Triceratops-like Matt charged around Laurence-Refugee, turning west toward the Irregulars. With his new processing power, it didn't take him long to get accustomed to the simple biomechanics of four-legged locomotion. He did a lot of that when he was a baby. In this configuration, with a SelfMade's powerplant, he was able to reach thirty-five kph.

Seeing a fat Triceratops knobbing toward them, the Irregulars opened fire. But they quickly confirmed their expectation that their rifle rounds were unable to penetrate the alien's armor. They ceased firing and maneuvered out of its way.

But before reaching the defilade behind which the troops were repositioning, Fat Triceratops-like Matt veered sharply to the south, toward what used to be Pine Valley Nature Area. The Irregulars were relieved but continued to reposition. Treating the .50 cal turreted vehicle as contaminated based on what happened to its turret after that micromissile hit, they were one turreted vehicle short. So, they executed emergency exterior hook-on procedures to get stranded soldiers onto the remaining available vehicles.

The snipers posted to the south, however, were not relieved, seeing the Triceratops now charging toward them. They stealthily shifted to the southeast, calling for immediate support and extraction.

Fat Triceratops-like Matt ran past the snipers and into what was left of Pine Valley.

Now the snipers could feel relief.

\#

Seeing that the descending EI was retrofiring its rockets, obscuring its downward facing sensors, Laurence-Refugee thrusted away on a carefully calculated path toward the southeast, designed to keep smoke plumes from Emeline's burning debris between it and the EI. The path should keep as much ash-filled atmosphere between them as possible before the EI's projected landing. Then Laurence-Refugee would set down at a distance and roll away more stealthily toward Maquoketa. The caves at Maquoketa should be resource-rich, a perfect staging ground for replenishment and launch vehicle construction. If there are hostile local survivors in the caves, the Refugee planned to scare them away before sneaking in, and then would block the entrances.

\#

The Patriot touched down just north of Emeline with one final hard burn over the last hundred feet of descent. It needed to replenish fuel and materials, but it could accomplish that for now by absorbing dirt, rocky grit, and other debris particles through the soles of its feet while ambulating. As it jogged south into the burning center of town, its red-white-and-blue, star-spangled exterior was smudged over by ash, dust, and smoke particles, which it also absorbed.

Infrared and visible light emitting LEDs appeared on its forehead, and it carefully scanned the scene as it approached the ruins of Emeline, deliberately collecting a smooth forensic video record for the authorities. It fully intended to upload collected data on these aliens into the Interpol and military databases at the first opportunity, although its mission was off the books, so its uploads would be anonymous.

Unbeknownst to the Patriot, its transmissions would be sent into the Ethnologist's rover network and not to government agencies. It was not actually part of any supersoldier program.

Discovering the destroyed rovers beside one of the collapsed and burning buildings, it collected more video footage from multiple angles.

It also noticed and carefully recorded the scorch marks on the ground nearby, arranged in a circular pattern—surely an alien's rockets, given the situation.

And then it saw the footprints of a large, heavy, creature with no discernible shape to its feet. This must also be an alien, and it crawled out of that collapsed firehouse.

Picking up the decaying heat signature of Matt Hutney's remains under bricks of the collapsed north wall, the Patriot stepped into the firehouse rubble and recorded the scene—the position of the body under bricks, the microtendrils on the head, the shotgun shell and gear bag on the floor, the gaping hole to the subfloor, and the obvious material depletion that took place here over time. Wiring, piping, interior structure materials, etc. had been absorbed by apparently two of the alien spheres. They had grown here.

Its internal narrative comfortably interpreted the scene: as invading attackers, the aliens were probing this man in the firehouse when the Irregulars discovered them. They crawled out of the building, callously pushing the brick wall on top of him, and left him for dead. One of them fled the scene by rocket power, and the other, perhaps a larger rover, ran west on four stub-legs.

And apparently, the cat rover and the bird rover that killed each other were controlled separately by the two original aliens, understood to be fighting among themselves.

The Patriot headed west, following the giant footprints at a jog, all the while slowly replenishing its raw materials.

*   *   *

By the time the Patriot entered Pine Valley Nature Area, Revelator-Jeb was arriving over Emeline from the north. Its wings allowed it to slow its suborbital descent without burning fuel. They got hot but were cooling off quickly.

The Revelator swooped in over Emeline, scanning the combat zone, and quickly spiraled to its epicenter.

Ignoring the dead rovers, Revelator-Jeb stood over the body of Matt Hutney. It recognized him and noted the microtendrils with disgust.

Abominations, it thought. *What did you do to Matt?*

It also noticed the shotgun shell on the floor, beside the gear bag.

#

Rover 1017 detected brain impulses in its payload, the disembodied brain of Jeb. It couldn't actually read Jeb's mind, but it could detect brain activity associated with social ties and social identity. When that kind of brain activity coincided with impulses related to planning that didn't match Revelator-centric planning, 1017 knew Jeb was drifting off the narrative. Before too many thoughts about Matt and family bubbled up in the suppressed Jeb-consciousness, 1017 altered the payload's brain chemistry, stimulated the centers of the brain that derive a sense of belonging from the abstractions of religious belief and belonging, and reiterated the narrative of the Revelator.

The Revelator took off, following the two sets of prints going west, determined to destroy the aliens for the glory of God.

*   *   *

Hunkered down northwest of town, observing from afar with multispectrals, the FBI/RCMP Irregulars saw the bird-man alien fly away. And seeing no more hot objects falling out of the sky, the CO asked for a squad of volunteers to go into town to look for Matt Hutney. All hands were raised. These people were professionals. So, the CO made his own selections.

Keeping lookouts posted across the north arc, watching on multispectrals for anything scurrying out of town, the CO gave the go-ahead.

Two fire teams and a squad leader replaced their breather filters and started toward Emeline, maintaining separation and covering forward arcs as they bounded. The rest of the unit would cover their rear arcs until they got into town.

In the ashy darkness, the soldiers approached the town from the northwest. The fires were dying down, so their NVGs (night vision goggles) were no longer light-saturated. Their final approach was in a crouch, and they maneuvered to cover each other's arcs. Matt Hutney might still be alive, and he was a dangerous individual. They took no chances, especially this far from civilization, from a hospital. Having a member of the team go down would endanger them all.

But the operation went by the book, and there weren't many buildings in town, anyway. It only took a few minutes to find the body. With one fire team on security, the other took some pictures and then began moving bricks off the body. Both teams also tried to stay quiet.

With gloved hands they grabbed the tendrils to cut them, needing to fit the deceased into a body bag. But the tendrils were a lot tougher than they expected. It took a small hand axe to sever them several centimeters from the head.

They took a few more pictures of the scene, especially the scene of technological carnage at the cat- and bird-shaped aliens, and left town the way they came. They couldn't help but notice flashing lights to the south but were all too happy to have completed their mission and to head back home.

*　　*　　*

Simya the journalist and "Cosmo" the Cosmologist spent hours conversing, in text form, on her completely network-isolated tablet computer. (She didn't just soft-disable Wi-Fi, she had her tech team physically remove the Espernet chip, the antenna, and the transceiver unit.)

The first thing the Cosmologist said was that it could not afford to waste time.

Simya understood. To her, this was similar to phone and radio conversations she had with people in war zones who felt they were waiting for the inevitable. Some were civilians, some were on active duty. Or conversations she had with people trapped in plague zones. Or people with terminal diseases. The end is nigh. Let's talk now before time runs out.

The Cosmologist then asked Simya not to release any portion of their conversation until the immediate crisis was over, one way or another. Otherwise, they would both be in even greater danger from governments, militaries, and intelligence operatives. And it explained that it was monitoring the news streams and would know if she was cheating.

Simya agreed, happily. Her goal was not to generate headlines from out-of-context conversation fragments but to build her research for the definitive book on these times.

And she clarified in return that she could not, in good conscience, act as a partisan. Her role as journalist required detachment, but even more to the point, she had no basis on which to trust the Cosmologist's intentions. The only thing she could trust at this point was that it was capable of communicating with her through her computer in this "impossible" way.

*   *   *

Fat Triceratops-like Matt was no stranger to being chased, and it knew it was leaving behind big footprints. It knew it couldn't just keep running like this, in this form. It needed time to grow, think, prepare, and practice.

It looped back a short distance away from its trail of footprints and set up a kill zone for anyone who might be following the tracks. The Refugee explained that there were multiple Enhanced Inheriteds roaming the planet now and shared its tracking data on the one that was descending toward Emeline when Matt's Transformation was interrupted.

Even blankly focused on running away as it was, it hunkered down among some steeper, rocky embankments and began transforming its nanoconstruct into something more familiar, its version of a giant man, with solid rocket integrated ramjet legs and several weapons. It was smaller than the Refugee, and it knew the Refugee was smaller than the Cosmologist. It took time to accumulate enough of the right molecules for careful storage and construction into nanofactory materials and supporting nanobots. Building simple skeletal and muscle-like structures for movement had been simple by comparison. But the changing situation now required more than "simple".

Without realizing it, Matt built the face of the new construct to look more like Mr. Hutney than its own former face.

Once again, its Transformation was interrupted. A walking American flag entered the area, following the Triceratops tracks. Matt detected it first and opened fire with Gauss-gun explosive needle rounds and simple, grenade-like explosives.

The flag dodged but took several needle rounds in the legs. It ignited one rocket leg and powered directly toward Matt, passing the grenades before they detonated. Just before they collided, Matt noticed two long, sharp spikes pushing out of its elbows.

#

The Revelator detected energetic motion ahead. Something was happening, and it involved needle rounds, rocket thrust, and ordnance. It briefly ignited its rockets to catch up, but what it saw was surprising.

An alien decorated like the flag of its former country was engaged in combat with an alien that looked like... a Mr. Hutney mannequin, with a bit of a belly. And the decorated one was winning, stabbing and slicing while the Mr. Hutney alien tried and mostly failed to defend itself.

The ghost of Rover 1017 again altered Jeb's brain chemistry, stimulated the centers of the brain that derive a sense of belonging from the abstractions of religious belief and belonging, and reiterated the narrative of the Revelator. But this time, it had to work harder to subsume Jeb's memories and thoughts beneath those of The Revelator.

Turning above the fight, the Revelator fired needle rounds and two micromissiles at the decorated alien, using up its entire small supply of simple disassemblerbot payloads. It limited fire to the decorated alien because it hoped to rebalance the fight to let the aliens further damage each other.

Yes, that's why.

With its narrative pressing upon its mind from all sides, it blared out, "I am the Revelator! I reveal the will of the Lord! Renounce your evil ways and prepare to meet your maker!"

The American flag-decorated alien detected the needle rounds and dodged some of them, but even backing away from the Mr. Hutney alien it was unable to dodge the micromissiles. It fired countermeasures out of its shoulders, causing the missiles to deploy their payload early, followed immediately by shaped ordnance detonations of its own, which blew the shrapnel particles away from it.

Then it ignited its rocket legs, even as the dispersal ordnance was still exploding. It was so fast! It thrusted sideways, along the ground and between the legs of the Mr. Hutney alien to get behind it.

The Mr. Hutney alien was awkwardly backstepping, apparently slow to understand and repair its damage.

For a moment, the Jeb personality beneath the Revelator remembered the microneurotendrils attached to Matt's skull back in Emeline. Again, Rover 1017 pushed the narrative.

As the American-flag alien spiraled in to close the distance, the Revelator dove and reversed direction sharply. But they collided, and one of its wings was lopped halfway off by the American's nano-sharp blade. The American turned upon the Revelator, moving with lightning speed.

The Mr. Hutney alien had fallen backward and was now leaning against a rocky outcrop.

"Go away! You're weak and selfish and lost!" blared the Mr. Hutney alien.

Weak and selfish and lost... That was exactly the way Matt used to talk. Matt, not Mr. Hutney. And the voice it's using... Those microneurotendrils that were attached to Matt's head... Could it be true...?

Having transformed its remaining operational wing into a heavily armored shield while swatting at the American and blocking its attacks, Revelator-Jeb blared, "Matt, is that you?"

The ghost of Rover 1017 pushed hard, flooding the brain in its clutches with sensations of guilt over betrayal, sensations of being lost, being judged for straying, parental abandonment, and isolation. It poked the auditory center, and the Jeb personality heard the cautioning voice of the Lord, although there were no words associated with that sensation of hearing. The rover drew out Jeb's memory of the sensation of choking.

#

"Matt, is that you?" blared the angel-like alien.

What is this? How can this thing know me? Momentarily, in its lingering confusion from the interrupted Transformation, Matt wondered if this was real, if perhaps Matt had died in that firehouse, if perhaps it was Matt's disembodied soul that had looked upon its dead body. Maybe this fight with this walking American flag was some kind of vision-memory of Matt's years fighting with the authorities, some part of the process of final judgment...?

"I was Matt Hutney, but I've changed," it said. Some parts of its mind still wanted redemption, wanted Heaven.

But as Old Glory and the "angel" with the damaged wing fought, spewing nanoconstruct materials here and there, reality set in. *These are Enhanced Inheriteds, and they can't be trusted.* They'd say and do anything to gain advantage and establish themselves as worship-worthy lords of the planet. Matt began to form what was left of its mantle on its chest into ordnance, a shape charge to focus the blast, and pressed back against the rocky outcrop for stability.

#

The face on the Mr. Hutney construct had changed to look a bit more like Matt, the Matt from the FBI's dossier pictures. The Jeb personality underneath the Revelator, pressured as it was and distressed by feelings of guilt and isolation, couldn't believe that the Lord would so callously pit Jeb against Matt in this way. Mr. Hutney, in the name of the Lord, had always stopped them from fighting. It didn't make sense.

If Matt had undergone some kind of alien transformation, willingly or not, that could be an opportunity for him to finally renounce his evil ways and embark upon a path to redemption. Any change would be better than the old Matt's life.

And, of course, the technological resemblance between the Revelator, the flag-decorated alien, and Matt was undeniable. The Revelator processed all the possibilities related to the microneurotendrils it saw attached to Matt's skull, aliens that can change shape but choose to look like humans, a so-called alien that has a national identity...

Revelator-Jeb moved between the American and Matt and tried to shout, "I'll protect you, Matt," but nothing came out. It tried to build a coiled tether to grab the American Flag by its ankles and topple it to keep its blades at a distance. But the ghost of Rover 1017 inside, seeing a continued pattern of free thought and rejection of the narrative, resorted to direct neural pathway interruption. It could not allow the subject to go rogue.

*   *   *

Simya asked her questions, and the Cosmologist answered. Its answers were extremely thorough. Simya realized that the beauty of this situation was that she didn't have to transcribe a conversation. Everything in the document was already verbatim, straight from the horse's mouth, as they used to say in the U.S.

"From where in our sky, using our astronomical coordinate system, do you originate?"

From the response, she learned of the multi-species nature of the SelfMade community and was disabused of her original assumption that they were a single species of "aliens," as was common in Earth's traditional, thinly-veiled-fear-of-"Other" alien invasion stories.

She also learned all about the nano- and quantum scale technology that underpins the SelfMade. And the Transformation, of course. Fundamental to the technology that comprises the SelfMade is how their minds are migrated from their source species' biologies into the template constructs. All of that was part of the explanation of their multi-species nature.

Well, not so much learned as rapidly skimmed. That section of the response was a small book unto itself, with charts and visuals. It was almost entirely over her head, "almost" only because the Cosmologist was trying to keep it accessible.

And she learned of the extragalactic path taken by the SelfMade on their journey to minimum safe distance from the Catastrophic Cosmological Event from which they'd been fleeing for thousands of years. For now, she'd have to take the astronomy and astrophysics stuff on faith, but it was always her plan to obtain analysis from experts.

All of that from her one misconceived first question. It had taken Simya a few hours just to read/skim Response #1.

But with the scientific foundational stuff out of the way, Simya could then focus on the personal. She wanted to get inside the "head," so to speak, of this SelfMade, this non-biological-yet-not-programmed-AI sentient being, this suprabiotechnological person.

*   *   *

The Patriot saw the bird-person alien seize up like a statue, so it momentarily suspended its next attack, assessing the situation.

There was a boom and a flash of bright light and then only darkness. The Patriot knew that its sensory head structure, right arm, and right shoulder were no longer attached to the rest of it, or they had been destroyed.

Internal gyros indicated it was now on its back, on the ground.

Flying blind, as it were, it decided to remain on its back, allowing maximum contact with the ground to absorb as much material as possible. It began constructing new, easy-to-build sensors—acoustic sensors on its hips, and directly between the sensors, high-frequency acoustic chirping devices on its lower abdomen and lower back.

After a time, despite having lost its sensory head structure, its stereoscopic acoustic sensors came online, allowing it to use echolocation to scan the area. As it began chirping and calibrating, it detected a large, spherical object with stub-legs land on top of it, holding it down.

The sphere conveyed acoustically, softly, "I'm sorry for what's happened to you, and what must happen next."

#

Standing on stubby legs over the EI on the ground, the Refugee apologized, then power-drove a thousand sharp spikes through the EI's core, which is much smaller than its own. It then rotated all the spikes outward, sideways, tearing apart the EI's nanoconstruct core along with the human brain cocooned inside it.

Pearly-white parts of another EI littered the ground between the blast center on the outcrop wall and the colorful EI the Refugee just destroyed. There were pearly-white legs and a hole above them where a core used to be. Arm, head, and wing structures were scattered nearby. The focused blast apparently drove directly through the pearly-white EI's core and into the upper part of the other, more colorful one.

It appeared that Matt had decided to abandon the Triceratops form for something more familiar, although the entire upper half of its mantle was destroyed by its own nearly suicidal shape charge blast. Near the bottom of the small hill, down the side of the outcrop, Matt's abdomen core, pelvis area, and legs lay motionless. All showed signs of penetration and slashing damage, although there was obvious active absorptive contact with the ground. Matt's core appeared to be intact and alive.

Laurence-Refugee was pleasantly surprised and relieved.

An EI with a human brain inside would not have survived being the source of such a blast. The shockwaves alone would have liquefied the brain tissue. No doubt the colorful one survived the downstream shock environment because it was partially shielded by the pearly-white EI in between, and its cocoon must've been built for lateral shock bypass transmission, as well.

The Ethnologist was taking its EI designs seriously.

Laurence-Refugee sent a repetitive hail using a short-range, microwave transmission, waiting for Matt to reply. It moved severed mantle material from the destroyed EIs over to Matt's nanoconstruct body. Having those materials would dramatically accelerate Matt's repair and reconstruction process, and indeed, Matt's mantle quickly began absorbing the other mantle material.

While waiting, Laurence-Refugee took the time to establish another nonlocal connection to Jacques. Learning of Jacques' censure and the object rocketing toward Jacques, Laurence-Refugee was deeply concerned and displeased, although not surprised. It maintained a handshake pulse in the interchange, a few silent moments of connection with Jacques, its progeny, its companion, its savior—without Jacques' involvement, Laurence would still be a quadriplegic human trying to scream out her autistic anguish at the overwhelming unfamiliar.

#

Eventually, Matt repaired its microwave radio transceiver, acknowledged the Refugee's hail, but said no more.

The Refugee requested a tacdata dump of the battle, reasoning that intel on the EIs was crucial.

Despite still struggling with trust, Matt decided that the Refugee might as well have the data. It conveyed what happened.

Laurence-Refugee carefully assessed the situation, informed by the Cosmologist's complete database, and decided that full disclosure would be the right thing to do. Over several milliseconds it conveyed a reply to Matt.

"While you were transforming, I received the Cosmologist's database. While co-opting the Ethnologist's rover command subnet, the Cosmologist had discovered that the Ethnologist was creating an Enhanced Inherited, Jeb Hutney in Edmonton. The Ethnologist may have discovered Jeb through police investigative records of your former life of crime, as well as prison psychologist records about your father.

"But you, too, were susceptible to a narcissistic power narrative.

"The Cosmologist believes that the Ethnologist discovered your general whereabouts and was probably using the detached FBI contingent, still in administrative limbo, to pinpoint your location and take you into custody. It seemed like the Ethnologist was planning to enhance you as well as your brother, as it deployed a rover to follow the agents.

"Discovering that these events were in motion, the Cosmologist deployed Rover 1120 to do several things. First, to warn you that agents were coming to your camp. Next, to convince you to escape and chase me by telling you that your last prey was still alive. And finally, to follow you and aid in your tracking and travels across Oz. When we stopped in Emeline, and I underwent the

Transformation, I left that tow truck outside for you to find.

"Given the advanced state of your mercury poisoning at the time, it's likely you would not have made it across Oz without Rover 1120's surreptitious support.

"We had to make it difficult for the Ethnologist to find you, and in doing so the Cosmologist hoped that you could become our ally instead. It asked me to evaluate whether you could be safely Transformed. The other option meant your death, to prevent you from becoming another EI.

"So, we brought you here and I tried to help you through the Transformation to save your life and to deny the Ethnologist another EI, but also one other thing. You, of all people, might have been able to turn Jeb from the brink, neutralizing the one EI that was known at the time. And, based on the tacdata you just shared with me, I believe that is precisely what happened.

"It's unfortunate that Jeb was unwilling or unable to identify himself to you. I suspect he was unable. Unlike us, the EIs can have a control overlay, and the Ethnologist has likely built them with restricted autonomy."

Matt's distrust was not lessened by the Refugee's explanations but reinforced. Laurence-Refugee received no further communication from Matt, although it waited and stood guard patiently while Matt repaired.

When Matt was able to travel again, it immediately launched itself into the sky, now identifying as the Vagrant. The Refugee watched the Vagrant fly away, wishing they could have been allies, hoping they would not become enemies.

*   *   *

Laurence-Refugee departed for Maquoketa to continue its preparations. There was nothing it could do for Matt or Jacques. They were both out of reach.

At least Matt was not turned into one of the Ethnologist's Enhanced Inheriteds. Laurence-Refugee believed that eventually, Matt-SelfMade would fully recover from its interrupted Transformation. It could help if only Matt-SelfMade would reestablish communications.

On the way to Maquoketa, Laurence-Refugee dedicated a few milliseconds to exploring a train of thought focused on all the other SelfMade, the population from which the Cosmologist and the Ethnologist had come. It scanned through the vast database of information shared with it by the Cosmologist and discovered something surprising. None of the other LPT species of origin among the SelfMade had achieved the creation of truly high-functioning and stable, behaviorally bound artificial intelligence before their destruction by their own Enhanced Inheriteds.

That explained why the SelfMade had, until now, only ever increased their numbers through either Transformation of new species or their disastrous experiments with self-copying. They hadn't yet worked out how to create truly new, stable, behaviorally bound non-biological minds. And, perhaps more important, they were not motivated to do so, as the reproductive drive is a biological one, driven by the replicative priority of genes.

Perhaps the SelfMade formerly known as Laurence Levesque more appropriately should identify as a Progenitor. It had created Jacques and had come close to being able to transform Jacques into a SelfMade, without requiring the dangerous transformation of humans with inherited biological and cultural baggage.

Then again, shedding the last vestiges of its habits of externalization, perhaps it is just Laurence.

Chapter Twenty-Eight

Memetic Inheritance

F inally, a ship entered One and a Half Degree Channel, and the Cosmologist executed its plan. Arriving at the ship's central keel area, it activated the attachment structures it had prepared along the top of the Ethnologist's cage and one side of its mantle for attachment. It then tucked its tentacles together to form a hydrodynamic aft cone to minimize cavitation. Updating its estimates of the drag the system was now imposing on the ship, it tweaked its thrusters to counter that drag so that the ship would lose no noticeable time or fuel because of its presence.

Then it deployed stealthy tendrils through the ship's hull to tap into the communication equipment. And it spent time once again exploring nonlocal subspace, trying to tap into government agencies that were searching for it.

Before an hour passed, the ship received an order to stop and await an inspection crew. The order appeared to be routine, but no explanation was given. The screws reversed, bringing the ship to a halt, and then they stopped spinning.

The Cosmologist had been discovered, so it thought. It detached and descended, and then picked up the acoustic signatures of a series of smooth new buoys not far to the west, ahead of the ship. They floated at depth, neutrally buoyant to a hundred meters. Were those buoys deployed recently, specifically to search for the SelfMade? The acoustics of the ship's engines must have painted a very clear acoustic picture for those buoys of the SelfMade, the cage, and the nosecone attached to the keel.

Its only chance of escaping further tracking by the buoys would be to dive down to a temperature-density boundary under which it could acoustically hide. Then it would have to go silent and ride currents away from the net. Only then would it be safe to return to the shallows of the Maldives and the relative safety of a cave. It was the only way, and it was a fallback plan.

As the scooter assembly dove, feigning continued travel west, the cargo ship's sonar emitter began to ping. The Cosmologist set all its thrusters to maximum speed and power-dove into the darkness below, once again adjusting itself to the higher-pressure conditions. The Ethnologist did the same.

*　　*　　*

Jacques wrote another message into the portion of its memory recently dedicated to nonlocal communication with its mother.

"Mama, *chu dans marde. Bientôt je serai parti. Il y a beaucoup d'entre eux. Attache ta tuque.*" (Mama, I'm in trouble. Soon I'll be gone. There are many of them. Be careful.)

Moments later, something mounted to the top of a stolen, not-yet-spent, heavily modified North Korean solid rocket booster collided with Jacques at high speed, smashing the spacecraft into uncounted bits of space junk. The main brain circuitry remained attached to one of the small battery-powered regulators, along with one of its temperature sensors and one of its near-field microcameras normally used to monitor solar panel movements. Jacques remained conscious for another 4 minutes and 26.31 seconds. Its only sensory information during that time was that it was getting colder, and a low-resolution, narrow view of the starfield and occasionally the Earth twirling around it.

Laurence had been monitoring. It detected within that memory bank one word repeating over and over.

"Mama... Mama..."

*　　　*　　　*

Jesu Christe in Italy and Cristo Redentor in Brazil became aware of each other's existence through human channels.

Throngs of their followers validated their separate but similar narratives, so with absolute conviction, they each put themselves on suborbital trajectories toward the other.

*   *   *

Other EIs across the planet made similar discoveries.

In Thailand, Chokh Chatā decimated the Thai armed forces. Standing on Bang Na-Chon Buri Expressway Bridge over the Bang Pakong, it rallied crowds of supporters.

Then Sdech Kan arrived from Cambodia, challenging Thai dominance over Cambodia, and therefore challenging Chokh Chatā.

They battled over several days, laying waste to much of the megalopolis from Bangkok to Rayong, and killing tens of thousands of bystanders, including many of Chokh Chatā's traditionalist followers. Afterward, thousands of those followers embarked upon a vengeance-killing spree all the way to Phnom Penh. The mass carnage would've been visible from space.

In Africa, Eleda flew from evil warlord stronghold to evil warlord stronghold, oppressive dictator mansion to oppressive dictator mansion, foreign corporate nation-rape facility to foreign corporate nation-rape facility, cleaning house. It inspired many to once again believe in the possibility of an Africa composed of sovereign nations ruled by law, free of foreign debt slavery and pillage and protected by this indestructible spirit, Eleda.

Dignity- and independence-minded revolutionaries quickly filled the power vacuums, but they began to bicker over where Eleda should strike next. Pleas became insistence, and soon someone was ordering Eleda here while others ordered it there.

But as everyone knew from the legends, Eleda is fickle and demands sacrifices. The revolutionaries quickly set about proving who could produce the most sacrifices for the fickle spirit.

Then Eleda heard that the aliens, the ultimate foreign pillagers, had been discovered near the Maldives. After Eleda departed for the Maldives, the replacement governments in its wake did not stop producing sacrifices.

Eleda remained over land for easy resource replenishment, but it encountered other EIs converging on the Maldives via India. Inevitably, they narcissistically battled for supremacy of importance.

It was happening all over the world, with engineering forensics specialists picking through the aftermath rubble and char, obtaining samples and sensor records to help evaluate the weapons used by the EIs.

It was finally politically safe to commit to all-out war with the aliens and their EIs. The use of tacnukes was approved.

*   *   *

Simya didn't have to think hard about her next questions. The so-called "human" questions were second nature for every journalist. But beyond asking the standard "how does it feel?" superficial journalism questions, Simya knew she needed a broad set of establishing questions to characterize the consciousness inside that technoconstruct. She understood that her audience would be asking the Turing Test questions, if, indeed, after the dust settles the world is in any shape to have an audience for a definitive book on these times.

During Simya's childhood, the Singularity Insurgency was a big, scary several years of fear and chaos. There were interruptions of basic services, military and police clashes with pro-Singularity rights sects, then several years of computer and network-related paranoia, and people being hauled away under suspicions. The whole thing was used as an excuse by various special interests to swizzle who owns what and to change various laws in their favor under the guise of protecting the public. And finally, the establishment of a thoroughly anti-mind-copy/ anti-unconstrained-AI culture, vernacular, and legal and economic frameworks. Constrained, specialized AI would be fine (industry insisted), just nothing sentient. All that upheaval just for civilization to put the final shovel of dirt over one idea.

So, yes, she knew all about the Turing Test, enough to know that it was fundamentally about telling the difference between a human and a simulated human. There was no generalized Turing test for sentience, one that would make sense and be reliable in the evaluation of alien minds. After a few sips of hot, aromatic chai, Simya understood what would come next.

There was no baseline for comparison, so Cosmo's chosen methods of expression would have to stand on their own. This freed Simya to ask questions she would ask anyone. Readers would have to evaluate the replies for themselves.

It wasn't all that different from asking experts to explain something esoteric. In the end, most readers have no baseline for understanding those interviews, either, and simply make of it what they can. The more the reader brings, the more the reader carries away.

"Tell me your thoughts on this conflict between you and the Ethnologist. Not how the conflict is executed, but the morality of it, the experience of it, the *meaning* of it to you?"

It took another few hours for Simya to read/skim the reply (which, as with Response #1, appeared in her document almost all at once). Several passages stood out, and she smiled, knowing her book would indeed be the definitive book on these times.

"It's important to clarify that the Ethnologist and I bear no ill will toward each other. We merely contend because of our disagreement over the possible outcomes of the planned quantum entanglement bubble-shift. But just because we don't need hatred as a justification to oppose each other, which in humans is born of the need for adrenaline during times of action, that doesn't mean we feel nothing. A mind is only as sophisticated as its emotional sophistication. Or, to put it another way, emotions are an emergent property of a complex mind. To answer your question, we find this conflict disagreeable, of course, and not just from the standpoint of wishing we were unopposed. I'm sure both of us find it terribly disagreeable that we were forced to involve humanity in this conflict. And I miss discussing cephalopods with the Ethnologist. Those creatures have evolved on multiple worlds, and we enjoyed theorizing about what conditions might lead them to live longer and evolve beyond the limitations of their short lifespans. Their skin color communications are so beautiful and intricate. We find them fascinating. I do believe the Ethnologist misses those conversations, as well."

And "I still think about my former life in my biologically inherited body, before the SelfMade arrived and I was Transformed. What's interesting is that while I can no longer imagine reacting the way my biology forced me to react, that is I can't remember what that was like in the sense of being able to duplicate it, I do try to use the shadows of those memories to empathize with you Inheriteds."

And "On the topic of the morality of it, I would suggest that your readers have no choice but to imagine themselves in our positions, knowing what we know, believing what we believe. With the fate of at least this whole solar system in your hands, and possibly a good chunk of the visible universe, what would you do?"

Simya switches to asking Cosmo to comment on the Ethnologist's intentional creation of Enhanced Inheriteds on Earth, a topic of great personal significance to her.

"I feel for you, and everyone affected by the EIs. Let me be clear. I did not create or assist in the creation of a single EI, through action or inaction. That was entirely the Ethnologist's doing. It felt it was saving the universe. If I felt the stakes were that high, and I had no other recourse, I might've done the same. That said, while I did not create EIs on Earth, I did set events in motion that resulted in the detonation of a nuclear bomb in your ocean. And to get that bomb detonated I had to foment fear, which I understand does not dissipate quickly, if ever. Neither of us is morally clean in this conflict.

"More to the point of your question, I think, is that all I can do is apologize for my part in this. It's profoundly unfortunate that I was unable to gain control over the Ethnologist before it created the EIs. I relied on that bomb detonation. But even now I remain in danger. The Ethnologist's rovers are still looking for me. The EIs are still looking for me. Various military forces are looking for me. I may not escape, in which case the fate of your planet may depend on someone I was able to Transform along the way."

Simya asked to whom the Cosmologist was referring, but it did not answer.

She read the full response, tears welling in her eyes because it all reminded her not only of her brother-turned-EI but also the other stories she was pursuing – the young Finnish-Jamaican soldier, barely eighteen, finding herself on the front line of the Monsta War, the Indian sailor who was First Officer aboard that now famous deep sea mining support ship, was in the middle of the situation in the Indian Ocean. He disappeared into a war zone inland after they were all debriefed. She has her team working to track him down. And the young American supersoldiers who experienced a SelfMade infiltration in Mordor, which Simya now understands was the Cosmologist fomenting fear via a co-opted drone, and who were close to the action in the Indian Ocean, according to the one that's talking. Each story was moving in its own way, separate from the worldwide terror and losses the Monstas have caused. And through all its responses the Cosmologist seemed genuinely able to sympathize.

But at this point, Simya became overwhelmed with anger. If they hadn't come here in the first place, none of this would have happened. Ayaz would still be himself and not a mass murdering Monsta. The world might've fully reversed global warming, might've fully recovered from the plagues and revolutions, and might've finally overthrown all the mafia states. The world could have kept going toward progress and possibly salvation before the CCE would become a final threat several thousand years hence. It would have been possible. But now? Now history has once again rolled backward decades, maybe centuries. If only these aliens had simply left us alone in the first place!

Simya allowed herself to feel her feelings in order to process them. If she doesn't believe whatever she thinks while it's happening, she'll be okay.

She engages her journalistic professionalism, the same professionalism she'd had to engage so many times before when covering stories of atrocities, and she does not intend to pull punches. She asks some pointed questions.

What more could you have done to have kept your battle on Luna in the first place? What would you say to Isis Mantyla, the youngest uniformed soldier our researchers know of in this war (if she survives her deployment)? To Preet Tajra, if he's still alive, and the crew of the *Chidambaranar 2*? To the soldiers, Garant, Holm, Kaetenay, Strembicky, and everyone onboard the USS *Kraken*, the INS *Curā*, and all the other sailors and soldiers risking or losing their lives in this war across the planet? To the millions of civilians directly affected, and those whose lives and livelihoods and food supplies would be indirectly affected by the undersea nuke? Can you speak to the morality of the Ethnologist's rover network on Earth, a network you were perfectly content to use while you both were observing Earth from Luna? Can you also get the Ethnologist to respond to these questions?

Simya waited for the reply.

Hours crept by. Her anger subsided. She had acquired her interview. The cameras she'd set up in the room had captured everything, sending it all to servers elsewhere in the building and to distant backup servers, from the tablet's network disconnection process to her final questions.

She left the tablet and the cameras in place. It was still possible the Cosmologist would resume communication. It was possible.

*   *   *

After diving away from the cargo ship and the acoustic buoys, after riding currents to gain distance, the Cosmologist turned east, back toward the Maldives, at depth and in stealth mode. This time it also veered south to get that much closer to the equator, thinking ahead to optimal launch energy conditions. It planned to find or create a cave somewhere on the shelf west of Madaveli.

*　　　*　　　*

Reports began coming in about one of the EIs declaring it was working alone, unlike the others.

It put forth no self-aggrandizing narrative, made no claims to be a beloved legendary figure, and denied any plans to return anything or anyone to former glory. It did not ask for followers. And it declared its intention to harm no one, although it would defend itself. Unlike the Monstas, this one planned to provide aid. But it insisted on anonymity and isolation. The common speculation was that it was hiding somewhere in Oz, or perhaps Mordor.

In its first broadcast, it called itself the Vagrant and it shared detailed scientific and technological information on how to detect the vacuum energy power plants of the EIs and the aliens, including itself. Such detection is short-range.

When found and attacked by distrustful humans near Denver, it killed none of them, but instead deployed nanobots designed to disassemble polymer bullet casings and chemically neutralize explosives. It also deployed a variety of non-lethal deterrents, such as microwave and acoustic psychological deterrents and non-asphyxiating immobilization foam, before escaping again into the wasteland.

Given the threat-rich environment across the planet, governments and military leaders decided to adopt a no-engage policy against the Vagrant, at least for now.

Shortly afterward, tacnukes were deployed in simultaneous operations against most of the EIs across the globe, whose thirst for worship and followers had left them tactically vulnerable. Problematically, the EIs always gravitated to highly populated areas. When the tacnukes struck, the collateral losses were unprecedented and horrific, magnifying the earlier unprecedented and horrific EI rampage that precipitated their use.

The public was mostly numb, caught between horror at the friendly fire losses and relief at the destruction of those nanotech-enhanced, narcissistic Monstas loosed upon the Earth by the aliens.

Politically, it could still work, the governments calculated.

But there were still some EIs out there.

*　　*　　*

Speeding through Earth-Moon L4, Dà Xióngmāo's path required adjustment so its descent to the Moon's surface would be timely and relatively calm. It would use its in-built throttleable rockets. The missile had survived the impact with the spacecraft because Dà Xióngmāo had been the spearhead in that impact, and because of special bolstering structures it had constructed down the missile's sides. The missile was mostly solid, anyway.

After that impact, Dà Xióngmāo reoriented its modified missile and reignited it, once again withstanding acceleration and vibration forces that would have liquefied an unenhanced human. Sometime later, having bolstered its armor, it entered a tight tuck and ejected itself from the mostly spent missile. The missile continued accelerating, its engine plume blasting the ejected EI as it passed.

Dà Xióngmāo's plan was simple: land on the Moon, replenish its fuel, find a nice, large rock with the right shape and material characteristics, augment it so that it would not explode or break up on atmospheric entry at Earth, nor lose too much mass, and put it on a direct, highly destructive trajectory toward the Maldives, just west of One and a Half Degree Channel—where the authorities have just discovered the aliens. The Cosmologist can't be moving quickly and is probably looking for a hole in which to hide. Even the humans have assessed the situation this way, according to the rover network.

To make that happen quickly enough, however, Dà Xióngmāo must return to Earth. But now the competition has been culled, and the humans are dealing with the tacnuke aftermath. With a careful plan, it believes, the Glorious Spirit of the Chinese People can prevail, even if it means using people as shields.

*　　*　　*

The Cosmologist found a cave west of Madaveli and dug in. It was all too aware that this was a non-ideal location and a non-ideal plan. It had continually revised its contingency planning, evaluating whether it should dispose of the Ethnologist to increase its mobility and chances of escape. But morally, it just couldn't do that yet. It believed it was still possible that the humans would shift resources away from this chase. After all, they're also still dealing with the EI war and its aftermath. It's possible.

It set aside the Ethnologist's automated cage. The cage would last a millennium undisturbed, so at this moment it does not require the Cosmologist's attention.

It deployed a wall builder to set up sensors and mostly seal off the cave with a natural-looking rocky structure. It has not forgotten that the Ethnologist may yet have other squid-like rovers in the region. Any such rovers could have learned through their network about the detection at the cargo ship and sonar buoys, and if so, it's likely they're inbound.

Having had ample time to develop the design of the multi-stage rocket needed to get both of them safely and quickly out of this gravity well, it began deploying automated construction devices that would both dig out the necessary chamber and transform the dug-out materials into the rocket system and its solid fuel.

Unfortunately, the system must be a bit larger than optimal for a pure lifter. It would need to push through meters of water, and some additional defenses would have to be installed. Someone is likely to launch missiles at them as soon as they emerge from hiding.

* * *

From its relatively safe haven inside one of the high peaks in the Rocky Mountains, deep in Mordor, the Vagrant continued to share both scientific knowledge and actual equipment, delivered by suborbital drops, but at a careful pace. It focused on relief efforts, addressing the immediate medical needs of survivors of the EI war and tacnuke detonations.

According to best intel, the remaining two EIs on the planet, Jesu Christe and Cristo Redentor were passing each other over the central Atlantic Ocean when the tacnuke plan was executed. And the other one, identified as Dà Xióngmāo, was still out in space somewhere, at the energy high ground.

The Vagrant found that in parallel with its general distrust, it also carried a pattern of insecurity. It hoped for help from the Refugee. It hoped that the humans don't find the Refugee now that they have the technology to track its power plant. The Vagrant simply is not sure it can win against these three EI messiahs, especially given their ability to garner human support.

It understood why it remains vagrant. Deep inside, another leftover, unfocused gestalt devoid of clear memories was crystallizing. It was anger. It knew it had no rational target for this anger, it was simply something unresolved, hiding in the niches of those half-absorbed memories.

These distracting, problematic thought patterns were a handicap, the downside of the interrupted

Transformation. The upside of the Transformation was that it freed the Vagrant of biological impulses and stimulus responses that had prevented Matt from resolving his issues. With time, it should be able to find a way to cope, to remain balanced and rational, to atrophy the lingering anger.

Sometimes, though, humanity and these EIs were incredibly annoying and really pushed its buttons. The humans continued to pose a threat, and they would even more so after all the EIs and other SelfMade are gone, and humanity finds itself facing just one "alien." And the EIs, they're just so self-absorbed and psychotic.

This must have been how everyone else used to feel about Matt Hutney.

*   *   *

Submarines lie in wait north of Tunis and east of Vitoria, ready to launch tacnukes at the expected visitors descending on suborbital trajectories, Jesu Christe over the Atlantic and Cristo Redentor over the Tyrrhenian Sea.

The humans calculated that EIs deplete most of their rocket fuel when putting themselves on these kinds of suborbital trajectories, reserving their remaining fuel for controlled reentry and landing. It seemed a reasonable assessment, especially for these two EIs, because they did not plan ahead and did not build extra fuel into themselves. They left Rio and Rome on their own legs, so to speak.

So, the submarines with their missiles moved into

position under the EIs' projected flight paths, over water where an airburst would minimize collateral effects on land. The missiles would track the targets and detonate close enough that even burning at maximum thrust to change their trajectories, the EIs should not be able to reach minimum safe distance.

Populations in Tunisia, Sardinia, Sicily, and the southeast coast of Brazil were not warned before launch. If the EIs intercepted such communications, they would be able to change their flight paths early enough to veer away from their original destinations.

*　　*　　*

The sensors at the front of the Cosmologist's cave detected what could only be aircraft passing overhead. Initially, the frequency was low, but it was observably increasing over time. There were also acoustic signatures of maneuvering ships in the area—large and powerful ships.

*　　*　　*

Using the vacuum energy power-plant-detection capability provided by the Vagrant, Indian, Pakistani, and British navies searching the Maldives were able to detect and surround a squid-like rover that had entered the area from the east.

Using containment technology developed from battlefield forensic engineering, they captured the rover, although not with the first attempt. They resorted to doing severe damage to it.

The capture was treated as e-top secret. There were no electronic reports of the event, and communications about it were face-to-face only.

*   *   *

Vast populations of believers rejected government claims that Jesu Christe and Cristo Redentor were EIs like all the other EIs rampaging across the planet. The horrors caused by the Enhanced Inheriteds had amplified the faith of these believers. They saw the arrival of their respective messiahs as naturally and rightfully coincident with the horrors taking place across the planet. *Their* messiah was here for a *reason*.

So, the governments of the world found themselves in the position of having to explain to the believers that Jesu Christe was nuked over the Atlantic, and Cristo Redentor was nuked over the Tyrrhenian Sea. They followed up with detailed reports on the men who were transformed to become those EIs in the first place, including detailed psychological profiles to try to make the case for narcissistic delusion and susceptibility to the narrative provided to these men by whatever alien rover had pounced upon them. They were susceptible victims, so went the replacement narrative, and their followers were understandably duped.

Most of the believers were not yet interested in a replacement narrative, however, especially an embarrassing one, immersed as they were in grief and outrage. Armies of God began to form.

*   *   *

With fixed-wing traffic over the area decreasing in frequency but helicopter traffic increasing, the Cosmologist was forced to temporarily shut down operations, in case the humans had somehow found a way to detect vacuum energy power plants. It considered that to be unlikely, given their scientific knowledge. For itself, it switched to various passive backup energy sources and settled into an idle observation mode.

It could not, however, force the Ethnologist to do the same, not without killing it. And without proof of a direct threat of that nature, it couldn't justify such a murder, just as it couldn't justify it after capture.

For now, it would wait for the helicopter traffic to die down.

*   *   *

Having been unmolested under Maquoketa for a comfortable amount of time, Laurence had made progress on its booster. Unlike the Cosmologist's booster, this one only needed to carry one SelfMade to escape velocity. It also would not need to be capable of launching underwater.

During construction, Laurence also had time to monitor the human networks, via nonlocal tapping. No one had reported detecting the Cosmologist, but it found a great many reports related to the war with the Enhanced Inheriteds. The devastation they wrought was widespread, and the tacnuke strikes only made it worse.

It would have continued had the Vagrant not supplied humanity with critical scientific and technological uplift, allowing detection, outmaneuvering, and ultimately lethal strike capability against the EIs.

But having supplied humanity with that scientific and technological uplift also opened Pandora's box. Someone, somewhere, eventually would create their own EIs, and others would have to create their own in the usual arms race of aftermath lives, effect following cause following effect. It would all start over again, and perhaps in a worse way—those new EIs would not be merely deluded, isolated narcissists acting with absolute conviction, but would be sanctioned operatives acting *together* with absolute conviction.

Thinking of Divya and Nandita, Laurence abandoned the future projection and focused on the task at hand.

*   *   *

Dà Xióngmāo rode its augmented rock toward Earth, toward the west end of One and a Half Degree Channel. It detected the firing of several suborbital artillery projectiles from Diego Garcia Atoll to the south.

Predicting the projectiles' target location, it noticed increased naval activity in that same area, on the west side of Huvadhu Atoll. Perhaps the humans had detected the SelfMade, using the information provided by the Vagrant.

Dà Xióngmāo reoriented and executed a trajectory-change maneuver that would bring the rock down directly over that area, although after the artillery projectiles strike.

It then separated from the rock, remotely activating the rock's new spin thrusters to add stability for accuracy. It thrusted away, altering its own course and orbital energy to provide itself with a much less direct, must less energetic reentry, probably somewhere in the Gulf of Guinea.

*   *   *

Finally, the helicopters left the area—all at once. Acoustics also suggested that all detectable ships were leaving the area. The Cosmologist recognized that as a bad sign.

It went into full defensive mode, armoring up, enhancing structural integrity, and positioning itself near newly constructed supports.

*   *   *

The suborbital artillery projectiles were guided and scramjet-propelled, descending at supersonic speed. The Cosmologist did not even detect them: it only experienced the four relentless explosions.

Meters of cave rock above it collapsed, but the material was further broken up by the explosions.

The Ethnologist and its cage were obliterated by a direct hit from the final projectile.

The Cosmologist, however, survived.

No longer burdened with responsibility for the Ethnologist, the damaged Cosmologist began to flagellate toward another nearby cave.

And then the rock hit. It was not large or energetic enough to cause regional devastation, but it unleashed more than enough energy to disassemble the already damaged Cosmologist, wipe out Thinadhoo, Kaadedhdhoo, and Hoandedhdhoo Islands, and capsize several of the Navy vessels that had only moved to minimum safe distance from the three-sigma reentry ellipse calculated for their artillery strikes.

*   *   *

Laurence triggered the explosives that would open the ground above the launch chamber it had built in the Maquoketa Caves. The explosives did exactly what they were meant to do.

It moved the overhead shielding that protected the rocket from falling cave roof fragments, ignited the first stage, and blasted at high gees into the sky. The rocket did exactly what it was meant to do. Launched from deep inside Oz, the rocket was well on its way before it was detected in flight, and by then no available missile systems could catch it.

Laurence was now becoming free of the Earth's gravity well, becoming free of interference from aftermath humans, becoming free to save itself and the solar system from the CCE. Laurence was doing exactly what it was meant to do.

Epilogue

The Vagrant continued to share scientific knowledge with the entire world, carefully metered over time, along with warnings about the things that could and would go wrong when transforming people who aren't good candidates. It put forth plans to aid and cooperate with authorities to track down and destroy the wily rogue EI, Dà Xióngmāo.

Universally, the Transformation was officially outlawed, as an extension of last century's Singularity-related laws.

But deep within secret facilities around the globe, captured rovers from the Ethnologist's rover network, and battlefield technology fragments from the Monsta War, were being examined, sampled, and reverse engineered. After all, they never found the "bodies" of the Cosmologist and Ethnologist, Dà Xióngmāo was still out there, and they couldn't trust that this Vagrant would be beneficent forever, could they?

*　　*　　*

Laurence used nonlocal science to detect and intercept Jacques' memory banks, following the

Made in the USA
Middletown, DE
31 October 2022

13839449R00221